To Have AND To Hold

ALINA COMSA

A DARK ROMANCE STANDALONE

Published by: Malum Canticus Books

Edited by: Malum Canticus Books

Cover design by: Malum Canticus Books

E-book ISBN: 978-1-0687806-0-8

Print ISBN: 978-1-0687806-1-5

CONTENTS

Trigger Warning List   VI

Blurb   VIII

Dedication   IX

1. Siah   1

2. Siah   5

3. Siah   8

4. Siah   11

5. Siah   15

6. Siah   20

7. Siah   24

8. Him   29

9. Siah   33

10. Siah   37

11. Siah   41

12. Siah   45

13. Him   50

14. Siah   52

15. Siah   55

16. Him 59

17. Siah 63

18. Him 66

19. Siah 71

20. Siah 77

21. August 82

22. Siah 88

23. Siah 91

24. Siah 99

25. Siah 103

26. Him 109

27. Siah 119

28. August 122

29. Siah 127

30. Siah 130

31. August 134

32. Siah 142

33. Siah 146

34. Siah 150

35. August 152

36. Siah 159

37. August 164

38. Siah 170

39.	Siah	177
40.	Him	181
41.	Siah	186
42.	Siah	191
43.	Siah	197
44.	Siah	202
45.	August	207
46.	Siah	214
47.	August	218
48.	Siah	225
49.	Siah	229
50.	Siah	237
51.	August	244
52.	Siah	250
53.	Siah	256
54.	Siah	262
Epilogue		269
Acknowledgements		274
About the author		276
Also by		277

Trigger Warning List

I take mental health issues with the utmost seriousness. I don't speak in the name of anyone but myself. The issues portrayed in *To Have and To Hold* are issues portrayed not as textbook and not generalised, but based on my opinions, views, or reactions. Not two experiences are identical, and not two individuals survive through them in the same manner. This is a work of fiction and must be treated as such.

If you ever find yourself in any of the situations depicted, please find help. You are not alone.

Sensitive subjects are touched in the book, either by mention or graphic depiction, and I've done my absolute best to treat them with the sensibility and care these subjects deserve. Regardless, the situations depicted may be triggering for some readers, so please check the list below.

To Have and To Hold has the following trigger warnings:

⊃⊂⊃⊂ Stalking
⊃⊂⊃⊂ Dub-con/Non-con
⊃⊂⊃⊂ Blood play
⊃⊂⊃⊂ Somnophilia
⊃⊂⊃⊂ Gun play
⊃⊂⊃⊂ Sexually explicit scenes
⊃⊂⊃⊂ Death of a parent (mentions)
⊃⊂⊃⊂ Child abandonment (mentions)
⊃⊂⊃⊂ Child abuse/negligence (mentions)
⊃⊂⊃⊂ Domestic Violence/Assault
⊃⊂⊃⊂ Entrapment
⊃⊂⊃⊂ Mental Health Issues (paranoia, depression, anxiety)
⊃⊂⊃⊂ Emotional/Mental/Physical abuse
⊃⊂⊃⊂ Medical Procedure – Birth Control

⪥⪥ Torture
⪥⪥ Emesis
⪥⪥ Gaslighting
⪥⪥ Suicide (mentions)
⪥⪥ Death
⪥⪥ Divorce (car accident – mentions)
Your mental health is a priority.

BLURB

My life's a cage. I was free for however many hours I laid in my blanket on a bench in a park, even though I have no memories of that. No one remembers their first day of life.

Then... then I was rescued. Taken to a hospital. Given a name that was never mine. And the foster care swallowed me whole and spat me out eighteen years later.

I've broken free of that cage, because I'm scrappy like that. Went to college, married a good man. Or so I thought.

Seems, in my journey to the rest of my life, I've also collected an unseen, but ever-present hitchhiker. No, he doesn't share my car for rides.

What does he do, you ask? He makes my skin prickle, my stomach fill with dread, and my heart race until I fear it will explode out of my chest.

The freedom I was so proud of is only an illusion.

That illusion shatters as soon as my brand-new husband slams divorce papers in my face and kicks me out of his house.

Alone and afraid, I'm spiralling, trapped in a new cage. This cage comes with fancy bedsheets, suffocating anxiety, and silver chains wrapped around my wrists.

How will I free myself now?

Do I even want to?

DEDICATION

To all the snobbish, stuck-up, pretentious people like me, may your obsessions run deep, your sheets burn hot, and your chains wrap up tight.

Chapter One

SIAH

My blood is foaming inside my veins, bubbling like champagne during New Year's Eve. My heart is racing, pounding relentlessly in my eardrums. An ice-cold shiver peppers goosebumps on my skin. The electric current of the chill seeps into my bones, curling around my spine. My lungs constrict, refusing to inflate. My eyelids spring open, my eyes unseeing. The lack of oxygen finally shakes me awake enough. I jackknife in a sitting position, spluttering and gasping for air.

"He's watching me," I croak, my voice raspy, my throat dried out. I clutch at my husband's forearm, my nails digging into his warm skin. "Henry, he's in the house. He's watching me. Wake up."

I blink as if in slow motion, my eyelids heavy, my eyes gritty, trying to force my pupils to enlarge and get used to the darkness of our bedroom. I know *he's* there somewhere, always watching, always following me. My stomach flips and churns, bile climbing up my esophagus, burning my throat.

My husband stirs next to me, the sheets rustling before a heavy exhale cuts through the silence of the night. "Siah... There's no one here. I checked every lock, every window, every nook and cranny before we went to sleep. No one's watching."

I curl my knees to my chest and bury my face in my palms. Defeat settles heavily on my shoulders, pressing over me like a stony boulder determined to crush me. It's been months... months of nightmares, months of barely existing on not nearly enough sleep, months of feeling the burn of *his* stare through the windows and the flimsy thickness of the brick walls. I might as well have lived in a glass house for all the good that it does at keeping me hidden and protected.

I'm out in the open, vulnerable, cut apart for *him* to look at and dissect.

My whole body jolts when a large palm settles at the base of my spine, rubbing soothing circles. "Babe, did you forget to take your meds again?" Henry's voice is gentle, but I hear the tiredness in his tone, the quiet 'get the fuck over it'.

The chill in my bones is replaced with pure fire, the fear chased away by anger. My person, my rock, my anchor... somewhere along the line, he stopped believing me. Maybe I'm selfish for wanting him to believe in me when there's no proof of someone following me. But he vowed to have and to hold me until death do us apart. To have my back and give me his support.

"I took my fucking meds, Henry," I snap. "For whatever good they do to me. That fucking psychiatrist is a crook. You think sedating me and keeping me sedated is the answer?" I sling my legs off the bed, the coldness of the hardwood floor under the soles of my feet barely registering as I straighten to my full height of five foot five nothing.

Another heavy exhale and more rustling. I can practically hear him rolling his eyes at my back. "What would you have me do, Siah? You refuse to sleep. In less than six months, you've gone from my lively, exuberant wife to a shell of a woman. When was the last time you left the house? When was the last time you greeted me with a smile? When was the last time you let me touch you?"

I spin on my heel so fast, I nearly trip, but I don't let my clumsiness deter me. My finger jabs in his direction, a hulking shadow surrounded by darkness. "That's the crux of it? I'm terrified to the very marrow of my bones every single hour of the day, but you're suffering because you haven't gotten your dick wet for a couple of months?"

"It's been half a fucking year!" he thunders, the rage in his voice palpable, almost alive in the small space between the two of us. "I can't fucking do this anymore. I can't wake up at unholy hours, scared out of my mind that something happened to you, and manically check every single square inch of this house. I can't continue to fight with the unseen ghosts in your head."

My heart drops to my feet, and I wrap my arms around myself to try to contain the hollow in my chest that spreads past my rib cage, threatening to consume me. "What are you saying, Henry?" I whisper.

"You need professional help, sweetheart. I'm not equipped to care for you," he says matter-of-factly. Just like that. He turns his back to me and stands, hands shoved deep into his sleep-tousled blond hair.

The hollow grows, spreading from my chest to my limbs. "You don't need to care for me, Henry. All I ever asked for was your trust," I breathe out, the words strained and gargled as they rip from my lips.

"And my fucking sanity, Siah. That's going down the drain right along with yours," he snaps, turning accusing hazel eyes to me. A soft click sounds, mellow golden light pouring between the four walls of our bedroom from the lamp on his nightstand. "I made an oath to my patients. They need me at my best. I'm exhausted beyond belief, constantly distracted because of you."

My knees tremble and buckle, and I lock my legs together to remain upright. "You made an oath to me, too."

His lips grimace in a line so tight the pink is chased away by strained white as he folds his arms across his bare chest. "Don't I wake up every night to look for imagined monsters under the bed for you? Didn't I accompany you to every session with your psychiatrist? Don't I make sure you take your meds each and every day?"

"The only reason you have to accompany me and make sure I take my meds is because you don't trust me. I told you time and again, someone is following me. Someone broke into our home, watched us as we slept. Some of my clothes are missing. Hell, even books, notebooks, my fucking underwear." I throw my hands in the air, trying to relieve the pressure caving my chest in.

He shakes his head, disbelief etched in every sharp line of his handsome face. "No one broke into our home, Siah. I showed you the camera feed. There was absolutely no one here. Your paranoia is only growing. I can't fucking deal with this anymore. I hate that we got to this point."

I lower my eyes to my feet, my pink painted toes drumming lightly against the hardwood floor. The one person I hoped to have my back is instead ripping my heart out of my chest. The feeling of being watched is not a new one to me. Over the years, it waned and ebbed, it tightened and lessened. When Henry came into my life not even three years ago, I clung to him with all my might, made him my safe space. I was foolish then, I'm still every bit as foolish now.

While, much like most of my feelings, I managed to conceal the fear embedded into my every cell for most of our relationship. But the oily sensation of being followed and under observation—like a lab rat—only intensified ever since we got married. In eleven short months, I quit my job, gradually decreased my outings until the only reasons to venture out the door remained the imposed psychiatrist visits, most of my friends have dropped me like a hot potato, and it seems like my husband is not far behind.

"You're leaving me?" I ask incredulously, my words cutting my tongue like sharpened razors.

Chapter Two

SIAH

Cold hands grip my shoulders and move me upright on the sofa. My vision is blurred out. My eyelids refuse to blink, my reflexes sluggish and painfully slow. They scratch across my dried-out eyes as they lower and lift, like a wiper on a windshield with not enough moisture and too much friction.

My chapped lips part, and hot liquid hits my tongue, sliding down my throat. "That's it, babe. One more." Her voice is warm, with just a hint of raspiness, a hint of familiarity.

I force myself to swallow right on the brink of a cough. More hot liquid, followed by something soft that disintegrates in my mouth, is fed to me. I'm just... existing. A shield of numbness and loneliness surrounds me. It's been maybe a week or a year since Henry packed his bags in the middle of the night and left me.

The safest place in this house was my sofa. So here I stay, away from the watching eyes following me through the windows. My muscles cramped some days ago from being locked in the same position for far too long. Sleep has eluded me for far too many hours. Every time I give in to the burning desire to close my eyes and rest for even a second, my skin prickles and the hairs at the back of my neck stand at attention.

I'm exhausted. I'm terrified. I'm alone.

The same cold hands pet my hair, smoothing it away from my forehead. A flash of red blurs in front of me, then the plane of my existence tilts until my head rests once again on the soft throw pillow of my sofa.

"I'm so sorry I didn't come earlier. I've got you, babe. Don't worry, I've got you," the disembodied voice whispers, the words floating in the stale air of my living room for me to catch. I barely hear them through the drumming of my heart, my blood flooding through my ears until all I register is the thunder-like sounds that have been my companions ever since my husband left me.

I jolt when harsh shouting reaches me. "You're a fucking asshole, Henry, you goddamn spineless coward…"

"I didn't know."

"It's your job to know. How could you, you selfish prick?"

I'm floating in nothingness, my body weightless in a pool of warmth. The cold weighing me down is washed away by a scratchy sponge. Circular movements against my skin start at my collarbone, down my arm they go, my stiff muscles softening under careful ministrations. A vice tightens on my forearm, a blink in time or maybe two.

"Get out. You don't get to see her like this. Get the fuck out."

The harshness breaks through the bubble of my dreamlike state.

"It's my fucking house. That's my goddamn wife!"

"Not for much longer, if I have anything to say."

Gravel pours through my pool of warmth, cementing my limbs, weighing them down. I sink lower and lower, until there's no air, no warmth, nothing left.

"Fucking hell, Siah! Are you trying to drown yourself? Are you that far gone?"

Fire licks at my lungs, my chest heaving under the torrent of coughs rattling at my rib cage, but the fog that settled over my mind thins, just the slightest bit. The underside of Henry's dimpled chin, covered in a smatter of scruff, comes into focus. The press of his wet white shirt against my naked skin chaffs as I rock into his arms at each step he takes away from the bathroom and into our bedroom.

"Just get her into bed and leave," Jayme, my best friend since college, orders him.

"I'm not leaving her like this. She's going straight to the hospital. She can't even care for herself," he bites back. My forehead scrunches in affront. I'm right here. Maybe I can't remember the last time I slept, or ate, or got up from that sofa, but I'm right here.

"You have no say over her anymore," Jayme pushes, a hint of victory in her voice. The crinkle of papers sounds as Henry lowers me gently onto the mattress. It takes more effort than I care to admit to curl into a ball, trying to make myself smaller, invisible, out of the reach of their vitriol and fight. "Siah signed your fucking papers."

I feel more than I hear his sharp intake of air. "S-she d-did?"

"What did you think was going to happen?" I force my eyes open, only to see my best friend in all her glory, hands on her hip, like a superheroine determined to save the day. The image of her dark blue jeans and pink T-shirt shimmers in front of me, like a mirage in a sandy desert. "Oh, that's rich. You thought she'd crawl on her knees and beg you not to divorce your pathetic ass? Get out of my fucking face, Henry, or so help me God…"

Darkness creeps at the edge of my vision, the sting of tears mighty at the back of my eyes. Memories play on slow motion in my mind, flashes of Henry slamming the entrance door, luggage in hand, the pimpled pizza delivery guy serving me with divorce papers two weeks after Henry left, my hand trembling on the document as I scribbled my signature anywhere a pink tab indicated, the hours upon hours of crying on the sofa. The fear comes back faster, the iciness of realizing just how utterly alone I am quickly follows.

My breath stutters in my chest, my heart sluggishly pumping life through my veins as I finally succumb to my exhaustion. Henry's cruel words are the last thing I hear before darkness consumes me.

"If she signed the divorce papers, then pack her bags and get out of my fucking house."

Chapter Three

SIAH

A displeased moan leaves my lips as the IV drip-drip-drips incessantly, the noise as torturous and annoying in the middle of the night as a power drill going off at 5 a.m., ripping you out from the sweetest dream, and thrusting you back into the land of living. The machine monitoring my vitals accompanies the IV drip, both apparently determined to keep me awake and infuriated.

"Turn it off," I mumble to no one in the dim night light of the hospital.

The scrape of a chair against marbled tiles has me jolting, the beep of the machinery intensifying to match my heart rate. A man dressed in dark green scrubs, a stethoscope wounded around his neck, steps cautiously closer to the bed. He gives me a restrained but genuine smile, his eyes crinkling at the corners.

"Mrs. Cavanaugh, you're awake," he rumbles, his voice deep and velvety. The center of my chest heats, a faint blush igniting its way through my skin, making me thankful for the dim light in the room.

"H-Hadley, Ms. Hadley," I correct. My recollection of the past month might be hazy at best, but the memory of my trembling hand clutching a fountain pen as I scratched my signature across the divorce papers is tattooed on my brain.

I spent two weeks alone, watching the entrance door, waiting for Henry to return. And then I spent another two weeks looking at nothing, knowing how alone I truly was. Knowing my husband chose to leave me in my time of need.

A paper straw is placed on my bottom lip, and I swallow greedily, the cool liquid soothing my dried throat. "Take it easy, darling. You don't want to get sick." I heed his advice, despite the urging of my body to drink as much water as I can before it disappears from my reach.

"What happened?" I pieced enough together from my hazy memory and my surroundings to know I'm in a hospital, but how and why I got here, now that I still need to know.

He gives me a wane smile, fleeting sympathy flashing through his pale green eyes, before they cool once again as he takes me in. He walks unhurriedly to the foot of my bed and picks up a chart. His jaw ticks as he scans the papers, his fingers drumming on the back of the clipboard. "Severe dehydration, malnourishment, severe sleep deprivation. You're lucky, Ms. Hadley, that your friend found you when she did."

If he's judging my poor life choices, I can't tell. His words are delivered matter-of-factly, almost clinical. A wave of shame crashes through me; he doesn't need to judge me. I'm doing enough of that myself.

I should've been used to people always leaving me, giving up on me. I just never thought I'd bring myself to a position where I'd be the one giving up on myself, but that's exactly what I did. Meeting Henry and realizing he had staying power made me complacent. Him leaving me blindsided me completely. It's not an excuse, though.

"When am I going to be released?" I ask, even though I'll have to figure out where I'm going to live. The simple thought of having to rent an apartment and live alone terrifies me. I force my face to maintain a fake smile for the sake of... I guess he never introduced himself. The monitor betrays my false composure as the beeping picks up in intensity again.

"I'm not sure at this point, Ms. Hadley. Currently, the IV provides you with necessary vitamins, so I can only guess that the doctors will want to ensure your body has recuperated from the ordeal it's been through." He clicks his tongue against the roof of his mouth, the sharpness of the sound reverberating through the small room. "However, the most pressing matter now that you are awake is a psychiatric evaluation."

I slump against the rock-hard pillow, letting the offense rush through me. I shouldn't be surprised, yet I am. "What's the eval for?" I hiss through gritted teeth.

He turns those pale green eyes on me, his face all harsh lines and somberness. "Your husband..."

"Ex-husband!" I bite back, all bitterness and restrained hurt.

He clears his throat, the corners of his mouth hitching up in the semblance of a smile. "Apologies, Ms. Hadley. Your ex-husband insisted you have been on medication for some months now, and that your psychiatrist is continuously evaluating you as you are suspected of paranoid schizophrenia."

My eyes roll so hard, I'm getting vertigo. "Of course he did. God forbid Henry Cavanaugh MD is ever wrong." His eyes sparkle with humor, and that immediately puts me at ease. He's not making any snap judgments about me. No preconceived notions, either. "How do I ensure a different psychiatrist evaluates me?"

He drops the clipboard back behind the foot of the bed and folds his arms across his chest. "You request a different one, Ms. Hadley. Do you not trust yours?"

I ponder his question. The truth is... no, I do not. And yes, I'm aware that only feeds into the suspicion of me being a paranoid schizophrenic. But my current psychiatrist, *Doctor* Christiansen, is also an old med school buddy of Henry. Each session with him, his preconceived notions took precedence over what I was actually telling him. I don't think Henry meant any harm, and I naively let him coordinate this process, deferring to him in my weakness.

It's time I get my life back on track by myself. At the end of the day, I can only rely on myself.

"I'd like a second opinion."

Chapter Four

Siah

Anxiously, I watch the clock, my thumbs battling in my lap. In twenty-four hours, I'll be out of here. In twenty-four hours, I'll have to re-learn how to live alone and be at peace with my loneliness.

To my surprise, Henry has more than once tried to visit me. I made sure, under no unclear or uncertain terms, that he was not to be granted entry. Sure, I'm a petty bitch. But he's the one who decided to celebrate our one-year anniversary with a divorce. Instead of helping me navigate my fears, he used them against me and, when he couldn't have his way, threw me to the curb. So, he can take his worry and shove it up his ass as far as it can go.

While legally he is still technically my husband, the beauty of an uncontested divorce where we all keep only the assets we've entered our marriage with is the short wait time until the dissolution of our union. It certainly helps that I want nothing to do with any of our shared things. All I need are my clothes—which Jayme has already packed and stored for me—and my laptop for work. I even left him my books. I can always buy new copies.

My psychiatric evaluation has been... surprising, yet at the same time not. Doctor Ferguson, a no-nonsense woman in her forties, has dismissed the paranoid schizophrenic diagnosis after our first meeting. Apparently, I do not, in fact, meet the criteria for the diagnosis. While she believes I have severe anxiety and my feelings of being watched need to be monitored, she cut me off the plethora of medicine Henry's buddy prescribed 'for my own good'. I am instead to take up therapy as soon as I'm discharged from the hospital, so that I get the necessary help I need to manage my anxiety.

The strange feeling of being watched has all but vanished the whole week I've been in the hospital. While my mental faculties have made a *miraculous* recovery, my body is slower on the uptake. Turns out, no eating or drinking anything for close to seven days is really, really hard on the body. Add in the lack of sleep, and my body has been as close to shutting down as it would ever get, except maybe in death... That scared the absolute fuck out of me.

Every morning as I look at my gaunt face in the tiny bathroom mirror, I promise to never neglect myself to this extreme, regardless of what shitstorms batter at my life. I am my own responsibility. My wellbeing is my right to maintain and protect.

"Boy, have I got good news for you!" Jayme bursts through the door of my hospital room, arms full of coffee and donuts. My mouth starts watering as soon as the bittersweet scent of the dark roast reaches me. My arm extends of its own volition, as if pulled by an invisible string, my fingers twitching in a silent 'gimme' demand.

"You bustin' me out of here earlier than planned?" I ask, a hopeful note in my tone.

She plops down on the bed next to me, pushing the box of donuts between us. With a huff, she blows away the curled tendrils of red hair covering the rich brown of her eyes. "Nah. Sorry, dude. You shall be unjailed on the 'morrow, still."

I shrug my shoulders. It was worth the ask, although I'm not as excited to leave as I make it seem. I still need to figure out where I'll live and how to make my new home a place where I'm feeling safe enough. The feeling of being watched might have disappeared, but I know, *I know,* he's still out there, lurking, watching, waiting.

"Remember August?" Jayme's question takes me out of my head.

"The elusive stepbrother?" I pop an eyebrow. I've never met her stepbrother. The one and only time I spoke to him was at our college graduation. My brave best friend tried—unsuccessfully, might I add—to hide her disappointment at him missing the festivities. So, I sneakily appropriated her phone and told the bastard off when he dignified to answer my call.

She grins at my question, her pretty face lighting up from the inside out. "The one and only. Anyway, he's away, and shall remain away for a good while, according to him."

"That's a surprise," I mutter sarcastically. If there's one word invented to describe August St. Andrew, that's 'away'.

"Well, this instance might be the only one when I'm happy he's not here," she says, the reproach sharp and clear in the brown depths of her eyes. "Look, you're going to hate me for this, but I promise, he's a vault."

I sit up straight, my stomach flipping and curling into itself. "What did you do?"

Her cheeks redden, the plethora of freckles on her skin fading under the strength of her blush. "I wrecked my head the whole week about what to do, and then it dawned on me when I spoke to him. His house is a fucking fortress. Security system, cameras, restricted access—Fort Knox is a joke compared to his home. All he asks is that you keep away from the third floor because that's his work-office when at home."

My heart accelerates, thumping furiously inside my chest. Adrenaline and relief course unbidden through my veins. My major worry is all but eradicated by the most unexpected person.

I lean forward and clasp Jayme's hand. "Thank you, friend. And thank August, too. This is..." I don't get to finish putting my gratitude into words as I burst into tears, heart-wrenching sobs rattling through me.

She draws me into her arms. The familiar scent of vanilla, freesia, and plum—flowery and fruity, just like her—envelops me. I allow myself this moment of weakness, a blip in time, before I draw back and rein the torrent of salty tears in, wiping all traces of weakness from my face with the back of my hand.

Jayme doesn't make a big deal out of me losing my composure, but shoves half a chocolate donut into her mouth, chasing it away with a hearty sip of her coffee. Once she's thoroughly chewed through the dough, she picks up her phone and rattles a series of numbers.

"I'll text them to you, just in case. It's August's personal phone. I'll forward him your number too, so he can send you all the details you need to access his house. He's very... protective of it. So he doesn't share any details if he doesn't have to."

Worry streaks through me, my fingers twitching on the paper cup in my hand. "If this is too much of an imposition to him, I'll find somewhere else to live. I can stay in a hotel until I get rent sorted."

She snorts a very unladylike laugh. "As if. Nah, dude. He was happy to help. As happy as August gets, and the circumstances allow." Her hand swishes back and forth in front of her, hot liquid spilling over the rim of her own paper cup. "Honestly, he said you can do whatever you want in the house. Treat it as your own. Except for the third floor. You can't gain access to it, anyway. He has a special code and whatever—I sorta dozed off when he started ranting about security."

"Security sounds great just about now..." I sigh wistfully.

Chapter Five

SIAH

I whistle sharply as the dark gates part to allow us entry into August's drive. His home is surrounded by lush forest on three sides where it's perched on a hill at the edge of an exclusive neighborhood just outside of Seattle.

The skies are dark and overcast. Heavy clouds hang so low on the horizon, I feel like I can just stretch out my hand and fluff the swirling, angry darkness with my fingertips. Jayme drives slowly through the metal gates and parks her car in front of the large garage next to the three-story house.

I'm not surprised to see the house in modern lines of metal and glass, as tall and dark as I imagine its owner to be. I've only ever seen one picture of August with Jayme, taken shortly after our college graduation, when he took her on a holiday to Hawaii to make up for missing that important milestone in her life.

According to Jayme, August is extremely fond of his privacy due to the nature of his work—he owns or consults for a security company, she was vague on the details—so pictures are an absolute no-go with her grump of a stepbrother.

I couldn't discern much from the picture she showed me, since it was taken in a gloomy bar, with only Edison bulbs for illumination. All I could tell was that August St. Andrew is tall, dark, and can glare at a phone like no other. To say I am curious to actually see him is an understatement.

There's a reason I worked as an editor before my fear got the best of me six months ago. Both Jayme and I were first employed as journalists for *Debatable*, an online magazine. The magazine prides itself on quality content, well thought-out articles—from celeb gossip to famine in underdeveloped countries—and only deals with facts that can be verified. But my curiosity has always been my downfall. There's not a mystery in the world I don't like and chase after, like a hyped-up bunny chasing after a carrot. Being an editor kept me both safe and sated my curiosity.

Until I got scared of everything, including my own shadow, that is.

Debatable, surprisingly, did not have any remote jobs. The owners preferred us all to go into the office, unless out on assignment. While they understood my issues, they couldn't accommodate my need to work from home, so I had to resign. My love of writing took a massive hit, but now I'm channeling my passion into ghostwriting. It didn't feel prudent to take a leap and become a published author and have my name—not even a pen-name—out there in the wild, when I'm convinced there's someone following my every move.

I guess I'm not holding August's love of privacy against him, despite my curiosity, since I know all too well how my own privacy is a necessity, a lifeline even.

Ghostwriting is really not too bad. The assignments are diverse and challenging. Best of all, they pay really damn well. Which is a saving grace for my current situation. The last thing I need right now is to depend on alimony from Henry and drag out the divorce.

A shiver passes through me at the mere thought, goosebumps sprouting on my skin as I exit the car. A balmy wind, carrying a hint of salt from the ocean just below the hill, plays in my hair, tangling the chestnut-colored curls hanging heavy over my shoulders.

"It's going to take me a hot minute to get used to your hair," Jayme comments as she slams the driver's door shut.

I wink playfully at her. So, my hair might have been an impulsive move. I've worn my hair a light ashy-blonde ever since I aged out of foster care and started college. Eighteen years of 'Moussiah' as a nickname were quite enough at that point. So I got rid of the mousy, brown color, straightened my hair within an inch of its life, and wore it that way for ten long years.

Until now. Now, Moussiah doesn't sound so bad. Moussiah can blend with her surroundings, be one with the walls, never standing out, never drawing attention to herself. The very first stop we made after being discharged was to a hair salon where my hair got restored to all its natural glory. And by all its natural glory, I mean dyed in a color as close to my original one and had my curls moussed and conditioned and styled.

Show me a woman who has gone through a break-up or a divorce and didn't make a journey to the hair salon, and I'll show you a liar.

"It'll still be here when you do. The curls less bouncy and with a lot more frizz, but still here," I say, heaving up my luggage from the trunk of her small SUV.

It's pitiful, really, to see your whole life in two wheelers, a duffle bag, and a laptop backpack. The silver lining would have to be needing only one trip to carry my whole life inside August's monster home.

"Hurry up, would you?" Jayme shouts from the front door. "These blasted bags are cutting through my skin, I swear."

So maybe more than one trip, considering we bought off half of Walmart's inventory.

Sweat is dripping down my back as I climb the few steps leading to the door. I lean the wheelers against the black metallic wall and slide my phone out from the pocket of my jeans, tapping quickly to open August's instructions.

> Gate code: 29682091
>
> Front door - this only has to be done once. Press the green button on the bottom left corner.

August St. Andrew

My finger touches the cold metal, a shiver working up my spine at the contact.

> Type the overwrite token.

August St. Andrew

My eyes jump between the screen of my phone and the touchscreen keyboard on the panel as I carefully type the long combination of letters, numbers, and characters.

"Yes," I exhale when 'Access Granted' flashes on the screen and the red outline of a finger forms instead of the keyboard.

> Scan your fingerprint. Make sure the whole pad of your thumb is pressed against the scanner.

August St. Andrew

I, once again, do as instructed and press my finger tightly against the screen, rotating my thumb right and then left. The panel beeps once more, confirming the task has been completed, and the keyboard appears under my fingerprint.

> *Lastly, add your name.*
>
> *Once your fingerprint is registered, you won't need to do anything else. I'll adjust the security system so that you don't need to worry about the alarm being armed or disarmed. You'll always be safe in my home.*
>
> *Now, delete this message if you're done.*

August St. Andrew

A soft click comes from the door when the panel displays an 'Entry granted' message, and Jayme pushes it open. "Damn, that looked complicated," she mutters. "Come on, dude, I've frozen my tits out waiting. I need a hot cuppa ASAP."

My eyes widen as I take in the open concept of the first floor. Floor to ceiling windows greet me from every direction. The kitchen is tucked in at the far corner of the large space, separated by a dark island from the rest of the living area. On the opposite side, a couple of sturdy-looking leather couches are oriented toward a full wall adorned with a massive TV, a lone coffee table sitting in front of them. Last, as if forgotten, a loveseat is tucked into a corner, a side table next to it, with a book spread open on its shiny surface. Sleek, lustrous stairs, right in the center of the room, divide the open space, leading to what I presume is the second floor.

Sparse. Dark. Sleek. And empty.

I can't help the foreboding feeling rushing through me. My brow furrows as shame battles for dominance inside my chest. August has been kind enough to open his home to me. Who am I to judge how he prefers to live?

My phone pings from my pocket, and I slide it out once again.

> *Siah,*
>
> I apologize for the work-in-progress that is my home.

I'm afraid I don't spend much time at all there, and when I do, it's mostly on the third floor.

The kitchen is fully functional. A laundry room and a gym are in the basement. The master bedroom and guest rooms are on the second floor. Unfortunately, only the master is fully furnished. It's yours.

I've scarcely used it. As I said, most of my time is spent in my office.

If you're uncomfortable, let me know, and I'll arrange for a guest bedroom to be furnished for you.

Welcome home.

August St. Andrew

I swallow down the lump of emotions lodged in my throat. A tendril of unease curls at the bottom of my stomach. I feel as if I'm pushing him out of his own home, but that's silly. He wouldn't have offered if he didn't want me here, right?

Besides, once the divorce from Henry is finally complete, I'll start looking for a place to live. Maybe in a different city. Hell, a different state. I'll put as much distance between me and my follower as I possibly can.

And I'll be out of August's home before he returns.

Chapter Six

SIAH

My fingers fly over the keyboard, the story I'm writing flowing as I lose myself in the forbidden love between a high lord and his lowly servant. Papers are strewn across the gleaming surface of the glass desk I'm sitting at. Heavy rain hits incessantly at the large window, Douglas firs bending every which way under the unforgiving gusts of this early fall storm.

It bothers me none. Jayme was right, August's home is a fortress. Never in my life have I felt quite this safe. Not as a child growing up in foster care, not as a young adult navigating college life with nothing to fall back on, and not as an adult being tossed aside by the one person I thought would be my ride-or-die.

My fingers falter over the keyboard. Thoughts of Henry always bring a bitter taste to my tongue. My heart constricts painfully in my chest, and the back of my eyes burns with unshed tears. The past two weeks in August's home have been... illuminating. So have the therapy sessions I'm attending on the daily. Too many questions are weighing heavily on my shoulders.

Who are my parents?

Why did they abandon me?

Did they ever name me?

Do I actually love Henry or was I in love the whole time with the future I thought the two of us would have?

Maybe I've spent far too much time with my nose in romance novels lately. Maybe my promise to choose myself is the driving force behind my feelings, or lack thereof. But ever since I woke up in the hospital, I've been cognizant and determined to move on with my life. I haven't missed him. Not one bit.

Twenty-one days. That's all it took for me to see the forest for the trees. To glimpse at the elusive distance separating the two of us during our relationship and our brief marriage.

Henry Cavanaugh didn't love me. He loved the arm candy I became to feel worthy of a man such like him. He wanted a worldly wife who depended solely on him. And I, foolishly, let him dress me, let him *care* for me. The lonely, unwanted child inside of me rejoiced, for I had finally found my family. A lovely portrait of smoke and mirrors, the paint only just surface deep.

My soon-to-be ex-husband is not a bad man, by any means. A little narcissistic, a little vain, but his heart was in the right place most of the time. Except, of course, when the woman he pledged to love for life was in dire need of his support. And then his heart preferred to unburden itself from those pledges.

He was only too happy to issue me with an ultimatum; either I was going away for a wellbeing retreat—he mispronounced his attempt to have me locked up and sedated out of my mind while he posed the image of a concerned husband—or divorce.

I might be unsure if I had truly loved him, but his actions still smart against my skin. The sting of rejection still makes my stomach churn. And his continuous need to control me sparks a new tendril of fear and rebellion inside my chest. I refuse to be discarded but kept on a loose fishing line to be reeled in when his ego demands it.

So the plethora of messages he keeps bombarding me with sits in my inbox on my phone—read but never answered. He's like a Swiss clock in his delivery, precise, on time, and thoroughly unwanted.

> Siah, you're being childish. Where are you?

Henry Cavanaugh
Delivered September 8th, 11:34 a.m.

> Siah, stop ignoring me.
> Christiansen tells me you haven't attended any of your sessions with him, nor have you picked up your prescription. I'm worried about you, darling.

Henry Cavanaugh
Delivered September 9th, 11:34 a.m.

> *You are still my wife. I have the right to know what's going on with you. Your bitch of a friend refuses to tell me anything. It doesn't have to be this way between us, Siah. Answer the phone, darling. Let's meet and discuss. It doesn't have to end this way.*

Henry Cavanaugh
DELIVERED SEPTEMBER 10TH, 11:34 A.M.

I suppose I should be grateful that I can have my coffee in peace before he fucks up my day with his insistence. As far as I am concerned, he stopped being my husband the second he packed a bag and left me alone to my fears in the middle of the night. I owe him absolutely nothing, no response, no conversation, from the very moment he chose to file for divorce and have me served with the papers like a coward. The time for conversation was at the end of July once he had time to think through his hasty decision to leave, or all throughout August.

Had it not been for my best friend, I would have died by my own unintentional hand three weeks ago. He hadn't checked on me for a full month, not once. Not until Jayme returned from her assignment overseas and, concerned with my lack of response, came barreling down the door.

While his messages dripped of fake concern when I was first discharged from the hospital, as the days wound by, the concern was replaced with contempt, hatred, and vitriol.

> *For fuck's sake, answer your goddamn phone.*

Henry Cavanaugh
DELIVERED SEPTEMBER 20TH, 11:34 A.M.

> *You're an ungrateful cow, aren't you? If you don't answer your fucking phone, I'll report you as a missing person.*

Henry Cavanaugh
DELIVERED SEPTEMBER 21ST, 11:34 A.M.

Now see, that particular message got my blood boiling. I was oh so tempted to reply and tell him where to shove his threat. But I knew all too well he was trying to get a reaction out of me, so I didn't give him the pleasure of knowing he got one. It also gave me a sick sense of satisfaction to deny the great Henry Cavanaugh what he wanted.

August's home has given me a sense of indestructible safety. Like I can't be touched between the steel and glass walls of his house. I can't be reached, and I can't be found.

My eyes find the small clock on the taskbar of my laptop. *11:33 a.m., here we go. Three, two, one... 11:34. Ping!*

> *You fucking bitch. I should've known better than to marry white trash. Poor little abandoned whore. Are you still being watched, Siah? Are you still begging for attention, crying wolf to anyone who'll listen? Have you dug your whoring claws into the next poor unsuspecting man? Does he know you are still married to me?*

Henry Cavanaugh
Delivered September 22nd, 11:34 a.m.

I close the lid to my laptop and shove my phone in a drawer, then lean back into my comfortable, buttery-soft office chair. A deep sigh escapes my lips as I stove away the tears brimming at the corner of my eyes. In my head, I count the days until we're officially divorced, and I'll be able to block his number without repercussions. So far, he stopped only at threats. At least, if he proves to be difficult and tries to delay our inevitable parting, I'll have material aplenty to use against him.

It's my only saving grace and the sole reason I haven't blocked him yet.

Chapter Seven

Siah

My days are quiet, and I love the solitude. My mental health has never been as strong as it is right now. The therapist I've been seeing religiously every day this past month has suggested we reduce our meetings from daily to twice a week. As minor of a suggestion as that is, it feels like a major victory to me.

After the six months spent on a cocktail of drugs that made me sleep more than I was awake and, when awake, feeling like my emotions were not my own, I'm happy to be without any right now. I'm free to feel my own feelings, free to deal with my sadness and my worries. That's another small victory I didn't know before how much I should appreciate.

Henry's messages have turned particularly nasty, so while I still haven't blocked him, I muted his contact. I don't need to poison myself with his hateful words, meant only to hurt me. He's part of my past, and that's where he needs to remain.

And so, my phone has been quiet apart from the occasional call from Jayme. She's once again out of state on an assignment, shaking it up with professional storm chasers, on the tail of a series of tornadoes that have been plaguing the Southeast. While I miss seeing my friend, I also miss her doing my grocery run for me. For the past three days, I have been living on freezer meals, and my stomach is not a happy camper.

I'll have to siphon any and all traces of courage I have left and venture out by myself for the first time in months. Just the thought has my knees trembling. Since yesterday, I've been making a mental pros and cons list between going out myself or doing my shopping online and having it delivered. Neither option is appealing to me.

Apart from Jayme, only August's personal assistant has visited once. It was at August's bidding, when he arranged furniture to be delivered and installed for one of his guest rooms. Which turned out to be my new office. To say I was surprised is an understatement. Not because of the visit. But because of my landlord's thoughtfulness.

I guess my best friend told him what I do for a living, so he created a perfect space for me to focus on my writing. He also ensured I'd know beforehand when his assistant, Robert, arrived, together with the delivery guys. All throughout, August assured me no one knew—including Robert—that I lived there. Jayme greeted them and led them to the room to become my office, then escorted them out when they were done.

Deep down, I'm convinced that changing my hair, having my location disabled on my phone, and not using my credit cards was instrumental in deterring my follower from finding me again.

I've gone paperless with my bank and rented a PO Box for anything else. When Jayme visits me, she stops by the Post Office and brings me anything I might have received. Of course, this arrangement works only when my best friend is actually in the city and not chasing the next story for the magazine.

A feeble plan forms in my mind. There's no real way to know if it'll work in the slightest, but it's better than leaving an online trace with my credit card and August's address.

> Hi August. Would you mind if I borrowed one of your cars for a quick shopping trip? Jayme and I were supposed to go buy a car for me, but with everything… Well, we forgot.

Me

Am I feeling like an ungrateful bitch taking advantage of his generosity? That'd be a resounding yes. He refuses to take any rent or bill money from me. But I made sure to set aside a lump sum—and will continue to do so every month I live in his home—and transfer it to him when I move out.

The screen on my phone doesn't fully dim before it illuminates once again with a new message.

> There's a locked black box in the garage as you enter through the kitchen door, on the left-hand side.

August St. Andrew

> *Access code: 15062016. The keys are there. Take whatever car you want, although, if you're going shopping, I'd suggest the SUV. It's large enough to fit most things you may buy, and small enough that parking won't trouble you.*

August St. Andrew

> *Alternatively, I could always arrange for grocery delivery for you.*

August St. Andrew

Dear God! Who is this man? Although it is appealing to have him deal with groceries, I can't be in his debt any more than I am right now. It's also important to me to regain some semblance of independence. I don't want to live my life in fear. I don't want to be locked within four walls, depending on others to help me with basic necessities.

> *Thank you, August. I'm so grateful to you. I promise I'll return your car in the same condition I borrowed it.*

Me

> *Of that I have no doubt, Siah. Safe travels.*

August St. Andrew

My belly clenches as I read his words. The memory of his rumbly, gravelly voice, like a thunderstorm on its march to destruction, washes through me, and liquid heat pools between my legs. My cheeks redden, both with embarrassment at lusting over someone who's helping me, but mostly... with desire.

A surprising side-effect of the medicines leaving my body is my newly found libido. I've never had the highest sex drive. Whether that's by nature or nurture, I don't know. I kept away from men during high school and college. The last thing I needed was to get pregnant and risk having my child end up like me—abandoned in foster care because I couldn't provide for them. My sexual needs ended up repressed by a healthy dose of caution and fear.

Fear seems to be the motif of my life so far.

My first sexual experience happened just after I got hired at *Debatable*. My first assignment for the magazine was a satirical piece on clubs being the hunting grounds of supposedly civilized men, written in contrast with Jayme's piece that made an analysis on the mating habits of primeval men. Isn't it ironic that I fell prey on those hunting grounds?

I can't bring myself to regret the experience. If anything, my only regret is not having seconds, or thirds, or fourths. Blind Date was one of those clubs for the bold and daring, bored with the normal experience of overflowing drinks and overcrowded dancefloors. As soon as I entered the darkened, mirrored hallway, an attendant put a flimsy blindfold over my eyes. Dense enough to conceal distinctive features, sheer enough to not trip over my own two feet.

And so, in the obscurity of my blindfold, I danced the night away in the middle of the club. Until a pair of large hands gripped my waist, and a strong body curled around my back, narrow hips guiding the movement of mine. Maybe it was the dangerous appeal of the darkness, or maybe my lack of faith in anything romantic, but the stranger seemed like the best choice I could make to finally understand what it felt like to have a man move inside of me.

Boy... did he move.

How he found an empty office at the back of the club is beyond me even now. One minute, we were writhing against each other to the beat of sensual songs. The next, I was on my back, my hands clutching the crisp material of his shirt as he fucked me ten ways to Sunday. If I close my eyes, I can still taste on my tongue the burnt amber and spiciness of the whiskey he must have drunk before he kissed me like he'd never come up for air.

As with any fairytale, at the stroke of the clock—or phone notification, as it was my case—the magic vanished. My caution returned, and before he could zip his trousers up, I was out the door and driving like a bat out of hell to the little studio apartment Jayme and I shared.

I've never forgotten one single second of that night. Of the man who showed me that one-night stands don't have to be a cheap experience, and chemistry goes a long way to make up for lack of skill.

Maybe that's why it took me three years to give another man a chance. Henry was... not disappointing. Tall, handsome, with a protective streak a mile wide, he swept me off my feet. So what if my orgasms were few and far between? His easy-going nature and kindness more than made up for the extra dash of chemistry that was missing between the two of us. It was only at the very end, when my rose-colored glasses shattered into a million pieces, that I saw he wasn't protective, but controlling. He wasn't easy going, but indifferent. My missing orgasms weren't because of a lack of chemistry. He got his, so any extra effort wasn't warranted.

When my meds all but eradicated the little sex drive I had, his kindness also vanished into thin air. Any kind of act of service toward me became a barb to be used at a later date to showcase my redundancy and lack of usefulness in his life.

I know for a fact he's not the one behind my many nightmares. He's not my follower. The fear started burrowing into me far before Henry, even before my Blind Date stranger. But my soon-to-be ex-husband sure as fuck used my fear against me to control and, eventually, get rid of me.

Shaking my head to dispel the cloud of negativity hovering over me, I climb into August's car. The leather smells new, with barely a trace of burnt amber and sandalwood permeating the cab.

It's time to be a big girl now.

Chapter Eight

Him

The little blue dot flashes against my screen, moving slowly over the map, no doubt because of the mid-afternoon Seattle traffic. My fingers fly against the keyboard, the images of a dozen traffic cameras flickering to life on the screens mounted on the far wall of my office.

The corners of my lips tip up. My jaw nearly cramps under the effort. I haven't had many reasons to smile in this lifetime. Not until her.

"Where are you going, little mockingbird?" I murmur as I drum my forefinger against my lips, my eyes not missing anything on the screens in front of me. Not the rich chestnut curls bouncing on her slender shoulders, not the nervous swipe of her tongue across her full pink bottom lip as she signals a turn and parks her car in front of her bank.

Without looking at the keyboard, I bring up on the screen next to me all her banking accounts. A few clicks, and the live feed of the security cameras from inside the bank is in front of me. There she is, my little pet, fidgeting from one shapely leg to the other as she waits in the queue to be seen. She smiles softly at the teller, and my hands fist under the bolt of jealousy crashing through me.

I crave all her smiles for my own.

I want her smiles, her tears, her fear, her love. Everything Siah Hadley is, I need like my next fix.

I jump to my feet and pace the entire length of my lair. Back and forth, back and forth. It's all I can do to expel the burning energy thrumming through me like a live wire ready to electrocute and fry.

With the corner of my eye, I see her walk with a manager to one of the back rooms. The hollow echo of my sigh bounces off the walls as I tap on my keyboard with more vigor than intended to bring up the feed from the manager's office.

"Mrs. Cavanaugh," comes the stiff voice of the asshole, "is my understanding you wish to withdraw the entirety of your savings account?"

Siah crosses her legs and leans forward. "Ms. *Hadley*," she bites out, overemphasizing her surname. That's a good girl. If I hear one more person referring to her with another man's surname, I'm not responsible for my fucking actions. "And yes, I need my savings account in cash, except for five thousand dollars."

The manager clasps his meaty hands on top of his desk, a frown marring his pudgy face. "May I ask why do you need so much cash?"

That's an answer I too am interested to hear, except I don't like the way he questions her. *What are you planning to do, little mockingbird?*

"With all due respect, you may not. My money, my decision, Mister..." Siah trails off. It's only too bad the camera in his office faces the asshole, and I can't see her pretty face. I'll have to be content with looking at her long hair, imagining the softness of all those silky strands wrapped around my hand.

"Peterson." He clears his throat, his cheeks reddening with affront.

Get over yourself, you spineless cunt.

"Mr. Peterson, do you question everyone holding a bank account here about what they do with their money?" Siah asks, her tone calm and polite, despite the obvious challenge in her words.

"My apologies, Mrs. Ca... Ms. Hadley, I'll see that you have your cash ready for you. If you'd be so kind as to take a seat in the waiting area, it should take no longer than fifteen minutes." He stands abruptly, towering over her, but my brave brave woman only leans back into her chair.

"One last thing," she says, rummaging through her bag before producing a piece of paper she pushes over the desk to him. "Please change my emergency contact from Mr. Henry Cavanaugh to Miss Jayme St. Andrew. Here's a copy of the Temporary Orders from our divorce proceedings, and a copy of Miss St. Andrew's contact details. I tried to update everything online, but for some reason my banking app kept freezing."

Of course it kept freezing, my love. Over my dead fucking body, anyone else but me will be listed in any official documents.

Except she's not ready. Not yet.

I tap the screen on my tablet a few times. Jayme St. Andrew will have to do for the moment. Until Siah is ready to accept that she's mine. She *always* has been only mine.

The burner phone—a clone of Siah's—vibrates next to the keyboard.

I'm sick and tired of these stupid games you're playing, Siah. You locked me out of your banking account? What the fuck?

Henry Cavanaugh
Delivered September 28th, 11:34 a.m.

My jaw clenches. Before I realize what I'm doing, the sound of plastic and glass shattering reaches me. *Great. Another phone gone.* Now I have to spend another hour setting a clone up again.

It was my own goddamn mistake that this asshole has gotten this far—dating *my* Siah, marrying her, divorcing her. The cockroach doesn't deserve to breathe the same air as my beautiful mockingbird, nevermind taking any more time of her day. Three years have been plenty enough.

I've been living in hell ever since she married the dickless insect. Images of them together torture my every waking hour. Knowing she slept next to him, kissed him, made love to him, makes me sick to my fucking stomach.

I'm not wasting another fucking minute. Anyone daring to get between me and my little bird will curse the day they were born.

My eyes are trained on Siah as she once again follows Peterson inside his office. He passes her a sealed black bag with the bank's logo on the front. "There you have it, Ms. Hadley, seventy-five thousand dollars in cash. We were also successful in updating your details, as requested."

Siah shakes the asshole's meaty hand, and I barely stifle a groan. My palm itches to feel her soft skin against mine. I bet she feels like the most expensive of silks. My cock twitches in my trousers, the bastard as eager as I am to feel her wrapped around me as I fuck all my pent-up frustration into her.

As she sashays her way out of the bank and to her car, a message she sent out earlier pops into my head. For fuck's sake, she's just going to stroll around through Walmart aisles with a shitload of cash stuffed into her purse?

I grab my personal phone from the pocket of my trousers and hit the first contact. One ring, two, he answers on the third.

"You summoned, *Master*?"

"Sarcasm is the lowest form of wit," I reply, rolling my eyes.

"That's 'cause I'll never match your intellect, oh wise one. What do you want?"

"You're a pain in my ass. Shadow Siah, make sure she gets to her home safe. I've sent you the tracking code."

He's quiet for a second. I know he disagrees with my plan, and I usually value his opinion, but he hasn't lived in hell for the last six years. He has no idea what it feels like to lose the one person you want the most.

Besides, he owes me, and he fucking knows it.

"And if she recognizes me?" he finally answers.

"You better think quick on your feet then. Otherwise, what use are you to me?"

Chapter Nine

SIAH

"Calm down, Siah. No one is watching you," I mumble, trying to encourage myself as I park the car in its designated spot in the garage.

This past month I became complacent, let my guard down. I allowed August's fortress of a home to lull me in a false sense of safety. Anger and fear war inside my chest, my skin sprouting goosebumps ever since Walmart. Did *he* happen upon me by accident?

Sure, I'd been anxious as I drove to the bank, but apart from anxiety, there has been no burn against my skin from eyes unseen. The condescending asshole of a bank manager was annoying, but as I left the bank—cash in tow—and headed to the hypermarket, there were no forebodings feeling accompanying me.

As I pushed my overflowing cart, turning veggies one way and then another before tossing them with the rest of my shopping, smelling the sweetness of the fruits, for a brief half an hour, I felt like Siah of the past—normal. And then the back of my neck prickled. A coil of electricity tensed inside my stomach, my veins flooding with nauseating ice, and I knew. *He* was back.

Watching me.

Following me.

Hunting me.

It took every ounce of courage I had built up inside of me for the past month to not ditch my cart in the middle of the aisle and run for the safety of my car. I carried on, finishing my shopping, tapping the soles of my Converse impatiently as each of my items were scanned and bagged, then cautiously walked to my car. My knees trembled as I shoved the bags into the trunk. My hands shook as I nearly sprinted across the parking lot, returning my cart to its rightful place.

But not even the comforting scent of burnt amber and sandalwood managed to calm my racing heart.

I don't know how I got home in one piece. Not with my eyes focused more on each of the mirrors, trying to see if any particular car was following me. Not with my choppy breath making it hard to stay alert and present.

"Fuck," I sob. "Fuck, fuck, FUUUUCK!" I yell louder and louder as I hit the center of the wheel with the pad of my palm. Bitter tears are pouring down my cheeks, my throat swollen with pent-up anger.

My body sags against the leather chair as the adrenaline leaves my bloodstream. As soon as the massive metal gates closed behind me, the intrusive burning feeling against the back of my neck disappeared. By now... he knows where I'm hiding.

My only saving grace is that I'm fairly certain he won't be able to access August's home. Not the way he was able to break into the house I shared with Henry. Because I know with every fiber of my being, he's been in that house. He watched us sleep. He watched us...

"Let it go, Siah. You're safe here," I croak, willing the words I'm saying out loud into reality.

I press my trembling thumb against the cold button of the remote. A whirring sound travels through the large garage as the door lowers until I'm sitting in complete darkness. The thumping of my heart is ridiculously loud in the close confines of the car, with my eyes robbed of any light.

I thought it before, but it hits me right now exactly how alone I really am.

How vulnerable.

Whoever it is, stalking my every move, has backed me into a corner with only two choices. Isolate myself inside a house that's not even mine, or risk myself every time I step foot out of those daunting gates.

He's never hurt me before—and I know it in my gut 'he' is correct—but who's to say his patience won't run thin, and observing from a distance would no longer suffice to satisfy whatever depraved need he has that keeps him following me?

Both choices are a prison. One simply has a larger hunting ground.

There's no one in my life to notice if I'm gone. No one to miss me.

Sure, maybe Jayme will notice eventually. Once she's back from whatever adventure she's on with the magazine. She'll have her morning coffee one day, and a random thought would have her check her phone and see a long time has passed since it chimed with a message from me.

And by that time, it would be too late.

The house is eerily quiet, with only the rhythmic chopping of my knife against a wooden board for background noise. I don't dare listen to music, or even turn the TV on. My body is wound too tight, my senses in overdrive.

I took my time in the car to compose myself. Then I did the numerous trips back and forth between the garage and the kitchen, carrying my groceries in. The shelves in the pantry are heaving now. I actually convinced myself they'll fall from where they're secured to the wall under the weight of all my cans and bags and cartons. Only after I pushed against the glossy wood, testing its resistance, my fears were laid to rest.

The freezer is also full. All my fresh vegetables are cut and chopped and minced and stored neatly in containers. If I'm careful, I'll have at least two months' worth of supplies for fresh dinners.

The flat of my knife scrapes against the wooden board as I push the last of the mushrooms inside the clear ziplock bag. My movements are apathetic, robotic, my limbs laden with worry and anxiety.

I can't keep living like this.

I need to make a plan, *fast*. The cash I have is not a lot in the grand scheme of things, but should be enough to keep me going until I replenish my emergency funds. All I need is a car, and then I can drive myself out of this godforsaken city. Hell, out of this state.

Maybe I should move to Panama, or Costa Rica, or any other country south of the border. Live my life on the beach, golden sand between my toes, much too warm sun above my head, and change my name to Esmeralda, or Paloma, or Salome. Now that's a prison I could get behind.

Still alone.

Still confined.

But with thousands of miles between me and my stalker.

Free.

As crazy as an idea as that sounds, a wave of renewed energy flows through me. I hurry through cleaning the kitchen, taking a shower, and getting ready for bed. When I'm in the middle of the enormous king-size mattress, with the velvety headboard supporting my back, I position my laptop on my lap and fire it up. Maybe I'm not ready to book the next ticket out of the country just yet, but getting the outline of a plan... It gives me hope that maybe, just maybe, I have a chance of actually living my life.

I open my Notes app and start making a list—used car, best country to live in South America, classed by cost of living in a major city, crime rates, and medical care. These items should keep me busy for a while.

In bold, red font I type out my deadline, December First. I should have enough information by then to be able to at least go on a long trip. My divorce from Henry, unless he plans to give me trouble, would also be official in a couple of months. And if I'm being careful, all the groceries I've bought today should last me until then.

A thunder-like rumble echoes through the ceiling, reverberating through the wall. My limbs freeze and my body locks up. An inhale is trapped in my lungs, a faint burning sensation flaming under my rib cage. I don't dare breathe. I don't dare blink. *What was that?*

Like a frightened deer sensing a predator on its tail, my ears perk up, every cell in my body standing at attention, anticipating, waiting, fearing...

Seconds pass as slowly as centuries but, apart from the violent swish of my blood against my eardrums, no other sounds are to be heard. Not even the wind ravaging through the trees outside.

My hand moves as if in slow motion, like every movement would alert whatever is on the floor just above me to my presence. My fingers hook over the edge of my laptop, and gently, carefully lower the lid, until I'm once again plunged into darkness. I drag the device quietly across the sheet covering my lap and hide it under the soft cotton.

Then it's my turn to slide stealthily under the fuzzy, gray blanket, until I'm covered from head to toe, a cotton armor against the things that go bump in the night. My hand, shaky and uncoordinated, finds my phone under the pillow. I've got one thing going for me, and that's my habit of keeping my phone on silent and on the dimmest setting for brightness. A soft tap, a long push on the side button until the volume is as low as it gets without being completely muted.

One ring.

"Hello?" Gravel, rasp, velvet. "Siah, are you there?"

A choppy exhale. "August. I'm scared."

Chapter Ten

SIAH

I curl under the cover of my soft blanket, my phone pressed tightly to my ear, my eyes squeezed shut.

"What happened? Where are you?" August's voice reaches me faintly from the speaker. Tension drips out of each word. There's no concern I detect. And why would he be concerned? It's not like we really know each other.

"Siah? Are you still there?"

I gulp. The deep grumble of his voice is barely audible through the rushing of my blood against my eardrums.

"I think there's someone on the third floor," I whisper, wincing as I brace for his laughter and ridicule.

A sharp intake of breath floats from the phone. "Impossible!" His denial is firm and resolute.

Defensiveness rises inside of me. Here we go again. Another person thinks I'm a lunatic. What was I thinking reaching out to him?

"I know what I heard, August!" I hiss through clenched teeth, tears building up on my lashes. "I'm sorry I bothered you." *God, what am I going to do now?*

"What did you hear?" he asks, a bite to his tone I don't care much for, but at least he's not laughing in my face.

"Something or someone fell up there, hard enough for me to feel the vibration against the headboard of your... uhm... the bed," I rush out, willing him to believe me.

Some distant rustling and crackling comes through the line, a gentle, hushed hum accompanying it. "I'm sharing my screen with you now," he says.

"W-what?"

"Accept the request on your phone." An order, but there's a gentleness to his tone that wasn't there a few seconds before. I move the device from my ear, holding it in front of my face. The pad of my finger barely touches the notification bar when the screen changes to a live feed.

I squint at the video, but the image is too dark to see anything of substance.

"... outside... sur... Siah."

"One second," I whisper. I pat blindly with my palm on the nightstand until I find what I'm looking for, then connect my AirPods to my phone and push one against my ear. "I missed what you said," I tell him as I increase the brightness on the screen enough to realize what I'm seeing is the outline of the house and some leaves fluttering in the wind in front of the camera.

"Outside surveillance. You're in the bedroom, right?" A shiver crashes through my spine as his rumbly voice embraces me, so much clearer and defined through the AirPod.

"Yeah," I breathe, my cheeks reddening. My flustered state has nothing to do with the fright from earlier, and everything with the man on the other side of this call.

"Turn on the lights and move in front of the window on the left wall."

"B-but..." I sputter.

A deep sigh laden with impatience comes so forceful through my AirPod, I can almost feel his hot breath fanning across my shoulder. The fear still swirls in the pit of my stomach, but his larger-than-life presence gives me a boost of courage even through the phone.

"I think you and I are similar," he murmurs as I slip one leg and then another from the protection of my fuzzy blanket. "Sometimes it's difficult to take people's word as absolute truth. Sometimes, we just have to see for ourselves to believe."

Maybe it's my guilt at bothering this... stranger with my fears in the dead of the night that makes me imagine things, but a faint trace of hurt trickles through his words. He doesn't like my lack of instant obedience. My chest constricts, everything in me compelling me to lessen his burden, to reassure him.

"I trust you," I blurt out, then gasp, because the certainty hits me with the force of a freight train. I *do* trust August. At first, just enough to move into his home without thinking his generous offer had ulterior motives. When I chose to call him instead of Jayme, I trusted him with my vulnerabilities, too.

Which is insane.

I was abandoned as a newborn, just... casually left in my Sunday-best onesie on a wooden bench in the middle of the park.

I was abandoned as a child. No one wanted to adopt the half-feral toddler with crazy curls and defiant eyes. Unless you were blonde with clear sky-blue eyes, or some exotic nationality that would boost your potential adoptive parents' standing in their gated communities, no one was interested.

The one time I gave someone a chance to stay, he abandoned me, too.

Clearly, I'm not the best judge of character.

My trust issues run deeper than the Mariana Trench. Yet, I'm learning to trust August St. Andrew.

"And I believe you," he says, his voice deeper, gruffer, hypnotic. "Lasting trust can only be earned, though." He pauses for a heartbeat. His next words send my heartbeat into overdrive. "I'm determined to do the work, Siah. Now, turn on the light."

My teeth sink into my bottom lip, trying to contain the whimper crawling up my throat at his order. I pad quietly to the wall and flip the main lights on. Light flickers from the screen of my phone too, the window to my bedroom fully visible now.

"The glass is programmed to remain in one-way view during the night," he murmurs in my ear, and a blush rises from my chest to my face. "I overwrote that for right now. Go stand in front of the window."

As soon as I'm perched in front of the large floor-to-ceiling glass panel, a pained moan and a slew of curses fly from the other end of the phone.

"August? Are you okay?"

"Yeah," he barks, gruffness and crushed gravel coating his throat. I hear a distinctive swallowing sound, the deep, satisfied exhale after a drink hitting just the right spot, a sharp smack of lips, then gravel again, smooth and velvety once more. "Sorry, I... uhm... stubbed my toe."

A hysterical giggle slips past my lips before I can lock it inside. Over the past month, I've built this image in my head of August. *Strong. Infallible. Untouchable.* Stubbing his toe is so imperfectly human it makes my stomach flip and butterflies take flight inside my core.

The dark timbre of his laugh mingles with mine and, for a second, I forget how to breathe. I forget my fright, my loneliness, my abandonment.

For one second in forever, I lie suspended between space and time, and I am happy.

My return to reality is imminent, though, when his laugh cuts off as abruptly as it started, and I'm left staring at the image of myself. My head is a mess of brown curls, settling over my shoulders like a crumpled mantle. I shift my legs. The image on the phone shifts with me, revealing the too-big-for-my-feet navy blue socks, covering my calves and stopping just below my knees. To complete my perfectly disheveled appearance is the softest of T-shirts, white and flowy, the hem hitting me mid-thigh.

Shit. I should've asked for permission before helping myself to his clothes.

"August, I..." I start to apologize, but he cuts me off.

"Now you know the feed is live. You've seen it for yourself with the camera aimed at the master bedroom. I can turn on the lights on the third floor remotely," he rasps. "Watch the screen."

My eyes stare intently as the video feed splits into four rectangles. My image sits in the top left corner. The top and bottom right show different angles of a massive office space, a dim red light cast over the entire floor. Bottom left is mostly darkness, with a glowy base, from what I assume is the brightness spilling out of my own window.

Light floods my screen from all three rectangles at the same time. I drink in the mystery of his private space as it reveals in front of my eyes—the wall of labeled metal drawers, the opposite wall heaving with books, the wall of dark glass in front of which a large desk with multiple keyboards and screens is placed, the comfortable-looking black leather chair, the smaller window behind it, and the minibar on the fourth wall, the soft fabric couch pushed against it.

What I don't see is anything broken, fallen, or disturbed.

It's painfully obvious that the third floor is completely and utterly... empty.

Chapter Eleven

SIAH

Absentmindedly, I'm playing with my fork, dragging around the bowl what's left of my chicken, bacon, and avocado salad. My chamomile tea sits half forgotten, so I chase the bite of salad with the lukewarm liquid.

The trees outside my window bend every which way, rain pelting down without mercy. It's been storming for close to two weeks now.

The start of this storm caused one of the old Oregon White Oak trees in August's backyard to fall against the wall. The huge tree-trunk, bereft of leaves, clipped the corner of the house before trampling down and landing against the back porch.

August sent me a time-stamped video from the camera feed the very next morning, showing the terrifying moment the tree fell.

He also told me Robert would be at the house later that day with a crew to have the tree removed and the roof and walls inspected.

They only had access to the shed attached to the garage, and I watched as they worked diligently, chopping, cutting, and sawing. I wondered the whole time if they felt my eyes on them, if unease and a sense of urgency curled around their spines as I looked on, or if they breathed a sigh of relief as soon as they cleared the massive gates of my gorgeous prison.

Jayme still has one more week of chasing tornadoes and men chasing tornadoes, so I haven't dared to venture out again. I shovel the last slice of avocado into my mouth, chewing slowly and methodically. My appetite is close to zero. But I'll be damned if I'm not making sure my body gets all the nutrients it needs. I'm not putting myself through another hospital stay.

Although, since the day of the great shopping spree, I haven't felt like I'm a tiny bacterium wiggling my way through saline solution under a microscope. I'm not allowing the hope that maybe he doesn't know where I now live to grow, though. I was caught off guard then because I became complacent. Until there are a couple thousand miles between mc and whatever lurks in the dark... and broad daylight, I won't rest easy.

My laptop pings, notifying me of a new email, so I push the lime-green bowl aside and check my inbox. A faint smile graces my face when I see the headline.

Noelle Lemieux: I love it! On to the editor now!!!

Cuniculus Inscius,
You wonderful, incredible, merveilleuse writer you. Thank you so so much. I absolutely adore the way you brought my story to life.
I've sent you the final payment. Are you one hundred percent sure you don't want to be credited for writing it? I want to brag to everyone about you.
All my love,
Noelle.

My smile grows as I finish reading. Noelle's book is both a memoir and a love letter to her husband. It did my heart a lot of good to write their story. A few clicks bring up my bank account, where I see I've already got the money. She likes to receive confirmation directly from me.

Cuniculus Inscius: Re: I love it! On to the editor now!!!

Noelle,
I'm honored and thrilled the manuscript is what you wanted. I fell in love with your story, and I desperately wanted to do it justice.
No credits necessary. You loving it is more than I could ask.
Don't forget to let me know when the book hits the shelves.
Congratulations!!!
My sincerest regards,
Cuniculus Inscius
PS: Payment received, thank you.

A yawn overtakes me, and I stretch in my comfortable chair, arms thrown over the soft back until I feel my shoulders pop, and then I relax into the buttery leather. I've spent the better part of the day searching for used cars online and saved a couple of ads that caught my eye. If the cars are not sold by the time Jayme is back, I'll ask her to come with me to check them out.

As each day passes, I'm more and more convinced I need to move away. I can't continue living like this, always looking over my shoulder, always sleeping with one eye open.

Another yawn forces its way through me, powerful enough to make my jaw crack. I barely cover my mouth in time with the back of my hand. I've always hated it when I had to see down people's stomachs because they're too lazy to cover their fucking mouths when yawning. Even Mr. Perfect-Manners Cavanaugh forgot more often than not to cover his mouth. I took sick pleasure from shoving my middle finger between his lips after repeatedly telling him that every time he yawns for everyone to see, he's likely to deepthroat a ghost's dick.

A pleasant weight fizzles through my limbs, my eyelids blinking slower and slower. There's nothing wrong with an early night sleep. I've been sorely lacking in the good rest department. In fact, I've taken to sleeping in August's T-shirt and socks ever since the night of the fallen tree. The faint traces of his cologne still clinging to the fabric bring me a special kind of comfort.

August makes me feel protected and safe, even from afar.

That night, I reached for his clothes as a way to make myself feel less alone. With my adrenaline still high after my shopping trip and fear embedded deep into my soul, the sight of his belongings hanging next to mine in the walk-in closet was like a balm to my loneliness. A foreign sense of belonging sprouted from all the barren, decimated-by-dread land inside of me.

I fell asleep to the sound of his voice in my ear as he read me the Sports section of a random newspaper. And when I woke up, the first thing I saw was a text he sent in the middle of the night. *"My T-shirt and socks have never looked better."* I took those words as his approval and carried on borrowing them.

Nearly dozing off as I rinse my salad bowl and fork, I quickly dry them and put them back in their rightful place before dragging my feet up the stairs and into August's bedroom. I rush through my nightly routine, washing my face and my teeth, applying a moisturizer mask I leave soaking on my skin as I change into a black T-shirt that almost covers my knees and long European football socks.

I snicker out loud to myself as one of the few happy memories from the foster care home plays through my head. One of our care workers, Oliver, was from the UK. He went red in the face, with a bulging purple vein pulsing across his forehead every time someone said 'soccer' instead of football.

"Bloody hell! I've said it once, I'll say it a thousand times. There's a ball, and it's played strictly with your feet. FOOT and BALL. Football!"

Ollie was one of the few who treated us like children and tried to give us as normal a childhood unwanted souls could have. The least I could do for him was to call his favorite sport by the name he preferred.

Once I'm dressed and my curls twisted in a protective braid—which will most likely come undone as I toss and turn—I peel off the soggy paper mask from my face and throw it in the bin. I massage the remaining serum of the mask into the skin of my neck and make sure the bedroom door is locked. With my AirPods charged and ready, I slide into bed, curling up in the middle of the mattress under a weighted blanket I found at the bottom of August's closet the other day. I start my classical music playlist that I found relaxed me enough to slow my anxious thoughts while still allowing me to hear any strong noises, and let myself fall asleep.

Chapter Twelve

SIAH

My skin prickles and my nipples furrow into tight pebbles as cold air washes over my naked body. *Naked?* My sleep-addled brain is slow on the uptake. Am I dreaming? Am I awake? I try to push myself up in a seated position, but my arms won't respond to my command. A pained gasp spills past my lips as I slowly slowly rouse myself awake. I pull sharply and whimper when silky material tightens around my wrists, my biceps and shoulders burning from the awkward position I've been restrained to.

"W-wha..." I cry out, but I'm immediately silenced by a warm finger pressing against my lips. My eyes spring open, but a gauzy black material covers my face. All I can see is the outline of a shadow bent over me.

"Hush now," the darkness whispers back to me, the quiet voice resembling the rumble of a thunder just after a lightning strike.

My heart pounds in my chest. The light piano notes still playing in my AirPods are drowned out by the rush of blood in my ears. Icy claws of dread slash into my spine, forcing my back to bow right off the mattress. A pitiful whimper escapes my throat, and I feel his shiver on the finger... *thumb* still touching my lips. His skin is both rough and pure velvet as he hooks the calloused pad over my bottom lip, trailing it down my chin, across my jaw, and finally resting over my pulse point.

The shadow grows larger as he moves closer to the bed. Spice, firewood smoke, and cardamon notes overwhelm my senses. How can a monster made of nightmares and shadows smell so good? He nuzzles his scruffed cheek to the sensitive skin of my jaw. His teeth scrape down the column of my neck. Hot lips replace the thumb over my pulse point, where he presses an open-mouthed wet kiss against the crazed-out flutters of my heartbeat.

My hips buck clean off the bed, wetness gushing between my thighs where my clit throbs against the maddening need misting over my body. Apprehension curls in my stomach, warring with the perverted desire rising in my core.

"Your fear is exquisite," he murmurs against my skin where my pulse is hammering away in frenzied flight. Fingers trail across my collarbone and over my breasts, feathering over my tight nipples. A needy mewl rips from my throat, a plea for more, a supplication to be released. "I bet your lust tastes even better than your fear." The growl in his voice speaks more of a threat than of prediction.

"I must be dreaming." I whimper the words as his fingers tickle over the side of my waist. My belly hollows under the trail of incinerating goosebumps his touch leaves in his wake.

"If *I'm* dreaming, then I never want to wake up." Another whispered threat, more goosebumps pepper my skin under the cocktail of need, lust, and pure and utter dread his gravelly voice promises.

I fight against the restraints constricting my wrists as his hand slowly and leisurely parts my thighs. A sharp inhale drowns the mournful violin notes in my ear. "You're wet for me." The shock in his voice is incontestable. His satisfaction, heady and thick, permeates the cool air of the bedroom.

"Pleeease," I cry out when his finger circles my clit, the brief contact sending jolts of pleasure through my core. My pussy clenches painfully around nothing as my hips rock, chasing his touch once more. I've never felt so empty and so full in my life.

He grunts in response, his free hand clamping over my thigh, pushing my leg against the rough material of his jeans. His hard cock is unmistakable, even through the coarse fabric. "You're going to sing for me, little mockingbird?"

The shadow doesn't really want a response, nor am I able to give him one as he robs me of all my words when he plunges a thick finger inside of me that I feel everywhere. I scream and cry and moan and protest as he withdraws as abruptly as he entered me. Before I can draw a quick breath, two fingers are thrust into me, the pad of his palm pressed firmly against my needy bundle of nerves.

"I could listen to your song all day, every day, for the rest of my life." He chuckles darkly, all gravel, and smoke, and coarse murmurs, as he moves his fingers inside of me unperturbed, in and out, in and out, in long, controlled strokes, all the while grounding the roughness of his meaty palm against my clit.

My inner walls quiver, my breasts tingle, the heel of my free leg anchoring into the mattress, pushing my hips up in a lovely, frightful chase for completion.

My need builds quickly inside of me, my skin heated, burning under the flames of his stare. I can't see anything but the hulking shadow looming over me. Instead, I feel everything, his eyes carving a path of destruction on my body, his hand owning me, his hard dick jolting for me, his palpable want for me to succumb to his every whim. I chase the end of his delicious torture, not a single thought of fight crossing my mind.

I want. I need. I let him take.

Not even the twinkling sound of a belt being unbuckled gives me pause in my hunt to fall apart at his beck and call. His cock falls heavy and hard, twitching when it lands over my knee. He takes himself in his hand, stroking his hard length. His knuckles move back and forth over my leg, faster and faster, in tandem with the fingers plunging into me, the boiling heat of him a mark on the sensitive skin of my inner thigh.

My cries are incessant, my shoulders straining under the tight constraints of my wrists as my arms pull taut over my head. "Oh god, please, please," I keen as my walls clench like a vise around his fingers. The maddening throb pushes me over the limit of what I can take. My orgasm explodes from my lower belly to the tip of my toes, through my oversensitive nipples, leaving my body a writhing mess on the crumpled Egyptian cotton sheets.

"You're fucking gorgeous when you come for me, little mockingbird. Your victory notes are the soundtrack to all my filthy dreams," he murmurs. "Look at you, soaking my goddamn hand. Allow me to return the favor." I melt into the bed under the symphony of praise, blasphemy, and lustful grunts spilling past his lips as he empties himself all over my stomach and tits.

I sigh, sated and fulfilled, under the claiming swipes of his large hand as he massages the proof of my end and his beginning deep into my skin.

His cool, minty breath fans over my heated cheeks as he whispers into my ear, "You're mine, little mockingbird. I dare you to run away from me. There's no hole you can crawl into where I wouldn't find you. Not a place on Earth is obscure enough to conceal you from me."

Firm lips touch my forehead, then the tip of my nose, and lastly, the delicate indent in my chin. My heart rate goes down in tandem with the delicious throb of my core. Adrenaline leaves my body, the sore and exhausted muscles of my shoulders sagging against the pillow.

"Who are you?"

"I'm yours," is the last thing I hear before blissful oblivion overtakes me once more.

I bolt upright in bed as the first rays of sun hit my face. The events of the night crash through my memory in a hazy reel. A foreign soreness twinges between my thighs as I stretch my legs and back. I push the weighted blanket away from me and blink furiously at the sight of my sock-clad feet, the black and white wool stopping just below my knees. The hem of the black T-shirt is twisted around my waist, just above the elastic of my damp panties.

My dream... nightmare... *wet nightmare* comes back to me in flashes and fragments of fear and craving. My cheeks flush as remnants of my unconscious lust return to me.

The screen of my phone flickers from my nightstand. My arm shakes when I stretch across the mattress to reach it. An email blinks at me from the dimming screen. My fingers tremble as I swipe on the notification bar. A single email received a minute ago, at 6:42 a.m., stares back at me. I touch the pad of my thumb to the alert, gently, softly, as if the sender would bite the fleshy appendage clean off my hand.

Unknown Sender: I'm starved for your song

It's a disservice to me to call yourself a dumb bunny. You shouldn't hide in warrens, even if you're trying your best to burrow away from me. Siah, stop hiding. Sing for me, instead. Your pleasured notes will be the highlight of my day. Every day.

Your eager hunter.

PS: Mimus polyglottos sounds so much better than cuniculus inscius.

My phone drops to the mattress.

"You're going to sing for me, little mockingbird?" The voice, foreign and deep like the rumble of an earth-shaking thunder just after lightning strikes, sounds in my head, as real as if my nightmare was more than the culmination of adrenaline-filled waking hours and my newly awakened libido.

A single, faint red circle surrounds both of my wrists.

"What the fuck happened last night?"

Chapter Thirteen

Him

I'm unsure if I should be enraged, offended, or turned on as I watch Siah scrub away all traces of my touch from her delicious skin. Maybe all the above. I loved my claim on her far too much. She's my complete weakness, my imminent doom. I know it now as surely as I knew it six years ago.

She's in my blood, like a deadly poison, binding with my every cell, bringing excruciating pain and the most exhilarating relief.

I've lost so many years at her side. Would we have ended in this hell of our own making if I'd chosen differently? Or would I have spent the last six years drunk on happiness, no trace or trail of sharp, jagged edges and overwhelming bitterness?

Alas, here we are. A flighty little mockingbird tempting me beyond belief and the hardened monstrous hunter ready to worship at her dainty feet.

I turn away from the screen with an angry huff. My cock jolts behind my fly, hard and wanton for another taste of her. I cup myself through the material, the zipper pressing painfully on my heated flesh. Squeezing tighter, I release a guttural groan as the excruciating desire lessens, the blood pooling in my groin stopped in its maddening flow by my tourniquet-like grip.

As sensual and tempting as the image of her wet, naked body, lathered in foamy suds is, I feel the loss of my claim like I would the loss of a limb. She's so deeply embedded inside of me, the mere distance between us feels like pure and utter agony.

I fear I'm reaching the end of my rope.

I've made one mistake after another in my cautious debate of whether to approach her. Only forced to act out of character when she ventured to give to another what is rightfully mine. Her body, her smiles, the deepest and darkest of her secrets, Siah Hadley is mine.

I shift on my feet, my hand still gripping the base of my lust for her. The shower beckons me, the allure of cold water beating across my overheated skin, but I refuse to wash away her sweet scent of honeysuckle and jasmine. I swipe my tongue across my bottom lip, where I can still taste the desire that was coating my fingers just a few hours ago.

Only one other time I've had her like that. Needy, achy, desperate for me and what only I could give her. And she ran away from me. Doubts plagued me, keeping me in the shadows, convincing me she was better off without me. It took me three agonizing years of watching from afar to realize there was no one better for her than me.

And then my only friend got hurt, and the scarce spark of humanity left in me demanded I see him alive and well and taken care of.

I paid for that humanity on my return, when I was rewarded and slain by glittering dark-green eyes, bright with happiness, and a smile that would bring a lesser man right to his knees. And all directed to another.

The cunt who wouldn't go away. The plague of a man who went ahead and married the woman I love despite not knowing myself what love is.

I don't even blink as I release myself and grab a dart from the cup behind me and send it flying straight between Henry 'The Dead Asshole' Cavanaugh's eyes. He winks at me from the blown picture on my dart board. The pride of knowing he'd just bagged the greatest treasure known to man bleeding all over his arrogant face.

So maybe I'm a masochist who allows himself to look at that false happiness on display each and every day. But I need the pain. I need the burning reminder of what I stand to lose if I don't get over myself fast.

I send a second dart flying, piercing right where his shriveled heart would be.

"Patience," I chastise myself. Soon enough, it won't be an image I'm throwing darts at to dispel my hatred. No.

My little mockingbird better learn fast; a beast has only so much restraint. She'll learn to accept me, or she'll fight me tooth and nail. To her misfortune, I'm equally fond of both her choices.

If she runs, I'll make good on my promise and chase her.

She'll look as beautiful and lovely waiting obediently for me in our bed at night, as she'll look tightly restrained by silken scarfs, her wrists and ankles reddened by the constraint.

Either way, she'll wait for me.

She'll sing her pleasure and fear only for me, every day until the day I die.

Chapter Fourteen

SIAH

I tighten my arms around Jayme's waist. It's so good to have her back. So, so good. I'm not one for physical displays of affection, regardless of who that person is, but the loneliness this past week got to be too much. I drove myself crazy each and every day after that strange, strange dream. The walls are suffocating, closing in on me, and trapping me into their glass and steel confines.

Her hands settle on my shoulders, her deep brown eyes assessing every inch of my face. Her bow-shaped lips purse and her freckled nose wrinkles. "You look like shit," Jayme concludes.

I roll my eyes playfully. *Well aware, J. Well fucking aware.* Not that I'm neglecting myself again, but sleep is hard to come by when I'm both afraid to my very soul to dream again... and ashamed to the very tip of my toes because I want to dream again. Instead, I spent nights on end tossing and turning, taking power naps when the exhaustion got to be too much. But the reverse smoky-eye situation I've got going on, and the chalk-white complexion of my face... well, there's nothing I can do about that.

"Had trouble sleeping," I mumble. I owe her the truth after the scare I put her through just over a month ago when I ended up being hospitalized.

Her eyes immediately soften, pity and worry battling for first place in her gaze. I hate that. I hate, hate, hate it. So I break away from our hug, despite the calm it brings to my torment, and put some distance between the two of us. My fingers tangle in my curls as I brush my hand through my unruly hair in an attempt to hide my anxiety.

"It's like before?" she whispers, dread dripping from each word.

I pull at my hair and wince in my haste to slash my hand through the air. "NO!" I say, louder than intended. "No." My voice is softer this time. "Nothing like before. I've been having weird dreams, and so my sleep has been restless and unfulfilling." I give her a wane smile and grab her hand. "You, on the other hand, look absolutely radiant. What the hell are they putting in tornadoes nowadays?"

Jayme gives me a sly grin in return. Although the worry is still alive and well in her eyes, like the gracious person she is, she allows me to change the subject. "Oh, I've been visiting the Emerald City once or twice." She laughs, wiggling her eyebrows.

"Oh, *Dorothy*. Do share. Let me live vicariously through you. Tell me all about your stroll down the yellow brick road. Were there lions, and Tin Men, and Scarecrows?" I gasp and mock-shiver, making her laugh once more.

"Lion, Tin Man, Scarecrow. Lion and Tin Man. Lion and Scarecrow. Lion, lion, lion. BOB."

"Where the fuck did BOB come from?" I giggle, but still blush furiously at her implication. I give her a wide smile and a wink as we sit down at the kitchen island with a huge cup of coffee each, and I lose myself in the stories of her sexual adventures.

That's how it has always been with us, ever since we found ourselves sharing a dorm in the first year of college. I'm the serious, withdrawn side of the coin—and have been even before my fears got the best of me—and Jayme is the fun and free side. She never told me many great details of her upbringing, just the cliff notes; her father up and leaving Jayme and her mother without a word when she was eight years old; her mother meeting August's father and marrying him when she was thirteen.

There were no happy stories of a blended family and a loving stepfather. Only hero-worshiping ones of an older stepbrother, who moved out as soon as he graduated high school, just after their parents' wedding, but still made a point to visit as often as he could and spend time with her.

Despite the lack of details of her upbringing, I know—in the only way a kindred spirit knows—her childhood was lonely and cold and rigid. So now she's free, and warm, and surrounding herself with people without being tied down by any. On the surface, Jayme is a social butterfly. On the inside, there are only two people in this world she cares about—me and August.

So, if the occasional romp in the sheets brings her the happiness she needs, as long as she's being safe about it, I'm here to cheer her on.

I went down the marriage road and put my trust issues aside, chasing the mirage of a white picket fence and family and companionship. Where did that leave me? One month away from the final divorce mediation meeting and hiding away in a stranger's house from eyes that burn my skin in the darkness.

"So..." Jayme looks at me, both her eyebrows high on her forehead.

"So what?" I ask, confused. I might have trailed off in my mind. Living alone does that to me. I retreat deep into my head, so used to having no one to talk to.

She crosses her arms under her breasts, pushing them forward. Gotta admit, I have some *major* envy of my best friend's cleavage. Think... melons to peaches. Involuntarily, I lower my eyes to my tank top and my barely there tits and scrunch up my nose. Eh, at least I don't have to wear a bra for support, and I'm spared of back pain. Besides, my ass compensates for my lack of balcony.

"This won't do. Come on!" She claps her hands, making me jolt. "You have thirty minutes to get ready. I'm taking you out."

That freezes me to the spot. "O-out?"

"Yes, out. We'll go to a bar, share the largest platter of spicy barbeque wings, stuff ourselves full of fries, then roll like over-inflated beach balls back home. You need some people-ing, even if you don't interact."

My teeth worry over my bottom lip. Last time I ventured out, the feeling returned. I know he's watching, the email from last week proved as much. I should tell Jayme. I should tell my therapist. I should tell someone... anyone.

But, as so bitterly proven before, I sought help and lost my credibility in the process.

Chapter Fifteen

SIAH

The Flame&Stake bar and grill is loud and crowded for a middle of the week, early afternoon. It may have something to do with the absolute piss-poor weather. October has definitely not been kind so far. Pelting rain, frigid winds, clouds so dark and menacing it feels like nighttime is just one blink away.

My eyes dart around the cluttered space, all burned browns, lacquered wood, peanut shells for floors, and lazy old-school rock music. But Jayme swears by their wings. The words 'multiple orgasms for taste buds' were uttered reverently, lips parting, eyes rolling to the back of her head. My stomach growled. Decision made.

So here I am, looking and feeling as out of place as a demon in church. My hair is thrown in a haphazard bun atop of my head, a couple of curled tendrils framing my face. Dark wash jeans with a high waist might have been a bad idea. I can't exactly pop the button open and lower the zipper if I'm gorging myself, since Jayme insisted I wear a red bodysuit, with lacy long sleeves. She also put a touch of makeup on me. Apparently, it will not do for Seattle to think I am ground-zero for a zombie apocalypse.

We find two empty stools side by side at the far edge of the bar, so I cover the rounded seat with my leather jacket since there's nowhere else to hang it. The bartender notices us as soon as we arrive—by us, I mean Jayme—and comes over as soon as he's finished with the drinks he was preparing.

"Afternoon, ladies." He greets us with a smile, his white, straight teeth gleaming under the warm lights above. "What can I get you started with?"

His hazel eyes slide right over me, stopping dead on my friend's cleavage. I shrug to myself. I'm not here to flirt with anyone, and I've got to admit, the flowery top Jayme is wearing fits her spectacularly. She's drop-dead gorgeous, even if occasionally she has a hard time believing it.

"My... aren't you a tall drink of water?" She grins at him, tossing her long hair over her shoulder. Obviously, there's a yellow brick road here somewhere, too. "I'll take a non-alcoholic IPA, whatever you have on tap. And my friend over here,"—she tosses a finger over her shoulder in my direction—"will have a can of Coke Zero, from the fridge, no ice, no glass, unopened. What's the wait time for a Wingasmic platter?"

His forearm flexes and strains as he pours her a pint, the glass frosty on the outside. I find myself fascinated, watching the veins under his tanned skin contracting and relaxing with each of his movements. Objectively, he's hot. I'm nearly divorced and clearly not dead—if I'm judging myself by the weird dream the other week, not dead and slightly kinky.

A tap on my shoulder has me swiveling on my chair to face my friend. "You've zoned out again."

"Sorry, babe." I give her a sheepish smile. "I got a new assignment for a romance book a couple of days ago. Let's just say it's heavy on the arm porn. Just doing my research."

Her brown eyes widen as she taps a long purple fingernail to her chin before startling me out of my chair with her high-pitch squeal. "Oh my god! You were checking out Tall Water's arm porn."

My palm flies to her mouth, trying to quiet her. "For fuck's sake, keep it down. I don't need the whole bar to know."

"But this is great progress! You're not withering away in August's home. There's still some hot red blood pumping through those veins of yours." Her lips twist in a grimace. "Speaking of blood..." Jayme jumps from her stool and bends to kiss my cheek. "Give me five. Gotta deal with a situation."

Before I can protest being left alone and offer to join her, she scurries away to the restroom. Tall Water slides the frothy mug in front of Jayme's seat, the amber liquid sloshing against the still frosty glass, then bends over, giving me a view of his jean-clad ass, and retrieves a chilled Coke for me.

I pop it open and take a welcoming sip, the bubbles sizzling on my tongue, but nearly choke as I feel his eyes studying me. "You're a writer, then?" he asks, hands shoved down the pockets of his jeans. His posture is that of a cool boy. I get no weird flirty vibes from him, so I relax in my seat.

"Ghostwriter." I shrug, toying around with the pull tab.

"So you write other people's stories for them?" He pops up a dark brow.

"Essentially. There are a lot of people with many great ideas. I just help them put their ideas on paper."

"And using the bartender's forearms for inspiration," he teases. My cheeks flush scarlet, in direct competition with the lace on my body suit.

I did say the words, so I will own to them. "There's a compliment hidden there somewhere. I do apologize for objectifying you, though."

His customer-service smile turns genuine. "I appreciate it. Both the compliment and the apology." He winks, genuine regret flashing over his face when he's called to the other side of the bar by another customer. I wave him off and take another sip of my Coke, struggling to swallow when I'm once again tapped on the shoulder.

"I wasn't zoning out again, I pr..." My words die a fiery death on my lips as I turn around and, instead of finding Jayme, I see Henry standing right in front of me. His blond hair disheveled, his normally clean-shaven face is hidden under a thick layer of scruff, just a touch darker than his hair.

He scowls at me and moves to take the seat Jayme occupied, but I'm faster, slapping my palm on top of the lacquered wood and stopping him in his tracks. His eyes, dark and unsettling, narrow at me, his thin lips pursing in displeasure. A tired sigh escapes him before his entire body softens. I jolt when his palm cups my cheek, my back hitting the edge of the bar. I shake my head to dislodge his hand, but he trails his forefinger down the column of my neck, his palm snaking like a rope around my nape. "You look good, Siah," Henry murmurs, bending his head and kissing my forehead.

The ocean-fresh scent of his cologne—the same one I'd carefully chosen and gifted him for his birthday not even seven months prior—invades my senses. My stomach flips, nausea churning anew inside of me. I don't want his touch. I absolutely do not want his nearness.

"Henry... Please, step away." There's a fearful tone to my voice. I've never feared Henry before, but these few months without him and the horrible way he left me in the middle of the night have stripped him off that pedestal I had him on. He's just a stranger now. And strangers are unsafe.

His fingers tighten around my nape, his hot breath mingled with alcohol vapors washes over my face. "You're my wife, Siah. I'm allowed to touch you."

I splay my palm over his chest. His heart is galloping away under my touch, his skin boiling-hot even through the thick material of his cardigan. Gently, I push him away. He doesn't budge. "Henry, please." I keep my voice even and as calm as I can muster. I've never seen him so… unhinged. Henry was always cool, calm, and collected. He claimed these traits made him a good doctor. He's nothing of the sort now.

"Is there a problem here?" Tall Water asks from behind me. My heart sinks to the floor when I see Henry's nostrils flare and his cheeks reddening under his scruff.

"Why? You're back here to flirt with my wife some more?" he spits, pushing me further into the bar top. I whimper in pain as the curved ledge digs into my spine. I put more force behind my attempts to increase the distance between us, but his grip on my neck tightens even further, his hold on me so strong that white spots dance in front of my eyes.

A large palm clamps over Henry's shoulder, startling him. Familiar pale green eyes stare at me from behind my ex-husband. "You have three seconds to remove your hand, or I'll remove it for you. One…"

Except there's no time for the handsome nurse visiting me that first night during my hospital stay to finish his count, when two things happen simultaneously: the fire alarm starts screeching bloody murder and Henry shoves me from where I'm precariously perched on the stool.

The last thing I see as my arms flail about, trying to find purchase *somewhere*, is the nurse tackling Henry to the ground. My forehead hits the edge of the bar top, blinding pain engulfs my head, and darkness consumes my vision.

Night night, Siah!

Chapter Sixteen

Him

"Are you sure you know what you're doing?"

"Get out of my fucking way, Sinclair," I bark. My arms tighten around her limp, delicate form. She's the only thing that stands between me and the soon-to-be dead motherfucker. I draw a deep breath through my nose, trying to silence the noise in my head, the chaos demanding blood and suffering and pain. He'll get what's coming to him. But Siah comes first. Always.

"You're being reckless," my friend accuses. "I can look after her."

"No one fucking touches her," I snarl, my teeth grinding. "Sort out the god-damn mess in the bar." I walk away, my steps light on the concrete at the back of the building despite the storm raging through me.

I keep my eyes focused on the car parked fifty feet or so in front of me. If I look at her beautiful face, if I see once more the blood staining the creamy pallor of her skin or the nasty bruises mottled on her forehead and seeping down to her eye... *Keep it together.*

The back door of my car slides open, hovering over the roof like a broken wing. I lean down and place her with utmost gentleness across the leather seat, then take off my suit jacket and fold it neatly, carefully, and use it as a pillow for Siah. When I'm satisfied she's comfortable, I walk to the trunk and remove a black suitcase. A quick scan of my fingerprint has the lid springing open.

I disinfect my hands and don a pair of latex gloves. I disinfect those for good measure, too. Lifting each eyelid with care not to provoke her any more pain, I shine the light of a penlight into her eyes. The fiery bands constricting my chest loosen a notch when her pupillary light reflex kicks in, her pupils constricting and dilating as expected. My hands shake as I unseal sterile gauze and clean off the dried blood. Rage blasts through my veins anew as instead of white, silken skin, I find red and dark purple bruises all over the left side of her face.

Unblinking, I stare at the wounded mockingbird passed out in my car, committing to my memory each bruise, each blemish, the size, the borders of each, the small cut above her perfectly shaped eyebrow. I memorize it all so I can replicate it on that motherfucker's face.

Henry Cavanaugh may not be aware just yet, but seven minutes and forty-two seconds ago, he just signed off his death warrant.

With tender fingers, I prod at the line still lightly bleeding on her forehead. The skin is scratched, but not completely split open, so I clean it with feather-like strokes of the gauze and close it with a band-aid.

My smartwatch vibrates on my wrist, and I sneak a peek.

> *Her purse is with D. The friend is freaking out, searching for her like crazy. SFD sent two units.*
>
> *Incoming, 5 minutes.*

Unknown Number

I return to my Aid Kit—can't call it a First Aid, since I have a mini-pharmacy here and enough surgical tools to equip a Trauma Room—and find the vial I need. I prepare a syringe, tapping the glass tube with the back of my finger to ensure no air bubbles remain. With the needle still capped, I lay the syringe next to her slender neck.

Now, for the hard part. I tunnel my hand between my jacket and her nape, gently lifting her head. Her adorable nose scrunches as soon as I wave the bag of salts above her upper lips. A pained moan spills from her pretty mouth, her irises frantically moving behind her eyelids.

"That's it, little mockingbird. Open those beautiful eyes for me," I coax her, my stomach tight, every muscle in my body coiled and tense, waiting for her to wake up.

If she has a concussion... everything I planned goes straight to hell. My patience is running thin, but I still want her to have time to come to terms with who she is to me and accept the inevitability of her fate. To willingly acknowledge that she's mine to have and to hold. Her injuries change everything. I wanted her to learn to trust me and come freely to me. But I'll take, if I must.

Her last visit to the hospital left me nearly blind with rage. I've been too lax, too complacent, too much of a fucking idiot wishing upon stars with my dick in my hand. Not anymore.

"Ow," Siah cries, her hand jerking up to her face. I catch her cold fingers in my gloved hand and press each limp digit against my lips.

"Be still!" I admonish, but don't mask the tenderness from my voice. She's the sole recipient of it, even if she doesn't know it. "I know you're in pain. I feel it as if it were my own. But I need you to be brave and open your eyes, anyway."

She winces, her tiny frame startling when the loud alarms of the fire engines sound down the street. We're running out of time. I place her hand over her chest and tilt her chin up with my thumb. "Siah! Open your eyes!" My voice is hard now, the command unmistakable. Her eyelids flutter, pitiful mewls pouring from her throat, each slashing at me, the agony throbbing in my chest echoing hers.

"W-wha... w-whe... h-he..." she mumbles, her eyes wide and panicked. My forefinger feathers over her plump lips, and I curse myself as I start hardening behind the fly of my trousers.

Not the fucking time.

"Tell me your full name," I grunt, ready to get this over with before I'll have to explain my presence here to the Seattle Fire Department.

"Si-Siahhhadley," she slurs, mashing her first and last name together, but I understand her just fine. Another constricting band around my chest collapses.

"What day's today?" I press, urgency flaring at my back. We're nearly out of time, the blaring sirens nearing.

"We's'ney, t-twe-ee-nty fff-rree ten." She forces each letter out, my good girl. Pride blossoms inside of me, awe at the strength of this woman warming my body.

"That's right, little mockingbird. Today's Wednesday, October twenty-third," I confirm for her, drinking in the relief painted on her unmarred right side. "You'll sleep now," I find myself telling her. "And when you wake up, am afraid you'll remember naught of this. But fret not, my love, I swear you'll remember all our next meets from now on."

She gasps as the needle pierces her neck, and I watch with rapt attention as her eyes turn glassy and her lids lower as if in slow motion before she once again grows limp in my arms. I pocket the syringe and press my lips to the tender place on her neck where the smallest drop of blood bubbles to the surface. I groan when the tip of my tongue collects the sweet coppery taste of her essence and make a silent oath to myself as I breathe in her nearness.

This is the last drop of blood Siah will ever shed.

And Henry will bleed all of his to pay his debt.

Chapter Seventeen

SIAH

I stare at the blinking cursor on the dimmed screen of my laptop. My body is strangely numb apart from the blinding migraine that starts with the precision of a Swiss clock every late afternoon.

The email from my divorce lawyer stares right back at me, like a monster trapped behind a glass screen, pacing and snarling as it decides whether to maim me or set me free.

Two more days until Henry and I are no more. No more ties—emotional, legal, or otherwise—except for a piece of paper that will collect dust in one of my folders when all is said and done. No more vitriol filled voicemails; no more poison spilled in text messages. I shudder under the weight of the memories plaguing my every waking moment. Guilt is mixed in that particular cocktail of emotions, too.

Meeting Henry three years ago gave me so much hope. His boyish grins, the way his hair would flap over his forehead, the cutest of cowlicks just so to the right at the edge of his hairline. He made my stomach whoop and my hopes soar.

I guess it's easy to be happy when everything falls in a neat little line and you stroll on a perfectly manicured street in broad daylight, sunshine, and flowers, and birds chirping. There's no worry or stress in that fairytale.

Except I forgot that my life is anything but a fairytale. And while plenty of good things happen in life, good things don't just happen to the likes of me. If growing up in a foster care home taught me anything, it's that as long as you know your place, keep your head down, and mind your own business, you get to see another day bruise-free.

There is no fairness, and the light at the end of the tunnel is a freight train that'll run me over without a second thought if I stray from the path.

And I *have* strayed from the path.

I don't know which version of Henry I'll see at the mediation. It's silly to yearn for a last glimpse of the man I thought was in love with me. But I do. Not because of any lingering feelings of love I might have for him. Right now, with the yellowed and sickly purple bruises staining my skin, it's almost impossible for me to believe I've ever loved him. But because I don't want to end this chapter in my life, lugging after me a truckload of resentment and fear.

I'm still in disbelief over his actions. My memory of Wacky Wednesday is hazy at best. I recall going to the bar with Jayme. I recall Henry encroaching on me, sucking the air straight from my lungs with the menace swirling around him. And I recall him shoving me. Was he trying to hurt me? Was he trying to protect me? Now, that's unclear. From then on, I feed on snippets—deafening fire alarm blaring, gloved hands touching my face this way and the other, the rumbly purrs of the Earth cracking open, but instead of swallowing me whole, it spoke to me. Dark blue skies, a whisper or two lighter than midnight. A lightning storm making the fine hairs on my body stand to attention, and me... floating in the eye of the storm.

My memory makes no sense.

I... make no sense. I haven't in a while.

Then waking up in my own bed—well, August's bed—as if nothing had happened, if I were to ignore the black and blue painting of horror on the left side of my face. I lost... twenty-four hours. According to Jayme, Devon—that's Tall Water's real name—carried me to his car. Elijah—the nurse dude—checked me over for signs of concussion and drove me home. I mumbled sufficiently to have Elijah take my phone and call August, who was kind enough to unlock the doors remotely. My lost day was apparently spent in the care of Elijah, who stayed to look over me and ensure I didn't have a concussion.

Unfortunately, Jayme was also hurt during the madness that ensued when the fire alarm went off. Instead of evacuating calmly and in order, people panicked and started shoving at each other to make it out the door first. So my best friend found herself in an ER for hours, waiting to have her ankle x-rayed. Luckily, all that got damaged was her freedom to wear high heels for two to three weeks while her sprained ankle heals.

And I'm back to my daily therapy sessions. The first night home after Elijah left, I couldn't sleep. I blamed the day-long nap I unwittingly took. But when the second night rolled in, and I was wide awake staring at a darkened ceiling, I knew it wasn't an overabundance of rest that kept me alert. Once again... it was fear.

I push away from my desk and, with heavy feet, descend the steps leading me to the kitchen. Grabbing a bottle of cold water from the fridge, I twist the cap and swallow in greedy gulps the refreshing liquid and the evening dose of my meds.

With the increased frequency in therapy sessions also came a magic little pill. It doesn't completely knock me off to dance with the fairies and butterflies in La-lah Land, but gently presses against the brakes of my mind, slowing it enough for me to doze off.

My limbs soften as I shove my clothes down on the heated tiles of the bathroom and climb in the glass enclosure of the shower, letting the hot water spray over me. The sweet honeysuckle fragrance of my body wash fills the bathroom as I cover myself in suds from neck to toe. Once every soapy bubble finds its way down the drain, I wind a fluffy black towel around myself and release my hair from the tight bun I had it in to avoid getting it wet.

My fingers are sluggish and slow as the medicine works its way through my bloodstream, but five thousand curses later and ten cramping digits, my curls are somewhat tamed in a protective braid. I swipe my tongue over my teeth, the sharp menthol taste of my toothpaste sizzling over my taste buds. My skin is still overheating from the hot water, so I dodge August's drawer of cloudy-soft T-shirts, and borrow a silky button-down instead, the coolness of the material bringing a brief reprieve to the strange oversensitivity trying me.

All I have to do now is lie in bed, close my eyes, and give in to the relaxation amplified by my sleeping pill. Soon after, a warmth settles over me. It starts at my back, like the gentlest of pressures mixed with the embrace of a weighted blanket. Steel bands fasten around my waist, a cage of security of my own making. The darkness takes over.

And so I sleep. Warm, weighted, obscured.

And safe.

Like every night this week.

Chapter Eighteen

Him

Siah stirs in my arms, her round ass pressing against the rapidly growing erection in my boxers. I hold my breath and stifle a groan. I'd just about sell a kidney and half my liver to feel her wet heat wrapped around my cock. My balls draw up, heavy and aching, and I can't help but thrust my hips against her firm ass, letting my shaft slide between her cheeks.

Lowering my head, I nuzzle my face in the whirlwind of curls sticking up everywhere. "Be good now, little mockingbird," I whisper in her ear as I toy with the hem of her sleeping T-shirt. A smile tugs at my lips as I tighten my hold on the curve of her waist.

Fiery satisfaction has more of my blood rushing to my cock. I'm preening like a goddamn peacock, knowing she's sleeping in my clothes. Sure, replacing all the T-shirts, socks, shorts, and underwear in the drawers with mine took entirely too fucking long and ate precious minutes in which I could've slept next to her. But at least, the storm raging in my mind and chest will give me a slight reprieve during the nights I can't be here, knowing she'll sleep covered in me and mine.

If she's noticed yet the difference in scent, or how the clothes hang just a bit looser on her, that they're just a smidge larger than before, she hasn't shown it. But then again, the fucking sleeping pills have her all out of sorts.

The only thing that brings me comfort is that I was able to watch over her sleep the whole week. It's been my greatest honor to hold her in her slumber and keep her nightmares at bay. Knowing she was hurt when I was standing not even thirty feet away broke something inside of me. The fear in her eyes, the skittishness in her every move, her setback called to me. I'll free my wounded mockingbird from her cage, if it's the last thing I'll do.

She whimpers softly, and I splay my hand under the T-shirt, covering her soft belly almost entirely, and press her closer to me. "Hush, little mockingbird," I hum, my lips feathering over her earlobe. My cock throbs where it's wedged between her ass cheeks, and I give into the temptation, sucking the fleshy soft part of her ear between my lips. Her hips jerk, and the whimper turns into a wanton mewl.

Desire spreads like wildfire through my veins. She's a goddess of sin and allure. I'm burning up for her. It's been too fucking long since I've last lost my mind and quieted the storm. And she's the only woman in this world to bring me quiet... peace.

Fuck it.

Like a dog in heat, I rub myself against the plumpness of her ass, wishing with all my fucking might to lower the elastic of my boxers and plunge my cock into the enticing heaven between her legs. But I'm denying myself once more. The next time we're one, she'll know exactly who owns her. She'll know exactly who she owns. She'll look me in the goddamn eye and sing my fucking name as she comes on my cock.

While my blue fucking balls could star in a sequel of *Avatar,* I can still take care of her needs. I gently trail my fingers on her abdomen, cupping one small breast with my palm—my much larger palm that covers the delicious softness entirely. I groan deep into my chest. The absolute maddening pleasure of feeling her smooth, creamy skin under my fingertips is almost too much for my starved state.

I thumb her nipple, a gentle brush with the pad of my finger. The little bud hardens under my touch, and my hips ground into her. I have no control over my body. My most basic urges take over, and I flip her on her back, pushing my way between her lovely thighs.

I'm jeopardizing everything for a taste of her. I'm risking her waking up and finding me here. Too soon, it's too soon. Yet, my mouth waters, and my cock lengthens, pushing through the band of my boxers. Wetness seeps from the oversensitive head, hot and sticky on my lower abs.

There's not enough light in the room to allow me to feast my eyes, to sate my hunger for her. But I live in the dark, I don't need light to guide me. With a flick of my wrist, I pull the weighted blanket aside. My movements are brisk and efficient. This is not the time to savor but to gorge.

She's exquisite in her vulnerability. I was *so* fucking wrong to think her fear was the sweetest of all. Her sleeping form, limbs soft and malleable in her slumber, brown curls fanned across the pillow, vulnerable and just ready to be taken... this is the sweetest version of her. *My perfect prey.* And I'm about to taste all that forbidden heaven, meant just for me.

With trembling hands, I grip her thighs, resting them up against my chest. I lean down and kiss the graceful arch of her right foot, then turn my head and kiss the other. Gently, tenderly, I peel off her lacy panties. I'd give away half of my bank account just to see the exact color of them. Crumpled in my fist as they are, I bring them to my nose, inhaling deeply. Honeysuckle, jasmine, and something that's uniquely Siah—tangy, spicy, and absolutely fucking maddening—invades my nostrils.

But a tender sniff would never be enough to douse the thirst raging inside of me.

I throw the scrap of lace over my shoulder in the general vicinity of my discarded clothes. This is the trophy I'm taking with me tonight. Let her wake up in the morning, satisfied and overstimulated, with her panties missing. It's past time she learns she's not as alone as she fears she is.

Lowering my body to the mattress, I nearly fucking weep when I find myself face to face with her wet pink pussy. "Fuck," I grunt, as my hips press against the firmness of the bed, jolts of electricity sparkling at the base of my spine. I arrange her legs over my shoulders, my elbows splayed wide, bracketing her rounded hips. With a palm clamped around each of her thighs, she opens up to me like a midnight flower when moonlight hits.

I lower my head and, reverently, press a soft kiss to her glistening folds. I'm immediately rewarded with a reflexive arch of her back.

"You're so fucking responsive to me, little mockingbird," I murmur, helpless in front of her magnificence.

I can't prolong this torture anymore. I won't.

Wasting no more time, I lick a path from her entrance to her clit, sucking the swollen bundle of nerves into my mouth. There's no finesse to my technique, no control either. I lick, I suck, I bite, I taste. Her decadent flavor floods my mouth, the heat of her arousal scorching my tongue.

I need to feel more of her. I need all of her.

Her hips start to circle, sleepily chasing my mouth. I throw a forearm over her lower belly, to keep her still right where I need her. My free arm stretches until my fingers find the softness of her breasts and the tightly pebbled buds—the fucking crown jewels pinched between my fingers.

Breathy moans spill from her beautiful mouth, while mine devours her throbbing pussy. I risk a glance up, past her hollowed stomach, up her delicate rib cage, over the majesty of her teardrop breasts, the paleness of her skin a stark contrast against my tan, to the slender column of her neck, parted lips, and wide-open eyes, staring right back at me.

I freeze.

The thundering drums of my heart vibrate through the mattress. One second. Two...

"Pleeeaaaaseeee," she cries out, her imploration the greatest symphony to reach my ears.

I am powerless to resist her song. When she sinks her dainty fingers through my hair, nails digging deep into my scalp, drowning my face with the flood of her arousal, I nearly fucking come on the spot.

A growl rips from my throat, and she echoes my call with a needy mewl. I squeeze the soft flesh of her breast in my fist and loosen my hold over her lower belly, just enough for her to grind leisurely against my mouth.

And so she dances for me. And so she sings.

The walls are reverberating with the enchantment of her moans and the low bass of my grunts. The sheet's rustling increases in tempo as her hips rock and mine thrust. My tongue seeks, prods, and discovers. When the pressure in my lower back reaches nuclear levels, I let myself detonate. Pure fucking fire draws my balls tight as my boxers and abdomen grow damp with my release.

"Oh... oh... oh fuck," she screams for me, so prettily, with such blinding desire, I almost come a second time. I bite down onto her throbbing clit, just enough to infuse her end with a touch of pain, and she soars.

"Fly for me, little mockingbird!" I murmur as my tongue soothes the sting of my bite with gentle sucks and teasing rapid flicks against her trembling, silken flesh. Her thighs clamp down around my head, the flutters of her sweet pussy sizzling on my lips. I lap up the dulcet reward of my efforts, not allowing a single drop to go to waste.

Her pleasure is mine. Her pain is also mine.

Her every breath, and every heartbeat, and every single one of her surrenders.

Siah Hadley is mine.

And if, by some kind of cruel fucking cosmic joke, I am denied, if I can't have her, I'll burn the world to the fucking ground and build a cage for my pretty mockingbird from the ashes to ensure no one else has her.

Chapter Nineteen

Siah

The alarm on my phone blares through the heavy blanket of sleep I'm cocooned in. I rouse with a gasp, my eyes still scrunched closed, as I pat around blindly for the infernal device. My fingers, finally, find purchase, and the sound cuts off, leaving me in blessed silence.

I sag against the pillows, my body achy and tired. A heated debate is taking place within me—keep sleeping or wake up and face the world. I don't want to leave this bed. What I want is to hide under my weighted blanket and not have to think about the way-too-real drug-induced dream I had last night.

My back arches in a stretch, my muscles tensing and relaxing as the last traces of sleep vanish into thin air. My hips and thighs are sore, as if I've put my lower body through an excruciating workout yesterday. My eyes spring open, the dove-gray ceiling above me feeling much closer than ever before.

Ragged breaths shake against my rib cage, my heart pumping furiously inside my chest. Are the walls closing in on me? Is this the moment where my bedroom turns into a box? My thighs rub together, and a shiver runs through me as my skin burns from the friction. I fish the sheet at my side, willing the room to halt its shrinkage.

I furiously think through everything I remember from the dream last night. The darkness of the room, the bottomless eyes peering at me from between my legs, the infinite waves of pleasure my nocturnal orgasm brought. The vague sense of wrongness throughout it all.

It was a dream, wasn't it?

My hormones are going crazy in their newly awakened state. The chemicals in my brain are wreaking havoc on my neurons. The beta-blockers helping with my panic attacks and the sleeping pills are just the cherry on top of this fucked-up cocktail.

I force my fingers to pry loose off the crumpled sheet. I urge my legs to swing to the floor. I beg my lungs to open up and allow oxygen to flow freely. With shaky movements, I pick up the blister of beta-blockers from the nightstand and pop one on my tongue. Water sloshes over the rim of my glass as my hand trembles uncontrollably. I barely manage to take a sip to wash the pill down, as most of the water seems to spill over my cheek and onto my chest and lap.

"August said no one can enter this house unless he allows them in," I say out loud to myself, hoping the words sink inside my fight or flight instinct and quiet the panic alarm rattling my mind.

I shove the now-empty glass back onto the nightstand and push to my feet, beelining straight to the bedroom door. My fingers curl on the metal handle of the knob. It doesn't budge. While the door can be unlocked from the outside with a key, it can only be locked from inside the bedroom.

Relief bubbles up inside of me.

Next on my checklist are the windows. One—locked, two—locked, three—locked, four—locked. My shoulders lower from next to my ears, and I take the first full breath of air this morning.

It *was* just a dream. A slightly disturbing, highly erotic night hallucination, but nothing else.

I shuffle my still trembling legs to the bathroom, wincing when the sensitive skin between my thighs rubs together, sharp pinpricks chafing. Bending down, I remove the socks and throw them in the laundry basket like a basketball. The T-shirt, damp as it is, follows. My panties... "Where are my fucking panties?" I shriek, patting my warm and very much naked skin with my palms.

My knees buckle, and I lean against the cold marble sink, goosebumps exploding across my body from the sudden chill. I put panties on before I went to sleep. I'm fucking sure I did. *Didn't I?*

I touch the back of my hand to my forehead, feeling for what? Can you feel forgetfulness like you do fever?

"Those fucking meds," I mumble under my breath. They may help me sleep, but they also make my mind foggy as hell. And with the looming divorce mediation twenty-four hours from now... maybe losing sleep is better than proving Henry right tomorrow. He'd be in seventh heaven if I show up scatter-brained and confused as hell.

With robotic movements, I turn on the shower, letting the nearly boiling water cascade over me. I tip my head down, my curls hanging heavy over my back. Slowly but surely, the heat and oppressive steam loosen my tight muscles, lulling my body into a relaxed state.

Gently, I run my soapy loofah over my shoulders and collarbone, across my breasts and armpits, then lower on my belly and thighs. The sting is still there, and a hiss spills past my lips as my skin smarts under my ministrations. When I'm done with my legs, I quickly shave them, then rinse out the sponge and razor. Pumping the intimate wash cap, I rub the smooth gel between my palms and start washing between my legs.

"Fucking Eve choking on an apple," I curse, as what feels like a bolt of electricity runs through my core at a simple graze of my fingertips. I'm sore, so extremely sore and swollen. My flesh feels overstimulated, like just after being ravaged by an intense orgasm and any following touch brings more pain than pleasure.

What did I do to myself last night?

The large metal gates open silently. I have to ask August who is greasing these things, because I've been living in his home for two months now, and I haven't heard as much of a squeak or a creak from them, not even after a heavy downpour.

I look left and then right before merging onto the main street. To preserve whatever is left of my sanity, I've decided to sleep tonight on Jayme's sofa. I could use her emotional support right now, anyway. All my shields need to be up and impenetrable for tomorrow. A good night's sleep—without erotic dreams and rogue orgasms that leave my vagina aching—and a safe place where I can attempt resting without the aid of any meds should help me be ready for the meeting.

As soon as tomorrow, I could be a free woman.

I flick the indicator on and guide the car into a parking lot. My eyes dart to the rearview mirror, then back around the lot. Shifting the car in reverse, I use the camera to safely park it before removing the keys from the ignition. I take a deep breath and, once more, scan my surroundings.

"Okay, Siah. All you have to do is walk across the lot. Thirty feet, if that."

I grab my purse from the passenger seat and exit the car. The frozen November air stales my breath for a second, and then my lungs remember their most basic function and start inflating again. The indicators flash as I press the lock-button on the remote, but I still try each door. Just in case.

Once satisfied the doors are secure, I hurry across, the click-clack of my heels against the wet concrete echoing through the space. By the time I push open the door to the clinic, I'm panting, a fine line of sweat trickling down my spine.

"Good morning! Welcome to Sundale OB-GYN," the bubbly receptionist greets me.

"Morning," I mumble, my mouth hidden in the collar of my winter coat. My elbows touch the wooden partition of her desk. "My name's Siah Ha-...uhm Cavanaugh. I have an appointment with Dr. Gutiérrez."

She gives me a sunny smile, red lips stretched wide over white, straight teeth, as her fingers fly over the keyboard. My teeth ache from her joy, her happiness itching under my skin. When was the last time I smiled like that? When was the last time I felt relaxed, and at peace, and not constantly having to look over my shoulder? "You're just on time. Go right ahead to Consultation Room Four. Dr. Gutiérrez will be right with you."

"Thank you..."—my eyes dart around her desk until I find what I'm looking for in the form of a shiny nametag proudly displayed next to a vase of roses—"Michelle. Can I also have my name and details updated on your system?" I rummage through my bag and find a copy of the document I need, sliding it to her. "My surname needs updating."

"Sure thing. Leave it with me, and I'll have it done by the time your appointment is finished."

I nod in appreciation and throw Michelle a wave over my shoulder as I head to the room she indicated. She's new. Sundale is my preferred clinic, and I have been registered with them since college. I haven't seen her before, on any of my previous visits. I gently knock on the door of the Consultation Room, then enter.

Dr. Gutiérrez swivels in her chair and pushes her round glasses up on her nose. The thick, golden frames always bring a smile on my lips. With her angular chin and round cheekbones, the glasses give her an owlish look. "Good morning, Siah. It's good to see you. Please, take a seat." She stands and gestures to one of the available chairs.

"Thank you, Dr. Gutiérrez. It's good to see you, too. Although I'm not looking forward to this visit."

She furrows her brow, forefinger at the ready to push up the glasses once more on her nose. "I suppose you're not. But I'll be quick, and I'll make it as painless as possible. One less thing to worry about for the next three years." She smiles wryly at me.

"Speaking of less things to worry about, I know we've discussed this before as a potential solution for menstrual pain and heavy bleeding..." I trail off. My periods are brutal. Short of getting a hysterectomy, I'm at my wit's end with the pain every single month. Birth control pills are not an option for me. I've tried both the implant and the shot when Henry and I had the "exclusivity" conversation. My body wasn't fond of those either. So we've had to continue to use condoms. Neither of us were ready for children. Then we got married, and my mental health took a dive into the ocean not to be seen again for months.

The medicine prescribed to me to *help* with my unconfirmed schizophrenia diagnosis made my sex drive a thing of the past. It also made it impossible for me to tolerate a hormonal coil. But now, I might actually have a chance not to have to beg for death every month.

"You want an Intrauterine System?" she finishes for me.

I nod. "I'd like to try, yes. Not sure if my body will tolerate it, but I'm definitely willing to try."

She claps her hands and stands. "Alright then. Ideally, I'd have it fitted right as a new menstrual cycle starts. It would make it more effective as a birth control measure."

I feel my cheeks heating up, and I cough in my fist to clear my throat. "That's not an impediment. I'm not currently... engaging in any sexual activity." Unless she's counting wet dreams in the middle of the night, but no one got pregnant from a dream before.

"In that case,"—she taps on her tablet, her finger scrolling on the screen a couple of times—"I have an opening for just before Thanksgiving. November twenty-sixth works for you?"

I nod again. I'm starting to feel like the bobblehead Ollie from the foster home used to have on his dash. A tablet is thrust in my face, and I jump, my eyes narrowing against the brightness of the screen. "Consent form," Dr. Gutiérrez explains. "Sign with your finger at the bottom when you're done reading it. For the IUS, I'll need to do an STD test. The results should be back in a week. Since I'll have you on my table in a minute, I might as well do it now. If there's anything concerning with the results, we'll call you to make an appointment and assess the situation. If not, I'll see you in three weeks."

Quickly scribbling my name over the consent form, I pass the tablet to her. "Understood. Thank you."

"Okay." She smiles, snapping a pair of blue latex gloves on her hands. "Put on this gown and hop up."

"Uhm... one last thing," I find myself saying. "Ever since my medication was switched, my sex drive... well, uhm... it went into overdrive. I'm experiencing... a certain kind of dreams and wake up feeling uhm... sore and sensitive. I think maybe there might be something wrong with my hormones?"

Her arms are jerking, as if reflexively she'd like to cross them over her chest, but all gloved-up she can't. "Nocturnal emissions are quite normal, unless they're disturbing your sleep or they're disturbing in nature."

She's stating a fact, but I hear the question hidden in her last words. I wouldn't say they are disturbing in nature, but my dreams *are* a smidge kinkier than my sex life has been so far. "They're... intense."

"I can certainly draw some blood up after the appointment and have your hormone levels checked if you're worried about an imbalance. The IUS should help with that, too."

For a third time in less than five minutes, Siah the Bobblehead makes an appearance.

Let the fun begin, said no woman ever.

Chapter Twenty

SIAH

I'm staring past Henry's shoulder at the large picture window behind him. Seattle's skyline is as gray and muted as the heavy rain clouds hanging over the city. I tuned out the two bickering lawyers twenty minutes ago. I'm also tuning out my-very-soon-to-be ex-husband's stare.

Ten seconds, that's all I allowed myself to look at him. His puppy eyes don't work on me anymore. The regret plastered all over his face does nothing to me. I rather enjoyed seeing his mouth twisting up in a grimace as his eyes scanned the fading bruises on my face. I could've worn makeup. But, as it turns out, I'm a petty bitch. And this petty bitch really wants him to see what he did to me.

"Ms. Hadley?" My lawyer, Daniel Greystone, draws my attention. He's a shark dressed in an impeccable Italian three-piece, his blond hair slicked backward, his eyes permanently narrowed, as if his mission in life is to glare at everything around him.

"Apologies," I mutter, "I got distracted." Tilting my head back, my eyes search his. "What do you need from me?"

"Just read over the summary and, if you're happy with it, sign at the bottom." He pushes a stack of papers in front of me.

I scan through each line carefully, trying to block out Henry's long-suffering sighs. We each keep the money we entered the marriage with—fine with me. Henry keeps the house. So he should, since he bought it before we met. I have no interest in the halfway we went on mortgage and bills during the time we lived together. As far as I'm concerned, I paid my rent. Any other common goods Henry can keep. I have clothes, my important documents, and my laptop.

Alimony? None necessary. I don't need any money or support from him. In theory, I earn more than him. In actuality, he has a trust fund the size of Texas. Or so he claims.

I scribble my name at the bottom. That's it. The end.

I push the papers back to my lawyer. He'll do what he has to, and I'll receive the final paperwork sometime in the following weeks. My chair makes an unholy noise as the wooden legs scrape across the laminate floors. Try as I want, there's no hiding my cringe. Fitting, though, for the situation we're in.

My eyes seek Henry's for what is, hopefully, the last time, as I clasp my hands in front of me. "Keep well, Henry. Look after yourself."

Without waiting for a response from him, my lawyer escorts me out of the room with a hand hovering above the small of my back. The brief elevator ride to the lobby is done in silence. He got me what I asked for—a quick divorce and not much fuss. As the doors slide open and we step out of the carriage, I turn to him and extend my hand for a shake.

"Mr. Greystone, thank you so much. I appreciate your professionalism and support."

He gives me a crooked smile and shakes my hand firmly. "My pleasure, Ms. Hadley. Life's too short to be married to the wrong person. I'll send you my final invoice once you receive the court-signed documents."

I nod in appreciation. "Goodbye, Mr. Greystone. It was nice working with you."

My heels click hurriedly against the marble floor of the reception as I push through the massive glass doors at the entrance. The wind whips my hair in every direction, and I sputter when a rogue curl finds its way down my throat. Jesus, I'm barely a free woman, and my own hair is trying to kill me. Wouldn't that be something? Death by hairstyle.

I pull my warm knee-length trench coat tighter around my body to shield myself from the cold air outside, nearly sprinting to my car. If it weren't for these goddamned heels, I would've actually run. As it is, I lengthen my stride and hope I won't break an ankle.

"Siah!"

I startle when I hear him yelling my name, but don't stop. "Come on, come on, come on," I mumble under my breath, wishing August's car would magically appear in front of me.

"Siah!"

Dammit, he sounds closer. My steps become quicker, my balance on the fucking heels decreasing in direct proportion with my speed. "Where are you, little vehicle?" I breathe a sigh of relief as I turn the corner on a side street and see the sign for the parking lot where I left my car.

A tight grip encircles my upper arm, and a scream rips from my lips when I'm spun around. "Goddammit, stop ignoring me." Henry's clean-shaven cheeks are red, and his chest is heaving. Whether from extortion or anger, I couldn't tell.

I plant my palms firmly on the center of his torso and push with all my might. He's caught off guard by the way his eyes widen and the step he took back, but his grip on me still doesn't falter.

"Let me go, Henry," I hiss, looking around. There are plenty of people around us but, while everyone is openly staring, no one dares intervene. Fuck.

He shoves his free hand through his hair, messing up whatever neat comb-through he had going on for himself. His hazel eyes bore into mine, contrite, pleading, desperate. "So that's it then? Three years down the drain, just like that?"

I twist my arm, trying to break his grip, but to no avail. "For god's sake. What is wrong with you?" My heart is pounding, and black spots are dancing at the corners of my eyes as adrenaline floods my veins. I need to get out of here before we have a repeat of the bar incident. "Henry, you left me. You filed for divorce. What do you want from me?"

He pulls me to him until our pelvises touch and our chests collide. For any onlookers, we look just like a pair of lovers embracing when he sneaks his hand around my waist. "I made a mistake, Siah. Yes, I filed for divorce, but not for one second did you fight for us." He draws me closer, and I force a step back, attempting to put some semblance of distance between us.

"Fight for us? When should I have done that? In the middle of the night, while I was fighting a panic attack on my own in your living room as you packed your bags and went on your merry way?"

"Siah..." He sighs, his eyes closing tightly for a brief second, as if scrunching them shut would stop the truth of my words from hitting him in the face.

"No, no. You want to talk. Okay... let's do this in the middle of the fucking street, Henry." I wiggle some more, but he's like a goddamn wall. Unmovable. "Maybe I should've fought for us when I got sick." I stop for a second, the thoughts in my head spinning and swirling. "Unless that's what you wanted." A shudder wracks my body as ice-cold realization settles inside of me. "You fucker, that's what you wanted," I accuse. "You wanted me to beg you, to depend on you." My eyes narrow, and I drop my voice to pure lethal steel levels. "Take your fucking hands off me, or I'll start screaming bloody murder until my lungs collapse."

"Don't do this," he pleads, the look in his eyes almost manic. "We were good together. I took care of you, didn't I? We can still be good together."

My head shakes reflexively, dismissing every word out of his deceiving mouth. Nausea swirls in my stomach. Has he always been this manipulative? I thought my *follower* couldn't be related to Henry because I've felt those eyes on me many times before I ever met him, but what if I'm wrong? The fear only escalated once he and I got married. Was this just an elaborate mind-fuck game to get into my head and isolate me from everyone else?

"Ntz, ntz, ntz." I gasp as pale green eyes bore into the side of my face. Elijah is anger incarnate as he strides toward us. "Doc, you really haven't learned your fucking lesson, have you?" he says as a greeting.

"She's my fucking wife," Henry yells. My shoulders automatically rise to my ears, my eardrums thumping painfully.

Elijah is unphased, not even sparing him a side eye. "Do you want to be here with him?" he asks.

"Siah, please..."

I look directly into Elijah's eyes. "No."

He lunges then, quick as lighting. Before I realize what happened, Henry's grip on me disappears, his arm is twisted at his back, and his cheek is flush to the brick wall of the building behind me.

The smile on Elijah's face is sinister and cruel. A tendril of fear curls in the pit of my stomach. Elijah is not... not a dangerous man. The predatory flash in his eyes is unsettling. Between the two of them, right now, I don't know who's more unhinged.

He tips his chin in my direction. "Run along now. Go to your car."

I'm torn between getting myself to the safe confines of August's SUV and getting between the two men. Henry might disgust every cell inside of me, but I don't want to see him harmed. "B-but..."

"Go, Siah. I'll let him go as soon as you're gone. I promise."

I don't know this man from Adam. There's no way for me to be sure he'll keep his word. But my prolonged presence might escalate things. So I turn on my heel and rush to the parking lot, Elijah's words traveling through the noisy street.

"I thought you were smart enough, Doc, to heed my first warning. For your pitiful sake, I hope you heed my second."

Chapter Twenty-One

AUGUST

F uck this job. Fuck incompetent people. Fuck entitled arrogant pricks who don't have two neurons to rub together.

I pace the living room floor of the penthouse like a caged animal. My fingers hook into the knot at the base of my throat, and I all but rip the goddamn tie and throw it across the room.

"So what did you do about it?" I growl at the person on the other end of the phone.

"Did you actually want me to do something about it?" he replies casually, his voice bored and uncaring. "I simply *followed* your orders, boss."

I pinch the bridge of my nose between my thumb and my forefinger, willing the tension headache pounding behind my eyes to settle down some before my brain starts leaking through my ears.

"You fucking lost him!" I shout. "You had one goddamn job, and you fucking lost him."

An offended sigh. I can practically hear his eyes rolling from the other side of the phone. "At least, I got you tickets. First class, too. You know, you really ought to be more grateful. It's Thanksgiving in a week. Show some goddamn festive spirit."

I chuckle ruefully, each grating sound dark and filled with unrestrained rage. "You're testing my patience."

"W-whaaat... ch... ch-ch... I'm going through a tunnel. Can't hear you, ch-ch."

"Don't be a dickhead. Who's picking me up from the airport?" I ask. It's better that I focus now on my upcoming holiday trip. Since I'm traveling so *far away* and all.

"Jayme. If you call and ask her. As far as you're concerned, I'm busy this weekend. My phone will live in an eternal tunnel from Thursday to Monday.

But, if you ask nicely enough, I'll drive you back to the Sea-Tac on Tuesday morning," he quips before the line goes dead.

Fuck! I scrub my face with my palm, then shove my fingers through my hair and pull. This is not... ideal. Directing my pacing to the minibar next to the window, I pour a measure of Macallan. The burn of old, rich whiskey should take off the angry edge my voice carries. I drop on the couch, my bent legs spread wide, and rest my elbows on my knees.

This whole fuck-up with our latest job is the reason my one motto in life is *If you want things done properly, do them yourself.* I might have an unholy amount of money and power, but even I can't be in two places at once. And the last place I want to be right now is here.

There are two aspects to my business. The advertised side—my cybersecurity software is second to none. The front side is all about cybersecurity and surveillance. I design and create custom made cybersecurity systems, my team tests the heck out of them, and then we sell. Simple as. Occasionally, if a breach—*fucking impossible*—or an error is encountered, I'd do an in-person diagnosis and fix it.

And the damned reason for this trip. There's no saying no when James St. Andrew calls and demands that I help his crooked friends protect their assets. Not yet, anyway.

The obscure side... we're a very useful tool employed by Elijah's military contacts or various police departments—rarely by the FBI—to help. That help mostly comes in the form of information mining or finding people who do not want to be found. In plain English, if it's on the Internet, I know it. And I know it first.

The obscure side currently stares at me from the screen of my tablet.

Unknown Sender: The Syren

Mr. St. Andrew,

Your target is a female, Caucasian, mid-build, height unknown, presumed to be in her mid-twenties to mid-thirties. There are no known photos of her. No camera feed either, since she seems to know where to position herself not to be seen. Gender and age are based on witness accounts—which, at best, is unreliable. Her body count, that we've so far managed to piece together, is 13. Her victimology is all over the map. She does not discriminate. Religion, age, social standing, there's no sense to her hunt.

Three things her victims have in common—they're all males, over eighteen, resid-
ing on the West Coast.
She lures them in, and absolutely all of them have been found dead precisely
twelve hours later.
Her cooling-off period seems to be as erratic as her target choice.
Attached there's a list of all her victims.
Find her.

I trace the untraceable. I find all those who wish to stay hidden. And hand-de-
liver them to the authorities requesting my help. With a flick of my finger, I
forward the email to my second-in-command. Right now, I have more pressing
matters than an erratic serial killer. You lock up one, ten more pop their ugly
heads.

Tipping my head back, I relish in the coolness of the glass against my lips. The
second sip I keep on my tongue until every nerve ending burns and grows numb
under the sweet smokiness of the whiskey, and only then I swallow. Onto the
next phone call. It doesn't take me long to find her contact. A foreign warmth
spreads through my chest when she answers before the first ring fully ends.

"Hi August! To what do I owe the honor?"

"Hi Siah," I purr. Yeah, I fucking purr—a tiger tamed by a butterfly. Go
fucking figure. "I... ran into a bit of an issue at work, which has me coming back
to Seattle."

I don't finish my explanation when she interrupts me. "Oh. Well, I can be out
of your hair by tomorrow."

My stomach tightens. An uncomfortable jolt twists up my insides as her
words echo in the empty living room. "No, no, no." Shit, I sound like a pussy.
"Coming back for a few days. I'll leave again on Tuesday next week. If you're
uncomfortable with me at the house, I'll get a hotel room." I hear the idiocy of
my words. I truly do, but she has the tendency to reduce me to an idiot *nearly*
every time I talk to her.

"Good grief, August. Why would you stay at a hotel when you have a perfectly
good home? Don't be ridiculous." I lean back on the couch and undo the button
of my trousers. It's all I can do to release the pressure in my groin. Fuck, I need
to get laid. It's been a while... "—sleep on the couch, and you'll take back the
master bedroom."

"I have a perfectly good pull-out couch on the third floor, Siah. It may not
look like it, but it turns into a king-size bed." The glass rim is pressed against my

bottom lip as I tip back my head and savor the burn of the whiskey. For good measure, I smack my lips together, so I can feel the elusive note of antique oak on my tongue. I bet her kisses taste exactly like that—rich, sweet, spicy.

She clears her throat, and I hear her soft breaths through the speaker of my phone. "When are you getting here?"

"Tomorrow morning."

There's a hitch in her breath. Anticipation? Dread? Anxiety? A low, self-deprecating laugh. "Well, I look forward to finally meeting you, August."

I lick the drop of whiskey from my lip. "Yes, Siah. I look forward to officially meeting you, too. Sweet dreams."

The call ends, and I'm left to stare at an empty wall in the darkened penthouse. Siah Hadley... intrigues me. More than I care to admit.

When Jayme, my stepsister, and Siah ended up sharing a dorm, I did my due diligence for my peace of mind. My stepsister is a strong woman, but she was starved for friends at that time. I simply wanted to ensure she didn't end up rooming with someone who'd take advantage of her kindness or treat her like shit. Siah was... plain enough for me to rest comfortably at night, without worrying about Jayme.

Until she called me and ripped me a new—or several—asshole for disappointing Jayme by not coming to her graduation. I was already on my way when the hellion stole my phone number and took matters into her delicate hands. Two minutes, thirty-two seconds—that's how long it took for my curiosity to be piqued.

And ever since then, Siah Hadley has slipped through my fingers.

The leather crinkles under me as I shift, a low groan ripping from my throat. She has been through hell and back lately. The least she needs is me lusting after her during our... brief cohabitation in the daylight.

My fingers fly over the keyboard of my phone in my attempt to distract myself from all the nighttime-suited images rushing through my head.

> *Any nefarious plans for tomorrow morning?*

Me

She's quick to respond. She always is.

> *World domination postponed 'till after Thanksgiving.*

Jayme St. Andrew

> *That's too bad. Would picking up your favorite brother from the airport count as a consolation prize? Say 7:30 a.m.? Breakfast on me.*

Me

> **Gif of a puppy wearing a party hat**

Jayme St. Andrew

> *It's unholy o'clock! Better add an Extra Large Coffee. I'll be there with bells on.*

Jayme St. Andrew

> *Unfortunately, I know you enough to know that might indeed be the case.*

Me

> **Gif of Homer Simpson disappearing in bushes**

Jayme St. Andrew

A stray, a hacker, and a stepsister walk into a bar, and...
Knock-knock.

I slap my palms on my knees and stand to my full height, rolling my eyes.

"And apparently do fuck all because of unwanted visitors," I mutter to myself as I stride to the entrance. With the most pleasant smile I can muster, I open the door with a flourish. "Good evening, Helena."

"Oh, August. Hi, darling boy." She pushes past me and beelines straight to the kitchen, where she deposits a paper bag onto the dark counter. "I brought you dinner." She smiles brightly, her hands clasped in front of her.

Helena is a beautiful woman, even as she's nearing fifty. Elegant, gracious, submissive—the perfect wife for the perfect asshole. She and her daughter, Jayme, are the only reasons I still keep in touch. If it weren't for them, well, my father could rot, as far as I'm concerned.

"Thanks. You didn't have to. I planned to order in and have an early night. I'm leaving for Seattle tomorrow," I tell her. It's not her fault she married my father. She tried to do her best by me and also protected Jayme fiercely when I wasn't there to intervene. Why she's still with him? Not for me to judge.

"You're leaving already?" She gasps, the disappointment clear on her face as her brows furrow. "I... I hoped you'd join us for Thanksgiving dinner."

She's been pushing for years for family dinners, holidays together. Not in the St. Andrew household. We're no white picket fence, happy family kind of people.

I settle my hand on her shoulder and give her a light squeeze. Placating her costs me nothing. "I'm sorry, Helena. Unfortunately, business never stops, not even for Thanksgiving. I was only in town because of that mess with Crenshaws. I have very urgent... projects that need to be overseen. Exceptions were made when Father called in the favor for his friends. Now, I must return. I figured, since I'm stateside, I might as well see Jayme, too."

She cups my cheek and affectionately pats the five o'clock scruff I'm sporting. I miss my fucking beard, but Father's circles require a certain kind of appearance—pompous fucking cunts that they are. "You're a good man, August. Thank you for looking after my baby girl. Send her my love. I wish she'd come visit more often."

I grunt in acceptance, but there's no point explaining to Helena that her daughter is a smart woman, and as long as James St. Andrew is alive, there's absolutely no fucking way in hell I'll allow Jayme anywhere near him again.

Or Siah, for that matter.

Chapter Twenty-Two

SIAH

The coffee mug shakes in my hand. Or maybe's my hand that's shaking. Who the fuck knows at this point? My anxiety is at an all-time high. The house is fine. I cleaned it yesterday—after the shocking phone call with August—to within an inch of its life. Hell, I even polished the locked door to the third floor. Everything is gleaming. It practically sparkles brighter than a diamond in the sunlight.

I spin on my heel to face the entrance when I hear the lock disengage. Of course, my whole body is a live wire of bubbles, as if some sort of internal jacuzzi turned on and jets of air and pure fucking torment are blasting at my insides.

"Cool and collected now, Siah." I give myself a pep talk. Because pep talks always work. Especially when I'm hyped up on caffeine. THEY. ALWAYS. WORK. That's why I'm convinced I'm being followed, just divorced Henry, and I'm living in a stranger's home.

Hot coffee stings my skin, and I drop the mug like... well, like it burned me because it fucking did.

"Holy mother of boiling shit on a liquid stick," I cry out as I dash to the sink and run cold water over my smarting skin.

A throat clears at my back, and I feel the blush barreling up my neck, aiming straight for my cheeks. This is so not the first impression I wanted to give August. We keep... meeting in the most unfavorable of circumstances. The first time we ever spoke, I shouted at him and called him a selfish bastard. The second time, the selfish bastard offered his home for free to the paranoid, crazy lady. And the third time...

Heat envelops my back. Not the kind that sears through my skin and blisters painfully. The kind in which I bask at the end of a long day under the embrace of my favorite blanket. Spice, cardamom, sandalwood, one after the other, each fragrance hits—first my knees, making them weak, then my stomach, causing it to flutter, and lastly my heart, quickening my heartbeats.

Electricity crackles across my skin as a large, warm hand closes around my wrist and rotates my hand around the icy-cold stream of water. "Allow me, please," he rumbles, with a thunder-like quality to his voice that makes me smell petrichor in the air, even though summer is long gone. "What happened to you?"

"Coffee attack," I squeak.

He crowds me against the edge of the sink as he stretches to pick up a paper towel from somewhere above my head. *Holy hotness Batman, he's huge.* I half-turn in his direction. My forehead barely reaches his collarbone. I tilt my head back and barely suck in a breath. Dark blue eyes streaked with golden flecks, like lightning in the night, stare back at me. Straight nose, dark pink lips that look plump enough to lick, a neatly trimmed beard covering a strong jaw, tousled, thick, jet-black hair—this is no poorly lit bar picture.

August's mouth twitches in a semblance of a smile, while I keep staring at him like I've been frozen-dumb with my eyes on him. I flinch when the abrasive paper towel rubs against my still smarting skin. "I'm sorry," he rumbles, "I just need to dry your hand."

I close my eyes and nod. At least the sting gives me enough sense to break eye contact. The last thing I need right now is to lust after my best friend's stepbrother. Talk about fucked up. Sure, it's nice to know I'm not completely dead inside and living my best fantasies only in twisted dreams. But... yeah, not going there.

My eyes are still closed when he takes a step away from me. I don't need to see him to know. Every cell in my body is feeling the absence of his proximity. "I need to grab something from my suitcase. Stay away from rogue coffee until then."

And my nipples tighten at his teasing tone. I've never been more grateful in my whole life for bras with extra padding. I'm a woman; I'll forgo a bra every time I can get away with it. Meeting someone for the first time isn't really a get-away-with-it kind of situation. And smart thinking of me, too. Right now, there's no need for my nipples to salute the room like dutiful soldiers. No sire, no way.

I shake my head to dispel whatever pheromones August's cologne is infused with and slump into the closest chair, on the opposite side of the island from where my traitorous coffee still steams. By now, my face must be as red as the irritated splatter on my hand.

Speaking of reds... "Where's Jayme?" I ask August, not daring to lift my eyes from where they're fixated on my hand. For sure, he looks as good from the back as he does from the front, and I really don't think my ovaries can take much more.

I don't care what the test results from Dr. Gutiérrez said, there's something unnatural happening to my hormones.

"She had to drop by *Debatable*. Said she'll be back for dinner," he informs me. His long, thick fingers, with perfectly manicured squared nails brush over my wrist, spreading a glossy colorless unguent over the raised edges of the first-degree burn now fully formed on my pale skin. "This should help numb the pain. It also keeps blistering and scarring to a minimum." A last brush of his index finger over my battle wound lingers a second too long and has my throat drying instantly.

"Thank you," I mumble, swiveling on my chair to watch him as he walks to the sink and washes away the unguent from his palms. And yup, I was sadly very, very much right. Wide shoulders, barely contained by his gray button down, strong back tapering down to narrow hips, and—*mother of god, the squats this man must do*—a firm ass embraced by his dark trousers.

Well, one thing is for sure. August St. Andrew is one magnificent man.

And I'm well and truly fucked.

Chapter Twenty-Three

SIAH

To say Jayme is in a good mood it's an understatement. She's been one huge smile all evening. There's no denying the love she has for her brother and her happiness at having him home.

August has kept his word and spent most of the day on the third floor. If it weren't for the occasional thumps in the ceiling, I could've sworn I was home alone. Weirdly enough, the thumps helped assuage an old fear of mine. The ceiling is not soundproofed. If at any point someone is upstairs, I'd be able to hear them walking about. Especially in the dead of the night, when silence reigns, and even whispers are deafening.

He's now changed into a pair of dark wash jeans that look... custom-made just for his ass. I've learned today that I do possess quite a bit of self-control, because it took everything in me not to drool all over my glazed baby-carrots when he got up from the dining table and went to the minibar to prepare a whiskey for himself and a glass of whatever concoction Jayme's drinking. He had to bend just so to retrieve the glasses, and I nearly fell off my chair.

It also doesn't help that his light blue T-shirt sits so snugly on him, I can see every flex of his abdomen and chest.

And so the first dinner together went. Jayme chatted happily about everything under the sun, content—her words, not mine—to have two of her favorite people under the same roof for the first time in ten years. August, polite but aloof, made small comments here and there, allowing his stepsister room to just be her lovely exuberant self. And then there was me. Shoveling carrots into my mouth like they went out of style, chewing each bite twice the recommended amount, just so I could keep my moans and inappropriate thoughts to myself.

Some friend I am.

"Oh!" Jayme shrieks all of a sudden, making me jolt in my seat. "Shit, Siah. I forgot to tell you..."

I tilt my head in her direction, a questioning eyebrow high on my forehead. She leans across the table and grabs my hand. "I'm the worst, I swear. I'm so sorry."

My stomach bottoms out, and a black hole of anxiety opens up inside of me. "What happened?"

"Davina called a staff meeting for tomorrow morning. Last chance for her to ensure a couple of us go into the long weekend with our holidays ruined, I'm sure. I tried to wiggle out of it, but she wouldn't have it." Jayme rolls her pretty brown eyes, genuine disappointment tugging down at the corners of her lips.

And then it dawns on me. "Oh." Well, that's... inconvenient. "No worries, babe. I'll book a taxi or an Uber or something."

She squeezes my hand, sympathy pouring out of her. "I'm really sorry. I promise I'll be here as soon as the meeting ends, with an entire aisle of ice cream and chocolate in my bag."

My cheeks pink up. I'm no prude, but I also don't particularly want August to know my business. Not this one, at least. I remove my hand from hers and wave her off. "Honestly, it's not a problem. Work comes first."

"What's that?" August asks, looking at me over his glass, the deep amber of his whiskey swirling as he tips the rim to his mouth.

"Nothing important." I shrug. "I have an appointment tomorrow, and Jayme offered to drive me, but now she can't."

"Is there something wrong with the SUV?" Worry swims inside the navy-blue depths of his eyes.

The SUV? Oh! Hello, thy name is Mortification.

"It's a doctor's appointment. She needs someone to drive her back home." Jayme oh so helpfully clarifies.

My eyes dart to the stairs just behind my chair. If I'm quick about it, I could climb them and hide in my bedroom in thirty seconds flat. Or maybe forty. Fifty, at most.

"So then I'll take you," August declares, as if it is a done deal.

I stand from the table and nervously start collecting the dinner plates. "I appreciate it, but it's fine. Honestly. I'll just take an Uber. Traffic's a bitch with last minute Thanksgiving preparations. Everyone—and their mothers and their pets—is out shopping."

My belly flutters when he leans back in his chair, elbows resting on the armrests, strong thighs parted. He looks so casual and chill, with just the faintest trace of tension under his skin, as if he could pounce at any second.

"Siah," he purrs my name, causing every cell in me to stand at attention, not just my nipples with their newfound duty. "I'll take you."

Jayme lifts her glass in August's direction. "Thanks, big brother. You're always at the ready to save my ass."

One good thing about being embarrassed down to the last toenail is that I can't find it in me to worry about lurching ex-husbands or stalkerish eyes. Instead, I just worry my fingers in my lap, stealing glances at the somber man in the driver's seat.

August is both what I expected and completely surprising. He's quiet, an observer, able to blend with the shadows and flirt with aloofness, sometimes even coming across as borderline indifferent. At the same time, he doesn't need to speak a word for me to be conscious of his presence. He feels larger than life, taking up all the air in my vicinity. I'm painfully aware of every single movement he makes, every twitch of his lips, every flare of his nostrils, every flex of his muscles.

I discreetly turn my head to the window and yawn in my palm. Sleep last night was... restless, at best. Ever since I've divorced Henry, the quality of my sleep has grown exponentially. Even my peculiar dreams have dwindled. My paranoia has slowly decreased, too. Spending all night tossing and turning, my ears perked up, eager to hear any sign of August upstairs, was disconcerting.

He guides the car close to the curb in front of Sundale and, without a word, opens the door and exits. *Okay then.* I clutch my purse in one hand and make a grab for the door's handle on my side, when it pops open, startling me. A large palm with splayed fingers offers itself to me. With a small gulp, I place my hand in his, shuddering as the warmth of his skin seeps inside of me despite the frigid temperatures outside, and let him help me out.

He doesn't hold my hand for more than it's necessary for me to get out, and I shove down the disappointment bubbling inside my chest when he releases me. "How long do you think you're going to be?"

"Shouldn't take more than half an hour," I murmur.

He tips his chin in a nearly imperceptible nod. "I'll go find a parking space, but I'll be back here when you're done."

"It's fine. Just message me where you are, and I'll meet you there."

That has him smirking, then bending down and kissing my cheek. I swear, I feel the soft graze of his stubble everywhere. "See you in thirty."

And... I just lost at least twenty IQ points. Just like that. A brief brushing of lips and the feathering of stubble, and I'm struck dumb.

"Y-yeah. Thanks... S-see ya," I stutter, then promptly spin on my heel and march inside the warm reception of Sundale.

Michelle smiles when she sees me come in. Her red lips gleam under the fluorescent lights. "Good morning," I greet her as I approach her desk. "I have a 9:30 with Dr. Gutiérrez. I'm Siah..."

"Hadley," Michelle finishes for me. "I remember." Her smile widens even more. "Forgive me for being forward, but I just love your curls."

That has me smiling right back, pride shining through me as I bounce one with my palm. "Thank you, Michelle. I'm quite fond of them myself." In three short months, I've learned to appreciate them. Moussiah is nowhere to be found anymore.

She slides a tablet over the tall reception desk to me. "Please verify your insurance and contact details, then make your way to Consultation Room Five."

I scan quickly through the information on the screen, updating my address with the PO box I rented. The last thing I need is for Henry to receive any more information about me. One smart move I made when we got married was to insist on keeping my own health insurance rather than have him add me to his plan. One less thing to change on the divorce side of life.

Once I'm done with the paperwork, I say my thanks to Michelle and make my way to the consultation room. Anxious butterflies take flight in my stomach, and my insides feel all twisted up. I don't care what anyone says, spreading your legs in front of a stranger will never not be embarrassing for me. Blame it on my upbringing, where little girls were shamed, tecnagers were called whores, and young adults were made to doubt their morals, but I've never not been nervous when visiting an OB-GYN or exposing my... intimate parts.

With Henry, it took me a good while to feel comfortable and relaxed while naked in front of him. And even my first sexual experience with a stranger at the Blind Date Club, I wasn't technically... fully naked. The office was dark, the blindfolds were on; he couldn't really see me.

I knock gently, then push through the door. "Good morning, Dr. Gutiérrez!" My voice shakes, and I swallow down my emotions. It'll be fine. Millions of women go through this.

"Good morning, Siah." She smiles prettily at me. "Come, have a seat."

And not one second too soon, as my knees threaten to give out from under me. I slump in the office chair she patted and fold my arms across my chest.

"Okay. You're here today to have an Intrauterine System fitted, or what we call a hormonal coil." She pushes what looks like a leaflet with information about the coil. "The device will be effective for five years. After the time has passed, it will need to be replaced. However, it can be removed at any time, should you wish to have any children earlier than that, or if you have any issues with it, or if you simply want to have it removed."

"Understood." I nod for good measure.

"Great. Now, as with any medical device, there are some risks associated with the hormonal coil," she begins. By the end of the five-minute spiel, my head is spinning. Looks like I'll be spending the next five years of my life with my finger inside my vagina, looking for coil threads. Oh joy!

"Please remove your underwear and make yourself comfortable on the chair. Ensure the skirt of your dress is high enough on your waist. Nurse Merrington will be assisting me today. She's only here for your comfort. So feel free to squeeze her hand and breathe when she tells you to."

I stand up on trembling legs and make my way to the chair. My comfortable cotton panties are shoved in my purse, and I try to forget all about them as I lean back on the crinkly paper towel. Nothing screams awkward like panties in a bag and ass hanging half off a chair while your legs are spread about in stirrups. Best day of my life.

A curtain is drawn around me, and the face of a thirty-something woman hovers at the corner of my eye. "Hello, Ms. Hadley. I'm Nurse Merrington. Don't worry. Dr. Gutiérrez is the best at what she does. Try to relax, and we'll have you out of here in no time."

The sound of a curtain being drawn once again echoes around me, but I don't dare look anywhere but at the ceiling. "Thank you, Nurse Merrington. I'm... just a bit nervous."

"I'm here if you need me," she reassures me, her voice calm and soothing.

"Okay, Siah. I'm going to insert the speculum now. This will feel just a bit uncomfortable."

Sure, if by uncomfortable she means splitting my vagina apart, then it's just a tad uncomfortable, I agree. I suck in a breath and will my thighs to stop shaking. My heart pounds wildly in my chest as I feel her working between my legs.

"Now, I'm going to rub a numbing agent on your cervix, which will hopefully make things easier for you, then sterilize the area. Expect some tingles and a cooling sensation."

I nod, my eyes still firmly planted on a hairline crack on the otherwise pristine cream-colored ceiling.

"You're doing great," Nurse Merrington praises. "For the next step, it's very important that you keep breathing, okay? Dr. Gutiérrez will measure your uterus, and this will come across as a pinch. It might startle you, but it will only last a couple of seconds, okay?"

I focus on her words, determined to follow them to the letter, except the pinch feels very much like all my internal organs are being vacuum-suctioned through my vagina, never to be seen again.

"Breathe, Siah. Come on, breathe for me," Nurse Merrington coaxes me.

My lungs burn as I release a deep exhale. She was right about the duration, but fuck me, if it felt anything like a pinch.

"Almost there, Siah. You're doing amazing. I'm now going to insert the IUS. In about ten seconds, you'll feel a cramp forming. This is your uterus contracting around the device as I place it in the right position," Dr. Gutiérrez advises.

Great. I can't wait. I simply, simply *love* cramping.

"Motherf..." I gasp when the strangest, most mechanical and unnatural cramp spirals in my lower belly, stealing the air from my lungs and searing my insides together.

Dr. Gutiérrez gently pats the inside of my thigh. "You're all done, Siah. Relax for me now as I remove the speculum. Don't try to get up. I need you to remain here for another ten minutes to ensure you will not faint. The cervix doesn't like to be poked around, and when it happens, one side effect is a lowered heart rate and a lower blood pressure. On rare occasions, fainting occurs."

The speculum is as *uncomfortable* going out as it was getting in. I remain staring at the ceiling, barely murmuring a thank you to the kind nurse—who went ahead and took my legs out of the stirrups as I scooted up on the chair—and Dr. Gutiérrez, while my uterus starts a civil war against me.

Yes, I was told to expect period-like cramps immediately after. They'll also most likely continue through the day and, if I'm really really lucky, tomorrow too.

Other super cool things to look forward to are light bleeding and spotting. I'm just ready now for that light at the end of the tunnel, when in two to three months, the coil will hopefully reduce the normally heavy flow of blood during my period and some of the pain, too.

"I've left a sanitary pad for you," the good doctor tells me from somewhere behind the privacy curtain.

I slowly push up on my elbows, and when my head doesn't start spinning, I shift my legs off the chair. With shaky fingers, I make quick work of donning my underwear and sticking the pad, then smooth my flowy skirt down my thighs.

"You look a bit pale," she observes. "Are you feeling faint?"

"No," I rasp. "Just some cramping, but not lightheaded."

Her smile is sympathetic. "Unfortunately, the cramping is there to stay for the rest of the day. I saw in your chart the medicines you are currently on. My advice would be not to take any painkillers. A heated pad or a hot water bottle should help with the pain, though. However, if the cramping gets unbearable or if you're spiking a fever, please call the practice immediately."

"Understood. Thank you, Dr. Gutiérrez."

She pushes to her feet and opens the door for me. "You're very welcome. I know all you want to do is lie down right now, so I made a note for Michelle to call you tomorrow and set up another appointment in about two weeks' time. It's recommended I do a quick check to ensure there's no sign of pelvic infection or inflammation. Very rarely, the coil will tear through your uterus, but that usually happens when a coil is fitted soon after giving birth. The uterine walls are very fragile then. It's best, though, to verify it all works as it should."

I nod again and say my goodbyes before limping out toward reception. My whole body halts mid-stride when I see August standing up from one of the chairs in the waiting room, his forehead crinkled with worry, midnight blue eyes scanning me from head to toe. I don't miss his sigh of relief either when he finds me no worse for wear.

Silently, he walks to me, and with a large warm palm at the small of my back, he ushers me out the door and into the waiting car.

And if for the one hundred and twenty-three seconds it took us to reach the car, I leaned back into his touch, well, I just had a plastic device shoved up my vagina and stuck into my uterus.

Sue me for enjoying the comfort of his presence.

Chapter Twenty-Four

Siah

Maybe it was a bad idea to have this procedure done just before Thanksgiving. I bring my knees to my chest and burrow deeper into my blanket. This pain is exhausting. I beelined straight to the couch as soon as we got home. I got too relaxed in the car, with the heated seat providing comfort on the drive back. As soon as I exited, and the frigid wind wrapped around me, I immediately felt the need to double over. There was no way I would've made it up the stairs and into the bedroom.

So, now I'm just lying here, soaking up the cramps and the mortification. To make matters worse, instead of minding his own business and going to the third floor as he did yesterday, August hovers like a worried mother hen. He'll wear a path in the hardwood floor as he keeps pacing from the kitchen to the living area.

I'm not sure at what point the pain gets the best of me, but between the warmth of the blanket and the sheer exhaustion of the cramps, my eyelids become heavier and heavier, and I blissfully fall asleep.

Flashes of gray, dark and light, paint my restless dreams as my weightless body levitates. I'm as heavy as a bird. *Little mockingbird,* a dark gravelly voice whispers in the spiral of my dream. My stomach swirls and churns, agonizing stabs of pain bending my wings. Despite the tumultuous air flows spinning me around, I land gently on a cloud, goosebumps ruffling my feathers.

Lightning strikes my center, a patch of fire ignites, branding my skin. The flames are purifying, incinerating away the agony tensing through my weightless body. A mournful song chirps from my mouth as the spiral of hurt unwinds from my core.

"Siah, wake up. Siah!"

The cloud I'm resting on shakes, roaring thunder barreling through the softness. From above, the sun is shining majestically, its healing warmth spreading along my back and side.

"Siah, open your eyes, darling. Let me see you're okay, and you can go back to sleep."

My limbs press into the rapidly firming surface of the cloud. My body lengthens and expands, the weightlessness evaporating as if it never were. My belly feels hot, too hot. But the cramps are nearly gone, only a dull echo remaining. A solid wall of heat rests at my back. I shift around and blink open my eyes, only to find worried pools of midnight skies staring back at me.

"Thank fuck," he exhales, his lips twitching in the semblance of a smile. "Sorry to wake you, but you were crying in your sleep. It was obvious you were in pain," he whispers.

"August," I croak.

"I… uhm… called Jayme. She said to put a heating pad on your lower back and one on your belly. I tried to wake you before, but you wouldn't." I hear his words, but I barely comprehend them. All my attention is focused on the fingers trailing softly across my forearm. "I hope they help," he continues.

"T-thank you." My voice is gritty. Embarrassment and a foreign kind of emotion unfurl in my throat. He looked after me. He cared for me.

He squeezes my arm, then lets go. "Alright, I'll let you sleep. I've put your phone next to you, so message me if you wake up and need anything."

Before I can respond, he climbs off the bed and walks out the door, taking all the warmth in the room away with him.

What the fuck just happened?

As it turns out, Jayme was one of the people to have their holidays ruined after her work meeting the other day. Our plan was for her to come to August's house early in the morning and help me cook Thanksgiving dinner for us. Instead, I'm alone in the kitchen, peeling potatoes like they offended all my ancestors and my hypothetical children.

August has been decidedly cold ever since he carried me to my bedroom two days ago. I'm starting to get a bit offended. I understand it was an uncomfortable situation, but he could've just let me be and carry on doing whatever it is he's doing. He stepped up instead, and then all but vanished.

I mean, I didn't have hopes of us becoming best friends and braiding each other's hair. But... I don't know. When he called to say he was coming home, I was excited to meet him and see who the elusive August St. Andrew was. Sure, he owes me nothing. If anything, I'm in his debt. And his behavior makes me feel like I'm an imposition more than ever.

To make matters worse, I find myself attracted to him. I can, at least, admit as much to myself. Not that I am in a position to pursue this attraction—my friendship with Jayme means too much to me to betray it like this. That, and the desperate need inside of me to heal mentally after the disaster that was the end of Henry and me. But it's still disappointing to find myself attracted to someone, only for that someone to avoid me like I'm the plague.

I cube the potatoes and wash the excess starch, then move them to a pot and let them simmer.

There are silver linings to this situation. My resolve to pack up and leave is greater than ever. I haven't felt anyone watching me or following me in a couple of weeks. It doesn't mean my pursuer is still not out there. He's never had a pattern. Sometimes, I'd feel like I lived under a microscope for weeks on end, then he'd disappear for weeks or months. Like it happened before I married Henry. For almost a full year, I felt like a new person. Not constantly looking over my shoulder, not feeling the burn of foreign eyes boring into my skin, just a normal twenty-seven-year-old. It gave me the push I needed to accept Henry's proposal and sign the marriage certificate. For all the good that it did me.

I can write from anywhere. Maybe I don't need to do anything as drastic as moving to a foreign country, although mild temperatures and a sandy beach sound just perfect compared to the doom and gloom that is Seattle in November. The only thing keeping me here is Jayme. And if worse comes to worst, I'm sure she would support me.

As an abandoned child, all I've ever wanted were roots. We humans always want that which we could never have. So instead of pursuing roots and never achieving my goal, what if I embrace the lack of gravity tying me to one place? I've never been an extravagant woman, so if I'm careful with my money and frugal,

I could milk my savings for years to come. Plus, every writing gig could fund my travels.

Constantly moving about would most definitely also make life more difficult for whoever is following me. They might lose interest if I'm not in their immediate vicinity. You know, out of sight, out of mind.

I wipe my hands on the black apron, about three sizes too big for me. I had to wind it a couple of times around my waist, so it looks more like a dirty skirt than an apron, but at least I won't have any grease-covered clothes. Grease is a right pain to remove from fabrics.

Armed with oven mitts, I carefully slide out the tray where a medium-sized turkey is currently roasting. A mixture of thyme, sage, rosemary, and garlic aromas fills the kitchen, making my stomach rumble and my mouth water. I baste the turkey one last time, then slide it back into the oven so that the skin gets nice and crispy.

Setting a timer for the oven and a second one for the potatoes, I return to my bedroom and take a quick shower. I don't have time or energy to do anything fancy with my hair, so I just let the curls loose on my back. If I end the night looking like Medusa, so be it. A pair of stretchy black leggings and an off the shoulder green cashmere sweater-dress later, I'm ready for the feast.

I hurry down the stairs just as I hear voices coming from the entrance. I stop dead on the last step when my eyes find familiar pale green ones and a smirk to match my surprise.

"Hello, Siah! Happy Thanksgiving!" Elijah says, Devon waving at me from behind him.

Chapter Twenty-Five

SIAH

I groan as I rub my stomach. My leggings might be stretchy, but they're no match for my appetite. Good grief, I haven't eaten this much in a long, long while. And that's nothing compared to what the three hulking men put away.

I thought I was going to live off leftovers for the next two weeks, but now I'll be lucky if I have a slice of pumpkin pie left to eat with my coffee tomorrow morning.

"You outdid yourself today," Jayme says. I tilt my head to the left, just enough so I can see her in the periphery of my vision. That's about all the movement my food-baby allows.

The dinner went well, if I go by all the moans and grunts and barely any word in-between from my companions. I got over the initial shock of seeing Elijah and Devon and slid into the role of host quickly enough. Apparently, Jayme bumped into them when she was stopping at a bakery to pick up the pies for today. When she learned they had no plans, she invited them over as a thank you for looking after me during and after the Henry-being-a-cunt at the Flame&Stake incident.

What surprises me, though, is the undercurrent of tension wafting off August. His handsome face is an unreadable mask carved of stone. He hasn't as much as twitched in a semblance of a smile, nor has he made the slightest effort of making Elijah and Devon feel welcome. His rudeness irks me. I understand this is his house. I also understand he's not great at... people-ing. But it was *his* sister inviting them. He should take his displeasure out on her, not on the innocents.

"You really did, birdie," Elijah comments, his signature arrogant smirk plastered on his face.

A choking sound comes from August, who sputters in his whiskey. "Excuse me," he coughs, pushing back from the table and hurrying away from the room.

"Who pissed in his cranberry sauce?" Devon asks.

"Now, now, husband. Behave." Elijah laughs. "Moody is August's default setting."

Now it's my turn to choke on my iced Coke Zero—my alcohol ban is really inconvenient right about now. I could really use a tequila or ten, but it's a *bad* idea to mix my medicine with fun liquids.

"Wait, you guys know August?" I say at the same time as Jayme shouts, "Wait, you guys are married?"

Devon laughs, but my attention is drawn to Elijah, who has an *oh-shit* look on his face, none of his arrogance to be seen.

"Elijah is a former Special Ops," comes from behind me, a second before I feel his comfortable heat at my back. His fingers brush against my shoulders before his hands latch onto the backrest of my chair. I lean forward to cut the physical contact before I embarrass myself with the mother of all blushes I feel forming on my chest. "My security company often has military contracts," August clarifies.

I'm still as confused as before. They showed no sign of knowing each other throughout the dinner. And Elijah's comment shows a greater familiarity than the 'sometimes we worked together' explanation August threw our way.

Jayme's not interested in August's friendships—or the lack thereof—though, chatting away with Devon about his marriage to Elijah. If she's disappointed, she doesn't show it. Sure, I'm surprised too, since I remember Devon clearly flirting with my friend when we went to the bar, but I guess that's bartender life. You want good tips, you work the room. Or maybe they have an open relationship. Who am I to judge?

"Thank you for your service," I reply to Elijah. He inclines his head in my direction in acknowledgement, but I don't miss the shadows swirling in his freakishly pale eyes. "So, what made you become a nurse?"

Devon swivels his head toward me so fast, for a second, I fear he's given himself whiplash. "A nurse?" His laughter booms out of his chest. In fact, he's laughing so hard, he's just about to fall off his chair.

"What's wrong with being a nurse?" I ask, confused, but also offended. If he's one of those *dude-bros* with preconceived notions on jobs suitable for men and women, then I want nothing to do with him.

Devon sobers up and side-eyes Elijah, who's tapping his bottom lip with his index, but otherwise remains quiet. "I'm sorry. There's nothing wrong with being a nurse, and I'm truly sorry if my reaction came across that way. My husband here," he says, flicking Elijah's nose and causing him to sputter, "is a paper-pusher. He's out of the military but is now a CFO for a company still tied to our Department of Defense."

Elijah lifts one eyebrow, challenging me to ask the question sitting on the tip of my tongue. A swell of unease churns in my stomach. My head is swimming. I need to get away from everyone. I push away from the table, not even minding when the backrest of my chair hits August. "Excuse me..." I mumble and speed-walk to the stairs.

"Siah?" I hear August and Jayme call after me, but I ignore them, taking the stairs three at the time until I finally find myself in my bedroom. I slam the door shut and lock it from the inside for good measure.

My back hits the wooden shield protecting me from everyone on the other side, and I let myself slide down until my ass hits the floor.

It can't be.

Elijah was there that night at the hospital. He was wearing scrubs. He read my chart. He had a stethoscope, for fuck's sake.

He was there at the bar when Henry grabbed me and got between the two of us. Sure, one could argue that his husband works there, but... what were the chances for the both of us to be there at the same time?

He brought me back here and, allegedly, cared for me. Did he really? I remember close to nothing from those initial twenty-four hours—just waking up and constantly falling back asleep.

He was there, after the divorce meeting, when Henry made a spectacle of himself in the middle of the street.

He knows August, the man in whose home I live.

And he just so happens to bump into Jayme and get a dinner invite?

What are the fucking chances?

I shove my fingers in my hair, pulling at the roots to get the pain to center me. To stop this fucking merry-go-round I find myself on. Why would Elijah be the one to follow me? I've never seen him before that night in the hospital. Am I so desperate to know, I'm reaching for answers where there aren't any?

Maybe Henry's friend *was* right. Maybe I am indeed being paranoid.

A knock on the door has me startled, and my hand flies from my hair to my chest, where my heart is pounding wildly.

"Siah?" Elijah's voice comes muffled through the slab of wood. "Did I do something to offend you?"

I draw my knees to my chest and rest my cheek on top of them. What is he doing here? Do they all know? Are they all in on this twisted fucking game?

"Siah, are you okay?" he insists.

"I'm fine," I croak, tears burning behind my eyes as my limbs grow cold with fear. "I'll be right back. Just need a minute."

"Look..." A faint thump comes from the other side. "I'm sorry if I did or said anything to upset you. Devon and I will take our leave now. Thank you for the wonderful dinner."

No. He can't leave. I need answers.

I scramble to my feet, my fingers clumsy and uncoordinated as I struggle to unlock the door. I breathe a sigh of relief when the resounding click lets me know I've finally been successful in my attempts, and I shove the door open.

Elijah looks sincerely upset. His brows are drawn tight, his lips pursed. He takes a step back as soon as he sees me in the doorway, as if to appear non-threatening.

"I'm sorry."

I ignore his apology. It's answers I need, not empty words.

"Why were you at the hospital that night?"

His eyes widen—genuine surprise washing over his face. "That's why you thought I was a nurse?"

"And you helped me out when Henry got me hurt. You got me out of the bar and brought me home and cared for me..." I'm rambling at this point, my verbal spillage only stopping when I see his grimace. Regret? Guilt?

He walks backward until he hits the opposite wall, as if he's trying to put as much distance between us as possible, folding his arms across his chest and resting one ankle on top of the other.

"I volunteer at the hospital, Siah," Elijah says matter-of-factly. "I do have EMT training, but that's not here nor there. Usually, I spend my volunteer hours on the Burns floor. That night, I was going home. A friend of mine works in the Intensive Care Unit. She was running ragged for close to twenty-four hours, so when she saw me leaving, she asked me if I could just sit in your room for a while in case you woke up." He shrugs. "She needed a break, but you were on 'watch', so someone had to be around. I didn't see any harm in that, so I just sat around, waiting for her to come back. You woke up first."

I lean against the door frame as I process his count of events. It makes sense, it's plausible. The simplest explanation is usually the truth. But... why do his words feel oily, why do they ring untrue to me? I can't put my finger on it, but I'm one hundred percent sure he's holding something back.

"And the bar?"

He sighs, running a palm over his face. "I was already at the bar when you came in. My work hours are... unpredictable, even if I'm only a paper-pusher, as Devon put it. Whenever I have some free time, I like to spend it with my husband." He lifts a shoulder up, then drops it in a careless shrug. "I saw you, but we were strangers at the end of the day. You were pretty out of it when we met at the hospital. I figured you hadn't recognized me, so I minded my own business. And then I saw him getting aggressive with you."

"And you made my business yours." I sound ungrateful. I'm not.

"I'd intervene if I saw any man getting aggressive with a woman. And believe me, if I hadn't, Devon would have. He was just about to jump over the bar to get between the two of you."

Truth, but also... lie. What is he not saying? Or am I now too deep into my paranoid feelings that I'm just resistant to accept the truth?

"Did you know this was August's home when you brought me in?"

His eyes shutter. His face smooths of any and all traces of emotion. Whatever I could read on him before, it's gone now. If I look at him or I look at the wall, there's no difference; both are the same—impenetrable, silent, unreadable.

"I did," he says tentatively. Cautiously.

I draw in a quick breath. "Did you know before?"

He blinks. Once. Twice. "Not until I realized where the GPS in your car was taking me."

LIE!

The feeling of unjustness is so strong inside of me, I recoil off the door frame.

"Look... As far as I'm concerned, I just happened to be in the right place at the right time. I'm sorry I freaked you out. If this is too weird for you, I'll keep my distance."

Keep your distance. Yes, please!

"Did August know of all this?" I don't know why I asked the last question. I don't know what difference it makes.

"I know everything that happens in my house, Siah," comes from the top of the stairs, startling me. "I think it's time for you to leave now." This is directed at Elijah. He tips his chin in my direction, then strides past August, clapping him on the shoulder.

My mind is still spinning. Confusion, betrayal, and hurt swirl inside of me. So I take a step back, and then another, and then another, and then slam the door closed.

I don't have it in me to rehash the conversation with August.

Crawling between the cold sheets, I curl up in a ball in the middle of the bed and let the tears freefall on my cheeks.

If my instincts are right, there's nowhere safe here for me.

If my instincts are wrong, I just humiliated myself and made August look bad in his own home.

Fuck!

Chapter Twenty-Six

Him

I pace the floor at the end of the bed. Anticipation and anger war for first place in my veins. Fear has my heart pumping so vigorously, it just about cracks a rib. Too fast. Everything it's moving too fucking fast. She's not ready.

This will either make or break her.

She's still too fragile, still healing.

I hate being backed into a corner. Decisions being forced on me when I'm not prepared to make a move yet make my skin crawl, as if a million fire ants march over my body.

My shoes make no sound over the hardwood floor as I pace another length of the room. The only sounds that accompany me are her soft, even breaths and my blood rushing through my eardrums. I'll hear her sing soon enough.

My cock is painfully hard in my jeans, wearing a permanent indent from my zipper, but that's nothing new. Her fear is the most exquisite aphrodisiac. I bet my life her surrender will be even sweeter.

She's my calm and my peace.

I had to stand by and watch her make a thousand and one plans to leave. As if she'd ever be able to escape me. As if I wouldn't follow her to the very edge of the world. I love her fear, but I detest her torment. And I really fucking resent that I'm the reason she's torturing herself mercilessly.

She can't fucking leave me.

Another length of the room is eaten up quickly by my long strides. I'm getting restless. I'm getting impatient. The all-consuming need I have for her flames inside my chest, an eternal ache just beneath my skin that has no alleviation but for her touch. I yearn for her with every cell in my body. I'll self-combust if I don't get my fill of her soon.

It's been too long since I've last touched her.

Between my business and her visitors and all the turmoil she's been in after they left, it's been too fucking long.

But now she wants to leave. Next goddamn week.

If I have to keep her chained to this fucking bed until she understands well and truly the only direction she's running to is my arms... then so fucking be it.

In three long strides, I'm at her side. The mattress dips under my knees, but she doesn't stir. She's been crying herself to sleep all fucking week. I long to taste the saltiness of her tears on my tongue. But first things first.

Grabbing the blindfold from my pocket, I fix it across her eyes and tie it behind her head. I can't help myself. I lean down, burying my nose in her soft, wild curls and inhaling deeply.

Jasmine.

Honeysuckle.

Pure, sweet Siah.

From my other pocket, I grab the titanium chain I had made just for her. One end winds twice around her left wrist. When I'm satisfied that it's tight enough she can't take it off, but loose enough for her to maintain feel in her hand, I clasp the mechanism at the end to the middle ring of the link. Gently, I scoop out her right arm from under the pillow and bring it to the small of her back, then with quick, efficient movements, I wind the other end around her wrist and lock the binding down.

The titanium gleams in what little light is illuminating the room in such beautiful contrast with the pale-creaminess of her skin. I can't help but stop for a second to admire my handiwork.

Next comes out my pocket-knife. A perverted sense of satisfaction runs through me when I hack through the silky material of her tank top. She's taken to going to bed in her own pajamas this past week. The disappointment left me breathless and unable to sleep at night. My lungs fill for the first time in forever as I remove the scraps of material and throw them next to the bed, revealing the delicate contours of her back and her perfect porcelain skin.

Sure, I could've removed it before I tied her up, but there's no sense to risk her waking up and making my life difficult before I'm ready to up the difficulty level.

Mindful of her bound hands, I move Siah to her back and take off her sleeping shorts, leaving her in only a white lacy thong. My mouth waters at the promise of sweetness that is so prettily covered underneath the flimsy lace. For a second,

I consider removing her panties too and adding them to my collection, but I'll enjoy them better when I rip them off her body later on.

I slide out a second chain—an identical match of the first one, just longer—and wind it twice around her slender neck, like a choker. I nearly fucking choke on my own tongue just taking in her devastating beauty. My cock jolts impatiently behind my fly, currents of pain and pleasure running through my groin.

With one hand under her knees and the other supporting her back, I lift her off the bed and carry her at the foot of the armchair I positioned next to the door. Siah stirs then, which is just well enough, as I'll need her awake and cognizant soon.

With careful, gentle movements, I arrange her in the position I want her in. Asleep as she is, it looks uncomfortable as fuck, but she won't have to stay that way for long.

I made sure to replace those damned sleeping pills of hers with a *much* weaker version. Strong enough to get her asleep fast and have her slumber deeper than natural, weak enough so that she can be roused quickly and be aware of us.

No more forgetting of our nights together.

No more forgetting me.

I promised her she would remember our next meeting. This is me fucking keeping that promise.

My clothes find their way onto the hardwood floor, and then I position myself in the middle of the bed. The long, slender chain connected to her neck is wound tightly around my right hand. Long enough for my little mockingbird to feel free, short enough to pull her back to my side when she wanders too far away. *Perfect.*

Patting around under the pillow, I find the remote I dumped on the bed earlier, and, at the press of one button, warm lights flood the room. The strategically placed baseboard lights are one of my best ideas—it took a bit of care and sneaking about while she moped around in her office a couple of days ago, but I got them installed. They give enough light so I can delight myself in Siah's body, but stop her from seeing anything more than outlines and shadows through the blindfold. A little throwback to when I've had her for the first time.

I'm a romantic, after all, and everything I do is simply an expression of the all-maddening passion I have for her.

A grunt rattles my rib cage as I palm my cock, stroking myself while I take in the perfect picture that Siah makes. If I could bear to allow anyone to see her vulnerability, I'd have her drawn like this, and the painting hung above my fireplace. Knees parted, pretty pussy covered in dainty flowery lace, creamy skin all exposed, rosy nipples crowning the soft swell of her breasts, delicate collarbone, slender neck adorned with chains. Siah is my goddamned demise.

I pull the chain taut and watch in fascination as her lips purse and her forehead furrows. All my blood rushes to my cock, and I cuff myself at the base, controlling my frenzied excitement. My little mockingbird is about to give me the performance of a lifetime, and I'm a mere mortal, powerless in front of her magnificence.

The chain slackens as I unwind it once from around my hand. The silvery rings brush against her chest. A flick of the wrist has them swinging. A soft moan escapes her gorgeous lips as they touch one sensitive nipple, then the other. I groan loudly, my mouth watering when the pretty buds tighten in response, and swing the chain again.

Her hips buck, a fraction of a movement, barely there, but I don't miss it. My balls draw up, tingles dancing across my spine as I imagine the pristine white lace darkening with the slickness of her arousal.

"Come play, little mockingbird," I rasp, my voice rough with desire. "Wakey, wakey." I pull the chain taut once more, just enough so it tightens around her neck.

She jolts then so beautifully, my stomach bottoms out. Fuck, I want her.

"W-what?" She shimmies her shoulders, her melodic voice gritty with sleep.

I love her confusion, those fleeting seconds between sleep and awareness when there are no shields for vulnerability. The fragility and elegance of everything Siah is enslaves me to her wicked charms.

My patience has all but run out.

"Come to me, little mockingbird," I beg her.

A pained whimper leaves her pretty mouth when she realizes her hands are bound behind her back. I lick my lips, tasting her sweet, sweet desperation in the air between us. Her breaths quicken, her chest moving up and down erratically. What a pretty sight she makes. My beautiful, wounded mockingbird. ALL. FUCKING. MINE.

"W-what? Whe...? Who are you?" she cries, and I nearly come on the spot as her song bounces between the darkened walls of the bedroom.

"I told you, my love, I'm yours."

Siah startles then, leaning back against the armchair. Her indecision is written all over her beautiful face. I don't need to see her eyes to know what she's thinking. Try as she might, she can't escape me.

We're inevitable, Siah and I.

Her elbows find purchase on the cushion of the chair. Her legs tremble as she slowly lifts herself up until she's standing at her full height. "Such a good little mockingbird. So obedient," I praise. She's deserving of my praise and of the whole world laid at her feet. I intend to do just that.

"W-what do you want from me? Is this some sort of sick game?" she hisses.

The vitriol in her words hurts my chest. There are no games between the two of us. She's caged herself so deeply, so thoroughly, she can't escape. I'm her freedom. My only consolation is that I know she'll sing a different tune soon enough. I hope...

"Come to me and find out," I beckon, pulling at the chain and forcing her to take a step in my direction.

"Stop," she cries. "Why are you doing this?"

"I told you before. Because I'm yours," I reply sincerely, all my feelings for her infused in my words. Impatience eats away at me. Her beauty calls to my soul. I need to feel her, taste her, feast on her gracefulness. "Come to me and find out for yourself."

"You'll let me go if I do?"

NEVER.

It's on the tip of my tongue to shout my vow to her, but it wouldn't get us far. "I intend to persuade you to stay," I say instead.

She whimpers then, but puts one foot in front of the other, eating up the distance between us. I keep the chain taut, making it easier for her to find her way to me. Her hips swing harmoniously with each step she takes until her knees hit the edge of the bed, the vibration traveling through the mattress and straight to my groin.

"Please let me go," she whispers. "Whatever it is I did to you, I'm sorry. Please, I won't say a word to anyone, I'll disappear."

Her words have pure and sudden rage boiling in my blood. Over my dead fucking body, she'll ever disappear from my life. I'm on my knees in front of her in less than a second, my large palm cradling her damp-with-tears cheek. I should resist, but I can't. *I won't.* For far too long, I've denied myself. I deserve a goddamn reward. As the salty wetness, mixed with the sweetness that only Siah has, touches my tongue, I grunt deep in my chest.

My hips shift, my cock bobbing between us, straining to reach the wet hot promise between her legs. "The last thing I want, little mockingbird, is for you to keep quiet about me. Sing as loud as you can, my love," I murmur in her ear, reveling in the delightful shudder of her body.

With hungry lips, I trail a path of kisses from her ear to her jaw. Her protesting whimpers turn into breathy moans when I nip at her chin and suck on the delicate skin of her neck. I lean back, pride swelling inside me when I see the dark-purple mark forming against the creaminess of her skin. *My mark.*

"Please…" she cries, but I swallow her words with my lips as my mouth slants over hers. My stomach flips, my blood ignites like white phosphorus in contact with oxygen, and my groan of bliss disappears in her mouth. I lick at her bottom lip, coaxing, begging, pleading she grants me entrance. When her lips part, I'm ready to worship the ground she walks on.

My tongue sweeps inside, dueling with hers, tasting her sweetness and her wanton. Siah matches me stroke for stroke, her lips moving against mine with the same intensity and passion I'm pouring into our kiss.

I grab her hip and pull her closer to me, my cock trapped between us. Her pleased mewl at the feel of my desire for her has me throbbing, my fingers tightening their grip on her. All the hell, all the pain, every horrible memory torturing me for years is eviscerated by her. Siah is my reward, my fucking prize. I'm so lost in her fervent kisses, so adrift in my need, that it takes a minute for the pain to register.

My bottom lip smarts as she viciously bites into it. *Naughty, little mockingbird.* A coppery, metallic taste floods my mouth, washing away all her sweetness as she tilts her head back, cutting our kiss short.

I swipe my thumb over my lip, a crimson smear staining my fingerprint. I press the fleshy pad to her mouth. "Suck!" I order. "You want to draw blood, now you get to taste the reward of your efforts."

She cranes her neck further back, stubbornness written all over her face despite the trembling in her knees and the wetness slicking her thighs so strongly I can smell her desire for me in the air.

"Ntz, ntz. Good girls get praised. Bad girls... It's high time you learn what they get." I force my thumb past her lips, rubbing it against her tongue. Despite herself, she twirls it around my finger, licking me clean. Her teeth tighten for a fraction of a second around me, a little threat, a final push to show me she still has control, before allowing me to remove it.

Silly little mockingbird. She'll get to know that she has all the control. Always. I'm but a mere pawn, worshiping at the feet of his Queen.

I press a hard and fast kiss on her mouth, dirtying up with my blood those pretty, swollen lips of hers. "Get on your knees," I bark.

This, she obeys quickly, lowering herself on the hardwood floor. I wind the chain around my hand until it tightens just enough around her neck to see her pulse fluttering even in the low lights.

I cup her cheek. My thumb, still slick with her saliva, smears the crimson stains around. "Open your mouth, little mockingbird. Let me see how beautiful you look stuffed full of my cock, wearing my blood as your lipstick."

Her lips part, her pink tongue slicking over her bottom lip. Harsh pants leave her, her chest raising and falling in quick succession. I climb down from the bed and step in front of her, my feet bracketing her knees. The head of my cock, angry and oversensitive, touches her bottom lip, and the first swipe of her tongue has a litany of curses spilling past my lips.

Nothing feels like her mouth. Hot, wet, eager. She brands me with her essence, pure hellfire raining in my veins. Her velvety tongue sends electric currents through my cock as she flutters against my weight. The silver barbel crowning the glistening head disappears between her lips as I guide myself inside her mouth in slow, gentle, tender thrusts.

As if I'm not about to fuck her mouth until I'm ready to pass out at her feet.

"I dare you to bite me," I grit out. "Just know, we're not leaving this room until my cum drips out of you. We can do this the easy way or the hard way. The choice is yours."

And then I shift my hips forward until my cock hits the back of her throat. Her mouth is like a goddamn wet dream. All my fantasies come to life cannot do her justice. I retreat, then slam home again, and again, and again, getting her ready.

Siah hollows her cheeks around my length, her tongue massaging the underside of my cock, swirling around the blunt ends of the piercing, and I just about have a seizure.

My legs are shaking, barely supporting me upright. Pleasure, too much pleasure courses through my veins. My skin feels too tight for my body to encompass every sensation I'm feeling. I'm mindlessly thrusting inside her exquisite mouth, one hand buried deep in her silken hair, holding her still, anchoring myself to earth.

She's my mockingbird, but I'm the motherfucker about to take flight.

I push forward, eager to have her ring my cock with her mouth down to the base. I tighten my hold on her hair when she tries to move her head back. "Fuck, you're just about to kill me, aren't you?" I grunt when her throat constricts beautifully around me as she chokes on my length. I feel every flutter, every spasm, every contraction.

Fire rages through me when her lips finally touch my pubic bone. I hold her still for a second, her delicate gags and my strained breaths the only sounds to pierce the silence of the night. This is what heaven feels like. Her mouth, fitting me like a glove, is the reason men go to war. I pull at the chain and feel her throat tighten around me. "Fuck, fuck, fuck," I moan, unable to control the tremble in my knees and the stars exploding before my wide-open eyes when she hums deep in her throat. I'm just about to die, and I'll be damned to all hell and back if I won't die with her wrapped around my cock so intricately, we won't know where I end and she begins.

I didn't plan for this today.

But I can't take it anymore.

I pull out of her mouth forcefully, her ragged pants and distressed coughs spurring me on.

"Get on your hands and knees," I grit out, my jaw clenched so hard my teeth are grinding together.

Siah scrambles on the bed as I loosen the chain enough for her to move. The sight of her arched back and round, firm ass nearly has me undone. I'm feral, reduced to my very basic instincts. A savage animal rabid at the sight of his mate.

I grab her hips, shoving the scrap of lace aside, and slam home, burying myself to the hilt inside her tight, wet channel. "Oh gooood," she moans long and hard, her voice raspy and raw. I swell inside of her, satisfaction flooding my veins at knowing I got her voice all gritty. It was my cock slamming into the back of her throat. Me. Me. Me.

I fuck her in deep, long strokes, tingles racing up and down my spine as the room fills with her blissful song accompanied by rhythmic and fast slaps of skin against skin and savage groans ripping out of my chest. She's drenched for me, her arousal dripping onto my balls and down my thighs. Her walls clamp down on me, hindering my movements, but I tighten my hold on her hip and fuck her like a mindless beast.

That is what I am for her. Mindless. Lost. Adoring.

She's got me wrapped up around her pinky finger with no will of my own.

I wound the chain around my wrist again, the cold titanium links rubbing against her clit with every thrust. I tilt my hips higher, the crown of my Prince Albert hitting against that magic spot inside of her that has her legs shaking and her mewls frenzied. "Fuck, oh fuck," she cries. "Harder."

My palm splays between her shoulder blades, and I push her down against the mattress. The moan she rewards me with as the chain rubs deeper against her sweet, oversensitive bundle of nerves is unholy.

Just what I desired.

Sweat peppers my back, my heart hammering in my chest as I pound into her six years' worth of frustration. All the years of despairing since I last had her. All the fear and the agony I felt when I thought her lost to me. She takes it all and begs for more.

The bed creaks, her cries of bliss and pleasure intensify, my grunts complete our symphony.

"I'm so close," she pleads. "Don't stop."

I move my chained hand between us, my fingertips touching the magic connection of where we are joined. I coat my fingers in our combined pleasure, my thrusts not faltering once, my pace grueling and punishing. She bucks wildly against me when I press my thumb against her puckered hole, her pussy fluttering madly around me, pushing me past the no return point.

She floods my shaft with her release, her whole body trembling and convulsing. "God, oh god, AUGUST!"

I freeze inside of her. My heart fucking stops. I grip her neck tightly and plaster her back to my chest. "You don't get to say a name as you come when you're not fucking ready to know mine." And with that, I slam my lips over hers in a bruising kiss to swallow down all her traitorous sounds and forbidden names.

The sweet flavor of her mouth combined with the heady taste of me and my blood stains my tongue. My hips start again their punishing pace, all sloppy jerks and deep-rooted thrust. Whatever control I had flies right out the window. All I want is to conquer, take, punish, own. She mewls and shakes in my arms as her pussy strangles my cock like a vise when her second orgasm hits her. And I let go, spilling into her all that I am. My heart, my soul, my essence, my trust.

My head drops to the crook of her neck as I let the burn in my muscles settle and my heart return to normal rhythm. Siah grows limp in my embrace, her breaths soft and steady, even as her slick, hot pussy still flutters and pulses around my cock.

I band an arm around her, holding her close to me for just one second more before I release the chain from around her neck. I'll keep this memory. One handed, I free her arms from their constraints, letting the chain dangle from her left wrist. She'll have this trophy.

The first of many.

Gently, I lay her down in the middle of the bed, her head cradled by a soft pillow, her wild curls crowning her like a tiara. Her panties, stretched out and soaked with our combined release, snap easily in my hold. They are now the crown jewel of my collection.

Dimming the lights, I curl at her back, my fingertips tracing random patterns on her arm.

"Sleep now, little mockingbird. Next time we meet, you'll come while staring into my eyes and really crying out *my* name."

Chapter Twenty-Seven

SIAH

Step one, flush all my sleeping pills down the toilet. Step two, sleep on the couch. Step three, avoid the chain hidden under my pillow like the plague. Step four, constantly repeat to myself that, at the bare minimum, I'm not insane.

Actually, scratch that. The quality of my sanity is highly debatable. My head has been on a rapid-spin cycle for the past week, gyrating uncontrollably with my newly found knowledge. It only took me paying a steep price to acquire it—drowning every day into overwhelming shame and guilt.

My stalker is real.

I suck in a breath as my heartbeat turns erratic and my stomach flips.

My erotic dreams are not dreams but reality.

A wave of heat warms my core, while bile floods my mouth. I swallow it down, relishing in the pain and burn that comes with it.

I had sex with my stalker.

This is what hurts the most. I woke up blindfolded, bound, and on my knees. My body shook under the avalanche of fear barreling through me. And yet... I was more aware than any other time when I thought I was dreaming. I could see more, feel more, understand more. I wanted it.

I draw my knees to my chest and cover my face with my palms, allowing my shameful tears to fall free. My self-righteousness screams inside my head that I did what I did out of self-preservation, my survival instinct kicking in. I'm so willing to give into that train of thought, to convince myself my morals are still intact. It would be so much easier. But if I'm not honest with myself, what am I doing here?

My phone rings again. Jayme's picture flashes at me from the too bright screen. I hit the big red reject button. I can't talk to her. Not yet.

A shudder rattles my chest as another wave of guilt and shame washes through me with renewed strength.

What would I say to my only friend? That, if I'm being honest, when I woke up restrained and blinded, I felt more desire than fear? That I allowed him to fuck my mouth and then fuck me like a common whore and came twice? Or that, when I came, it was her stepbrother's name I shouted?

Yes, *he* scares me.

But the absolute raw truth of it is... never for a second have I felt in danger around him. In fact, deep down, I'm convinced that if I told him to stop at any point, he would have. If I'd put up a fight, he wouldn't have fought back.

A sob wracks at my ribcage, more hot tears pouring from my eyes.

Everything I held true about myself has been eviscerated by my newly found knowledge. Having it confirmed that he is real doesn't bring me any closer to knowing who he is and why is he doing what he's doing. He broke into August's home. More than once.

So much for *"I know everything that happens in my house"*. So much for being safe here.

He collared me like a pet. Humiliation and arousal flood my veins. It's all I could think about the past week. If the five grief stages are denial, anger, bargaining, depression, and acceptance, the five insanity stages are humiliation, shame, guilt, arousal, and repeat.

I can't even begin to entertain the thought of August *actually* knowing what happens in his house. Because if he does, and he lets it happen... Where does that leave me?

Does he know? Does Jayme? Elijah, Devon, Henry? Are they all in on this?

What would they have to gain?

I'm no one. I have no real money of my own. I own nothing of substance.

And, if it's just a long elaborate game of tormenting me to see what's my breaking point... they're all a bunch of sociopaths. While I might as well believe that of August, since clearly all the men I've ever been drawn to are deranged, warm sunshine personified, Jayme absolutely cannot be.

"Aaaagggghhhh!" I scream my frustration into the empty living room, the harrowing sound bouncing against the dark and depressing walls. My fists hit the cold leather on either side of me, harder and harder and harder, until I'm breathless with physical exertion, my arms heavy and sore.

He knows that I'm planning to leave. *He* doesn't want me to.

I haven't said a word to anyone of my plans. I wanted to arrange a dinner out with Jayme at her favorite restaurant, bribe her with a ton of good food, get her tipsy on however many cocktails it took to get her to her happy place, and then break the news.

What I have done is type them on my laptop. Which means... he somehow has access to it.

I push to my feet, my knees still shaky and weak as I walk to the kitchen like a newborn fowl just learning to trot. Removing a bottle of water from the fridge, I forgo a glass and down the whole thing in a couple of gulps. I might not be hungry and vomit any and all sustenance I try to shove down my throat, but I'll keep trying.

Renewed hope surges inside me.

He's watching me, of that I have no doubt. I'm pretty sure at this point there are cameras everywhere in this house, including the bedroom. If August put them there and *he* hacked into the feed or *he* installed his own, I can't know. I don't need to.

What I need to do is keep Jayme safe, the only one I truly think is innocent in this whole mess. So I have to keep my distance. What if, once I leave, he'll try to use her against me? What if he shifts his focus on her? No, I need to be smart about this.

I'll complete all the assignments I have lined up, go about my days as usual. I'll keep Jayme at bay, justifying my absence with the increased workload. My assignments, once complete, should fluff my savings by nearly ten grand. Once I get where I need to go, I'll find a way to legally change my name. And also find a way to start from scratch as a ghostwriter.

New website. New email. New bank account. New everything.

It fucking hurts to have to start from zero.

It's debilitating to feel like my life is not my own.

But I can't give up.

I won't.

He calls me his little mockingbird.

And now he gets to watch me mock him, and then fly free, away from his reach.

Chapter Twenty-Eight

August

> I'm probably breaking her trust right now and flushing ten years of friendship down the drain, but I'm worried. Have you seen Siah? Have you spoken to her? Short of breaking down your door at the house, I don't know what else to do.

Jayme St. Andrew
Delivered December 13th, 01:24 p.m.

> Do I need to spell it down for you? I need an access code to the house. Or for you to let me in. Please, August. I have a bad feeling.

Jayme St. Andrew
Delivered December 13th, 01:32 p.m.

> August? Please answer your phone, or call me back, or send me a message, or a smoke signal, or something. I'm very much close to calling the police and asking for a welfare check on Siah. Please.

Jayme St. Andrew
Delivered December 13th, 01:45 p.m.

Shit.

I loosen my tie as worry swirls in the pit of my stomach. I flip the crystal lid from the neck of the bottle and take a good swig of smokey, amber liquid. Fuck bothering with a glass. To say today was a clusterfuck of epic proportion is an understatement.

I hate my family. I hate this fucking state.

All I want is to, once and for all, cut all ties with them and finally be free. For years, the piece of shit that is my father has held me back; held me down by my neck as I drowned in self-hatred and bitterness. Unknowingly to them, Helena and Jayme have been his pawns to hold over my head.

Helena is blissfully ignorant. She sees the arrogant, narcissistic psychopath as a 'traditional manly-man'. I can't help it; I scoff in my expensive as fuck whiskey. James St. Andrew is not a man. He's a plague, an infection, a deadly cancer.

And he's infected me.

I'm all that stands between him and Helena and, ultimately, Jayme.

My stepsister knows not all is right with him. And, if she hasn't seen it, she's felt it. The darkness and malice inside of him cannot be contained by a practiced fake smile that never reaches his eyes. She *knows.* The only reason she's escaped his clutches so far is because he's taken to ignoring her. As long as he has me to focus on.

I made sure Jayme was not tied to him or indebted to him in any way, shape, or form. If she needed money, it came from my pockets. If she got in trouble, I was the one she called to bail her out.

The only weakness we both have is Helena—more Jayme's than mine. But my stepsister loves her mother, and I care for my stepsister, so whatever hurts Jayme, hurts me.

Unfortunately, I still don't have a solution on how to rescue Helena from his clutches. As far as I've seen, he's always treated her well—provided for her, spoiled her, and kept her in the dark. Whatever his wife doesn't know, won't hurt her.

The truth of the matter is, James St. Andrew might have been a good man once. Whatever shred of humanity he had in him dwindled the minute my mother gave birth to me. Suddenly, he wasn't the center of her universe anymore. He had to share the spotlight with me. Something he'd resented me for my whole life. The rest of his humanity shattered when my mom died. The very second

Felicia St. Andrew took her last breath, so did whatever good lived inside of James.

In his dark and twisted mind, I took his wife away from him.

So he's made it his life's mission to take everything from me.

I banked my first million the day I turned eighteen and sold my first phone encryption app. Back then, I was still plenty naïve, thinking that with money I could finally buy the freedom I craved for. I planned for years. Only to have those plans crash and burn a couple of months before my birthday when he married single mother Helena and adopted her thirteen-year-old daughter, out of the goodness of his charred heart. And thus tightening the noose around my neck.

He didn't have to tell me why he married her. I *knew*.

Fifteen years ago, I made a choice not to be selfish. I'm still paying for my choice, although I can hardly regret giving Jayme the chance at a happy and fulfilled life. Even at eighteen, I knew I was too far gone. But the pigtailed redhead, with stars in her eyes and a quick smile, still had a shot at happiness. She was hurt by her father's betrayal, sure, but her faith in humanity was still intact. There was no darkness in her coppery-brown eyes, no memories of locked closets, days of hunger, or emotional torture wrapped around her spine. I banked on her because I knew, deep down, I was damned.

Now... I'm facing the same choice. Choose myself and my one shot at happiness while setting fire to everything I've protected so far, or fully become my father in a futile attempt at martyrization.

Decisions, decisions.

"Oh thank god, August! I'm already worried sick about Siah, I don't need to be worried about you too," Jayme shrieks from the other end of the phone. I don't hide my wince as I move the device away from my ear and set the call on speaker.

"Apologies. Just got home. What happened?"

As if I don't know.

"I haven't been able to reach Siah in a week. This is not like her. Sure, she'd sometimes lose herself in one of her assignments, but she always gets back to me within a day or two."

"So what? You want to invade her privacy to confirm she's well?" I ask, taking another swig of whiskey. The burn of alcohol feels good as it warms me up from the inside out, loosening my tight muscles.

She sighs mournfully. "I failed her before, August. Five months ago, I was having a grand ole' time on my assignment and didn't pay attention to her absence, and she ended up in the hospital. I'm worried."

I know what I need to do, but knowing doesn't make me less hesitant. One minuscule error, and everything I've worked for crumbles like a house of cards.

"Opening the live feed now..." I trail off. Siah will be pissed when she finds out we're essentially spying on her. But Jayme needs to be placated, and the last thing Siah needs is the police breaking down her door for a welfare check.

"Thank you, thank you. You're my favorite brother."

"I'm your only brother," I deadpan.

"That I know of," she teases.

Really not. I made thorough checks over the years to ensure there weren't any other offspring of James walking around, clueless of the demon fathering them. Her piece of shit father, on the other hand, did humanity a favor and understood that him perpetuating the species was a *bad* call. As soon as he left Helena and Jayme behind, he got a vasectomy. Even the dumb are smart at times. For whatever good it did him, when he ended up taking his own life six years later.

"Okay. As far as I can see, Siah's in her office, headphones on her head, typing away at her laptop."

Jayme's breath hitches. "So then, why isn't she answering her phone?"

I mull over my answer. Regardless of what I say, her feelings might get hurt. "I don't know, Jay. Let me look back through the feed. Do you have a specific time you called?"

"All day today," she's quick to clarify.

I backward the security videos taken by the cameras. "Well, she's sleeping, she's eating," I narrate for my sister's benefit. "It looks like she didn't have the phone on her all day."

"So she's just sucked in with an assignment?" Relief and disappointment hit me from the other end of the phone.

"Looks that way," I agree. "Jay, I'm not comfortable doing this. You asked me to let her stay in my home, but I refuse to spy on her. She's entitled to her time and her space without us interfering."

Another sigh full of dejection from my sister has guilt swirling inside me. "I know, August, believe me, I know. But Siah has no one else to look after her. I'm it."

And me too, but I'm smart enough to not say that out loud.

"Will you be home for Christmas?" Jayme asks. "I'll be gone on a two-month assignment in January, and I'd really love to see you again before then."

If everything goes to plan... "Can't make any promises. I'll try to be there. Maybe clear it out with Siah first. My last visit didn't exactly end on a positive note."

Another sigh, embedded with regret this time. "I'm sorry for how she reacted. She has these... episodes, for the lack of a better explanation. Her paranoia gets the best of her and..."

"You don't need to explain," I cut her off. "Your friend is going through a lot. I told you I was going to be out of Washington for a while. I'll see what I can do about Christmas."

"Thanks, August. I'll leave you to your day. Or is it evening? Morning? Night?"

I chuckle. "Don't be nosy. Leave me to my time zone."

"Have a good time zone, big brother. I love you."

I turn my attention back to my laptop's screen, watching the woman bobbing her head to music only she hears, her dainty fingers flying over the keyboard.

"What are you up to, Siah Hadley?"

Chapter Twenty-Nine

SIAH

How ridiculous it is to be constantly looking over my shoulder.

I don't know if he's not coming anymore because he's lost interest now that he fucked me, or because he enjoys playing mind games with me. Does he like me afraid and paranoid? Is that what gets him off?

Try as I might, I cannot figure out who he is, what he wants from me, or what his endgame is.

Five days away from Christmas, and I've never felt more alone, more isolated. Jayme keeps calling, keeps messaging. I keep avoiding her, leaving my phone on silent mode on purpose and 'forgetting' it in different rooms. She wants to spend the holiday with me, and I'll give her that. She'll be gone on a long assignment come January, and if everything goes to plan, I'll be gone soon after.

It breaks my heart to just up and vanish from her life, but this is the way it must be if I want to keep her safe and out of his radar.

I spent the past two weeks working tirelessly on my assignments. All but two are completed. By the time I'll be ready to leave, those two will be done as well. I've also compiled a list of things I have to get in order before I disappear.

It's become my obsession to go over the list.

1. Get a full panel STD test because spreading your legs every two weeks in front of your OB/GYN is becoming somewhat of a hobby.
2. Find if there are hidden cameras in the bedroom. Four cameras, one in each corner, a fifth in the bathroom, none in the walk-in closet.
3. Buy a burner phone.
4. Buy a new laptop.
5. Buy a car; pay cash.
6. Give up all medication. Mind clarity trumps fear.
7. Complete all assignments.

8. Withdraw all your money.
9. Close all bank accounts.
10. Cancel insurance and health insurance.
11. Buy a SatNav.
12. BE FREE!

There are plenty of other things I need to do, but those can be planned and looked into once I've put at least a thousand miles between me and this city.

Apart from my assignments, everything else I'll need to get done in a very short time frame, a couple of days at best, just before Jayme leaves. As soon as she's gone, so will I. My biggest issue is finding a car. I can't go online, since I'm convinced he's tracking my cyber-footprints. I also can't buy a burner phone now and risk him finding it when he visits.

His absence doesn't bring me any relief. If anything, it ups my anxiety. My head is a mess of fear, dread, and—much to my shame—anticipation. Giving up my meds cold turkey was a bold, but terrible choice. Every creak, groan, and thump makes me jump. The panic attacks in the dead of the night are brutal. The nightmares are horrendous, and I wake up sweaty and cried out, my throat raw from screaming. All of it is taking a huge toll on me.

What's worse... I miss him.

I shake my head, trying to dispel my shame. to no avail. When he's not here, I fear him down to the smallest atom in my body. But when I feel his warmth on my skin, his gravelly, hushed voice tickling my ears, the possessiveness of his touch, all my fear is forgotten, replaced with thrill and want. For the few hours he's with me, I'm powerful and strong.

And I miss him. I miss that heady feeling of empowerment he breathes into me with his praise and his punishments.

My laptop pings, and I jump in my fancy leather seat.

August St. Andrew: Christmas visit

Hi Siah,

I'm sorry to spring this on you. My schedule unexpectedly cleared for the next week, and I was planning to stay in Seattle over Christmas and potentially the New Year.

Would this be an issue with you? I know my last visit didn't exactly end on a positive note, and I'd hate for you to be uncomfortable with my presence.

It is important to me that you feel safe in my home.
Please let me know.
If it's something I did last time, I'd appreciate if you'd tell me so I can avoid making the same mistake twice. Whatever it is I did, I'm sorry.
Sincerely yours,
August St. Andrew

My heart starts pounding as I read his email. My instincts are screaming at me not to trust him. He has hidden cameras in the bedroom, and not so hidden ones throughout his home. My cheeks heat as I realize he could've seen everything that happened to me. Even if he doesn't understand that the nightly visits are not welcomed, he still has the ability to see me do everything I've done.

And that's the best-case scenario.

The scenario in which he's not involved with the psychopath following me.

I, of course, cannot keep him out of his home. Jayme would be devastated. So I have to play along. This puts a kink in my plans, because I need to be extra careful with every step I make. The list must go. My money needs to be hidden, too. I can't afford for my only means to freedom to be taken away from me.

Siah Hadley: Re: Christmas Visit

Hi August,
I apologize for the way I've behaved at Thanksgiving. I can't even begin to tell you how sorry I am. Unfortunately, I was all out of sorts, and as much as I hate to blame my pesky hormones, I still have to point an accusatory finger at them. The IUS messed me out more than I care to admit.
I have since stocked up on chocolate and ice cream. It's safe to return. :-)
Jayme will be thrilled to have you here for Christmas.
This is your home. Please, don't feel like you need to tiptoe around me.
When do you expect to be here?
Kind regards,
Siah Hadley

I lower the lid to my laptop. There's no need for me to read his response now. He'll be here when he'll be here, and I played my part of the game.

The only thing left to see now is if on this board game I'm a pawn or a Queen.

Or maybe I'm just the dice spinning mindlessly on a corner.

Chapter Thirty

SIAH

My teeth are chattering, and my breath turns into a milky fog in front of me. I burrow my chin deeper into the furry collar of my winter coat. Jayme hooks her arm in the crook of my elbow and steers me on the ten thousandth lap around the Christmas tree farm.

"I'm so glad you finally agreed to get out of the house. The fresh air will do you good." She sighs happily, leaning her head on my shoulder for a second. It's an awkward position, considering I'm vertically challenged, and she could spit atop my head if she wanted to.

"You mean frozen air?" I huff. "Any colder, and I could have my body cryogenically preserved."

She throws her head back and laughs her delighted, throaty laugh. Warmth curls in my stomach. We won't get many more moments like this one, so I'm holding on to right now with all my might.

I nearly trip over my feet as she stops abruptly in front of a large evergreen. "Aww Siah, look at him. He'd look so handsome in front of one of the floor-to-ceiling windows in the living room, all decked out in silver and red."

Narrowing my eyes, I study the eight-foot-tall behemoth critically. She's not wrong. Dense, dark green, prickly needles adorn the multitude of branches. Perfectly proportional from top to bottom, her choice is a Hallmark staple Christmas tree. I bet it also costs an arm and a leg and at least half my liver.

"Uhm... He?" I pop an eyebrow and question her word choice instead, while internally I fumble for a justification as to why I don't want to fork hundreds of dollars for something I'd have to throw away in a week.

"Mr. Twinkly Lights," Jayme clarifies.

It's my turn to laugh now. "Of course you named our Christmas tree. Sorry, babe, but I think we'd be better off with a potted tree. That way, we can replant it in August's backyard after the holidays. I just can't convince myself to pay an absurd amount of money and let it die."

She slaps a gloved hand to her chest, her misty breath fanning over my face as she gasps theatrically. "But... Mr. Twinkly Lights and I have plans. Hot chocolate, red baubles, electric fireplace. It was going to be romantic as fuck."

"You can be romantic as fuck with Mr. Potted Lights, too." I placate her, patting her arm in a *there, there* gesture.

"Siah? What a surprise!" A masculine voice comes from behind me. A voice I recognize all too well and fills me with dread and apprehension. My eyes go wide and my stomach bottoms out. By the scowl on Jayme's face, I don't need to turn to know who I'm about to find.

I take a deep breath to center myself, the frozen air seizing my lungs, while having a silent conversation with Jayme, begging her to not make a scene and just... let it go. I plaster a fake smile and spin on my heel to greet him.

"Henry, what a surprise ind..." The words die on my lips as I take in his companion. Straight, ashy-blonde hair nearly to her waist, petite frame, dark green eyes, and rosy cheeks—she could be my younger sister. *What the fuck?*

"Oh, how rude of me." He leans slightly toward the woman clinging to his arm, gazing adoringly at her. "Hannah, darling, this is Siah, my ex-wife." He turns to me then, a sickly-sweet smile on his face. "Siah, this is Hannah, my girlfriend."

I'm sure I have a deer-caught-in-the-headlights look on my face. As if threading through water, my hand extends in her direction. "Nice to meet you, Hannah." *Seriously, what—and I can't stress this enough—the fuck?*

She clasps my gloved hand with her own, shaking mine twice before gently squeezing my fingers. "You too, Siah. I heard a lot about you. You seem to be doing better." Her voice is sincere and kind, but confusion clouds my mind.

What did the asshole tell her about me?

I step back into my friend. "This is Jayme, my best friend." I feel more than I see the wave Jay gives her over my shoulder. *Holy sentient shitballs, we have got to get out of here.* "Well, it was nice to run into you. Jay and I have a Christmas tree to buy," I say in an awkward attempt to skedaddle.

"I just wish August could've gotten home sooner," Jayme says with a disappointed sigh. "No matter. He'd be happy out of his mind when he sees the tree you've chosen. I swear to God, you could take a sledgehammer to one of his windows, he'd still praise your interior decorating skills."

I feel like a ballerina, constantly spinning on my toes, when I turn sharply to my friend and whisper-hiss, "What the flipping heck are you doing?"

"Who's August?" Henry asks, his voice deep and rough.

The dread in my stomach intensifies. I just wish Jayme left it well alone. I'm not in a pissing contest with my ex-husband. He has moved on... *ish*, considering the similarities between Hannah and me, but clearly the man has a type, and he's not my problem anymore.

I open my mouth to clarify and get out of this awkward situation, but Jayme's faster. "Siah's boyfriend. And my stepbrother."

A cruel smirk twists Henry's face. "Is that so? Well, I guess congratulations are in order."

I flick my eyes to Hannah in a silent apology. Her brows are furrowed, and her pouty lips tug down at the corners. "We better get going," I hiss to my friend. "It was truly good to see the both of you. Merry Christmas."

With that, I grab Jay's arm and half-drag her, half-march her to the potted trees aisle. I'm fuming inside. If it weren't for the beanie stuffed over my ears, surely steam would billow out through my eardrums. "What the fuck, babe?" I snap when we're a safe distance away.

"Don't you *what-the-fuck* me, Siah. He was rubbing that skank in your face," she whisper-yells, ripping her arm from my hold and cocking a hip.

"I don't care. And she seemed like a nice woman. Honestly, I know you can't stand Henry, and I can't say I'm too fond of him myself, but Hannah's not to blame here." I throw my hands in the air, suddenly exhausted. "There's no reason to antagonize him. I don't care what he does and who he does it with. That era of my life is done and dusted."

She loosens her fighting stance and throws an arm over my shoulders, pulling me into a half embrace. "I'm sorry, Siah. I hate what he did to you, and I hate that he keeps trying to worm his way under your skin."

"Henry stopped meaning anything to me the minute he walked out the door when I needed support the most. Him popping up like a nasty rash everywhere I am? It's annoying, but doesn't affect me. Let him peacock all over the place with his new toys and his new life and his new personality transplant. Once he sees he gets no reactions out of me, he'll let me be."

Jayme kisses my cheek and tightens her hold on me for a brief second. "Alright. Let's buy ourselves a Mr. Deep Roots."

Oh, for fuck's sake.

Chapter Thirty-One

AUGUST

SeaTac is ridiculously crowded. I guess no one gives a flying fuck about today being Christmas Eve. My hope was to get home two days ago, but my asshole father demanded I personally oversee the installation of the new cybersecurity system for his friend's company. While an installation as such is a play in the park for me, it does take time and patience—both of which I'm in short supply of.

But the delay wasn't without rewards, either. As much as I hate my childhood home, and I'd rather crawl over hot rusty razors than be there, it also got me access to his study. The last domino piece I needed is now in place. All I have to do is give it a little push, then pour myself a whiskey and take slow, satisfying sips as I watch his empire crumble around him.

Jayme might never forgive me.

But at least she'll be safe.

And I'll have a chance at happiness.

Wild, luscious curls draw my eye. In a sea of thousands of people, I'll never not seek her out first. I stifle the smile threatening to overtake me and lengthen my strides, beelining straight to where Siah is waiting for me.

She'd ever so kindly agreed to be my ride home.

I've always played on the safe side, kept my distance, and watched from afar. Soon enough, I'll be able to cross the line. I can't blame my aloofness only on dear old daddy. Whether my upbringing made me unfeeling and uninterested, or I was born this way, I don't know. But no other woman has held my interest, not until I met the equally caged and safe-playing Siah Hadley.

To say the events of my last visit itch beneath my skin like a million splinters is an understatement. Hopefully, this holiday goes better. Regardless, I'm a determined man. And when I want something, I get it. Time, effort, cost—nothing deters me from achieving my goals. Luckily for Siah—or maybe unluckily—my sights are set on her.

I circle around Baggage Claim. There's something to be said about traveling light. Most of my possessions are in my home, anyway. I barely keep a change of clothes in my penthouse in Phoenix. It should get on the market in about a week's time, anyway. As far as I'm concerned, whoever buys it can take everything. I have no need for mementos from the city that was my prison my entire childhood and teenage years.

In a move that's bolder than everything I've done as far as Siah's concerned, I wrap an arm around her waist and pull her to my chest, kissing the top of her head. She smells of jasmine and honeysuckle, of home, and I don't miss the opportunity to bury my nose in her silky hair.

She startles in my arms, a minute jolt if that, but it's enough to fill my veins with anger. *We'll have to work on this.*

"August, you're here," she stutters.

"Thanks for picking me up." I give her one of my most charming smiles and drag my palm to the small of her back. "I'm ready to get home."

She allows me to lead her away from the bustling Arrivals' area, and I tuck her in to my side, shooting daggers with my eyes at anyone daring to get too close to us.

"I didn't know if your flight would be delayed," Siah says, craning her neck to give me a brief look, "so we're in the Terminal Direct Parking."

I rub my thumb across the indents of her spine and frown. She's not wearing enough layers for the nasty wind that's sure to whip across from all directions once we hit the parking building. I stop in my tracks, hooking a finger in the cordon of her coat to stop her, too.

"Wha...?" she questions, but cuts off when I make quick work of unbuttoning my jacket and drape it over her shoulders. "It's not necessary. I'll warm up on the ten-minute walk to the car," she protests, trying to shrug it off. Too bad, I quite like her wearing my clothes, our scents mingling.

"Non-negotiable," I tell her firmly, gripping the lapels and closing them tighter around her. Trailing my fingers on her arm, I interlace our hands and start again toward the car park. I'm not savoring at all the feel of her icy-cold fingers in mine. I'm *really* not enjoying the way her small hand fits perfectly into my much larger one. And I'm definitely not walking around with a hard-on just because she's near me. I have more class than that.

Not...

We're both quiet as we reach the Skybridge, our eyes glued to the windows. Mount Rainier looms, tall and dark, in the distance, thick fog mantling its base, the white, snowy peak piercing through the heavy clouds. Planes taxi back and forth just below us. The Skybridge truly is an engineering masterpiece.

As soon as we exit the skywalk, she tightens her hold on my hand, making my insides flutter, and guides us through rows and rows of cars until we reach my SUV. I release the handle of my carry-on and shove my hand in one pocket of my trousers, hitting the fob of the remote I designed—so all my cars respond to one key, not just the individual ones.

Siah, elbow deep in her purse, gasps as the indicators of the car flash. "Oh, how did you...?"

"Know which car you took?" I shrug. "I didn't. I have a... master key."

Her cheeks pinken so beautifully, it takes all my fucking self-control and then some not to cup her face, feel the silkiness of her skin against my roughness, and maul her mouth right here. Instead, like the civilized man I pretend to be, I take a step away from her and open the passenger door.

Her dark green eyes search my face. Cold sweat peppers my spine as her gaze prods and dissects. Soon enough, all my secrets will be hers for the taking. But right now, I'm not ready to share.

Worst of all, she's not ready to know.

There's something different about Siah. I can't quite put my finger on it, but something's changed since the last time I saw her. There's an air of solitude in her vicinity, wrapped airtight around her petite frame. The silence is unnerving.

By nature, I'm a calm guy. It comes in handy since my job—and my past—brings a lot of stress. Making quick, smart decisions under pressure is my norm. The cybersecurity tools I develop, those too require an enhanced sense of patience—from writing the code to running the tests to debugging and smoothing out kinks. I don't fiddle with my fingers; I don't bounce my knee under the table to expel nervous energy.

But her eerie stillness makes me want to run circles around the table just to infuse some energy into her listless demeanor.

I pick up our plates, the chicken Alfredo still steaming. Hints of garlic and the sharp tang of Parmesan waft in the air, making my stomach rumble. Siah goes to the wine fridge and takes out a bottle of Pinot Noir. Her eyes widen as she turns around to face me.

"Are we not eating at the island?"

"I thought that Christmas tree of yours could use some company." I wink, my lips stretching in a boyish grin.

She visibly gulps, her eyes darting to the opposite corner of the open floor space, where her overly decorated six-foot potted evergreen stands proudly. "Mr. Festive Baubles does look a bit lonely."

I choke on a cough. "Maybe he's just embarrassed with his name."

Her shoulder lifts and falls in a careless shrug. "He can take it up with Jayme, then."

I follow her to the living room, my eyes glued to her hips swinging like a pendulum all the way to the coffee table. I made sure earlier to move the table closer to the tree, so we could use the multicolored lights for visibility, instead of the main ones overhead. The electric fireplace is on too, so the light is low and warm. And dare I say... romantic.

She's barely been divorced for eight weeks, but time is ticking, and I have to make my move before it's too late. I'm doing my best to give her the space she needs to process everything she's been through in the past few months, but at the same time, assess for myself if this wild attraction I feel toward her will lead us anywhere.

If I move too fast, she'll spook and keep me at bay. If I move too slow, well, I won't stand by and watch her go through another divorce.

I place the plates on the glass surface of the table and lower myself to one of the throw pillows I've left earlier on the floor for us. She follows suit. If the distance—or lack of—between us bothers her, she doesn't show it. I uncork the bottle of wine and pour us a glass each. My brows furrow as I watch the deep burgundy liquid slosh and settle. She's not supposed to have any alcohol with her medicine.

Wisely, I keep my mouth shut as her long fingers wrap against the stem, and she lifts the glass to her nose, inhaling deeply. "I love the cherry notes and hint of earthiness," she murmurs, then takes a dainty sip, her pink tongue darting out to catch a rogue drop staining her bottom lip.

I fist my hands, gripping the edge of my cushion, to stop myself from moving. If I do, the first taste I'll have of the wine would be from her mouth. *Goddamn, I did not think this through.* "The 2021 Burgundy Valley Vineyard is incredible. One of my favorites, that's for certain."

She hums under her breath, the quiet sound going straight to my groin. Self-imposed abstinence is a bitch. I just have to keep my eyes on the prize and not allow myself to be led around by my dick. So if the teeth of my zipper are leaving a permanent tattoo on the bastard, then so be it. I long for the day when I'll be able to go to sleep and wake up with her in my arms, when just a brief shift of my hips would have me buried deep inside her tight little body. I miss her in my arms like an idiot misses the point.

And how the fuck is it possible to miss something you've never truly had?

"You know what's strange?" Siah asks, pointing with her fork at me. I shift on my cushion enough so I can partially face her and the table and give her a chin nod to continue. "I've known Jayme for ten years, but never met you. And now I'm seeing you twice in a month."

The bite of creamy, cheesy pasta turns to ash in my mouth. I chew through it, swallowing quickly. "You've never lived in my house before," I tease, hoping like hell she'll drop the one subject I have no desire to discuss tonight.

"Good point." She grins, but her eyes are clouded over. "Sorry for being pushy. It just dawned on me that, for as close as Jayme and I are, I never really got to know her family."

I lean against the loveseat, holding my plate with one hand and playing around with my fork with the other. "Did Jayme ever speak of our family?"

"Hmm, not much." Siah takes a small sip of her wine, her finger tracing circles around the rim of the glass. "I never really asked either. Family is a sore subject for me. If I'm not willing to talk, why would I force her, you know?" She draws her jean-cladded knees to her chest, resting her chin atop of them. "She mostly mentions you, how lucky she is to have you as a brother, how much she misses you."

I'm fairly certain she knows more than she lets on, but if she's playing her cards close to her chest for my sister's benefit or because she's fishing, that's still to be determined. I'm willing to bite, though. This particular shark is hungry, and not for chicken Alfredo.

Pushing the plate back onto the table, I swap my fork with my glass of wine and top myself up. I incline the bottle toward Siah, but she covers her glass. My earlier worries about her alcohol intake ease some, seeing as she drank less than half, but I'll still look into what's going on with her meds.

I bend my knees, resting my elbow over my right one and my head against the loveseat. Might as well get comfortable, if I'm having a heart to heart.

"We're not a close-knit family," I start, a hollow chuckle ripping from my throat. "Helena tries, but my father and I were never close, and that hasn't changed in the years they've been married."

Siah turns toward me, abandoning her plate. "Jayme loves her mom," she says with a small smile, "but I got the impression she's not Helena's biggest fan." Her nose scrunches adorably, and it takes everything in me not to lean across the space between us and kiss the reddened tip. "She really doesn't like your father, but she's never told me why."

I bark a laugh, startling her. "That's 'cause my stepsister's a smart woman." At her widening eyes, I'm quick to clarify. "James never hurt her. He's a cold man, who never had room in his heart or life for children. To him, Jayme was... decoration. A means to keep his wife happy and docile. It helped that Jay was never too demanding, nor was she causing trouble. And if she was, well, she had me to bail her out."

"You're a good brother." Siah gives me a warm smile, her fingers still swirling around the rim of her wine glass.

"When I'm not bailing on my sister's graduation?" I retort with a half grin.

She rolls her pretty dark green eyes at me, and my stomach flips in response. I'll take playful Siah at any time over the taciturn, withdrawn wallflower she's been all day today.

"I said good, not perfect." She winks, but her smile quickly disappears as she chews on the inside of her cheek. "What about..." She clears her throat delicately, as she busies herself with the ends of her curls.

Understanding fills my chest. I only debate inside of me for half a second. I told her once, long-lasting trust takes effort and work, and that I was willing to put in the work. "My mom?"

Siah nods, her chin brushing the top of her knees. "You don't have to, you know..."

"I lost my mom when I was five," I cut her off, my eyes trained on the flickering orange, golden, and red flames in the fireplace. "Her name was Felicia, and she was sunshine personified." I sigh when I feel her small hand squeezing my forearm. She remains quiet, and I appreciate her silence more than she could ever understand. Empty words can't fill an empty heart. "I don't remember much of her. She smiled a lot; she read me good night stories, and she baked these really incredible hazelnut and vanilla cookies." A fond smile tugs at my lips. Regardless of what shit life throws at me, I was loved. And Mom loved me fiercely enough for me to remember the warmth of her affection twenty-eight years after she passed.

Siah scoots closer to me and leans her head on my shoulder. I throw my arm around hers, so that she's cuddling into my side. Yeah, empty words don't fill an empty heart, but actions... actions kick-start it.

"What happened to your mom?"

"She developed a rare blood clot disorder immediately after my birth. She managed it through medications and check-ups, but she fell and hit her head a couple of days before her death. Not badly, from what I managed to find out. My father was away on a business trip, so she didn't end up going to have it looked at. A blood clot formed and caused a massive stroke. My father had just returned when she... simply crumpled to the floor. She was dead by the time they reached the hospital."

Siah pushes closer to me, her arm circling my waist and tightening around me. I rest my cheek against her head and bury my nose in her hair. The next words I whisper, "He blamed me. My birth gave her the disorder. I had an ear infection when she fell, and she was more worried about me than herself. In his eyes, I killed the love of his life."

I haven't said these words many times before. Once to my only friend when he was recuperating from his own tailored-just-for-him hell. A couple of times to my therapist. This is the first time guilt doesn't incinerate me from the inside out.

"That's bullshit," Siah yells, indignation pouring out of her. Her warm palm cups my cheek, her fingers brushing against my stubble, as her eyes pin me into place. "You know that, right? It's complete and utter bullshit."

She's resolute in her conviction, an absolute warrior fighting to absolve me of my guilt and silence my demons, all in one move. I can't resist her fire. So I don't. I'm a weak man when it comes to her. I dip my head and take her sweet mouth with mine. She's soft, and pliant, and tastes like all my filthy fantasies come to life. I kiss her gently, my lips moving against hers, conveying everything that words fail to do right now. Her fingers slide into my hair, pushing me closer to her.

I won't break that last barrier between us.

Not now.

Not yet.

Instead, somehow, I find enough strength—or maybe cowardice—inside me to slow our rapidly kindling fire and eventually stop. I kiss the tip of her nose and rest my forehead against hers.

"Thank you."

Chapter Thirty-Two

SIAH

M y pillow is hard. Not uncomfortably so, but not the cloud I'm used to have cradling my neck. My pillow is also warm. I want to nuzzle my face in that fuzzy feeling and sleep the day away.

Thump. Thump. Thump.

Slow and steady against my ear, the heartbeat of my pillow echoes through me. A full body pillow that I am hugging with all my might. So snuggly, so comfortable, so... wait? Since when do they make pillows with erections? Because there's an unmistakable hardness pressing against my lower belly with every breath I take.

"Oh shit," I mumble, sitting upright. A pained grunt heaves out of my pillow when I replace my belly with my knee. Strong hands grip my waist, making me yelp as they lift me up and onto the loveseat. Goosebumps sprout on my skin at the contact with the cold leather. I peer over the edge at the man cupping his groin, face red and scrunched up, pain etched in that throbbing vein in his forehead. "I'm sorry. I'm so so so sorry."

If the earth could open up and swallow me whole just about now, that would be ideal. Please and thank you. He rubs his palm across his face as I blink sleepy eyes at him, before sitting up in one go, startling the living mortification out of me.

"You woke up this morning and randomly landed on violence, huh?" August muses, his eyes still crinkling with the aftereffects of pain, but his plump lips tug into a lazy half grin.

Feeling my cheeks burn up with embarrassment, I cover my face with my palms. "I really didn't mean to," I whisper through my fingers.

"I know," he sighs. He kisses my forehead, nipping at my index finger with his teeth. I lower my palms just in time to see him nimbly stand up in one fluid motion. He picks up our plates, still on the coffee table from last night's dinner, then heads to the kitchen. Barely turning his head, he looks at me over his shoulder. "Coffee?"

"Yes, please." I fidget with the hem of my T-shirt for a second. "I'm going to go take a shower. Been living in these clothes for quite some time." Not waiting for a response, I jump off the couch and scurry to my bedroom, tripping over one of the cushions on the floor in my haste. His chuckle follows me all the way up the stairs.

I grab a pair of leggings and an ugly Christmas sweater Jayme insisted we must wear today, as well as a set of comfortable underwear and bra, and make my way into the bathroom. Peeling off my T-shirt, I chuck it into the laundry basket, then quickly shed my jeans and underwear. I was beyond disturbed to find that hidden camera in the bathroom, so I bought a big-ass Boston fern to hang strategically and hinder the view of the camera.

At least now, I have one room in this entire house to guarantee me some privacy. I turn on the water and climb into the shower, allowing the hot stream to cascade over me. As I wash my hair and go through my routine, my mind wanders to the man preparing coffee in the kitchen.

August confuses me. I don't understand where he stands, what his goals are. I'm still shocked at the vulnerability he displayed last night, talking to me about losing his mother and his issues with his father, kissing me breathless but not pushing me any further than a gratitude-filled kiss. My belly flutters as the memories assault my mind. My lips tingle as if the phantom of his mouth is in the shower with me, brushing, teasing, tasting.

I've admitted to myself that I am attracted to August. Very much so.

It's why I crave his nearness and feel the crackle of electricity in the air when we're both sharing the same space.

I've also admitted to myself that August cannot be trusted. Not with the cameras, and his elusiveness, and the mystery that shrouds his every word.

What is his connection to my stalker? Are they in this together? One breaking me apart during the cover of the night, the other crumbling my resolve and my sanity during the day?

And the most shocking admission of all... well, that leaves me with weakened knees and a weightlessness in the center of my body that's all together too uncomfortable to delve into.

Last night, as my goosebumps receded from my skin and my desire went from boiling to simmering, guilt reared its ugly head. I'm fucked in the head, that's what I am. Because... *Don't say it, Siah. Don't even think it.*

A sob shudders its way through my esophagus. My teeth ache as I try to contain it deep inside of me. I have to admit it. I have to admit it to myself so that I can breathe, so that I set it free in the Universe and it stops pressing against my lungs and my heart.

Kissing August felt like cheating on the monster of my nightmares.

My forehead touches the cold tiles of the shower as I lean against the wall in a futile effort to keep myself upright. Is this a variant of the Stockholm Syndrome? Am I developing an unhealthy affection for my captor?

He may not keep me chained in his basement, but the modicum of freedom he awards me does not change my situation. I live in captivity, and I am a pitiful prey.

"Thank you, thank you, thank you," Jayme squeals, tackling August to the floor and peppering his face with kisses. He sputters and barks a surprised laugh as she rolls to her back, holding her arm up, so that the twinkling lights sparkle through the crimson rubies of her new bracelet. "This is really thoughtful of you," she sighs wistfully, turning her head to wink at me. "And now we're matching."

We are. August gifted both of us a bracelet for Christmas. Mine has delicate pale diamonds, their hallo shining brighter than our Christmas tree, and elegant emeralds, their deep green color resembling the forests surrounding his home. Resembling my eyes. My stomach twists. Both pleasure and guilt swirl inside of me in a maddening dance that leaves my head spinning.

I tried to protest. To claim the gift was too much. And it is. Too thoughtful, too touching, too expensive, too... August. But he turned those stormy midnight blue eyes on me, a million promises and depraved threats shining in their depths, reducing me to silence.

He sits up, a shy smile on his lips. "You're very welcome. I've been rather absent in the past few years. Haven't earned your forgiveness yet, but I thought the bracelet would at least send me on the right path."

She leans her head on his shoulder and hooks an arm around his. I'm not jealous, I'm really not. She's his sister, she can touch him and hug him freely and without reservation. I'm nothing. An unpaying tenant at best, a disaster about to happen at worst.

"There's nothing to forgive you for, August. You're my rock. You and Siah, both. I love having you around, but I understand there are reasons—*solid* reasons—for your distance. You're my family. As long as you're happy and healthy, then I'm happy."

My eyes mist over, and I lift my knees to my chest. In a few short weeks, I'm going to be leaving all this behind me. Jayme is the only family I have. And the shadow is forcing me away from her. I should be angry, but all I feel is bone-deep fatigue and a blooming desire for the torment to end. I'm not thinking of all the other feelings he's evoking in me. No, those I've locked in a dusty drawer in the furthest recesses of my mind, never to be touched again.

If this is the last Christmas I get to spend with my family, then I'm going to make the best of it. So I fight through the numbness and plaster a smile on my face. I laugh with them, I play board games with them, I eat all the food I can fit in my stomach until my leggings feel too tight and my body deliciously sluggish as carbs weigh me down.

Merry Christmas to me.

Chapter Thirty-Three

Siah

August has taken to spending a lot more time with me. If he's not actively engaging in conversation, he's tapping away at his laptop or phone on the kitchen island while I cook. After I have to literally beat him off with a kitchen rag to leave me alone to my cooking.

There's a certain peace mindlessly cutting and chopping and mixing brings to me. Plus, with him here, I can't really delve into my escape plans. So I cook, and clean, and work on my assignments, and blush as I write away at my laptop as he throws me flirty smiles across the table and brings me snacks and drinks.

In an ideal world, this would be my life. The most handsome man I've ever met would give me his attention and his heart. We'd share a home, talk about our days, cook together, and go to sleep together.

Over the past four days he's made it a point to share little tidbits about his life—the rotten relationship he has with his father, the conflicting affection toward Helena, his longing for freedom, and his desperate wish to allow himself to be happy. Maybe not in so many words, but I can read between the lines. Almost as well as I can read his attraction to me in his eyes.

He's as subtle as a punch in the face in his wooing attempts.

His stolen touches thrill me. A brush of his palm against my lower back, crowding me against the counter as he stretches out to pick up a mug on the highest shelf, a teasing pull of a rogue curl—he's naughty and daring, and charging my skin with electricity.

But is he genuine?

Or is he on to me and trying to divert my attention?

My paranoid instincts are screaming at me that he's lulling me to a sense of security. I'm a directionless pawn on a 3D chessboard, and everyone can see the checkmate move. Everyone, except for me.

Do I let myself be captured, or do I race to queening the eighth-rank pawn and fight for my own checkmate?

I burrow deeper into my blanket, the bone-deep chill my depressing thoughts brought makes me shiver. My eyes are affixed to the huge TV hanging above the fireplace. I can't really tell what's happening on the screen; I am so lost in my head, I missed more than half the movie.

August shifts next to me, the leather under us creaking faintly. His legs are stretched out lazily, resting on the coffee table, one ankle on top of the other, his arms casually folded across his chest. I'd much rather watch his massive biceps test the strength of the seams of his black T-shirt than look at whatever alien is killing another stupid human.

He unfurls his arms and drops a large palm to one of my ankles, gently massaging it through the thick material of the blanket. Even with a fuzzy barrier between us, his heat warms me up, traveling through my shin, up my thigh, and straight to my core. His presence keeps me rooted to the spot, anchoring me in an otherwise stormy sea. Warring emotions swirl and fight inside of me. My paranoia battles against my desire, my lack of trust against the strange familiarity he brings me.

"What?" August murmurs, not taking his eyes off the TV.

"Hmm... nothing." I stretch out, pushing against his rock-hard thigh with my toes before relaxing back into the comfortable cushions of the couch. "Do you ever feel lost?"

Now he turns his head to pin me with his stormy eyes. "All the damn time, Siah." He's dead serious, too. I gulp, his gaze searing my skin.

"What do you do when you feel lost?"

August leans his head against the backrest, staring at the ceiling and the flirty shadows dancing on the gray expanse. I release a relieved breath. His eyes unnerve me. It feels like he's able to see right through me, down to my innermost thoughts, feelings, and fears.

"I've never been without a purpose," he says, his voice low and gravelly, wrapping around me tighter than my fuzzy blanket. "My first purpose was to get my father to love me." A self-deprecating laugh fills the room, the hand on my ankle tightening. "I sure failed in that one."

"August... you don't have to continue if it hurts you."

His grip feels like a cuff now, strong, unbreakable, secure. "Bottling all that poison inside hurts even more." I shift closer to him, my bent knees leaning against his forearm. "My next purpose was to get out of that house, of that family. Believe it or not, I failed at that, too." He grins now, but I see the grimace behind the mask; I see the still-gaping wound. He's bleeding for me right now, and I'm trapped inside a vortex, spun around until I can't tell left from right. "I failed on purpose, pretty girl. As soon as I saw a lanky redhead with doe eyes and her heart on her sleeve, my purpose shifted. Jayme *felt* like family since the very moment I met her. And so I knew it was down to me to protect her."

"From your father?" I'm making assumptions here, threading on a narrow ledge. There's no safety either side I fall, only deep, dark abyss.

His answer is a simple tip of his chin. "Once Jayme was out, my work became my purpose. Having my own money and resources, so that regardless of what life throws my way, I'd always have the means to start over."

"Have you never wanted a family of your own?" The words are out of my mouth before I can stop them, but since they're out there, I'm dying to hear his answer.

I shiver when he turns those deep eyes back on me. We're sitting much closer now. So close, his minty breath is washing over my face. Nervously, I lick my lips, my mouth suddenly dry. His attention never wavers, never strays from my eyes.

"For the longest time, I didn't think I deserved one," he admits.

"And now?"

A barely there twitch of his mouth steals my focus. The sadness in that elusive smile breaks my heart.

"And now... my purpose has shifted once more."

I don't dare read between *these* lines. Because what he's saying can't be. I cannot be.

He sighs and resumes his mindless caress around my ankle and calf. "Do you want a family of your own?"

Of course, he has to go there.

But if August can be vulnerable with me, I can be vulnerable with him. Too many people have taken pieces of me without my consent. The ones I have left, there's power behind choosing when and how to gift them.

"More than anything in the world," I murmur my greatest dream. "And absolutely not. I know nothing of my parents. I don't even know my name. I wear the surname of the firefighter who found me on a random bench in a park when he was going to work. Just me and my little bassinet. My first name, that's the nurse who looked after me before I was released to the foster care home." It's my turn for a self-deprecating laugh. "She had a wicked sense of humor. *Siah* means dark in Persian. In Hebrew, meditation. What do you think she saw first? The darkness inside of me or my contemplative spirit?"

He's quiet for a second, his white teeth biting into his bottom lip, mulling over my words.

"In Seattle?"

"Discovery Park. Isn't it ironic? That's where that poor firefighter *discovered* me."

He doesn't find my joke funny. Truth be told, neither do I. But then he goes and presses the nuclear button, shattering the earth beneath my feet.

"I can find your parents for you. If you want me to, that is."

Chapter Thirty-Four

SIAH

The wilted grass is wet and cold under my bare feet. I push myself harder, my chest heaving as I weave through the darkened forest. My hands are extended in front of me as I feel for the rough bark of trees, for anything that could trip me, delay me enough to give him a chance.

The eerie whistling comes from everywhere all at once, and my soul shrinks inside of me. I have to get out of here. I have to reach somewhere safe. Anywhere.

Sharp twigs cut in the exposed skin of my forearms. Stones and fallen branches scratch at the soles of my feet. I can't worry about that now. My body is cold, oh so cold. The pain of each wound, regardless of how tiny, is amplified by hypothermic numbness. My breath fogs in front of me, making it even more difficult to see.

I feel his presence at my back—he's hunting me. Silent in his chase, if he catches up to me, I'm done for.

I slip in the sticky mud of the forest floor, and my heart stalls in my chest until I manage to find a semblance of a grip, my toes digging deep into the drenched soil. "Keep going, Siah," I mumble to myself. My courage is gone, my resolve dwindling. I'm just fooling myself.

The only reason I'm not chained up to the rough bark of a tree is because he's enjoying the hunt. He thrives on my terror.

An owl takes flight somewhere nearby, its mournful song announcing my impending doom. I chance a look over my shoulder, but the darkness of the night is too impenetrable, too thick. And that small decision costs me my freedom.

His booming laugh is chilling, colder still than the frozen air outside, as I run straight into his rock-hard chest. Out of nowhere, heavy chains wrap around my wrists. Manacles are weighing down my ankles. I'm trapped.

He's all shadows and gloom. Only his stormy eyes burn bright as they focus on me, golden flecks glinting like lightning during the most violent of storms.

"I caught you, little mockingbird. And now you're mine, to have and to hold, until death do us apart."

I open my mouth in a silent scream, begging my throat to form a sound, any sound. Nothing comes out, just pure and utter desperation as I succumb to my fate.

Chapter Thirty-Five

AUGUST

"P-please, August! Please…"

I burst through the bedroom door, my heart aching at the anguish in her pleas. The lights are off, but I know my way through this room with my eyes closed. Siah whimpers, the sheets rustling as she tosses and turns.

"August, help." Her voice is rough, raw pain infusing every syllable. I hit the edge of the bed with my shin, and I crawl in next to her, gathering her in my arms. She struggles and fights me, her arms flailing about, but there's no strength behind her slaps as they connect with my shoulders and neck.

I position her sideways in my lap, tucking her head under my chin, as I gently restrain her wrists in one hand, to stop her from hurting herself.

"Shush, I'm here. You're safe."

I lean against the headboard, gently rocking her back and forth. Her skin is cold and clammy, a thick sheen of sweat coating her from head to toe. With my free hand, I brush her drenched hair away from her face, stroking her head soothingly.

"You're safe, baby. Settle down now." I keep my voice low and calming as she sobs and trembles in my hold. "I have you, baby, I have you."

Her heart is hammering in her chest so fast, I can feel the frenzied rhythm beneath my ribcage. Her fear saddens me. Right here, in my home, in my bed, in my arms, she's the safest she'll ever be. I need to do better; I need to reassure her more.

Nothing can touch her here.

"August, please, August," she cries out, her body jolting, then growing rigid and stiff.

I press my lips to the top of her head, tightening my hold on her, hoping the warmth of my own body and the pressure on her muscles will give her nervous system the restart it needs to allow her to snap from whatever nightmare has her trapped.

"Siah," I purr. "Come back to me, baby. I have you right now. I'm holding you. You're safe."

I repeat the words over and over, gently rocking back and forth, until her breath evens out, her salty tears stop pouring down her cheeks, and her heart returns to its normal rhythm, leaving my chest bereft and empty.

With my whole body curled around hers, I'm cocooning her in my strength. I bend my head, powerless in front of her pain, and, with the tip of my tongue, I taste the salty flavor of her anguish.

A couple of days ago, I offered to shed light on her roots. I can see now, in the pitch-darkness of my bedroom, how wrong I was. Sometimes, the unknown brings more mercy than the cold, hard truth. Knowing who her parents were, and how they are no longer, won't bring her any closure. Her mom loved her. The abandonment was an act of mercy, a sacrifice of love, not a cruel, uncaring dismissal. As soon as her mother escaped the clutches of Siah's piece of shit father, she went searching for her baby. She'd never stopped, not until a car speeding through a red light ended her life. Despite what Siah's imagining when she sits alone and creates scenario after scenario in her head, she was wanted.

She *is* wanted.

"August," Siah whispers, nuzzling her face in the crook of my neck. "You came."

"I always will," I promise, my words pure gravel and grit.

Her tears are soaking my T-shirt. My stomach flutters and my lips tingle. I long for another taste of her pain.

"It hurts." Her fingers curl in the soft fabric, and I grip her hip, my thumb rubbing soothing circles over her nightgown.

I hum deep in my throat. I'm well aware how much it hurts, how deep and burning that wound is, the throbbing nearly unbearable.

Her lips are hot as she presses wet kisses on the side of my neck, tentative and shy at first, growing bolder with every second I don't stop her. She shifts in my lap, raising to knees, and before I can react, she's straddling me, her mouth pressed to mine.

A blink. Then two.

"Siah..." I try to do the right thing. I swear I do, even though my cock is a steel pipe in my shorts, and my blood is pure molten lava.

She stills in my arms, hovering above me like a goddess of the night, her white satin cami nearly translucent in the darkness. "Make it hurt less, August." A beg, a plea, and a demand. And in the next breath, my hands are on the lacy hem. One breath later, she's in front of me, beautifully naked, pale full breasts with hardened little peaks heaving, small waist flaring into indecently round hips, her bare pussy soaking through my shorts. "Please!"

I dip my head and take one of her nipples in my mouth, my tongue licking and swirling, teasing, tasting, loving. Her hips buck against me, and the sweetest pleasured mewl pours from her lips.

My blood is buzzing in my veins, pure adrenaline flooding my body. I release her tight little bud with a pop and focus my attention on her other breast. Kissing, caressing, branding her taste into my tongue, my hands touching her everywhere. A handful of her plump ass, a loving stroke along her spine, a possessive grip of her neck as I kiss up on her chest, her slender neck, and finally, finally her mouth.

I nip at her bottom lip, and she opens up for me, granting me entrance, allowing this sinner through the golden gates of heaven.

Her own hands are impatient, pulling at my T-shirt, frustrated little growls vibrating from her chest when the material doesn't immediately succumb to her wants. I release my grip on her hip, breaking the kiss only enough to undress and toss the bundled fabric into the unknown of the night.

Siah arches her back, pushing her soft breasts, still wet from my loving, against my heated skin. "God, you feel so good," I grit, "So soft, so silky. You're fucking perfect, baby."

Her fingers flutter over my abdomen, trailing up on my chest. She flattens her palms above my heart and slants her mouth over mine. My heart rate speeds up in response, each pump stronger, faster, louder, as if trying to reach her through the layers of bones, muscles, and skin.

Stupid organ. My heart has always had Siah's name tattooed all over its chambers and atriums.

"Please, August. I need you," she begs oh so prettily that stars explode at the base of my spine.

"Take what you need. Take it all," I rasp, ready to lower myself at her feet and worship the ground she walks on.

She pulls at my hair, her hips moving faster and faster against me, her pussy rubbing against my cock. I curse through my teeth the chafing material of my shorts. I want to feel her heat, her dripping wet all over me. No barriers, no walls, no distance, no air between the two of us. She loses all sense of rhythm as she dry humps me when I cup her breast and thumb her pert nipple, rolling and pinching it between my fingers.

"August, oh god, please."

I clamp my free hand on her hip, guiding her movements, and thrust up as she gyrates and undulates on top of me. "I need... please... I need... AUGUST!"

She throws her head back, the ends of her silky hair brushing against my thighs. A pained moan rips out of her throat. Raw, needy, and the best fucking sounds I've ever heard. Bliss runs through me as the heat against my cock intensifies, reaching boiling point.

I can't bear the distance, I can't bear not to feel her clamp down on me, strangling my dick with everything she has. So before any slip of rationality and logic dares dispel the magic she's weaving between us, I free my cock from the cotton prison confining him with a swift shove down of the elastic band.

And then she rides me freely, wildly, the hardest parts of me touching the softest parts of her, the purest silk encasing steel. The groan crawling up my chest is inhuman, the satisfaction of feeling her flutters and throbs on my bare skin too much.

"August, August, August," Siah chants as she comes, and I know, right here and right now, this is the moment my destiny is sealed.

She slumps against my chest, her pussy soaking my bare lap. I wrap my arms around her as jolts of pain and denied pleasure coil in my groin. She's all but completely draped over me, and even if my balls turn purple and fall off, I wouldn't move an inch.

I run my fingers tenderly over the lovely indents of her spine, from her sweaty neck to the top of her ass, slowly, gently, savoring everything the goddess in my arms is. My eyelids fall closed, and I draw a deep breath in and relax under Siah's slight weight.

"Someone was chasing me through the woods," she whispers, her lips tickling the oversensitive skin just below my ear. "The shadow caught me. My fear choked me. I couldn't breathe, I couldn't make a sound."

"Shh!" I exhale in her hair. "I've got you."

She moves her hands to my shoulders and sits up. My cock jolts as her maddening heat surrounds the thick base. Her button nose rubs against mine as she smooths her thumb over my cheekbones. "I know you do. When I could scream, I screamed for you. And here you are."

I tilt my chin up, touching my lips to hers. "Here I am."

"I still need you," she whispers.

"You have me." My words are resolute, dripping with conviction as she drips with her desire for me.

Her hips once again start their hypnotizing roll against me. She moves with agonizing slowness, driving me to the brink of madness and back into her arms. My hips jerk up when she grounds her clit against the over sensitive head of my cock. The satisfied gasp leaving her throat reignites the fire always simmering for her.

Her graceful fingers wrap around me and squeeze, and my eyes roll to the back of my head. "You're so big," Siah whispers.

"I'm dying to see you stretched around me," I confess. I'm just about to sign over my life to her, if only she'd put me inside her tight heat and let me die a happy man.

Siah lifts high on her knees, and my hands immediately clutch her hips, holding her just above me. She notches the head of my cock at her entrance, and I swear my eyes fucking mist over. I thrust up slowly, just enough for her greedy walls to grip me, fluttering against the tip in greeting.

"How do you feel so good?" she moans, rolling her hips and taking me inside of her one torturous inch at the time. She works herself over my cock, up and down, up and down, mewling, and moaning, and making me lose my ever-loving mind.

My fingers bite desperately into her hips. It takes every ounce of self-control in my body not to fuck myself into her like a rabid animal. But this is her show. Siah needs to be in control right now, so I let her take from me everything she craves, every-fucking-thing she desires.

"August, god, I can't breathe. I feel you everywhere," she cries, moving her hips faster, rougher, until she's fully seated on my cock. "I need you, please, I need you."

And her words are all I *need*.

I wrap my fist into her wild curls, forcing her to arch her back. Her breasts jot out proudly, bouncing with every thrust up of my hips. I latch my lips around one nipple, sucking roughly at the hardened bud. She bucks into me, her movements just as frantic as mine. My balls draw up, heavy and aching, as I plant my heels in the mattress and wildly fuck myself into her from below.

Her nails find purchase on my chest, the sting of my skin as it breaks under her passion spurring me on. Siah is marking me as hers, her brand deep into my psyche. "That's it, sweet girl. Take me. I want to feel your pussy strangling my cock. I want to feel you flooding me with your desire. Take everything you want, baby."

She clamps down on me as I fuck her relentlessly, obsessively. The headboard bangs against the wall. The sheets rustle all around us. The slap of her peach-shaped ass against my thighs has me crazy. All to create a beautiful symphony for our frantic lovemaking.

I feel myself ready to explode, ready to fill her emptiness with all my fullness, so I tighten my hold on her hair, forcing her to stare directly into my eyes so she can see how she owns me, so she can see what she does to me. There's no looking away.

Just Siah and I, her pussy strangling my cock, my thumb rubbing circles on her clit, and her sweet, sweet surrender as her dark green eyes connect to mine, and she sings my name to all the high heavens and the deepest hells.

"AUUUGUST!"

I thrust up hard, rutting into her as my cock swells, and I spill my essence deep into her tight, wet heat. My guttural moan as I explode into a million pieces for her to put me back together rattles my chest, and my hips lift from the mattress. "Siah, fuck, fuck, Siah," I chant her name over and over as she milks me of my release.

I pepper her sweaty face with kisses as we both come back to Earth, holding her tenderly in my arms like my most precious treasure. Her body grows limp on top of me, and her ragged breaths slowly even out. I comfort her affectionately as she falls asleep, her drenched pussy still fluttering around me, still taking me, still holding me.

We're one step closer to happily ever after.

She came to me.

She came for me.

Willingly.

"Your name is Ava. It derives from the Latin 'avis'." I chuckle quietly, mindful to not disturb her peaceful rest. "Avis means bird, or birdlike." I kiss her forehead. "Don't you think it's fitting, my little mockingbird? I promised you'd stare into *my* eyes and cry out *my* name. This is me keeping that promise. Now, all that's left is for me to have and to hold you for the rest of our lives."

Chapter Thirty-Six

SIAH

I wrap my arms tightly around myself as I watch August's tall frame disappear from view. My whole body feels numb and cold, as if he held all my warmth and, with him gone, I'm left with nothing. My steps are slow and unhurried toward the parking lot. I don't even take the time to admire the exquisite views from the Skybridge.

My eyes burn as I hoist myself up on the driver's seat of August's SUV and his lovely, masculine scent of sandalwood and thunder hits me. Something shifted inside of me in the last ten days he's been home. Spending time with him, talking to him, sharing my vulnerability with him and cradling his in the palms of my hands, sleeping with him, it's all messing with my head.

Just before Christmas, I was looking forward to leave this city behind me and start anew. August gave me a precious sense of security, of being safe. *Him* making a swift disappearance also helped tremendously, even if I'm still looking over my shoulder constantly. Did *he* stay away because of August? Does *he* know I gave myself to August over and over and over, and I rang in the New Year with him buried so deep inside of me I didn't know where he ended and I began? Is *he* furious that my belly flutters when I think of my best friend's stepbrother?

Will *he* come back again? And if *he* does, what will *he* do to me?

My stomach flips. August brings warmth and hope. *He* brings darkness and addictive thrill. I can deny it until my eyes cross; my denial doesn't change the horrifying truth. I crave the safety August's touch breathes into my skin just as much as I crave the depraved fear *he* instils in me when *he* ties me up and sets me free.

I dread going home. The house is massive, and empty, and devoid of everything good now that its owner is gone. I'm exposed there—easy prey.

My phone rings from the passenger seat. Rain is pelting down on the windshield, so I'm keeping my eyes on the road as I hit the button to connect the call.

"What did you do, you fucking bitch?" Henry rages at me, his voice crackling through the stereos of the car.

Fucking great. Just what I need. "What do you want, Henry? I can't talk right now, I'm driving."

"I hope they lock you in the crazy ward and throw the damn key, you unhinged petty cow," he yells so loud, my ears are ringing.

I sigh and look in the side mirror as I merge onto the highway taking me to August's home. "Okay, Henry. I don't know what crawled up your ass and died there, but the second we divorced was also the second I stopped having to take your abuse. Whatever your problem is, it's no concern of mine. Don't contact me again."

Disconnecting the call, I frown. I already blocked his contact—both work and personal numbers—in November, which means he had to have called me from a new one. It doesn't matter one way or the other. There's a very high chance this phone will be left behind when I leave in two weeks. If I leave in two weeks.

I like August. I'm fascinated by him. But this phone call right here shows me once more how important it is to put distance between me and my current life. As intriguing as this man is and as much as he makes my body sing, my safety is more important. He doesn't know of all my baggage. At least, I hope he doesn't.

He seemed so honest, so open with me in the brief time we shared his home. But I can't shake the niggling feeling in the pit of my stomach that August knows more than he lets on. I can't shake my suspicions, either.

I have no answers, only questions.

My fingers drum impatiently against the leather of the wheel as I wait for the massive gates to open up and allow me in.

The best-case scenario would have him innocent of everything my mind casts against him. The stalker would move on to greener pastures, and August and I would live happily ever after.

But my life has never headed to an ever after. Not in twenty-eight years. Why would now be any different?

I collect my purse and my phone and climb out of the car. There's only five feet or so to the door leading to the house, but the darkness of the garage and the harrowing echoes of my shoes against concrete as I hurry have fear rise in the pit of my stomach. I slam the door closed behind me and lean against the sleek wood as I pant.

That garage really needs a window or ten, or at least some lights, because *Jesus Christ in a horror house,* my adrenaline is at an all-time high and my pulse is about to shred my carotid to pieces.

When I finally get my bearings, I drag my feet to the bedroom, letting myself fall face first across the king-sized mattress. The soft sheets still carry his scent. I wrap myself tightly in the duvet, closing my eyes and imagining August's arms are holding me instead. It's funny how it only took five days of sleeping in the same bed for me to get used to him next to me, inside of me, part of me.

It's too soon to fall in love. The abandoned child in me is starved for affection and stability. The adult is fearful and terrified.

> *Does it make me a simp if I tell you I miss you? Next week cannot come soon enough.*

August St. Andrew

I hide my smile in my coffee mug. For a stoic man, August is surprisingly sweet. We've been messaging back and forth for the past few days. He promised he'd join us for Jayme's birthday celebration. She decreed a night out to celebrate the start of her last year in her twenties.

In all honesty, I wouldn't mind at all dancing the night away with him and my best friend. Of course, I haven't said shit to her about all the horizontal, and vertical, and diagonal dancing I've done with her stepbrother. If he was bothered about me keeping my distance while she had dinner with us or spent time with us, he hasn't said a thing.

> *You make simpering look handsome. I cannot confirm or deny how deeply I feel your absence.*

Me

> *You'll feel my presence deeply, soon enough.*

August St. Andrew

> *How's your writing going?*

August St. Andrew

> *Is that a promise or a threat?*

Me

> *I'm nearly finished with it. I should take up crocheting or something, I won't know what to do with my life once I have some free time.*

Me

> *Both, baby. Both.*

August St. Andrew

A gasp spills past my lips as a picture of him lights up my screen. August, smiling and sweaty, brilliant sunshine behind him—he leaves me breathless.

> *I don't mind occupying all your free time. *smiley face emoji* *wink emoji* Are you not having any assignments pending? PS: Your turn.*

August St. Andrew

I lift my mug to my lips, making sure the "*Coffee spelled backward is eeffoc. As in, I don't give eeffoc until I've had my coffee.*" print is visible on the picture, and cross my eyes. The window behind me shows the darkened forest, the sun still about half an hour away from rising. My wild curls are piled in a messy bun atop my head, my breasts hidden under August's sweatshirt that I've stolen out of his closet.

> *I'm starting the New Year with a break. I'll reconsider my options at the end of the month.*

Me

> *PS: It's an absolute blasphemy to start your morning with a run. Are you even human?*

Me

> *You are absolutely mesmerizing. Remind me again why am I not there, enjoying a lazy morning with you?*

August St. Andrew

> *What happens at the end of the month?*

August St. Andrew

If I haven't completely lost my ever-loving mind the way I'm losing my heart to him, the end of the month would, hopefully, see me far away from Seattle. And, unfortunately, from him.

> *I wouldn't have to run if I had you to start my morning with.*

August St. Andrew

Well, that earns him a snort in my coffee. Maybe I need to break some eggs and make a cheesy omelet with everything he's selling right now.

> *January is always a trial month. The real New Year starts in February.*

Me

At least... that's what I want. Isn't it?

Chapter Thirty-Seven
August

The echo of my steps reverberates against the cold marble. I fucking hate this house and everything it stands for. Its lifeless walls, the show of grandeur, the expensive paintings and over the top furniture—every brick is a statement of the arrogance of the one and only James St. Andrew. But not for much longer.

The last piece of the puzzle is in place.

It's now more important than ever for me to finish this game and cut all ties. So I can finally be free. So I can cut myself open in front of Siah and confess everything I've done to bring us to this point. And then to hope she'll forgive me; to hope she'll still have me.

There are no lengths I wouldn't go for her.

"August, I'm so happy you're here." Helena greets me with a kiss on my cheek and an affectionate pat to my jaw. "Come, please." She gestures toward the dining room—the formal dining room, because of course there's more than one in this fucking museum of atrocities.

"Thank you for having me." I squeeze her arm and pass her the neatly wrapped gift I picked up for her on my way here. Because nothing says *I'm ready to dethrone your husband* like a Cartier bracelet and a bottle of Macallan for the soon-to-be-fallen king.

"We miss you kids, here. The house is far too empty without you." Helena smiles, leading the way through the large white doors.

As expected, my dearest father, my absolute role model, is already seated at the head of the table, nursing a glass of whatever poison he drinks to keep him going. It irks me to no end that I look at him and see myself in thirty years. The jet-black hair, dark blue eyes, tall and muscular frame—it's like looking in a fucked-up mirror of horrors. The only difference between us is the nuance of black between our morals.

He takes for pleasure. I take for defense.

He assesses me from head to toe, not bothering to stand and greet me. And why would he? As far as he's concerned, he's got me trapped, at his bidding. He both hates the sight of me and takes perverted pleasure out of making my life a living hell. Not for long, though. Not anymore.

"You look good, Father," I say, clasping the backrest of the chair to his right and pulling it for Helena to sit.

I'd normally sit to his left, but today I'm feeling just a little rebellious, so I take the seat opposite him, at the other end of the table. His clean-shaven jaw twitches, but that's the only outward reaction to my affront.

"I was expecting you to be back in Seattle by now," my father comments, sipping at his drink, the ice clinking against the glass as he settles it back on the table.

I drum my fingers against the arm of the chair and cross my legs, resting an ankle on the opposite knee. "Tomorrow."

"Ah." Helena's face goes soft as she pushes a strand of hair behind her ear. "My daughter would be so pleased to have you there for her birthday." She turns toward my father with a hopeful look on her face. "Maybe we can surprise her, too? It's been a while since we've celebrated a birthday all together."

His eyes narrow as he leans back in his chair, a cold smile tugging at his lips. "I'm sure the young ones would much rather not be held back by our presence, darling. Besides, I've heard dear Jayme is leaving in two days." His stare pins me to my seat, a victory flash shimmering in the lifeless depths. "Africa, is it? The girl is a daredevil. She needs to be... careful. Foreign countries are dangerous."

"James!" Helena exclaims, her mouth wide open and her eyes unblinking. "Are you trying to give me a heart attack? You know how much I worry for her."

He grabs her hand, kissing the back of it. "My apologies, darling. I didn't mean to frighten you." He's telling the truth. He meant to threaten me instead.

She's a loving mother, I'll give her that. But she's color blind, otherwise there's no explanation as to why she refuses to see the walking-talking red flag she married. The man is vile, despicable, yet she eats from the palm of his hand whatever bullshit he feeds her, then asks for more.

Dinner is a tense affair, as it always is in the house of horrors. This mausoleum resembles nothing of my childhood home. The minute my mother was laid to rest, he stripped every bit of warmth and color from the walls; he erased her touch from every single nook and cranny. I believe he loved her once, but as soon as she was gone, a switch inside of him flipped permanently, and all the light was snuffed out, leaving only all-consuming darkness.

Much like the closets he locked me in when he felt so inclined to punish me for a perceived wrong or another. Much like the words of hate he spew in my direction every time he opened his vile mouth.

Bile still burns in my stomach as flashes of twisted memories carousel before my eyes. Contorted images of a child, crying himself to sleep, hoping Daddy would love him, wishing for one more warm embrace from Mommy, blink in existence in my mind. Shattered snippets of a hardened teenager, scribbling plans of freedom in the thin air around him with a trembling finger, explode behind my eyelids. Hollow snapshots of an angry but otherwise unfeeling adult, with one foot on solid ground and one dangling above a permanent abyss, intermingle with all the rotten memories this house and my deranged father bring.

Only the scrape of cutlery against porcelain is heard in the wide room, despite Helena's best attempts at conversation. I'd much rather be lost inside the poison in my head than make small talk with the devil in a sharp suit. As soon as the plates are cleared, James pushes back from the table.

"Son, a word in my office?"

I drop the cloth napkin on the table and stand, too. Shaking my head to dispel the dark spiral clouding my judgment, I kiss Helena's forehead in passing and extend my arm, gesturing toward the hallway. "After you."

I trail behind him toward his stuffy, pretentious office. He lengthens his stride, making me smile. There's still something human in him, after all. He's not in a hurry to have a conversation. In fact, he takes pleasure from prolonging the torture and play mind games with his victims. But right now, he feels the predator at his back. All his instincts are riding him hard, demanding he get to safety.

I'd bet half my wealth, he's confused as fuck right now. James St. Andrew fears nothing and no one, yet his pulse is hammering right at the edge of the crisp white collar of his shirt. He puts the obnoxiously large desk between us as he takes a seat in his 'throne'. I walk to the large picture window on the opposite wall, my hands clasped behind my back, and stare at the lights showcasing the back garden—Helena's pride and joy—and the flowers that are in bloom even in early January.

"What games do you think you're playing, August?" he asks, his voice calm and controlled. He doesn't fool me one bit.

"Not playing any games."

He slaps his palms on the mahogany surface. "Bullshit."

I click my tongue against the roof of my mouth, spinning on the heel of my Italian leather shoes. "Ntz, that's quite a temper you have there, Father."

Red creeps from under the collar of his shirt, spreading up his corded neck and clenched jaw. I unclasp my hands and spread my arms wide around me. "I'd be careful with that blood pressure if I were you. Isn't it called the 'silent widow maker'? I'd hate to see Helena dressed all in black, mourning for her husband. She's such a lovely woman."

An angry-looking vein makes its presence known on his forehead as crimson colors his cheeks. "You selfish son of a bitch! You aren't satisfied with Felicia's blood on your hands, now you come for mine?"

I don't flinch at the same old reproach, even if my internal organs curdle together. Fucked, if I'd give him the satisfaction of seeing his words still affect me. I make a show of turning my hands this way and the other before sliding them in the pockets of my trousers, as I lean against a bookshelf, crossing my ankles. "My hands are pretty clean as far as I can see. Can you say the same? Threatening poor Jayme in front of her mother is a low blow, even for you. You're getting sloppy in your old age."

He sputters, his hands gripping at the nod of his tie, fingers furiously unraveling it until it falls crinkled and crumpled in his lap. "What did you do with my stocks?"

I shrug as I take measured steps until only his desk separates us. "Nothing."

"Don't lie, August. Every single fucking company I've invested in tanked in the last six months."

I trail a finger across the mahogany desk, imagining how good it would feel to see it splintered and burning to a crisp on the front lawn. "That's too bad. You're a lawyer, what do you know about investments?"

"You cocky bastard."

"Ntz, ntz, ntz!" I wag my finger. "Not a bastard. You did give me your last name."

The glass paper holder shatters on the wall behind me. I sigh, schooling my face into a mask of boredom. "I wouldn't be so hasty in destroying property. You might have to sell some of this shit since your bank account is draining fast."

His weathered hand, peppered with liver spots, tugs at a drawer so hard, it nearly flies off. He grabs a folder and tosses it to me across the desk, pictures falling out of it. My blood freezes in my veins when Siah's smiling face stares at me from the photographs. I open the folder, skimming through the images of her out shopping, getting dinner with Jayme, going as far back as her courthouse wedding with Doctor Asshole-Extraordinaire. What I don't see are any pictures from inside my home. Which means he doesn't have access to her.

"You think you're smart. Six years you've been pining after her, panting like a dog in heat whenever her name came up. So what? You're all man now and trying to put me in my place so you can claim your bitch?"

I don't react. My eyes are glued to her curly hair, hidden under a beanie as she smiles at Jayme, surrounded by Christmas trees. "I swore to you, August, on that rainy day in March twenty-eight years ago as they lowered the love of my life in the barren cold ground that you'll never be happy. I'll take every ounce of happiness from you the same way you took it from me. You never should've been born, you fucking waste of space."

I take a step back and give him a cocky smirk. "It's too bad you never did get around to that vasectomy." My smile drops, and I let him see instead all the darkness I inherited from him. If he thought he was cold and uncaring, he's about to meet his reckoning. "First Jayme, now Siah. You're full of threats today."

He opens his mouth to spew some more bullshit at me, but my time is running out. If I want to make the last flight out of Phoenix to Seattle and surprise my little mockingbird just before she wakes up, I better make this fast. "In twenty-four hours, videos and pictures of your nightly activities are going to hit every major news station in the state." I spread my arms wide and smirk. "Congratulations, you'll be known nationwide. They're also being delivered to your partners at the firm. If I were you, I'd save my breath and whatever is left of my money and start planning an exit. I believe the cops ain't too fond of sadistic lawyers fucking underage whores who look like his dead ex-wife."

I duck my head as he roars and throws a ledger at me. "You filthy, ungrateful motherfucker!"

"Touch one hair of Siah's head, and the cops will escort you in a black bag instead of cuffs." I smirk wider. "How's that for a threat?"

Giving him my back, I stride out of the room. There's no sweetness to this victory, just a huge void, swirling with bitterness. He had Siah and Jayme followed. I need to make sure whoever's on his payroll forgets their fucking names. I wouldn't put it behind him to do something to them just to fuck with me. He's plenty fucking arrogant for it.

But that's the thing with arrogance. It runs in the family. Apart from my looks, it's also a trait I inherited from him. And my mistake, too. I spent one second too long to gloat. So when the unmistakable click of a safety being pulled sounds, I know I'm too fucking far away from the door.

And like the coward James St. Andrew is, he doesn't even wait for me to turn and face him, but shoots me as I still give him my back.

Agony, fire, and desperation explode behind my eyelids. My steps falter when my knees go weak under me. Ice-cold dread spreads from my shoulder to my chest, then all through my suddenly lead-filled limbs. As my blood runs in hot rivulets, staining my skin, all I think about are the missed opportunities I've had with Siah.

All the air rushes out of my lungs. My knees hit the polished hardwood floor, and the last thing I see before darkness engulfs me is the freedom slipping crimson-red through my trembling fingers.

Chapter Thirty-Eight

SIAH

I stare at the wooden doors of the bar in downtown Seattle. The wind whips my hair everywhere, so I gather the rogue curls and twist them around in my hand, so they don't try to wrap around my neck and kill me. Wouldn't that be something?

My stomach churns, unease gripping it tightly in its nasty claws. I haven't heard from August in two days. He was supposed to be here with me tonight. Now... he's M.I.A.; Jayme hasn't heard from him either. She told me not to be concerned, he usually disappears like that—perks of his work.

Maybe this is the clean break we needed—him gone on a job, me... gone for good.

My back tingles. My limbs feel numb and heavy. I turn my head slyly and check the street over my shoulder. People are out for their evening stroll; others are hurrying to wherever they're going. No one is watching. I blow a relieved breath.

My stalker hasn't made an appearance for more than a month. Was him fucking me out of his system all that it took to get rid of him? I shake my head, bile pooling in my mouth. I'm a dirty, filthy liar. My skull needs to be cracked up and my brain checked for parasites... because, surely, I don't have feelings for two men. One in flesh and blood, who has always fascinated me in a measure or another; the other, made of darkness and shadows, who has always instilled fear and awoken my most depraved desires.

NO.

I refuse to let myself believe that. This must be a side effect of me quitting my meds. I've always been afraid of my stalker, of feeling the burn of his stare as his eyes caress my skin from the cover of the night. He haunts my nightmares. I have feelings for August, for fuck's sake.

"Are you coming in or continue to stare at the door some more?" Devon asks, startling me. He's none too happy to see me, judging by the scowl marring his handsome face.

I hug an arm around my waist, careful not to damage the gift I brought for Jayme. "Coming in... I think." I brush past him as he lights a cigarette, the flame of his lighter blinding me for a second. "Those are bad for you," I mumble under my breath.

He stops me, his fingers curling around my forearm. "You hurt him, you know? It takes everything in me to allow you past these doors and not kick you out on your ungrateful ass."

My heart stops. My body locks down. "Excuse me?" I exhale.

"I don't think I will. You hurt my husband's feelings. Elijah's been nothing but kind to you, and you treated him like shit. I get that you owe no one anything, but when people are treating you kindly, consider returning the favor."

His voice is flat and even, not a hitch in his breath or a stutter to his words to be found, as if he can't help himself but defend Elijah, but knows true and well he shouldn't bother because he's already labeled me as a selfish bitch.

Devon tips his chin toward the entrance. "Go on inside. Jayme's waiting for you. But, for what it's worth, until you pull your head out of your ass, this is the last time you're welcome in my bar."

I rear back as if he slapped me. I want to turn around and stomp my feet and yell to him about all the shit I've gone through in the past months. How I think his precious husband is an intricate part of a very elaborate mind-game someone is playing with me. But what difference would that make?

And, if Devon's in on the joke, him lecturing me right now just shows how deranged they all are.

I push through the door, my heart pounding in my chest as I scan the crowded area for my friend. She chose this bar for her birthday celebration, knowing well and truly what went down at Thanksgiving. Maybe she's not as innocent in all of this as I thought. Maybe August isn't either.

My phone vibrates in the pocket of my coat. I move to the side to not block the entrance, allowing the steady flow of people to walk in and out, and check the screen.

> *Goddammit Siah, you lying piece of shit. Answ...*

Unknown Number

That's all I can read of the message without opening it. Not that I have any intentions to. Henry has been blasting my phone for the past two weeks, calls after calls after calls, nasty texts after nasty texts. I made the mistake of answering him twice—once on the way back from the airport when I dropped August off, and once when I was at home. As soon as he started shouting and throwing insults at me, I blocked the number, but he keeps changing them.

I don't know what his problem is, but I'm done with him.

I freeze. I *am* done with him.

I'm done with the mind games, too.

I'm done with unreliable people.

I'm done second-guessing myself.

I'm done living my life in terror.

I'm simply... done.

I spin on my heel and exit the crowded bar. The sickening smell of exhaust mixed with rain overwhelms my senses.

"Where are you..." Devon asks, but I cut him off and push the carefully wrapped gift against his abdomen. My epiphany is riding me so hard, I can't even muster a smile at the grunt of pain whistling past his lips.

"Tell Jayme I love her, but that I had an emergency," I mutter as I climb down the few steps to the sidewalk.

"Siah, where are you going?" Devon shouts after me, but... you guessed it, I'm done.

My heels click-clack in a hurry on the wet cement as I walk to where I parked August's car. I don't need to buy a new one for myself. I'll get home, pack what I need to, call myself a cab, and have it drop me off at a bus station. From there... the world's my oyster.

I go over my list as I round the corner, visualising the paper in my head, the cursive swirls of the pen as they loop with each item crossed off.

1. ~~Get a full panel STD test because spreading your legs every two weeks in front of your OB/GYN is becoming somewhat of a hobby.~~
2. ~~Find if there are hidden cameras in the bedroom.~~ Four cameras, one in each corner, a fifth in the bathroom, none in the walk-in closet.
3. Buy a burner phone.
4. Buy a new laptop.
5. Buy a car; pay cash.
6. ~~Give up all medication. Mind clarity trumps fear.~~
7. ~~Complete all assignments.~~
8. ~~Withdraw all my money.~~
9. ~~Close all bank accounts.~~
10. ~~Cancel insurance and health insurance.~~
11. Buy a SatNav.
12. BE FREE!

This past week I've gone through the motions of preparing for my departure. If I'd decided to stay for August, I could've found new insurance, open new bank accounts. And if I decided to leave, well... I was ready.

Everything else on my list, I can buy once I get wherever it is I'm going.

The pain is sudden and sharp. My scalp boils as my hair is nearly ripped from the roots. I cry out, my surprise and hurt cut short when I hit face-first the side of August's car. My bottom lip splits on impact, and my mouth floods with the coopery-metallic taste of my blood. The alarm of the car shrieks, piercing the silence of the night, drowning out the sounds of traffic just a few feet behind me.

"You can't ignore me now, can you, bitch?" Henry's hot breath washes over my neck, and a full body shudder passes through me. He pats my pockets, his hand kneading over my breasts, pinching me cruelly through my coat, until he finds what he's looking for. The car beeps as it unlocks, and the alarm stops as suddenly as it started. I pinch my eyes closed against the onslaught of flashing lights from the dashboard and blinkers.

Oh my god.

He crowds me against the car, pressing his whole body around mine. There's nowhere to go. I have no escape.

"Henry," I croak, gurgling his name as I choke on my own blood. I blink rapidly, trying to dispel the haze that descended over my vision to no avail.

"I asked you to stop. I asked you to mind your own fucking business," he grits, the hold he has in my hair tightening. I can feel the strands ripping away from my scalp, sharp pin pricks all giving way under the extreme pressure of his grip.

My hands are trapped between my body and the wet, frozen frame of the car. His legs are bracketing mine. My breath is shallow and short, coming in quick bursts. The frigid air passing through my lips makes the split throb harder.

"Please," I cry out, my plea muffled and faint.

"Please?" he mocks. "That's what you have to say for yourself after you destroyed my goddamned life?" His laugh is cruel, chilling to the bone. Hot tears intermingle with the crimson rivulets still spilling down my chin and pooling on my chest.

Stars explode behind my eyelids as he smashes my head against the car once more. The pain registers a second later. My vision swims and nausea burns through my stomach and up my throat. My knees give out, but I don't crumple to the floor. He keeps me upright by my hair, my nose smashed against the uncaring window.

My head feels a thousand tons heavy, the hurt unbearable, the pain too much. Adrenaline floods my veins, warring with the numbness brought on by the resigned helplessness that has me frozen in its claws.

"You're not so high and mighty right now, are you?" Henry chuckles, bashing my head against the car repeatedly. "Poor little abandoned Siah, flapping about like a ratty ragdoll."

Darkness swims at the edge of my vision, his words slurred, as if I'm threading through water, only coming out at the surface to be dragged back into the violent depths.

He grounds his hips against my back, his erection prodding between my ass cheeks. This time there's no stopping the nausea. The swirling in my stomach intensifies, the burn eviscerating any semblance of control, and bile shoots out my nostrils and mouth, dripping down my chin. The sour, acrid smell has me dry heaving. My lungs constrict between Henry's hold on me and the pressure inside my body that doesn't cease to grow, consuming me whole.

His booming laughter echoes through the deserted parking lot. I sag against the car frame, my nails digging deep into the paintwork. I open my mouth to scream—for help, for August, for anything and nothing at all, but all I achieve is choking on my own blood and bile. There are no sounds coming from me, except for frightened whimpers and ragged breaths.

"You're going to get your phone, and you're going to message whoever you need to message and tell them to leave me alone. Then, you'll send another one, explaining how you've decided to get committed because the voices in your head got to be too much. A public apology to me will sweeten how your next days are going to go, you dirty cunt." He thrusts his hips against me again.

Who is this person? This demented, unhinged version of Henry I never got to see or experience before. Defeat overwhelms me. He's lost his ever-loving mind. I can practically feel my time draining through my fingers. I know without a shadow of a doubt that once he's done with me, he'll kill me. And until then, I'll wish he'd kill me.

He pulls my head back savagely, my neck bending almost to an unnatural angle. He looks down at me, his nostril flaring, his pupils blown. His knuckles caress the edge of my jaw affectionately, almost caring. My heart hammers in my chest, every single muscle in my body trembling uncontrollably.

"You were supposed to be my perfect wife, grateful and docile, willing and warm. I would have mourned you so beautifully, blaming myself when you finally succumbed to the demons of your mind. Instead, you destroyed me." I push on my tippy toes, trying to alleviate the burn in my scalp and the crick in my neck that leaves me breathless. "What do you know of my skills to expose me for malpractice, Siah? Why the fuck did you have to go there? I was willing to let you go, lose all the money I got for marrying you, and that's how you repay me?"

My head is swimming. His words don't make any sense. "I d-didn't do an'thing," I gurgle. Fresh blood pours down my cheek, my bottom lip swollen and heavy. Even my tongue feels heavy and numb in my mouth.

It's only what remains of my self-preservation instinct that has me move my palms in front of my body as he pushes me to the ground. The unforgiving, cold cement scrapes at my knees, bolts of electricity traveling through my bones, as I curl into a tight ball just in time for my shins to connect with his boots.

My throat unlocks, and a blood-curdling scream, so raw, so gritty that it scratches at the soft tissues of my vocal cords, rushes out of me, echoing through the deserted parking lot.

I'm not fast enough to protect my head. Agonizing pain explodes in my temple in the next second, seizing my whole body, and the night swallows me whole.

Chapter Thirty-Nine

SIAH

"Oh my god, oh my god, oh my god!"

Everything hurts. Cold, frozen water pours incessantly over me. I'm blind. I'm swimming in darkness, bound tightly in ropes and ropes of hurt. My entire body is one giant bruise. I can't move.

"Siah, babe, oh my god. What happened to you?"

I'm lost to the shadows, floating underneath the surface. The abyss is calling to me. Sweet, sweet numbness tingles under my skin, the promise of peace too decadent to ignore.

"Fucking do something!" A wail slashes through my just-out-of-reach heaven.

No. Come back.

Wings sprout from my back, the unused muscles twitching and contracting under the unfamiliar weight. I'm free. Free to fly, free to run, free to die. *Finally.*

A furious rumble rushes through my body. *I have a body?* Pulses of pain and agony stab at my head, and chest, and legs, yanking me cruelly back to earth.

"Are you soft in the head? What do you mean you're taking her home? She's fucking bleeding, you moron."

Let me bleed. Let me shed my empty shell and be free. I'm so tired. There's nothing for me here anymore. I strain, willing my wings to spread wide and mighty and carry me away from my torturous prison. I long for the light and its healing warmth. But the shadows clutch me again, cold seeping into my aching bones. I have no strength left to spare.

"I'm not leaving her alone. I'm staying right fucking here. Dare to touch me, motherfucker, see what happens."

I'm grounded. Pinned to soft, silky grass, gravity an unbearable force tying me into place. I can't move. Sparks fire up in my chest, my heart sputtering and stalling. *Stop, stop, stop.*

Rainbows are dancing behind my sealed-shut eyelids. A bright beam of light sears my pupils. *Let me in.*

"Where is he? I know you know more than you're letting on. Both you and August think I'm stupid. Where is he?"

Murmurs and whispers darken my sky. A thunderstorm is brewing on the horizon. I've been asleep for so long. I long to sleep for much, much longer. Exhaustion slashes at my skin as tendrils of awareness slap at my face.

"Her nose is badly bruised, but not broken. It will take the better part of a month for the bruising to recede. Her lip will heal on its own, but it will hurt for a good while. I'd recommend soft foods for the next two weeks—soups, smoothies—and using a straw as much as possible. I cleaned up her scrapes. They look worse than they actually are. Her leg is not broken, but she'll be in pain for a good while. It's best she doesn't put any weight on it for at least one week. Lastly, I'm worried about her concussion."

I'm worried, too.

Cool bliss settles over my forehead. I try to shift, but pain seizes my lungs, holding me tightly in its merciless grip. A soft blanket covers me, just gentle enough to not scrape at my burning, itchy skin.

"Mmm 'lo," I moan, my throat dried out and scratchy, my lips unwilling to obey my command.

"There she is," Jayme gasps, her low voice hitting my eardrums with the power of a church bell, if I were sitting between the brass walls during mass.

I hiss, but it comes out more like a strangled cry. "I'm sorry, I'm sorry," she whispers now. "Can you open your eyes for me?"

My eyelids feel sewn shut, so gritty and heavy, but I try. The glue holding them together slowly peels off and bright light assaults my retina. I scrunch them shut as pain stabs at the back of my head. Which is a bad idea, because my face doesn't feel in a better shape either.

"I'm fucking this up." More whispers. "Give me a second." Some shuffling, low curses, and a muffled thump reach my sensitive ears. "You can try again now."

I respectfully disagree. My whole body is bracing as I expect the onslaught of pain to stab into me again. The blurred, darkened walls of the bedroom greet me instead. My arm twitches, and I untuck it from underneath the blanket to rub at my eyes, but Jayme catches my wrist and stops me.

"Fuck me, you look like a vampire," the blurry image of my best friend whispers from above me.

A smile tugs at my mouth—another bad idea, as my bottom lip throbs and pulses and burns. "W-well you..." and that's all I manage to get out as a deep cough wracks my throat, and all the aches and pains and stabs return with a vengeance.

"Hush, babe. Don't speak." A paper straw is placed against my lip, and I involuntarily wince when the feather-soft touch feels like a punch against the raw mess. "Have some water. Small sips, okay?"

The room temperature liquid feels like absolute heaven in my parched mouth. It takes everything in me to remain patient and sip carefully instead of gulping the glass whole like my throat is begging me to.

Jayme smiles at me. Her warm brown eyes, crinkling with worry, dart to the door, then back to me. "Do you remember what happened last night?"

Tears well in mine as fear blossoms unbridled in my stomach. Rapid images of Henry's cruelty flash in my mind, his vile and vicious words a symphony on repeat in my ears. I close my eyes and turn my face away from my friend, nodding slowly.

"Okay, okay. You don't have to say anything. I'm here for you. Don't think of anything, just heal."

The weight of her palm against my forearm is comforting. I force my eyes open again. I need to look at her as I ask the next question. With a deep breath, I gather what remains of my waning strength.

"Aug...?"

Her frown tells me everything I need to know. The sharp shake of her head only drives the knife home.

She hasn't heard from him.
He's not here.
And I have no strength left.

Chapter Forty

Him

I kick my legs up onto the ratty table, crossing them at the ankle. I turn the volume up on the TV, to cover the pained groans behind me as my dart flies true and hits bullseye.

"Shhhh!" I hiss. "Don't you want to hear the late-night Breaking News? I thought a man as worldly as you would be interested in the happenings of the world."

My arm screams bloody murder when I casually interlock my fingers behind my head. I'll be fucking damned if my face shows even the slightest bit of discomfort. My stitches are probably ripped to shreds, but that's the hazard of the job. I'll find a poor sap to fix 'em right up.

On the TV, a yellow banner with black bolded letters runs the news of the day in a loop. "Acclaimed lawyer, James St. Andrew, arrested." Under the banner, images of a sprawling mansion with manicured lawns are shown, zooming in on a red-faced James. His head is down, and his hands are cuffed behind his back as he's being escorted to a police car.

I slap the flat of the knife against my tight and tip my chin toward the TV. "You really ought to choose better friends," I say congenially. As if at any second he'll walk out of here and go for a drink with his buddies.

The sound of his garbled laugh itches under my skin. He'll cry soon enough. I'll make sure of it.

"Did you enjoy watching all those videos of me fucking that whore? Tell me the truth, August, did you rub one off seeing her choke on my cock?"

I don't have to turn around and look at him to know my pocketknife flies true, while my right hand tightens around the wooden handle of my butcher blade. His yelp is music to my ears. And it didn't even draw blood.

Okay, I'm lying. My blade *for sure* drew a little blood. A nick, really, nothing more.

"You'd have to have a cock for her to choke on it." I lean my head back, just for funsies. He looks... idyllic, suspended as he is in bloody ropes and rusty chains. "See, I'm starting to feel like Jack The Ripper. He, too, was gutting prostitutes. Because that's what you are, isn't it, a prostitute?" I give him a wink, out of the goodness of my heart, of course. We're just two ole' pals, catching up on the good times. He opens his filthy mouth to protest, I'm sure, but my hand is faster. My dart flies just past his cheek. Well, that's disappointing.

"Nuh-ah-ah. My turn to talk. But then again, it might not make a lot of sense to you. Since my father paid you to remain married to Siah, yet she divorced your sorry ass less than a year later. Oh, don't give me that look." My forefinger wiggles playfully. Even on death's brink, the asshole still finds it in him to feel offended. "I'm well aware it was *you* filing for divorce. You know, for a doctor, you really *are* stupid. Did your arrogance eat all your remaining brain cells?" Shit, I really need to stand up. Blood rushing to my head when I'm still healing from a gunshot wound is really not conductive for business. "I wonder, if I carve you up like the filthy pig you are, what would I find inside?"

"You're a sick fuck!" he spits.

I've got to give it to him, his balls are bigger than his brain. Or he actually believes he's walking out of here. Either way, it doesn't do him any good. I lean forward and grab another dart from the table. My head swims for a second as my blood rushes away from where it all pooled around my forehead. There's something to it, though, because this time I don't miss. His high-pitched cry could put any coloratura soprano to shame as the tungsten tip buries into his sack.

"Sure am," I reply cheerfully. "But I'm a free sick fuck. You, on the other hand..." I flip the knife in the air, snatching the handle mid-flip, my eyes glued to the TV.

The police took their sweet fucking time to arrest James. I wonder how long would have taken for attempted murder. At least, the news stations were faster to expose his filthy exploits. His face has been blasted on the news for the past two days, while I was busy patching myself up.

Father Dearest deserves worse than public humiliation; much, much worse. But hindsight is twenty-twenty. His cowardice delayed me. And that delay got my mockingbird hurt.

"You're not going to get away with this!" he screams.

Fresh anger ignites my blood, and in the next second I'm on my feet, the rough wooden handle biting into the raw skin of my palm. The coarse fiber rope screeches when it slides against the metal pole as he flails about futilely.

My smile is pure malice. I let him read on my face all the nicely cruel things I'm about to do to him. Pain reverberates through my knuckles, pooling in the unhealed gunshot in my shoulder, when my fist connects with his nose. Blood explodes anew through his nostrils, and his eyes roll to the back of his head.

I welcome the hurt.

My fingers fist in his short hair as I tip his head down, making sure the asshole chokes on his fucking blood, the same way my mockingbird did less than five hours ago.

The rope around his wrists draws taut when his knees stop supporting him. The sickening pop of the humerus as it slides out of the shoulder socket is drowned out by anguished screams. I release my hold on his hair and take a step back, admiring the admittedly painful swing as he hangs from his wrists, the tip of his toes dragging across the floor.

Dejected, I sigh and wag my fingers in his face. "Now, why did you do that for? Didn't I tell you shoulder dislocation is exactly what would happen? You're a fucking doctor, Henry. You should know better."

With a put-out shake of my head, I walk to the far wall and, with one clean slash of the knife, slice loose the rope holding him up. Just as well... Much to my chagrin, I can't take from him every minute of terror he inflicted on Siah. If it were up to me, I'd keep him here for months on end, stripping everything from him, his skin, the meat from his bones, bit by bit, until the agony would've been too much, and his corrupted black heart would've given out. Alas, I can't do that.

I might have been blind with rage when I found him looming over her in that goddamn parking lot, but Elijah made sure some semblance of sense got through the thick, red fury possessing me. I'm no good to her locked up.

She needs to be protected. She needs to be cherished. She needs to be loved.

I can't fucking do that if I'm sharing a cell with Father Dearest.

So my rage has to settle with only inflicting wounds that can be masked by a nice purifying fire. After all, all demons burn in hell. Henry's no fucking different.

My smartwatch vibrates on my wrist. I wipe the sheen of foul blood from the screen on my jeans.

> She's awake and asking for you. Where the fuck are you?

Unknown Number

I look in disdain at the crumpled asshole shivering on the wet, dirty floor. It was clean some time ago, but, as it turns out, even the foulest of what this earth has to offer bleeds and pisses the same as any other human.

The sole of my boot presses into the bruised side of his face, his swollen lips touching the floor. He gags and dry heaves, trying to move away, but I press harder. They're only his bodily fluids, after all.

The depraved asshole laughed while Siah was choking on her own vomit. He can choke on everything he produces now.

His body convulses, trying to break free of my hold. He didn't have a chance when he had use of his arms. Now, all he's accomplishing is flailing about like a fish on dry land. Pathetic, disgusting, waste of fucking air cunt, I wouldn't even use him for compost. I bet all those pretty flowers in Helena's garden would just up and wilt instantly.

Henry Cavanaugh is a goddamn sentient poison.

And poisons need to be neutralized.

I touch the screen of my watch, leaving behind a bloodied fingerprint. Fuck me, I need to burn my clothes, my darts, and my watch just to get rid of his stench. Not a single fucking cell of this motherfucker needs to exist in the world.

> ETA - 45 mins. Celebrate with fireworks. Go big! Then go home.

Me

"Please," he sobs, giving up the fight, his body growing lax under my foot.

"Quiet!" I bark. The quicker I deal with him, the quicker I can be at Siah's side. "I can't fucking stand to look at you. If she ever finds out the truth, if she ever finds out why you married her, it will destroy her. You're a filthy parasite."

It's not just revulsion I feel. I'm drunk on guilt and rage.

There's only one reason Siah Hadley lays in my bedroom bloodied and battered right now. There's only one reason my exquisite little mockingbird ever came across the rotten piece of shit at my feet. There's only one reason James St. Andrew has his vile eyes on her.

And that reason is me.

My infatuation, my obsession, my arrogance.

I'll never live long enough to earn her forgiveness. But I'll sure as fuck crawl at her feet each day until our very last.

Chapter Forty-One

SIAH

I come to with a start as the bed dips and a heated weight settles across my stomach and my good leg. My heart instantly pounds against my ribcage and goosebumps sprout on my skin. A painful groan spills past my busted lip as I blindly reach with my bruised arm, and my fingers tangle in wet, silken hair. My blood rushes through my ears, the frenzied drumming of my heart all I can hear in the darkness of the night.

He's shaking so badly the whole bed vibrates with him, rattling my battered bones. What feels like steel encased in velvet coils around my waist, and I whimper pitifully as I shift under him.

He's back.

But my hands aren't weighed down by chains. Nor is there a collar around my neck. I can't smell anything but the congealed blood in my nostrils. He squeezes me tighter, his thumb lovingly brushing on the exposed patch of skin on my hip, where my T-shirt twisted up in my sleep.

I blink through my fear, but I still can't see anything except for his hulking, shadowed form draped over my lower body.

"I'm sorry," he whispers, pure, unadulterated regret coating his words.

"August?" I croak as my stomach flips and tingles. A sob burns up my throat, and I can't keep it contained. Hope blossoms in my chest as every single muscle in my body relaxes.

The trauma of the past day sure did a number on me if I stooped so low as to mistaken August for *him.*

"I'm so, so sorry, baby! I should've been here. Please, forgive me."

I curl my fingers in his damp hair and pull—with as much force as a baby carrot, I'm sure. But he reads my gesture for what it is and pushes up on his hands and knees, crawling up the bed until his shadow covers me from head to toe.

My sleep-addled concussed brain plays tricks on me, because the obscure man in front of my eyes is both August and *him*. The loving, protective touch of the man I'm falling in love with has sparks of electricity crackling beneath my skin. The current of danger, adrenaline, with a touch of forbidden of the man who haunts my dreams has my heart racing and my blood pressure spiking.

I tug at his hair, to pull him closer or push him away, I've no idea what I'm doing. My head is swimming, a dull pounding starting just beneath my forehead. I close my eyes, my hand trailing down his shoulder and over his corded biceps as he lowers in a push-up, gently touching his mouth to mine.

His choppy breath fans over my face and his lips part. Tenderly, his tongue delicately traces my busted lip as tears spring from my eyes at the gentleness of his touch. I gasp as a memory slams into me, of my tongue lapping at a busted lip and the blood smeared all over my mouth.

No. I'm going crazy.

Henry must have rattled loose something in my brain.

August must feel me stiffening under him and, with a regretful sigh, moves away from me, kissing the tip of my nose in passing. He settles his massive frame around my body, surrounding me with his strength and warmth.

His palm rests over my belly, the move both affectionate and possessive.

"Sleep now, baby," he whispers, his voice all choked-out and gravelly. And worse... all *him*.

I feel like I've been run over by a truck. Repeatedly. And then it backed over me some ten thousand times for good measure. I yawn and flinch when the simple gesture of opening my mouth has my lip splitting open again and my nose throbbing as if a hammer is continuously boinking me in the forehead.

The furnace I curled around in my sleep is hot and heavy and... *Wait, what?*

I blink my eyes open, the low daylight sending bolts of pain through my protesting eyeballs. "Holy fucking eclipse, someone turn that sun down," I rasp, my throat dried out and scratchy.

A raspy, woven with sleep chuckle breaks the silence of the morning. The heated bare chest pressed to my back vibrates with the low sounds. Soft lips touch my nape, sending tendrils of desire in my lower belly and making me squirm. He shuffles behind me, his hard cock pressing into my ass. A brief flash of a memory from the other night plays behind my eyelids, when a different man pressed into me. My body had a completely different reaction then.

My cheeks burn with humiliation as I taste bile in my mouth, remembering how I vomited all over myself and Henry just... laughed and made it hurt even more. My skin starts itching and singeing. A harsh demand to get under the hottest shower and bleach his disgusting touch from my skin rises in my chest.

With impossible gentleness, August curls his fingers around my biceps and rolls me to my back, looming over me in a lightning-fast move. My eyes burn, bitter tears gathering at the corners. His look murderous instead. The navy-blue of his irises is nearly taken over by the fathomless darkness of his pupils. His lush mouth is pulled in a taut line. His jaw clenches so hard, it looks like granite about to crack.

My arm screams bloody murder when I lift it to cradle his cheek and run my thumb through the prickly scruff adorning his skin. "That bad, huh?" I gulp, trying to dislodge the swirling mass of emotion stuck in my throat.

He squeezes his eyes closed. Anguish, agony, and heartache are etched deep in every line and contour of his face. He lowers his head and kisses what I presume to be an untouched patch of skin on my forehead. "You look beautiful, you always do," he murmurs.

I slap at his shoulder, hissing, "Liar," since I could see my reflection and the motley of bruises and swollen flesh disfiguring me in his eyes, but I'm soon distracted by... I touch his shoulder again and rub my fingers together. My stomach flips. Pure liquid nitrogen rushes through my veins, freezing me from the inside out. I don't dare look at my palm and confirm what my touch is telling me. "Is... is that blood?"

August jumps so fast out of bed, the blanket tangles around his strong legs as he lands on a crouch on the floor. "Shit!" he mutters. "Those fucking stitches."

I forget all about my battered body as I move to a sitting position. My head swims and my vision rolls, the image of August still crouching next to the bed with blood trailing down his massive shoulder moving in and out of focus.

"Lay back down," he barks, and I wince, scrunching my eyes shut, the power behind his voice amplifying my headache. Tender fingers grip my chin, soft lips touch to mine once, twice. "Lay down, baby. I'll clean up, and we'll talk after."

I let the cloud-like pillow cradle my head and my back, my thoughts racing in all different directions. *What the hell did he get into?* I can hear him padding to the bathroom, a door opening and closing, then the shower turning on. My skin bristles as the same feeling of being unclean and soiled unfurls in my chest. I could definitely use a shower myself.

Another door opens, and my eyelids spring open, blurriness and vertigo be damned. Jayme stares at me as she walks closer to the bed.

"Morning, Dracula." She winks, tossing her heavy mane of red hair behind her shoulder as she takes a seat at the edge of the bed. Despite the joke, she's subdued, so unlike her normal exuberance. She takes my hand and gives me a brief squeeze.

I open my mouth to greet her, but she releases my hand as if burned and jumps to her feet. "Is the shower running?"

Oh, shit!

"Uhm… about that," I croak and clear my throat to dislodge the lump residing there at the same time as she starts for the bathroom.

"Ouch, fuck," she curses as she trips over something on the floor. She bends down and picks whatever she tripped on up, turning to face me with wide eyes and jaw slack. "What's this?"

Blood rushes to my cheeks, and every bruise on my face starts pulsing under the onslaught as my eyes burn a hole in the distinctively masculine black hoodie and dark-wash jeans she's holding.

The door to the bathroom opens and, in a mantle of steam, with only a flimsy towel around his narrow hips, August steps out. If he's surprised to see Jayme here, he doesn't show it. Instead, he walks past her, kisses the top of her head, and plucks the clothes from her hands. "Picking after me again, sis?" he teases her before disappearing inside the walk-in closet.

Jayme is completely frozen in the middle of the room. I would've laughed if I weren't mortified to the point of wishing my bed would swallow me whole, never to be seen again.

"Jay?"

Her nose scrunches, her brow furrows, and then big ugly sobs rip out of her. Rivulets of tears are trekking down her cheeks as she plops down, hugging her knees to her chest.

"Oh my god, Jay!" I scramble off the bed, every bone and muscle in me protesting the abrupt movement. What feels like a thousand knives stab through my calf as I put weight on the leg Henry kicked at just the other night. Half limping, half crawling, I make my way to her and throw my arms around her shaking shoulders. "It's okay, it's okay," I whisper as we rock in place.

She sniffles and wipes her face with the back of her palm, dragging in deep gulps of air. I sit on the floor next to her, running my fingers through her hair as I give her the time and space to put herself back together and voice her thoughts once she's processed her feelings.

"Too much," she whispers, her voice cracking. I hum in response and rub calming circles on her hunched back. "You got hurt. August was nowhere to be found until he magically appeared in your bathroom. My mom calling me in tears because my stepfather's been arrested. It's too much, all at once."

I don't get to ask more questions about her stepfather when August walks back into the room. Wearing a pair of dark sweatpants and a black T-shirt that looks painted on him, he scowls at me like I personally offended all his ancestors. "What the fuck are you doing out of bed?"

I scowl right back, then immediately regret all my life choices when pain hits me square in the face, as if I took a sledgehammer to it. He sighs and, through the stars that explode in front of my eyes, I see him trail his fingers through his still wet hair, then pluck me off the floor and cradle me to his chest.

"I'll get back for you," he tells Jayme, then pins those bottomless midnight-blue eyes on me. "You have a concussion; you don't move out of here without the doctor giving you the all clear."

My response is a minute nod. I can't argue when my brain feels too big for my skull, the increasing pressure making it hard to breathe. He settles me down onto the soft pillows, tucking me into the blanket.

I hear only soft whispers and muffled shuffling as he helps Jayme up and, together, they walk out the room. The door closes resolutely on whatever they are discussing.

My body grows lax, all the excitement of the morning draining my energy far quicker than I expected. I close my eyes and allow myself to fall asleep once more, even though a thousand and one questions race through my mind.

Why was James arrested?

Why is August bleeding?

With one question, standing out against all others...

Why, even in the light of the day, I still feel that August is him?

Chapter Forty-Two

SIAH

The past three days have been... weird. August has taken upon himself to nurse me back to health. While I don't mind having him dot on me like I'm precious to him, I can't shake the niggling feeling in the center of my chest that something is not quite right.

Jayme barely said a word to me before she left for her apartment to pack. She had to postpone her work trip for a couple of days as she made sure I was on the mend and her mom was okay. August took care of Helena, from the little I have gathered when he spoke on the phone while he thought I was sleeping.

I couldn't check anything myself as the doctor gave me a seventy-two-hour ban from any electronics with a screen—phone, TV, laptop, my Kindle. So I had to be satisfied with the bare bones of information I got by eavesdropping. Whenever I ask August how he got hurt or what happened to his father, all he does is kiss my forehead and order me to focus on getting better and resting.

Today, my ban ended. So, as soon as August fed me breakfast and disappeared on the third floor to do whatever it is he does, I tiptoed down to the living room and made myself comfortable on the sofa. The boredom is eating me alive. If I have to stare at those gray walls for one more second, I'm liable to break something.

Sure, I am panting like a dog in heat from the effort of limping down the stairs and crawling to the couch, but I got there eventually.

I'm flipping through the channels like it's an Olympic sport and I'm going for gold, when a headline makes me stop dead in my tracks. Henry's picture is plastered across half the screen, his warm smile—so unlike the cruelty marring his features the last time I saw him—front and center. In a daze, I turn the volume up.

"...killed in a horrific accident in the early hours of the morning. According to initial reports, Dr. Cavanaugh was driving home from an unknown yet location when he swerved off the road. His vehicle collided head-on with a tree at high speed, resulting in a catastrophic explosion upon impact. Emergency services were notified by a passer-by and were quick to arrive at the scene. Unfortunately, nothing could be done to save the life of the highly respected Dr. Cavanaugh."

My eyes are glued to the screen showing the EMTs hurrying on the wet road, an ominous-looking black bag laid across a stretcher. My stomach churns and bile pools in my mouth. "What the fuck?" I whisper into my palms. An eerie chill spreads from my toes to the very tip of my nose, my whole body growing numb. "How... why... how?"

"Drivers are advised to proceed with caution as two northbound lanes remain closed for now. Black ice has been reported on long stretches of the highway. Congestions are likely to be expected throughout the day," the reporter continues as if she hadn't just earthquaked the entire foundation of my world.

Henry is dead.

My ex-husband, the man who assaulted me just days ago, is dead.

The hollow pit in the center of my chest expands, rooting me into place. I've tried not to think about him once my mind cleared after that night. Thinking about him and what he did to me would've only led to nightmares. My sleep is poor enough with my whole body being one giant bruise, I don't need the added stress.

My eyes start burning, and it's only then I realize I haven't blinked once since I saw the news. I turned to stone instead, right here in the living room.

Dead men cannot pay their debts.

Henry died like a reckless coward, still owing me.

He took from me, terrified me, left me powerless and helpless, and then he went and died, leaving me with more questions than answers. My stomach flips and contracts and, before I know what I'm doing, I bend over the edge of the couch, vomiting everything I had for breakfast this morning, bitter bile stinging the still healing cut in my lip.

A mantle of cold settles over my shoulders, so frigid, so cruel, even my bones are trembling. With a shaky hand, I wipe my mouth on my sleeve as I choke on a sob. I lower my forehead to my knees, trying to keep myself together, trying to keep myself whole.

"There you are." August's voice comes faintly from behind me. "I panicked for a second when I didn't find you in the bedroom." He chuckles, but his words barely register, as if I am underwater, sinking, drowning, disappearing.

"Shit!" A warm hand grips my shoulder. "What happened?" A squeeze—more like an anchor weighing me down—of his long fingers as he tries to gain my attention has me jolting, shying away from his touch.

"Siah, baby," he sighs, "let's get you cleaned up."

I don't answer. I can't. The water is pressing down against my chest, clogging my airways, burning through my nostrils and esophagus.

The voice of the news anchor suddenly cuts off. Silence, the sputtering thump of my heart, and the slosh of the mop against the hardwood floor are the only sounds in the room. I slump against the buttery leather of the backrest, making myself as small as my body can get, burrowing deeper under my blanket as I seek a tendril of warmth.

"You're scaring the fuck out of me, baby," August says. The cushion dips behind me, then blessed heat envelops me as he curls around my tight-as-a-ball body. "Tell me what you need."

I need what I can't have. I need Henry to look me in the eye and apologize for what he took from me. I need...

"Answers," I whisper, the one word broken and gravelly.

He shifts closers around me, his arms encircling my waist as he pulls me to his chest. A second later, I'm airborne. He tucks my head beneath his chin and walks me to the second floor in slow, careful steps. A surprised moan escapes me as the cold counter touches the back of my thighs. He grips my chin and tilts my head back, midnight-blue eyes assessing mine.

I shiver as I meet the strangeness in his gaze, that dead but all-consuming look both drawing me in and pulling me away. A glass of water breaks our eye contact, but the foreboding thread strangling my spine like a vise doesn't leave me. My fingers curl around the glass, and I take greedy gulps of water, rinsing my mouth, then spitting the foul taste of bile into the porcelain sink.

A brush and toothpaste are next. Mechanically, I clean my teeth, my eyes fixating somewhere on August's shoulder. August's shoulder that was bleeding profusely just days ago, and I still don't know why. What do I actually know about August St. Andrew?

He distracts me from my spiraling thoughts as he helps me rinse my mouth once again, then pats gently around my busted lip with a clean towel. His arms go around me, his steps sure as he heads toward the bed. "No." I pull at the collar of his T-shirt. "No. I've had enough of this room."

He stops abruptly, his hold on me tightening. "Okay," August drawls. "Where do you want to sit then?"

"In the backyard." I crave fresh air, and space, and... distance. I need him not to touch me and answer some questions instead. It's easy to lose myself into everything August is, but as startling clarity settles inside of me amidst the storm of grief, and guilt, and confusion, I'm starting to see that August might not be who he presents himself to be.

His heart is pounding beneath my ear. Maybe he realizes too that this time he can't shy away from us having an actual talk.

"You're impatient," he murmurs as he bounds downstairs with me in tow, grabbing a couple of waterproof blankets from a linen closet when we near the back door. "I need you to get better, Siah. The answers you're looking for aren't gonna help you heal. You're not ready."

Frozen air prickles at my skin as soon as he opens the door, my breath fogging instantly. "Do you think I want to be this helpless?" There's no hiding the bitterness in my voice. "I hate relying on you. If there's ever a choice between knowing and not knowing, even if being kept in the dark means mercy, I'll take the cruelty of the truth."

"You didn't want to know about your parents," he observes, and I immediately bristle.

Huffing a breath that blurs my view of the cloudy sky and gloomy forest around us, I say, "Because I already know the truth, August. Regardless of the circumstances, I was left on a bench in a goddamn park. If they loved me and couldn't keep me, if they loved me but were forced to abandon me, or if they didn't want me at all, I still ended up on that bench. *That* is the truth."

He hums deep in his chest as he lowers me on a wicker armchair, wrapping me tightly inside the blanket. The bite of the frozen air feels good against my throbbing face. The pressure around my eyes and forehead has lessened considerably in the past few days, even if my face still looks like I went ten rounds with a heavyweight champion and ended each of them with a KO.

The wooden pergola he has taken us to is masterfully crafted, with harsh twisted carvings in rough weathered wood. August fidgets with a heater attached to the vaulted ceiling, rubbing his palms in relief when flames come to life from a chained chandelier-like metal enclosure.

"What happened to you?"

The scrape of the wicker armchair next to mine stalls for a heartbeat. He slumps into it, the cushion creaking under August's weight as he spreads his knees and folds his arms across his chest. I can see the goosebumps on his veiny forearms, the fine dark hairs standing on end.

I avert my eyes and study instead the line of evergreens swaying in the wind just twenty feet in front of me. Maybe we'll both find it easier to talk with no eye contact.

He sighs and shifts some more. "James shot me."

I recoil in my chair and close my eyes tightly. The pain seizing my chest is unbearable. "Excuse me?"

"I got shot," he repeats gruffly, a hint of annoyance in his tone. "Would you look at me?"

I shake my head. "I can't."

"Siah, for god's sake, fucking look at me," he grits, his voice wrapping around me, snapping my neck in his direction. The force of his words presses against me, compelling me to open my eyes. His elbows are now on his knees. His eyes, cold and serious, are trained on me.

"How... when?" My tears are hot as they pour down my cheeks. I don't bother wiping them away since I know the torrent will not stop anytime soon. His whole body twitches as if it takes superhuman strength for him to remain seated.

"The day before Jay's birthday. Is why I didn't answer my phone and why I was late meeting you at the bar." His mouth curls down, his lips white he's clenching his jaw so hard. "One more sin on my father's filthy list of depravities."

I cover my mouth with my palm. "No," I breathe. "Is that... is that why...?"

His head tilts ever so slightly, the denial firm in the fathomless depths of his irises. "No. No one else knows except Helena, the doctor friend who patched me up, and... now you."

"Did you at least go to the hospital?"

August jumps to his feet, pacing the small space of the pergola. His laughter is chilling, colder than the air outside. "All gunshot wounds have to be reported to the police by hospital personnel, Siah. What do you think?"

Fear unlike anything else I've felt before seizes my lungs. Oxygen is hard to come by. I claw at the blanket strangling me as my body trembles and convulses.

"Fuck." The sickening crack of wood breaking barely registers as I scratch at my neck, desperate for a scrape of air, frantic in my attempts to resurface.

Warmth washes over my face, suffocating, cloying. I can't breathe.

"I'm fine."

White spots dance in front of my eyes, stained with crimson blood pouring out of August's shoulder.

"Siah, goddammit, I'm fine. It was just a graze."

The blanket finally gives way, and my erratic attempts at escape have me falling to my knees on the tiled, cold floor. My fingernails claw at nothing as icy knives stab at my palms, the skin growing redder by the second. My throat unlocks as I scream at the black swirls trapped forever in the marble. "LIAR! You're fucking lying to me right now!"

My head swims. He could've been gone. August could've died just like Henry did, and I would've been none the wiser. I went about my merry fucking day as he had a bullet inside of him. And now he gets to stand in front of me and act like it's no big deal?

My stomach heaves, but nothing comes out. I choke on nothing but pure adrenaline and terror.

I had to say I'd take cruelty. What the fuck do I know?

"You're not ready to know, little mockingbird."

Chapter Forty-Three

SIAH

Rough fingers wrap around my hair, pulling me to my knees. The burn in my scalp and the protest of the bruises that have barely begun to heal is enough to snap me out of my spiraling hysteria.

August is standing tall in front of me, his whole body shaking—anger, fear, and apprehension carved into the harsh lines of his jaw. Despite of the aggressiveness pouring in waves out of him, his words are low and soft as he murmurs to me, "That's it, baby. Look at me. Keep those beautiful eyes on me and me only."

Fresh tears spring in my eyes, the sting welcome and freeing. His fingers trail down my neck, wrapping around me like a vise. My throat bobs on a swallow as I dislodge the negativity and shock coating my tongue.

"Fuck," he grunts. "Do that again."

The frozen air around us charges with electricity. Heat pools between my thighs, and I rub them together, trying to alleviate the ache pulsing through my clit. *What is happening?*

August's eyes are pitch-black, his pupils blown wide, his nostrils flaring. Rage is still riding him hard. His neck is tense, dark blue veins accentuated by thick muscles, covered by tanned skin, and just on the too much side of a five o'clock shade.

"You drive me out of my goddamn mind," he says, tightening his hold on my hair. Between one hand collaring my neck and the other one fisting my curls, I'm at his mercy.

I've never seen him like this. A faint voice at the back of my head tells me I did. It screams at me that this is the true August St. Andrew. I've seen him many times like this in my nightmares, my dreams, and my barely awake moments when he'd made me his doll to play with as he pleased in the cover of the night. Until he decided to step out of the shadows and consume my days, too.

He sucks in a break and takes a step back, releasing my neck. "You're afraid of me."

The sting in my scalp increases as I shake my head, the burning sensation traveling down my spine, drenching my panties. "Yes," I confess. I swallow over nothing. "No," I deny in the same breath.

August forces me to my feet and up on my toes, which are getting numb from the frigid marble. "Which is it, baby?" His question is innocent, but the undercurrent of danger and threat in his tone wraps around me like a live wire, seizing me in its hold.

"Both," I whisper.

He crushes his mouth to mine, sucking forcefully at my bottom lip. The pain and surprise leave me breathless. A scream rips out of me when his teeth sink in my bruised lip—not enough to break skin, but enough for the split to open again. Mint, desire, and the metallic taste of blood flood my mouth.

My fingers curl in his T-shirt, pulling, pushing, demanding. His free hand finds my ass, cupping one cheek roughly, kneading, teasing, pinching. His cock is a steel pipe under the flimsy cotton of his sweatpants as he thrusts his hips against my belly.

"This is what you do to me," he grits in my mouth. "Drive me insane, dissolve every little bit of sanity I have left. I can't breathe, I can't think, I can't fucking exist when you're not around."

I drink in his words, let them poison me with his need. "August, please."

His hot greedy mouth trails my jaw, nips at my neck. Each brush of his lips, each lap of his tongue, each scrape of his teeth weakens my knees and makes my stomach flutter. Rabid butterflies ignite in my core as he finds my nipples through the fabric of my sweatshirt and bites down on the puckered bud.

"AUGUST!" I scream as liquid fire runs through my veins, exploding between my thighs.

"You keep pushing me away, baby. It does you no good. You'll learn, Siah, you're here to stay," he growls, ripping my sweatshirt over my head. My body is so overheated, I don't even care the temperature outside is in the low twenties. Despite the overhead heater, the wind howls all around us, whipping at my flesh in furious and merciless gusts. My nipples harden even more, the dusky ends turning red and achy.

His T-shirt follows the path of my sweatshirt, my eyes glued to the width of his shoulders, the bruised and crude stitching of the gunshot. My gaze moves lower to the rippling muscles of his chest. A smattering of hair darkens the expanse of his pecs, narrowing down in a smooth line, highlighting the valleys and peaks of his abdomen before it disappears under the elastic band of his sweats.

He slants his mouth over mine once more, his tongue plundering between my lips with unrestrained savagery. My face throbs, my bottom lip burns, yet I open up for him, welcoming his assault. Pained whimpers escape me, my breath shallow and strained.

My nails find purchase on his corded shoulders, holding on to dear life. His skin radiates heat, burning an imprint of his mark onto mine. My soft breasts are smashed against the stone his chest is carved out of, my belly rubbing against the undeniable hardness of his cock, fighting to reach me.

My leggings are the next to vanish in whatever place clothes disappear when the need is too much, the air too shallow, and time has lost all meaning. The cold bites, August soothes. My blood boils, August cools. I need him like I need my next heartbeat.

I don't know when I climbed him or when he wrapped my legs around his waist. My lungs seize and contract when my back hits a searing-cold wooden pillar. August cuts short our kiss, his eyes a whirlpool of desire, anguish, and threat. The shivers running like electricity through my veins have nothing to do with the freezing temperature, and everything with the hellish fire reflecting back at me from the darkness of his pupils.

The hand in my hair tightens its grip. I strangle his hips with my thighs when he releases the hold he has on my ass and shoves his sweatpants down, enough for his cock to spring free, bobbing against his abdomen. A flash of silver glints in the fading daylight. My back arches in a bow as August fills me to the brim in one harsh thrust.

He's too much and not enough all at once.

His head drops to the crook of my neck and, for one suspended moment in time, I feel everything. His strength, his control pulled taut just about to snap, the tension in his rock-hard muscles vibrating just beneath his skin, and the heat of his cock as he impales me between the wooden pillar and the brick wall of his chest.

My arms coil around his neck, threading through his damp hair. He releases mine, my curls falling free down my back. My scalp tingles as blood rushes back with a vengeance. Gently, suavely, he trails his fingers down my chest, thumbing my nipples, plucking and pinching until I'm a writhing mess, fucking myself on his cock in stuttered, uncontrolled jerks.

"Look how beautifully you respond to me," he groans, agony and bliss woven into each syllable. "Your body sings for me and me only."

"August," I moan as his hips push against me in response.

"You're never going to leave me, baby. I *am* yours and you are mine." A vow and a warning that send cruel thrills through my spine and make my pussy flutter around him. "You're so wet, so tight, so perfect for me."

All at once, his massive hands grip my hips, his fingers digging into my softness—unmovable, possessive, permanent—and he leans back, staring directly into my eyes. "There's no going back now, Siah." I cry out as he retreats painfully slow until only his thick head remains inside of me. "Take me, baby."

My head hits the back of the pillar, my shoulder blades rubbing painfully against the smooth polish as he fucks himself into me without mercy, his eyes never once leaving mine. Every nerve ending lights up as pain and pleasure, ecstasy and anguish, the end of the world and the start of madness, all swirl in my lower belly, growing, and growing, and growing with each frenzied thrust of his hips.

He's not fucking me. He's claiming me, owning me, possessing me, until there's nothing left of Siah Hadley.

August St. Andrew is branding my insides with his cock, recirculating my blood with his essence, and chaining me to him all at once.

He's not chasing my pleasure. He's not racing for his release.

He's rapidly, methodically, and without hesitation wiping me from existence and rewriting me as his.

My tits bounce, my shoulder blades burn, my thighs quiver as the crescendo reaches its apogee inside of me. I bow my back, the ends of my hair brushing against my ass, my eyelids fluttering closed.

"Eyes on me, Siah," August grunts, the order unmistakable ever through the haze of my impending orgasm. "Fucking see me. I'm the only one who fucks you. I'm the only one who feels this silken pussy choke the fuck out of my cock. I'm yours. Say it, Siah, say I'm yours."

He increases the punishing rhythm, and the world disappears from around me. All I see is body enveloping me. All I hear are his blissed-out groans and growls. All I feel is his thick, hard cock fucking me into oblivion.

"Oh fuck, August, I'm close," I cry out as he hits a particularly sensible spot inside of me that has my knees shaking and stars detonating in front of my eyes. He stills suddenly, pinning me between him and the cold pillar, lowering his head until his eyes consume me and his nose brushes against mine.

"SAY. IT. SIAH, and I'll let you come."

"You're mine, August. Let me have you."

My words are the catalyst for the animal in him to break through his cage and pounce free. His mouth is everything. His hands are everywhere. Inside and out, there's nothing left of me.

His thumb presses against my clit, his thrusts frenzied and out of control as his teeth sink into the delicate skin of my shoulder. Pain and fire collide inside of me, my pussy clamping down hard against his dick. My whole body seizes and contracts as my orgasm robs me of sanity and every one of my senses.

"August, oh god, yes, yes, you're mine, you're mine."

My head sags against the wooden column of the pergola, the frozen wind whipping through my curls. August wraps his arms around me, his body stiffening as he comes, my name ripping from his throat in an inhuman growl.

I rest my cheek against his shoulder as my pussy quivers through the aftershocks, dripping with our combined desires. My chest heaves, pushing against his. His heart beats so fast, so strong, I feel it between my lungs, replacing mine. August kisses the top of my head, his breath fluttering through my messy curls.

"I caught you, little mockingbird. And now you're mine, to have and to hold, until death do us apart," August murmurs, pure satisfaction and awe coloring his voice.

My soul just about leaves my body. The weight of his words rushes through me with the power of an avalanche, stealing my breath away. I open my mouth on a silent scream as terror seizes my throat. The world tilts sideways and then darkness swallows me whole.

Chapter Forty-Four

SIAH

I fist the silky sheets, a needy moan muffled by the pillow spilling past my lips. I hate my traitorous body. I hate that it responds so easily to his touch. I hate that I'm so used to his warmth, his strength, his passion.

The throbbing ache in my clit woke me up as he gripped my hips and stroked in and out of me lazily, tenderly. My moans and complete surrender accepted him even in my sleep. He's not hiding anymore. He has me, and he knows it. He holds whenever and however he wants.

"God, you feel so damn perfect." August shudders behind me, his pace quickening. My pussy convulses around him. My walls, slick with my arousal, clamp and release him, quivering with every maddening deep stroke. "You grip me so well. I'm gone for you. You hurt me so beautifully, little mockingbird."

My hips don't obey my wishes, but push back into him, the fire licking at my clit spreading through my body. His hand clamps around my calf, pushing my knee into the mattress, and then he surrounds me, pounding, driving his big, thick cock into me with abandon. I scream my release into the pillow as I detonate around him.

I scream my hate too, even if he doesn't know it.

"Fuck, Siah, fuck, you're gonna be the death of me, fuck," he groans his own release, his teeth scrapping my shoulder as he sags on top of me, his weight pressing me further against the mattress.

August kisses the back of my neck and down my spine, shifting to his knees behind me. I whimper and sigh as his cock, still half hard, slips out of me, his hot release dripping down my thighs and onto the rumpled sheets.

He bites each ass cheek in turn before dragging my hips up and shoving his tongue inside of me. Jolts of electricity quake my oversensitive flesh, a new wave of arousal spilling out of me. "You're fucking delicious. I'm starved for you," he murmurs, then buries his tongue in my pussy, feasting, licking, sucking, biting until I come a second time all over his face.

My eyes burn with the sting of betrayal and bliss.

He owns my body. He conquered my heart. There's so little left of me that doesn't bow down to him.

I let myself sag back inside the cover, evening my breaths despite my heart pounding so hard I'm sure he can hear it, and pretend to fall back asleep. He chuckles low in his throat, and my skin pebbles—because that's what my traitorous body does. My body is in love with August. He strokes my hair as he climbs off the bed. "Sleep, baby. You need to regain your strength."

He talks as if he cares. As if my well-being means something to him. August St. Andrew is a goddamn rotten liar and a despicable user of the worst caliber.

At least, my tears still belong to me as they slide bitterly down my cheeks and soak into the pillowcase. All this time... it was him. Following me, terrorizing me inside of my own home, forcing me into his, trapping me—this is his master plan, and I fell right into the cage he built for me.

He acts as if he didn't implode my world a week ago, like we're this couple in love and still getting to know one another. Like he hasn't stalked me for god knows how many years.

A sob crawls up my neck, and I stifle the pitiful sound in the pillow. He won't hear me through the pelting of the shower, but I don't know if his cameras are still working or if they're recording sounds, too.

God, at this point, he has numerous videos of us fucking in his bed, of me begging him, taking him, holding him. My stomach bottoms out, fear spreading through my limbs. He could release those any time he wants if I leave. He could release them anyway.

Does it even matter?

Not everyone watches revenge porn. And even if they do, my plan is to be as far away from people as possible. I'm done with everyone and everything. After finally finding out the truth, it's not like I'm going out there looking for a partner. My trust is in short supply, and August took a sledgehammer to the reserve and blew it to smithereens.

He's been keeping a close eye on me the whole week, never leaving the house, not going to the third floor until he thought I was asleep. Even then, I didn't dare move from the bed, knowing those fucking cameras were following my every move.

I'm biding my time, pretending right along with him that all is well in our gilded little cage. While my body needs no coaxing, craving his touch like an addict craves the next hit, I still have a small ember of survival instinct flickering inside of me.

And the first opportunity presenting itself, I'm taking and running with it.

He's been surprisingly indulging these past few days, allowing me to wallow and stare at the walls until my eyes are so dry it's painful to blink. It's morbidly funny to think it helps that so much has happened, his arrogance doesn't allow him to think my being withdrawn and quiet has anything to do with him.

In his self-centered mind, I'm traumatized after the beating Henry gave me. And I am. Henry haunts my most recent nightmares, in high competition with August. The burst blood vessels in my eyes still make me look like a vampire. The bruising around my face has faded from deep purple to sickly green mixed with blue centers and yellowed margins. I still can't put my full weight on my left leg, and the scrapes on my palms and knees are itching and sore. The headaches have lessened in intensity and frequency, but I still tire easily.

And this is just the physical aspect of it.

Mentally, I'm shattered. I've started taking my antidepressants and anti-anxiety medication again. I'm playing a waiting game of foul moods, crying bouts, and deep-rooted apathy as they work their way through my system, slowly stabilizing my brain's chemistry.

In August's mind, he's also thinking Henry's untimely death has taken a toll on me. Although, he's less understanding of that.

"The man was a vermin, Siah. He doesn't deserve to have you mourn for him."

I don't mourn Henry. The past months since our separation, through therapy and my introspection, I've learned quite a lot about our relationship. Henry never loved me. I don't know what possessed him to court me or to marry me. He love-bombed me at the start, swept me off my feet with the promise of stability and family, and then he controlled. I just didn't see it. He also planned to get rid of me, in cahoots with his psychiatrist friend—dope me up and have me committed.

Why? Fucked, if I know. His endgame? A goddamn mystery.

So I mourn his death. Because with him gone, so are my answers. So is my justice for all the fucked-up shit he did to me and for all the pieces of me he took and destroyed.

But it works for me.

As long as August thinks my recent trauma has me in its clutches and I'm still processing through it, he's giving me time to heal, at least physically. Mentally, I'm planning my exit strategy. All I need is him out of the house—thirty minutes to disappear.

The door opens, and I shift under the covers, faking a sleepy moan, stretching around the silken sheets. Groundhog day number nine begins. The heady aroma of scrambled eggs and bacon has my stomach groaning. I roll to my back and settle against the velvety headboard.

"Morning, baby." August smiles at me, carrying the tray containing my breakfast. He's deliciously rumpled. He's as handsome as he is a lunatic. His madness goes hand in hand with his beauty. That's how predators attract prey. They don't even need to chase. A smile of those full lips, a flash of white straight teeth, a wink of those deep midnight eyes, the prey falls straight into the lap of the hunter, begging to be slaughtered.

"Morning," I reply, forcing my own lips into a smile. I don't need to force much. My pupils dilate on their own accord, and they would since my body craves what my eyes see. My pulse flutters at the base of my neck, and he homes in on my reaction to him. By the self-satisfaction crinkling the corners of his eyes, he knows that if he peels off the covers, he'd find my nipples puckered and my pussy wet.

I'm ashamed of my body's reaction to him. But I will use everything I can to save myself from him. The man I thought I was falling in love with *and* the monster of my dreams.

As he hand-feeds me each morsel, chatting about meaningless stuff, smiling at me and kissing me between bites, I go over my *new* list.

1. ~~Morning fuck.~~
2. ~~Breakfast.~~
3. Movie downstairs.
4. Lunch.
5. Nap. Comes with pre or post nap fuck.
6. Whatever board game he thinks I'm interested in.

7. Convincing me to start a new assignment for work.
8. Pretending to want to know me, meaningless conversation.
9. Dinner.
10. Fuck.
11. Sleep.
12. Repeat.

Chapter Forty-Five

August

In a very sick twist of fate, this is the best day Seattle has seen for the beginning of February in decades. The sky is a sparkling blue, not a cloud in sight. Overhead, the sun is dazzling. Not even a soft breeze disturbs the air. The salty scent of the ocean and the resinous, sweet smell of evergreens overpower the sickly stench of white lilies.

Waves are crashing against the cliffs in the distance, a soothing background noise as the pastor drones on and on and on about the life and accomplishments of the distinguished Henry Cavanaugh. *Ugh.*

This is what I left Siah's side for, to listen to one hour of bullshit and pure rotten lies about the life of a bastard who deserved to die in far more excruciating pain than what he got. I've been *merciful*. When his fancy car hit the tree, he was already dead. He should've felt what it's like to be trapped by twisted metal and sharp steel. He should've drowned in fear as the flames licked at his skin, melting his putrid flesh from his bones.

Instead, he died like a coward, begging for his miserable life as he sat in a puddle of his own piss. A disgusting rat dying a disgusting rat's death.

Siah should have been here, to taste for herself the blessed relief as his sleek coffin is lowered into the frozen ground. Thanks to his cowardice, she's still not strong enough. Just the thought of her battered face has rage coursing through my veins. If I could kill him again, I would.

As it is, I'm half tempted to send out the video I got from the parking lot security cameras. To show all the mourners here, crying their fucking britches off for a goddamn sentient piece of shit with eyes, whom they're wasting their tears on. A rapist, a plague who assaults defenseless women, a sociopath who married a good woman for money after he blew up his trust fund on expensive toys and cheap whores, then planned to have her committed as a dangerous paranoid schizophrenic.

No. Henry Cavanaugh doesn't deserve the tears, the flowers, or the poetic bullshit spewed by the pastor.

Death was always coming for him, even before he dared to put his filthy paws on Siah.

And I'll sit here with lead in my stomach because that night was so easily avoidable. As much as I want to stand here and kick at his coffin and set it on fire until there's nothing left of him but brittle bones to be ground and released in the wind, I'm as guilty as he is.

It was my own goddamn ego what enabled Henry to go as far as he did. I wanted him destroyed. I wanted him to lose everything he held dear, every cent on his name, his reputation, and his fucking mind. Dismissing whatever else he might do, because in my eyes he was a coward. And cowards run and hide, they don't confront.

Except... cowards run and hide when they perceive their opponent to be stronger, smarter, better. While Siah *is* stronger, and smarter, and absolutely fucking perfect, her strength is not physical. He had no issues confronting her. He had no trouble attacking her, using a deserted parking lot and the cover of the night for his heinous deeds.

If I hadn't gotten there when I did...

My hands fist at my sides, the funeral program crumpling in my grip.

The memory of him standing over her, with his pathetic dick in hand as she bled, passed out on the cold, wet ground, will haunt me for the rest of my life.

I *did* that. I let it get that far.

First, I underestimated the evilness of the man who fathered me. Then, I underestimated Henry's cowardice.

What else have I missed?

My watch vibrates on my wrist, a message flashing from the darkened screen.

> I'm at the bar. Join me?

Unknown Number

> Business or leisure?

Me

> *Fuck business, man. I need a fucking vacation. Consider this my PTO request.*

Unknown Number

I stifle a chuckle. Apparently, it's not appropriate to laugh at funerals. Nope, it's only appropriate to bawl your eyes out and wail so loud even people who've been dead and buried centuries ago wake up from their eternal slumber. Like that willowy blonde hanging by Henry's mother. Another poor soul he trapped in his web. She looks like an uglier, faded version of Siah's before her long-awaited separation from the cunt. Sleek blonde hair, similar height, similar build, but that's where the similarities end. As much as he tried, he never would have gotten another Siah.

Her spark is impossible to recreate. Her smiles are uniquely hers—bright with an edge of mystery, like she's owning a secret and enjoys being its sole keeper. The softness of her skin, my palms tingle just imagining the rapture of trailing my fingertips across the creamy-white silk. And while her body has been designed to fulfill all my filthiest and depraved fantasies, it's her mind that owns me, it's her heart I crave.

No. There's no one else like Siah. Never would be.

At last, the pastor finishes his sob speech. Excuse me while I barf in my mouth. One by one, his family bend next to the hole where Henry is rotting—with a bit of divine fucking justice he'll have no godforsaken eternal peace—and gather fists-full of crumbly soil, spreading it over the toxic waste freshly laid to rest.

If it were up to me, I'd bulldoze right over his grave until nothing and no one would ever know a stain on humanity was buried there. Alas, no one asked me.

> *Consider your request approved. I'll be there in 15.*

Me

With a last look over my shoulder and a very mature decision to not whip my dick out and piss on his goddamn shrine, I make my way to my car. Luckily, I'm among the first to leave, so I'm not trapped in a sea of tears and sobs that are likely to make me run someone over, really give them something to cry about.

I spend the whole drive to Flame&Stake thinking of Siah. Not that I don't think of her twenty-four seven. She's always on my mind, in my heart, in my very blood. But now that we're so close to our happily ever after, I'm more terrified than ever.

I neutralized every threat in our path. While my father isn't yet worm-feed next to the roasted asshole, he'll be too busy preparing for his trial and living the rest of his life locked up to be a serious threat. Sure, I'm not making the same mistakes twice. I'm monitoring the evil motherfucker constantly. He so much as twitches in his sleep, I'll know. Due diligence is a small price to pay when it comes to Siah's safety, even if it grates on my ego.

My plans have contingency plans with contingency plans of their own.

If by some fucked up black magic curse, he squirrels his way out of prison or a life sentence, well... that's his death sentence. Purely for Jayme's and Helena's benefit, he's still alive to shade the earth uselessly. Although, part of me is still firmly convinced they would be better off with him dead.

I freed my little mockingbird.

And yet, she's still caged. Her beautiful green eyes, like the darkest of emeralds, are dull, lifeless. It grates at my insides that she's mourning *him*. What did he ever do to earn her sadness? It poisons me inside that she's thinking of him. He doesn't deserve not one single thought of hers; not her hate; not her grief; not her mourning; absolutely fucking nothing. If I could erase him completely from existence, I would. Wiped clean, just like a hard drive.

I'm sick to my stomach every time I look at her face, every time my eyes assess her now rapidly-fading bruises. I'm eager for the day his evil will be completely gone from her perfect skin and from her beautiful mind.

It's our chance to be happy. We've earned it.

Years of neglect, abuse, and abandon. Every tear, every heartache, all the seconds, minutes, hours, fucking decades spent questioning our self-worth and our miserable existence—we've paid the toll.

I park haphazardly in one of the employee bays and jog to the back door. If anyone has an issue with my car, they can take it up to Devon. The bar is technically owned by Devon, Elijah, and myself. My best friend and I are acting more like silent investors, just taking advantage of a fine whiskey every once in a while. Right now, I've taken it upon myself to nag Devon about every small thing under the sun.

I saw the video. I heard every single word he'd said to Siah. His only luck is being married to my best friend, otherwise I would've hung him from his miserable balls in the middle of the dance floor for daring to speak to her that way. I give absolutely zero fucks he was protecting his husband. Elijah was doing the job I asked him to do. He *knew* there could be consequences before Siah learned the truth. So he got his feelings hurt.

Big fucking deal.

I got my feelings obliterated when Devon left his sorry ass during Eli's last enlistment, and when his Humvee got blown to hell, I left everything to tend to his health. Changed his goddamned bandages, debrided his wounds, donated my fucking skin for grafts, only to return and find Siah married.

My palm meets the center of his back as I slap him in greeting. "Vacation looks good on you."

Elijah lowers his aviators, giving me a sultry smirk. "Yes, *Master.* I'm working on my tan, too."

"Fuck off," I grumble good-naturedly. "Why did you summon?"

He lifts the glass of bourbon, by the looks of it, to his mouth, the deep-amber liquid sloshing against the walls of the glass. "Cause it's nice to be the one doing the summons for a change." He scowls at the wooden bar top. "Thanks for dumping the Syren in my lap."

"You're welcome. Puzzles keep your old mind sharp. Besides, I have more pressing matters to tend to." I wave him off and plaster on my best resting asshole face as I bend over the bar and pick up the bottle of Macallan Devon keeps stashed for me on hand. Pouring a double, I clink my glass against his. "To summons and dead assholes. May they all burn in hell." The hearty mouthful of aged whiskey warms me inside out, and I slump on the barstool, releasing the tension in my shoulders.

"How did it go?" Elijah asks, his eyes fixed on his drink.

I smack my lips, toying with the rim. "As expected. Wailing circus, lies served on bread shoved down people's throats."

He snorts and shakes his head. "Just as well it is done. How's Siah?"

Well, that question just brings the tension right back. "Recuperating." I shrug carelessly, although I'm worried sick about her mental state. "Healing." Another shrug. I'm impatient, too. I'm ready for the ride in the fucking sunset with the woman of my dreams in my arms.

"That's not what I'm asking, and you damn well know it. How'd she take finding out what you've done?"

"Way to ruin a good fucking day," I mutter between sips. "She's not ready to talk. She hasn't asked one single question. I'm not going to start *that* conversation when she's still processing all the other shit."

"Fucking A. For a smart man, you're ridiculously stupid." He chuckles, derision practically dripping out of every pore on his body.

I bristle. "What's that supposed to mean?"

He downs what remains of his drink and drops the glass on the wooden bar top. His fingertips drum next to it, each tap of his finger driving me insane. "I've watched you pant for this woman for six years, August. Working yourself up over her to the point of insanity, of obsession. We've been through this too many fucking times before. I've listened to all the bullshit excuses you served up—not the right time, not ruining Jayme's friendship with her, you not deserving her..." He trails off, his eyes pinned to the window behind me.

"Your point?" I clip.

"You have her now, and you're afraid to hold on." Elijah runs his fingers through his short hair, cursing under his breath when he pushes his sunglasses off. "There were so many different ways to go about actually meeting her. August,"—he swivels in his chair, his pale green eyes boring into mine—"you're deluded if you think her finding out what you did isn't weighing heavily on her. I might not have watched her for six years, but I know enough. And if you think she's processing quietly and bending to your will, she's not the woman you fell in love with. Stop dicking around and talk to her."

I open my mouth to argue, despite knowing he's absolutely damn right, when the watch on my wrist vibrates in a specific combination that has my blood freezing in my veins.

"What now?" Elijah barks, clearly attuned to my body language and my foul moods.

I ignore his question, scooping my phone out of my pocket. My lungs burn as I hold my breath, dreading what I'll find when I log into that particular camera.

Siah's pretty face stares at me from the entrance to my lair. She knocks on the door, then pauses, as if she is waiting for a response. Looking left and right, she bites her lip, her fingers wrapping against the fake knob I installed on the door.

My final mistake unveils before my very eyes—getting careless with Siah and granting her unlimited access. The reader scans her fingerprints, and the door swishes open, startling her. She straightens her delicate shoulders and gingerly walks inside my lair.

"Oh shit!" Elijah exhales, drawing my attention to him. His eyes are wide and cheeks pale. "Fuck me, go. If you haven't talked and she finds it..."

I'm off my stool and out of the bar in less than thirty seconds.

She doesn't need to find it to leave. What Elijah doesn't know, but I'm all too familiar with, is that goddamn backpack she placed next to the door.

Her *escape* plan.

My chest constricts as pain consumes me. Red fills my visions. My hands grip the steering wheel as I peel out of the parking lot, my tires screeching on the cement until they find purchase.

My little mockingbird is leaving me.

Looks like there's a need for her gilded cage, after all.

Siah Hadley is mine. And it's past time she learns her place once and for all.

Chapter Forty-Six

SIAH

My heart is pounding. I really shouldn't be doing this. A cold flush washes over my trembling body as my fingers splay against the door. It opens with eerie silence. I look behind me at the stairs leading to freedom. It's not too late to turn around, grab my backpack, and run.

But curiosity has always been my downfall.

I have to know. My gut feeling is telling me that the answers I need are just behind this door. I pause for a breath. Two breaths. Right now, I'm not sure what's more important—finding out the full truth or my freedom.

My feet solve that dilemma for me. As a war between self-preservation and insane fantasies of happily-ever-after is wagging in my head, I take slow, silent steps past the door and into the mystery third floor August kept locked. Until now.

Is this a test? I gulp, my throat dry, my breath choppy. If it is, I definitely failed it.

I don't know what I imagined... Coffins? Medieval torture devices? But the third-floor space looking exactly as it was in the camera feed August showed me months earlier wasn't it. Except, that's not quite right either.

Light from the large windows floods the space containing the massive desk and comfortable-looking leather chair. The lone couch pressed against the wall keeps company to a minibar. A full wall of labeled drawers greets me as I clear the door. But it's so much smaller. *Definitely* not covering the entire house.

"What are you hiding, August St. Andrew?"

My feet are silent against the hardwood floor. I stop in the middle of the room, looking around, lost like a ship at sea. A gasp spills past my lips when my eyes are met with an intricate wall. Dozens of strings—red, green, blue—are spread on a blown-up map of the US. Colored pins, matching the strings, hold in place polaroid photos of various men. As I walk closer, I can make out on the edges of each picture names, dates, locations. In bold, black letters, 'The Syren' is written at the top of the wall.

My eyes are drawn to the lone picture pinned over where Seattle should be. *Corbin Davenport, October 22, 2015, Discovery Park* reads on the white edges. His eyes, dark green and calculating, stare back at me from the still-print. My stomach lurches and flips as I scan over his face. A strange sense of familiarity floods my chest, as if I've seen him before.

"What the fuck?" I breathe, my hand trembling as I press it against the hole blossoming in my midsection. I shake my head, puffing at a rogue curl hanging over my forehead. "You don't have time for this, Siah."

I turn my back to the mystery wall and walk to the metal drawers on the opposite side of the room. Pulling at any of them yields no results—they're firmly locked. What catches my attention, though, is that they're not pushed back against the wall. It only seems like it because they're ridiculously high. Who the hell reaches the top drawer unless they're a freaking giant?

I round the small space where the row finishes. Three black doors, at least five feet apart, line up behind the drawers. I push the first one open, only to find myself in a pristine but small bathroom. A toilet, a sink, and a cramped tiled shower are in here. By the row of masculine toiletries left on the marble edge of the sink, it's well used.

The second door is locked. Frustration bubbles up inside of me. The paranoid asshole keeps everything under lock and key. And to think I was the one about to be committed to an institution because of my suspicions and constant fear. If I had more time, I would've taken an axe, a chair, a goddamn bulldozer to the door.

The third one opens easily. Nothing but darkness greets me from inside. A foreboding feeling has me rooted to the spot, as if one step inside will see the door sealed-shut and me forever trapped. There's not much light coming in from the main office either, since the wall of drawers behind me touches the ceiling, blocking whatever sunlight spills through the windows on the other side of freedom.

Blindly, I pat with my hand around, but there are no switches to be found either. I can barely make up in the all-consuming darkness the outline of a bed pushed against a wall, and that's about it. At least, it's empty. There are no strange women chained up here. I'm not sure what would have surprised me more—finding a chained woman or not finding one.

I scurry back around the drawers and to the massive desk reigning absolute in front of a floor-to-ceiling window. An enlarged picture of Henry, with dozens of darts and even more holes, is tapped to the wall near the desk. "August, you mindless jackass."

Well, Henry was a jackass, too.

They should've coupled up and lived a jackass-life together, leaving me out of their fucked-up mind games.

I rub with the heel of my left palm the aching throb in my chest. Denial sits bitter on my tongue. I won't miss August when I'm gone. I can't miss him. If I do, then both Henry and August would be successful on their twisted mission to drive me insane. Any creature will develop a false affection for its captor if the captor displays glimpses of kindness. Humans, more than any other species, are designed to get used to the good and fast. We're engineered by both nature and nurture to find the positives in others and latch onto them.

Because... when all hope is lost, monsters rise from the darkness and blend with the light. Exquisite monsters, with midnight-blue eyes and lightning strikes in their irises.

I suck in a breath when the top drawer of his desk slides open. My fingers comb through the papers neatly stacked in color-coded folders. I read through each of them as quickly as my eyes process, but in most, the sequences of numbers and letters make no sense.

"Come on, Siah. Smarten up. He's a goddamn programmer, at the very least. Aren't all hackers allergic to paper-based information or something?"

I abandon the folders when my knuckles brush against what feels like a wooden cube. With careful movements, I slide the small black box from the furthest recess of the drawer. The lid flips open with ease. Bile explodes out of my stomach, pooling in my mouth, as a golden wedding band glints at me from inside the box. I swallow it down, pinching the bridge of my nose as I lean my head back. "Do not vomit, do not vomit, do not vomit," I repeat to myself through ragged breaths.

My fingertip feathers over the monogrammed initials permanently etched on the surface of the wide band. "What did you do, August?" I croak as my throat burns. My eyelids flutter closed as tears gather on my lashes. I don't need to look any closer at my dead ex-husband's wedding ring to know the coppery stain layering the dull gold is blood. His blood.

Dread curls around my spine. I need to leave, and I need to leave now. Fuck the answers. Knowing won't do me any good if I'm dead. Suddenly, the fine hairs on my arms stand on end. The entirety of my skin bristles as an eerie chill seeps into my bones. Slowly, I turn my head toward the window.

I watch rooted in place as the gates part unhurriedly and August's car barrels through them.

My heart stops. My breath falters. My fucking soul leaves my body.

I'm too late.

Chapter Forty-Seven

August

The gates take an impossible amount of time to open. I want to barrel my car through them. Fuck it, I can fix them later. But that would only make her fear me more.

I'm the goddamn king of underestimating.

With the corner of my eye, I watch her sprinting out of my lair and down the stairs. There's no time to switch to a different camera. Siah saw me returning through the window as she was snooping through my desk. She'll either make a break for it now or wait for me in the bedroom pretending that all is right in the world.

The past two weeks... this is what we've been, a game of pretense. My heart aches, and I rub the center of my chest with the pad of my palm to stop the hollowness from taking over. I held her in my arms, I made love to her... and she pretended.

It's not a blow to my ego. Fuck that.

I want her to want me. I need her to love me. What we have is real. The chemistry is real, the way my blood boils for her is real, her reactions to me are real. I go back in my head over everything we shared in the last fourteen days. She didn't fake her body's reactions to me. She came to me willingly, pliant and soft in my arms. She came for me willingly, too.

So her melancholy was because of me, not because she was mourning the depraved, rotting asshole.

If there's a situation where I could use some semblance of a silver lining, this is it.

All that's left for me is to convince her. Convince her of the certainty of my feelings and that we belong together. If my persuasion is not enough, well... One thing is guaranteed. Siah can't leave me. I told her I was hers. I told her only death can do us apart. The only way she'll be free of me is when I'm dead.

Who am I kidding, not even then. The way I feel her in every pump of my heart, the manner in which she consumes my every waking thought and all my dreams while I'm asleep... there can only be two endings for us—together, or with me rotting next to the rapist cunt.

I throw the car in park in front of the entrance and jump out. A quick tap on my wrist brings up the tracker I hid in her bracelet. I might not be able to check the detailed map on the small screen, but I see enough to know she's already running through the woods bordering the backyard.

"Fuck's sake," I curse under my breath. We're doing this the hard way.

I have to tread carefully. The last thing she needs is to injure herself again. With one hour until sunset, the light is diminishing rapidly, especially once we'll be in the thick of the forest. I calculate mentally all the places she could run to. To the West, less than a mile in, she'll hit the edge of the cliff and the ocean below. North, she'll have about five miles to the nearest house once she reaches the highway. There's always hitchhiking, but this particular section has been half closed for maintenance, so there's hardly anyone driving through it. South, forest and more forest, and that's my main concern. So many places to get hurt.

The sun might be shining today, but the forest bed is frozen at best, most likely muddy. The temperature will drop to below twenty during the night. Even if she doesn't fall or otherwise hurt herself, she'll risk hypothermia.

I run inside the house, kicking off my dress shoes as I go and quickly replacing them with a pair of sturdy hiking boots. It takes less than a minute, but it's precious time I'm wasting. A quick check of my watch has me sighing with relief.

"West it is." At least with the cliff, she'll be trapped on one side.

With my hiking backpack firmly strapped over my shoulders, I burst through the door and retrace her steps. I'm no more than five minutes behind her. My eyes are focused on the trees in front of me, ears attuned to every breaking twig, every rustling, dried-out bush.

On silent feet, I eat the distance between us. The hurt bubbling inside of me has me short of breath, my heart pounding against my eardrums. I can't focus on it. My single-minded objective is to find Siah and bring her home safely. The broken trust, the heartache—these are all things we can deal with after. After she's safe, after she's back at my side where she belongs.

I trek through the withered foliage, going deeper and deeper into the woods. The hike is slow. My boots are sticking to the muddy soil. She'll have an even harder time walking, but my frequent checks on her position show she's making consistent progress. A smile twitches at my lips. I might be hurt she's running from me, but I can't stifle the pride and awe at her strength and determination.

No more than an hour has passed with me trailing her, but the visibility is almost gone, the evergreens so dense, I can barely glimpse at the rapidly darkening sky above. A chilly wind howls eerily through the tree trunks.

My watch vibrates on my wrist.

> I'm following you both, on hand if rescue is needed. Storm front formed close to the coast. Heavy rain and strong winds expected. Orange alert issued. Get out of there.

Unknown Number

"Fuck!" I rub a hand over my sweaty face and push forward.

Fear unlike anything I've ever felt claws at my insides. An out of nowhere storm right now is a bad fucking idea if she reaches the cliff. Siah's slight frame won't need much to be pushed over if it gets too strong. Nevermind the slippery as fuck rocks and potential ice forming.

I shake my head, clearing all my doom's day thoughts. Stealth be damned, I'll deal with a bear or a cougar if I have to. I have to catch up with her.

Uncaring of the branches scratching at my face, I start running, my lungs constricting as I push through the slight incline of the hill. My boots get heavier and heavier the more mud they collect. Worry rattles at my rib cage as the wind picks up in intensity, the howls stronger, the whistling deafening.

"SIAAAAAHHH!" I yell, projecting my voice as loud as I can, the echo carried over in the wind. The light is almost completely gone. She must be scared out of her fucking mind at this point. Surely, knowing I'm here must be better than thinking she's alone and lost in the woods.

The watch vibrates once more on my wrist, this time in a string of notifications in a specific pattern. *Fifty yards.* Too far away still. The brightness of the screen, even dimmed, is still enough to have white dots pepper my view. I blink rapidly, continuing my advance toward her, cursing the fucking wind running rampant between the trees that stops me from hearing her.

"SIAAAAAAHHH!" I yell again, hoping beyond hope she would hear me and respond. My breath fogs in front of me, the milky-white cloud dispelling like a ghost in the darkness of the forest. I stop for a second, turning around in circles, listening for any sound she could make.

Nothing. Just unsettling silence and eerie, mournful gusts.

A new pattern tickles my wrist. *Twenty yards.* I look at the screen, my whole body turning to stone when I notice how close to the cliff edge she's gotten. *Fuck this.*

I turn on the lantern on my watch, revealing the sparse trees around me, and sprint ahead, weaving around them until I burst out of the tree line. The climb up the hill is treacherous, the ground peppered with broken stone and jagged rocks. I wave my wrist in the air, and a flash of white to the right, advancing slowly, but steadily toward the edge, catches my attention.

The wind is whipping savagely all around me, the gusts strong enough to make me pause and rob me of air when they hit me head on. My heart feels as if it's about to burst, the pressure of my exertion and the suffocating push of the wind constricting my lungs inside my chest.

"SIAH!" I bellow.

A whimpered shriek is her response as she falls to her hands and knees in the muddy, damp ground and dead grass.

I dump my backpack next to a hollow stump and, with renewed energy, climb faster. We don't have much time to get back to the house. Judging by the dark clouds hanging heavy and low to the ground, the sky is just about to slice open on us. We need to get ahead of the heavy downpour and seek shelter under the trees.

I slip and slide, my calves burning as I press the grated soles of my boots harder into the ground, my eyes trained on Siah. Fear grows inside my chest the closer she gets to the edge of the cliff.

"Fucking hell, would you stop running?" I bark, my calm all but vanishing.

"Don't come any closer," she yells back, her eyes wide, her lips almost blue.

I'm five flimsy feet away. She's less than ten from the edge. The breath trapped in my lungs rushes out in a stream of white fog as she stops when I stop. Her whole body is shaking. Whether from the cold, or from the exertion she's put her weakened muscles through, or both, I can't tell.

I stand to my full height, letting my arms loose around me. "What would you have me do, Siah? Let you fall to your death?"

She scrambles to her feet, yelping as the wind barrels into her, forcing her to widen her stance in order to remain upright. Quick as lightning, she looks over her shoulder at the angry ocean swirling at the bottom of the cliff. Big fat drops of freezing rain start falling from the skies, and I curse under my breath. We're definitely running out of time.

I reach my hand out to her and, lowering my voice, plead with her. "Come back to me, baby."

The indecision is clear on her pale face. Her hands are fisted at her side, her delicate jaw clenched. My stomach flips as she takes a step back, bringing her closer to the crumbling and abrupt rocky edge. All my muscles tense and flex as I ready myself to lounge at her.

"Why won't you let me go?" she screams, reading the intent in my eyes.

"You said it yourself, I'm yours. Wherever you go, I follow." My words reek of desperation and despair.

My truth doesn't mellow her. Pure venom is etched into the delicate features of her face. Her hatred is like a bullet to the heart. The disgust in her eyes eviscerates me.

"You're fucking delusional, August. Do you hear the words coming out of that traitorous, lying mouth of yours? You made me trust you. Trampled all over my life, made me feel seen, like I mattered. All the while, you were chaining me, transforming me into your mindless puppet." Another step back, and I die a thousand deaths.

I open my mouth to rebuff her accusation, but she'll never believe me, not now. Why did I think talking would solve anything is beyond me. Siah has never trusted words. She needs to be shown. A gust of wind has me swaying on my feet, but it's enough to have her distracted as she steps sideways to remain upright. I launch myself at her before I even realize what I'm doing, wrapping my arms tightly around her cold body.

My back hits the ground, the rocks jutting from the muddied ground digging into my sore muscles. Currents of electricity strike at the still healing wound in my shoulder. The entire upper side of my arm grows numb as pain detonates and spreads through my biceps and shoulder blade.

It takes but a heartbeat for Siah to shake off her shock. Her frozen hands slap at my face, neck, and chest. Her nails, sharp as razors, scratch at my cheeks, the sting amplified by the bite of the ice-cold wind. She's like a wild animal, fighting with all her might to be set free.

Tears burn at my sinuses, gathering at the corners of my eyes. She wants to be free of me. Free of the one person who loves her beyond belief and possibility. I bled for her. I'd die for her and her happiness. *Fuck it.*

I roll us over and pin her hands above her head and her legs under my knees with just enough force to keep her still. Her back bows, and she thrashes under me, her chest heaving, her breaths coming in ragged pants.

"STOP!" I bark. "Stop fighting me. Fucking stop."

She sags under me as if my words stole all her remaining strength, and her head lolls to the side, her eyes scrunch closed. Bitter sobs spill past her blue lips, defeat washing over her. "I hate you, August. I wish I'd never met you, wish I'd never known your name. I fucking hate you."

My fingers tighten around her wrists as I recoil, her barbed words slicing my heart open. "You don't mean that," I whisper.

Her mouth sets in a firm line despite the quiver in her chin. She lifts her head from the ground as rain pours down on us, drenching us from head to toe. Her eyes spring open, devoid of all light and hope.

"I hate you, August. I'd rather die than spend one more second around you." Her saliva is warm on my skin as she spits in my face.

The pain leaves me breathless. She might as well have reached out and ripped my heart clean out of my chest. My minute daze is all she needs. Her forehead collides with my nose, hot blood bursting through my nostrils, as her hips bridge high, and she throws me off her. In the next second she's on her feet, disgust and determination tattooed on the creases of her forehead as she turns to the edge of the cliff.

If it's the terror or the adrenaline, I don't stop to think. My body reacts of its own accord. Before I blink twice, I'm on my feet, my hand wrapped tightly around Siah's slender neck. Boiling hot tears are pouring down my face, washed away by the rain falling down on us without mercy. Her fingers dig into my forearm, rivulets of blood pooling around her nails. Her lips part on a silent scream as my fingertips find the pressure points I seek.

"Sleep now, little bird of prey. You eviscerated your victim, now rest," I murmur, my chest imploding with agony as her eyes roll to the back of her head and her body convulses before she falls limp in my chokehold.

Chapter Forty-Eight

SIAH

My head is pounding. My skull feels like it's about to split open right down the middle. The pressure behind my eyes is too much, too sudden. My stomach churns, nausea roiling through my insides. I groan and shift on the soft bed, trying to curl myself into a ball, to do something, anything, to stop this miserable pain.

A metallic chiming sounds as I turn, a pitiful whimper slipping past my lips. My eyelids feel swollen and heavy, too heavy to open. Instead, they press down on my eyeballs, causing my head to throb even worse. I drag my knees to my chest, but they don't fully reach, stopping just about halfway up. I kick around, trying to dislodge the sheets wrapped around my calves, the chiming getting louder.

My arm extends as I reach around to untangle myself, but my shoulder just about dislodges out of its socket as I'm stopped short in my efforts. Bubbles fizzle in my veins, my heart racing, as the reality of my situation starts to take shape in my mind. An onslaught of memories overwhelms me, images flashing one after the other behind my swollen lids—entering August's office, finding Henry's wedding ring in the drawer of his desk, the picture of my late ex-husband hung on the wall, numerous darts protruding out of it, the hidden rooms on the third floor I couldn't see when August showed me the live feed, wasting too much time as I searched through everything unlocked, running through the woods in a desperate attempt to escape my tormentor.

The most painful parts linger, seeping into my soul and freezing me from the inside out—August catching up with me, the embers of his obsession burning bright in those fathomless dark eyes. My resolve to meet my end still rides me under the overwhelming pressure in my head and the layers of shock and regret. The brief spark of desire to survive when he wrapped his fingers around my throat, makes my heart skip a beat or ten even now.

More clarity ensues as I fight my way to full consciousness. My body feels tired and achy, as if I laid on my back for too long of a time. I move each leg in turn, trying to alleviate the stiffness in my muscles. My ankles are weighted. I run a toe on top of my other foot, finding it bare. The coldness of a harness...*no, that's not right... a* cuff just above my heel gives me pause. I follow the buttery leather until I connect with smooth ridges and links. *A chain.* So my legs are restrained.

I bend the knee of that same leg, moving it toward my torso slowly, until the chain pulls taut and halts my movement. There is some slack, but not a lot. I also notice they're not tied together; the restraints are individual for each leg.

It doesn't take a genius to figure out my hands are also chained up in the same way.

My restrained limbs grow numb from the inside out. I'm well and truly trapped. There's no escaping August anymore.

The click of a door and the muted sound of it opening over a carpet have me shifting to my back. Even with my eyes still closed, the world tilts sideways then rights itself. My stomach flips as the pressure in my head increases and blood rushes through my ears.

"You're awake," August states, his voice devoid of any inflection or feeling. "I'm turning the lights on."

I make a noise of protest deep in my throat, but nothing comes out. My tongue sticks to the roof of my mouth, I'm so dehydrated. Light batters at my eyelids, the pain in my head reaching nuclear levels. The churning in my stomach swirls and gurgles, and I turn my head to the side as sobbing heaves wreck through my chest.

"Dammit," he bites, and blessed darkness replaces the knives stabbing through my eye sockets.

I jolt as a loud thump rings in my ears. The migraine currently busy killing me is both photosensitive and gifts me with phonophobia. *Great.*

"I'm going to help you sit," he whispers now. "Are you going to fight me?"

"No," I breathe, the sound so low I barely hear myself.

As if I could fight him. I wouldn't be able to overpower him when I'm at full strength, nevermind when I'm knocking on Death's door and debilitated by a brain-crushing migraine.

His palm cradles the back of my head as he lifts me to a seated position. My chin drops to my chest, and I sigh in relief as the pressure in my skull shifts and lessens a notch. He rearranges something behind me, his hands and arms brushing against my back every so often.

The clanking of chains has my shoulders reach for my ears as I'm trying to protect myself against the high-pitched sound. His hands grip under my arms, and I feel myself being lifted and settled still upright, with my back against a headboard, pillows cradling my hips and nape.

"Can you open your eyes?" August keeps his voice low, and I hate myself for feeling thankful. I shake my head, my throat too dried out to form proper sounds.

"Okay. Here, I have a glass of water for you." What feels like a straw is placed on my bottom lip, and I suck it inside my mouth, drawing the cool liquid greedily through it. I nearly choke as it rushes down my throat, the sting of it too much, too good, too little.

He lets me drink to my heart's content, not making a sound apart from his slow and steady breathing. A slurp cuts through the silence when all that's left at the bottom of the glass is air. He pulls the straw out of my mouth gently and sighs.

"I made you some soup. Didn't think you could handle anything heavier. Are you going to throw the bowl at me again?"

My forehead crinkles, my sinuses throbbing in response. "Again?" Sounds come easier to me now that my throat has had some lubrication.

"You don't remember," August states, a hint of disbelief in his tone.

He thinks I'm pretending, faking my confusion. "I don't have enough strength to fight a cobweb, never mind a fully grown man."

"I think you're underestimating your own strength, but I'll take your word for it. I'm trying to avoid either of us being scalded by hot soup," he states. I feel him moving, then the touch of a warm spoon to my lip. I open my mouth and slurp the rich chicken soup slowly, trying not to choke. Once again, he remains quiet, focusing solely on feeding me.

I have nothing to say either. I'm weak as a newborn kitten. There's no fight to be had, no fire left in me. All I want is for this fucking headache to either stop or to kill me. What's there to live for, anyway? I'll live and die as August's captive.

A soft fabric brushes against my lips, and I rear back, but I have nowhere to go.

"Just cleaning you up," he murmurs.

Tears spring behind my closed eyelids. Once again, I'm at his mercy. Food, drinks, basic grooming... I can't or am not allowed to do anything on my own. The spiraling unfurls inside my chest, rage rushing through me so quickly and violently I'm scaring myself. The spark of fire is doused quickly by hopelessness. I must have catastrophically fucked up in a previous life, and this is the purgatory where I'm paying for all my depraved sins.

Every single person in my life has failed me.

What is it about me that makes me seem so unworthy, less than human, to anyone else?

My body starts trembling so badly, even the mattress underneath me shakes. The tears I've so far managed to keep at bay pour freely down my cheeks. His palms cup my face, thumbs swiping my skin dry to no avail. August touches his lips to mine, a soft peck, then a second. I can't bear his touch. When he nears again, I turn my head ever so slightly.

His dejected exhale washes over the sensitive skin of my neck as he rests his forehead against mine. I hate myself even more that the small gesture lessens my pain even more, as if my body was in withdrawal, craving his presence, and the smallest of August-fixes is already working its magic through me.

"You still hate me." A statement, not a question.

He gave me chicken soup. I can give him truth.

"Always."

Chapter Forty-Nine

SIAH

He's hard, and thick, and warm, and pressing into me. Today's not the first time in my captivity that I've woken up with him curled all around me, crowding me in the twin bed. It's also not the first time his erection is present for the morning cuddles. My stomach burns and my lower belly heats. I'm fucked in the head. How can I be both turned on and nauseated by his presence?

"I know you're awake," he murmurs, his voice all sleepy and gravelly and oh-so-fucking-hot. His lips are tickling the back of my neck, his nose buried deep in my hair. I swallow down a moan as he grounds his hips into me, and the thick head of his cock slides against my clit.

"Difficult to sleep when I'm afraid of what you'll do to me when I'm unconscious," I lie through my teeth. I'm lying to myself, too. My mind is a mess as I go round and round in circles. Maybe it's the darkness of the room, or maybe the gentle way he constantly looks after me, but deep down, I'm softening toward him. I'm trapped, or so I tell myself, but do I really want to escape? Escape to where? Do what? My heart is screaming that right here, in this house, in this man I already have everything I've ever wanted. And all it's costing me is my freedom. My sense of self-preservation, on the other hand, demands that I fight for myself and my autonomy. The rage simmering beneath my skin is fueled by all the ways August has lied to me. His betrayal cuts deeper than my softening feelings. And so, I keep fighting.

The chains clang noisily as he flips me to my stomach and straddles the back of my thighs. I fight my instincts to buck into him, trying to throw him off. All I'll do is excite him more.

"Is that so?" he purrs, trailing his fingers on the length of my spine. "You mean to tell me that if I spread your legs, your pussy is not soaked and swollen with need for me?"

"You have your morning wood, I have my morning whatever," I retort,

"Who's delusional now, little mockingbird?" August asks with a derisive chuckle, pushing away from me.

I don't bother turning back to him. The room is always pitch dark unless he turns on a light or a lamp. So dark, I can't even see my hands in front of my face. He's built this cage just for me. Padded black walls, a single bed pushed against one of them, a small side table to hold a tray of food, a door, and nothing else. Should've just saved myself a trek in the forest and walked in here, closing the door behind me that day.

According to August, I've been here for a full week. Well, I guess, this is Day Eight. For the first four days, I've been delirious with fever and violent. I smiled the entire half hour he droned on and on about me throwing everything I got my hands on at him and, when that wasn't enough, my fists and feet took over. *Good.*

I remember none of it, but I'm not sorry in the slightest.

The chains are, apparently, for my own benefit. So that I don't hurt myself in one of my rage fits. Sure, we'll go with that.

"What do you feel like having for breakfast today?"

My answer is the same as for the past three days. "You letting me go and an extra-large coffee."

He chuckles darkly. "Pancakes and bacon will do." He kisses the top of my head, his steps light as he exits my cage. The room fills with light as he opens the door. I don't even get to open my eyes and study my surroundings as he quickly closes it, shrouding me in darkness once more. Joke's on him. I already know where I'm locked.

My migraine lasted for two full days. The bastard sedated me every time I tried to set myself free and *attacked* him. There's a reason the sleeping pills I was taking were the lightest my therapist could prescribe. My body reacts weirdly to sedation. It lasts longer than normal, makes me groggier, messes with my memory.

I don't know which is worse. Living my life drugged out of my mind, a meaningless existence I would not be aware of, or living my life aware, feeling every second escape through my fingers, knowing I have no will or power of my own, entirely at his mercy?

I flip to my back, contracting and relaxing my stiff muscles. Despite the long hours I've slept this week, I'm still bone tired and... numb. I'm not afraid anymore, I'm not much of anything anymore. His betrayal broke something inside of me. Instead of a heart, there's a black hole in my chest, consuming every molecule and atom of my make. Soon, all that'll be left of me is a shell.

My whole body flinches when the door pushes open. The small space is immediately inundated with the heady aroma of bacon and coffee. My stomach makes its hunger known, the gurgle rising from beneath the covers competing with those of savage beasts. So, you know, August.

"Are you going to let me see today?"

He hums, pondering my question, then answers with one of his own. "How's your migraine?"

"Better."

The bed creaks, the mattress dipping as he sits next to me, the side of my thigh brushing against his back. He follows his normal routine and cups my nape while fussing with the pillows at my back. The chains grow slack, and then I'm upright, leaning against the headboard. His wristwatch lights up, then a soft dim glow brings his face into view.

August looks impassive and... unkempt. His jet-black hair sticks every which way, his normal five o'clock shadow is a full-grown beard in dire need of a trim. He looks exactly like he is—savage. The most surprising of all are the dark circles under his eyes and his sunken cheeks. His elegant nose is no worse for wear, which is a pity. I hoped my forehead did some damage and messed up some of that inhuman handsomeness of his. So the ugly on the inside could easily be seen on the outside, too.

He balances the tray on his knees, eyeing the coffee still steaming on the side table warily. "If I pass you the cup, are you going to throw it in my face?"

I consider it. I really, really do. But will that anger him enough to kill me? If I knew for sure that it did and the end to this misery was guaranteed, I'd do it. Except, I've come to realize I really, really know fuck all about August. And I'd pretty much prefer myself pain free. There's enough agony inside my soul. I don't need a battered body to go with it.

Shaking my head, I make grabby hands toward of the coffee. He takes my word for it and gently transfers the hot cup into my palms. The first sip is bliss, warming me up from the inside out. The bitter aftertaste, mellowed with creamer and a hint of hazelnut, makes me hum with pleasure.

He cuts through the stack of fluffy pancakes, coating a little triangle in syrup and bacon grease, before loading his haul onto the fork and pressing it against my lips. I open up for him and chew slowly, savoring each morsel.

August never talks when he feeds me. His attention is dedicated entirely to the tray on his knees and my mouth as it wraps around the fork or spoon, whatever he's using at the time. He never hurries me either, but waits patiently for me to chew as slowly and as methodically as I please.

Yes, I've tried pissing him off by eating so excruciatingly slow, I bit my tongue in the process. There was no frown, no impatient growls, no twitch of his jaw, just infinite patience.

"I can feed myself, you know," I say as I blow gently into the coffee once the plate is cleared. "You could also remove the chains."

He shakes his head and opens his palm in front of me. I down the last sips of coffee before passing the cup back to him. His fingers tighten around it, his eyes fixed somewhere on my lap. "There's been little to be happy about in the past days," August muses, more as if he's talking to himself than to me. "Feeding you is one of the few things I'm happy about."

His words hit me with more force than I'd like, and I wheeze out a breath. He stands, holding the tray in one hand. "As for the chains... I don't trust you anymore, little mockingbird. I'll remove them when I'm good and ready."

With that, darkness descends once more into the room, and the door slams closed on my scream.

"I hate you, you fucking bastard."

The scent of smoked firewood, burnt amber, and sandalwood envelops me. Nuzzling my face on my shoulder, the soft cotton rubs against my jaw, comforting me, calming me.

"I miss you so much I can't fucking breathe." I jolt at the gravelly sound of his voice. My eyes spring open, only to see him sitting against the opposite wall, his feet touching the sideboard of my bed, knees slightly bent to accommodate his long, strong legs in the small space.

"Shut up, August," I snap. "Just stop already with the lies."

He thumps the back of his head against the wall. "I never once lied to you."

I huff in indignation, shifting to my side so I can have him in my view at all times. My body betrays me worse than the man sitting in front of me. My skin obeys him and only him. If he tries to touch me, if he gets in bed with me... I'm done for. I might not be able to run away, but my instincts are screaming that if I see it coming, it'll be easier to protect myself.

"So you didn't lie about being away for months and the house free for me to use?"

August drags his palm across his face, scratching at the unkept scruff on his jaw. "The house *was* free for you to use. And I was away..." He sighs. "Occasionally."

My stomach flips painfully, and I breathe through my mouth. It's one thing to suspect something. A completely different fucked-up cherry on top of a controlling, toxic as hell man to have it confirmed. "You've been here since the beginning. That's why you didn't want me to come to the third floor. You've lived here this whole time," I accuse.

The look he gives me is full of mirth and derision. "What would you have had me do, Siah? Put yourself in my fucking shoes for a minute. I had to watch you starve yourself, depriving yourself of sleep, just cuddled up on that fucking couch, while I was trapped all the way on the other side of the goddamn world. Jayme beat me to the line by one hour. I would've broken in and taken you to the hospital myself. In fact, I was on my way to do just that."

My cheeks heat under the scorching embarrassment licking at my skin. I'll never be able to live down my stupidity. I don't remember much about the days before I woke up in the hospital, but what I do remember... "I was scared out of my mind because you were watching me. That's why I didn't move from the couch."

He lowers his eyes, studying intently the blanket covering me. "I wasn't, Siah. Not then. Not in person, at least. Henry had... cameras all over the fucking house, before you even asked him to install some. I hacked into them."

"You're lying!" I shout. The hits just keep on coming. I asked for the truth, but the truth is too much. Like being submerged in boiling water, feeling your skin melt off your bones, the air molten lava down your throat, slowly and painfully suffocating you.

"Why is it easier for you to believe the worst of me, but still give that rotting cunt the benefit of the doubt, huh?" August sneers, disgust and condescension dripping out of his words.

I ignore his claim. While Henry was clearly someone I didn't know, all my survival instincts are screaming about August being the monster in my nightmares. I have to tell myself that so I can stay strong. So I don't give in to the charming allure and the false promise of forever.

"Why did I never hear you up here? How did I never see you?"

He rolls those mystifying eyes now. "Come on, Siah. Everything is sound-proofed. You heard me when I wanted you to. There are hidden stairs leading from the third floor to the basement. There's another garage underground. It opens up a little down the road."

What the fuck?

"You slept here the whole time?"

Based on his grin, the wicked, crooked grin that looks so out of place when he's the epitome of dejection, he did not. "Six years, Siah. Six excruciating fucking years." The back of his head thumps against the padded wall once more. "Most of the nights I've spent at home, I was right next to you. Best fucking sleep of my life."

My skin both heats and crawls. Outrage spills out of my every pore. The violation of every one of my boundaries clashes against the warmth curling below my navel. He couldn't stay away; he couldn't come any closer. I can't delve into this right now or I'll lose the very little sanity I have left.

"How about when you said I'd always be safe in your home?"

An affronted sound comes from him, somewhere between a growl and blatant denial.

"When were you not safe, little mockingbird? Everything I did, every single damn thing, was and continues to be for your safety."

I scoff, narrowing my eyes at him. "Sure, August. Stalking me from the shadows, breaking into Henry's home when we were married, forcing me to move into your house, chaining me, taking advantage of my body as I slept—everything's for my own good, isn't it?"

He leans his head back, lips pursed, a dark scowl on his face. He's rejecting my words with his whole body.

"I never really knew what love was. I know I had it for the first five years of my life, but I was too young to understand or to appreciate it. Then my mom was gone. It took me less than a couple of months after her death to understand what hate was, though. The dark closet I was locked into whenever James felt I was too much or I was living too happily still fucking haunts me. The missed meals, those I got used to the fastest."

My mouth falls open, and I quickly cover half of my face with the blanket. I don't dare make a sound; I don't dare breathe. August is not even looking at me. His eyes are trained on his knees, lost in the memories of his past.

"He never laid a hand on me. He didn't need to. I think he realized pretty early on, a physical punishment would never hurt me as much as taking away everything I cared about and destroying it." August laughs then, a sound so devoid of emotion, a chill rushes up my spine. "Father Dearest used words as his weapon of choice. I was a murderer, a leech, a life-draining monster. I'm the reason Mom died, after all, or so he said. So anyone who dared getting close to me, he made sure they ended up regretting their choices or hating me."

August scowls and pushes to his feet. A couple of steps have him looming over me. "You called me and threw in my face what a selfish asshole I was, how Jayme deserved better from me. You weren't wrong. Jayme would've been better off with me keeping my distance. Instead, in a two-minute and thirty-seven seconds' worth of conversation, where I barely got a word in, you managed to convince me that maybe my life had some worth."

He fists his hands at his side, his knuckles turning white, veins popping along his forearms. "And then I saw your tears as you hugged her and congratulated her. I saw you cheering for her harder than anyone in that auditorium has ever cheered for whoever they were supporting. You fascinated me."

"August..."

"Go ahead and call me a monster, too. Yes, I'm a selfish bastard." He shoves a finger in the middle of his chest. "I admit it, I know it, I fucking live it." He shrugs carelessly. "But six years ago, I found the goddamn reason I was put in this godforsaken world. And I was too emotionally damaged to know what to do with you."

He leans over and turns the light off, my eyes aching as they struggle to adjust to the darkness.

"I never knew I had the capacity to care about someone. How could I, when no one ever cared about me?"

My heart is pounding, just shy of breaking out of my chest. A smarting pain pulses at my bottom lip as my teeth sink into it. My fingers itch with the need to touch him, to take away his torment. But in the blinding darkness, the distance between August and me feels more impenetrable than ever.

He draws a sharp breath as he paces at the side of my bed before he speaks again. "At first, I wanted just a small glimpse, just to see if whatever dark magic connected me to you was real. Of course, I fell for you—irredeemably and completely—the more I followed you, the more I got to know you. You consumed me." August laughs then, each gravelly chuckle bitter and hollow. "Then I was afraid *for you.* What would he do to you if he found out how much you mean to me? So I worked and schemed and planned, and when I finally, *finally,* got the means to protect you regardless, I was stunted. I didn't know how to come to you. You married the demon-spawn. So... I had a final choice to make. I'd either let you go, or you had to come to me instead."

A sniffle. "I never really knew love, Siah. And then I met you. So, you see, I had no choice at all."

Chapter Fifty

SIAH

A heavy weight settles over my navel. Rough like sandpaper, hot like a furnace, it makes my heart race and my clit throb. I rub my thighs together to alleviate the ache igniting in my core. It helps nothing. I try to shift, but the weight pins me down.

"Stop squirming. I'm exhausted. Please, just thirty minutes," he mumbles from the shadows.

"For fuck's sake, August. Get off me, I don't want you here."

A truth and a lie—I don't know what I want. I have an unhealthy attachment to the man sprawled out over my legs and belly. He owns my fear with the same iron grip he owns my lust. My life is limited to the four padded walls of the cage he built just for me. I hate him for it. I *should* hate him for it.

"That's a filthy lie, Siah. I can smell your arousal, little mockingbird." He trails his fingers around my belly button, tickling the sensitive skin of my belly on their downward path. "I can feel the heat of your pussy at my fingertips." Electric sparks charge inside of me as he feathers his knuckles over my drenched seam, not quite touching, not quite hovering. "You burn so hot for me, baby, if I were to fuck you with my fingers, you'd scald my skin right off."

"Fuck you, August," I spit, infusing my words with as much venom as I can muster while my blood boils with need for him to do just that.

"With pleasure." He groans loud and needy before shifting his hips between my legs, my knees falling open as he widens his stance. I don't have time to breathe, or blink, or protest. He covers my mouth with his, grunting ravenously into me. I buck against him, trying to push him away to no avail. All I manage is to rub myself against his thick, hard cock.

"God, Siah, you drive me crazy. Please, baby, please," he begs, pure agony dripping out of his mouth and into mine. I swallow it all and guard it in my chest.

His hand comes between us, pushing his boxers down. His cock slaps against my pussy heavy and hot, a jolt of desperate need traveling through me as he grounds between my hips, notching the damp head at my entrance.

I strain against the chains, slapping my palms on his shoulders. He plunges his tongue between my lips and his cock inside of me in one swift thrust and shudders. "Fuck, it's been too long, little mockingbird, since I've felt you are mine. Keep pushing me away. Keep fighting me, baby. It doesn't change the way you want me, the way you soak these fucking sheets for me."

August plants his palms on either side of my head, looming over me, caging me in with his wide chest and strong shoulders. I'm lost. Withdrawing until only the very tip of him remains inside me, he plunders back in so hard the bed creaks. He doesn't give me any time to adjust or to simply breathe. Over and over and over he pounds into me like he'd been starved for a century and his favorite meal is right in front of his face.

"You fit me like a goddamn glove. Siah, baby, I can't... god, you're choking the fuck out of my cock."

The whole bed shakes. Wailed creaks of the wooden frame, wild rattling of chains, grunted moans, and panted breaths fill the air. I buck against each of his thrusts, meeting him halfway, letting him fill me with his vitriol and need. He's out of control for me.

My mind may despise August St. Andrew, but my body loves him desperately, burns for him incessantly in impossible flames.

His open-mouthed kisses are sloppy and wild. We're a battle of lips and teeth as he fucks my mouth with his tongue the same way he's fucking himself into my quivering pussy. Stroke for stroke, a tandem of lust, he takes me with everything he has. There's no slow burn, no gentle build-up. The fire in my belly sparks, expands, and detonates all in the span of three frenzied thrusts.

"August, fuck, yes, yes!" I scream as my pussy flutters and clamps down on him, coaxing his own release, begging for the thick hot spurts of his cum to paint my walls.

"That's it, little mockingbird. Drown my cock. Fucking take me." August comes with an earth-shaking roar, his hips wildly rutting into me until I'm full of him and he's spent of me.

He trails a path of open-mouthed kisses from my mouth to my neck, breathing only desperation across my sweaty skin, then nuzzles his nose in the hollow of my shoulder. His arms wrap tightly around me as he gives me his weight, cock still half hard pulsing and throbbing inside of my drenched pussy.

My knees are still splayed open, heels pressing into his rock-hard ass, as I squirm against the soaked sheets.

"Be still," he barks, the bite in his voice muffled by my sweaty skin and the post orgasmic bliss still riding him.

"Get off me, August."

"I haven't slept in days, little mockingbird. I can't sleep without you." Dejection takes over the bliss. "But I can get you off one more time before I pass out."

"Why are you keeping me naked?"

He nips at my nipple, a sleepy smile on his face. "You're soft, and sweet, and it makes me feel closer to you while you punish me."

I scoff. "As if. How about demeaning, degrading, and intimidating, and you like me to know how powerless I am?"

August lifts his head from my chest, supporting his weight on one elbow. "You're the most beautiful woman I've ever seen, Siah. Open your magnificent eyes and see the truth for what it is. Despite your skewed beliefs, you're the one with the power in this relationship."

I choke down the hysterical laughter bubbling in my chest. He's a fucking lunatic. There's no reasoning with him. He dares saying my beliefs are skewed. What about keeping the woman he claims to love chained in a cage is natural or normal?

His forefinger circles my breast, and I cross my legs together as best as I can. This is Stockholm Syndrome, nothing else. The sickening affection I have for him spreads like a poison through my body. His touch lights my skin like a Christmas tree. My mind is playing tricks on me. I *know* I hate him. The coiling desire in my lower belly is nothing but a manufactured product of futile dreams and disillusions.

He startles me when he sits up abruptly, swinging his feet over the edge of the bed. The wooden frame gives an ominous creak, then sags at a corner. Bitter tears pour down my cheeks as peals of laughter make it hard to breathe. He stretches a long leg on the floor to maintain balance and shoves his fingers through his hair.

"It's agonizing to know how low you think of me. It makes me fucking sick to my stomach."

It makes me sick to my stomach to see you in pain. But I'll be damned if I say that out loud. At this point, I'm as much August's victim as I am my own. Because I'm so close to just giving in... to just say *Fuck it* and be with him. Let him own me and control me. Be his mindless puppet.

Being locked in darkness leaves a lot of time for introspection. August put physical chains on my ankles and wrists, but I'm the one who caged herself a long time ago. I've exercised restraint in every single one of my choices—until I met him. If anything, he freed me. But I'm not so far gone that I'd admit this shameful truth. Not yet.

"Are you going to fix this bed?" I ask, pretending to be unbothered by the turmoil swirling deep into his midnight eyes. Petrichor rises in the air around us, I swear. He's about to bring lightning and thunder on me, and I'll welcome the storm.

August jumps to his feet, pacing the length of the bed. "I never cared for touch, you know?" he mumbles, more to himself than for my benefit. "It made it difficult to connect with anyone. I tolerated Jayme's, more out of fear of how she'd grow up than anything else. Helena is a great mother, but she was beyond infatuated with James. My sister was left aside. I protected her the best I could."

He laughs hollowly, his pacing incessant as if fire ants are eating at the soles of his feet. "My aversion to touch... I'm honestly not sure where it stemmed from. Maybe my fear of more people getting hurt if I accepted their affection and responded in kind. Perhaps I intuitively knew none of them were meant for me." He stops abruptly and turns to me, pinning me to the skewed bed with his dark, fathomless gaze. "Until you. I saw you, and my palms were itching to trace the softness of your skin. My chest felt empty without you in my arms. I saw you and I realized, Siah, that I've lived twenty-six years as an incomplete man."

I sit against the headboard, the chains loose enough to have just a little pull, a little discomfort against my ankles. My body is bared in front of him, but are his words that leave me naked, cut open at his will for him to peer at my insides.

Because I too have lived my life incomplete. He returned some pieces as he stoked my fear and gave fuel to my darkest desires during the night. He welded me back together as he romanced me in broad daylight.

"You are my only. My first, my past, my present, my future... I wanted you to know no other man. For no other man to know you, your kisses, or your embrace. There's so much selfishness in my love for you. I'm obsessed enough to admit your name is carved inside my chest. And I allowed myself to hope you'd be selfish for me, too."

My brain short-circuits. He's gone off the deep end. Three nuggets and five fries short of a Happy Meal. "What the hell are you talking about, August? You're standing here in front of me, claiming I'm the only woman you've ever fucked?" I cover my breasts with my arms as I fold them over my chest. "You're telling me you were a thirty-three-year-old virgin?" I mock.

He rears back as if I slapped him. I'm being bitchy, and I know it. Regret swirls in my stomach, forcing me to apologize, to soothe however I can the hurt staring back at me from the dark abyss of his eyes. But I bear down harder, hold on to my stubbornness. He's taking me for a fool.

"No, Siah." August shakes his head. "A twenty-six-year-old virgin, as you so delicately put it."

My heart falls to my feet and jumps in my throat at the same time. Air is hard to come by. My lungs strain and burn. "No..."

"I was ready then to make a move. For us to meet... organically. And we did, didn't we?" His eyes remain sad and lost, even as his lips tip into the semblance of a smile. He leans down, rubbing his nose against mine. "You sang for me for the first time, blindfolded and pliant. You soared for me."

"I don't believe you," I snap.

He chuckles ruefully, gripping the top of the headboard. His muscles strain, his abs flex and ripple as he crowds me until we're nose to nose, mouth to mouth.

"You ran away from me, and like a puppy in love with his feelings hurt, I gave you your space. Went back to Blind Date for months, you never did. And then you met Henry."

I tilt my head, our lips brushing as I hiss, "Three years later, August. Don't you dare hold over my head something you have no right at. My body, my choice."

"The trust fund your dearest Henry was so proud of? Fully funded by James. As soon as I was done waiting, Henry got into the picture. My father vowed he'll never allow me to be happy. He made good on his word when he got Henry in your face, and you fell into his goddamn lap."

He springs away from the headboard so fast, my head is spinning. His words make no sense. How would Henry even know James? "What are you saying, August?"

My mouth drops open as the door slams shut behind him. But he doesn't leave me waiting for long, as he returns not even a minute later. Cool air fans across my face when a blue folder lands in my lap.

"There was actually a moment, right when you met him." He chuckles brokenly as he shakes his head. "I put *your* happiness first. Sure, I looked in on him, but *nothing* stood out. Doctor Respectable was squeaky clean. James is not stupid—he knows a friend of a friend of a cousin of a friend. I found out the truth just moments before he put a bullet through my shoulder. You think you hate me, little mockingbird? Maybe we should see how you do with a gun when I turn my back on you."

I lie frozen as the door slams once again, rattling the broken frame of the bed. I can't think of August's parting words. The anguished pain in them nearly has me ripping my chains off and begging for his forgiveness just so I can see the agony in his eyes easing. Instead, I squeeze the folder biting at my fingertips. Anxiety grips my heart with icy claws, draining the breath out of me. Once I open it, I can't unknow whatever is hidden past the blue cover.

I've accused August of lying to me. I haughtily claimed I prefer the cruelty of the truth. What a stupid, naïve woman I am. He's giving me his truth, one morsel at the time, and I struggle to chew even the bite-sized grenades he keeps unpinning.

My eyes scan over the background check on the first page. The information printed black on white is not news to me. Henry *was* squeaky-clean on paper. There's no relief for me, because I know the worst is yet to come.

The next pages are statements from different banks, spanning ten years. I don't read these line by line. I don't need to, since August—ever so helpful—highlighted in red pen everything I have to pay attention to. Henry blew through his trust fund, draining it completely six months before he met me. Out of nowhere, five grand were deposited into an account I knew nothing of.

The date jumps out at me. He got paid on the same date we met.

I look further down. More money was transferred to him on our first date, then our first anniversary, then our wedding day. The sum grew with each milestone we ticked off.

His voice filters in my mind, the words I couldn't make sense of the night he assaulted me coming back to me with startling clarity. *"I was willing to let you go, lose all the money I got for marrying you, and that's how you repay me?"*

A contract between James and Henry follows, detailing all the payments Henry would have gotten had he stayed married to me. I skim over it, but my eyes are drawn to the last stack of papers, held together by a golden paperclip. Dozens of printed emails and text messages between Henry and Dr. Christiansen. My stomach churns and swirls, bile burning deeply through my throat as I read on about all the times Christiansen followed me, the things Henry took from the house to make me think my *stalker* broke in, the reports on my decline Christiansen sent to Henry while I was wasting away on his couch.

One single black and white photo is tapped to the interior cover of the folder of Christiansen, cuffed to a hospital bed, his cheeks sunken and neck corded and straining. Below the photo what looks like a fragment of a medical report reads, "Name: Christiansen, Darren; Age 32; Gender: male; Diagnosis: violent paranoid schizophrenia; Recommendation: full psychiatric hold for assessment. Permanent admittance to a psychiatric facility."

I slam the folder shut, throwing it against the wall, as far away from me as I can get it. I've seen enough. The back of my eyes stings as bitter tears gather furiously under my lashes. Everything was a lie. A hiccupped sob rips from my lips. I wanted answers. What need do I have for them?

I'm already well aware I've never meant shit to anyone. I'm just a disposable means to an end. And now I have the written evidence to prove it.

Chapter Fifty-One

August

"So, she knows everything?" Elijah pinches the bridge of his nose as I slide a cup of coffee across the island to him. His mental fatigue is practically blasting in waves out of his every pore—a living, breathing thing in the kitchen between us.

I shrug. Truthfully, I'm not in much better shape than he is. The last three weeks, everything has fallen onto his shoulders and, as intelligent as my friend is, when it comes to coding, he's simply not me. Work, Devon, keeping my kitchen well stocked—everything is taking a toll on him.

"Largely," I mumble, sipping the bitter dark roast. Perpetual state of exhaustion is the name of the game. A lesser man would've been dead by now with how little rest I've been getting.

I sleep when she sleeps. Easy enough, right? Wrong! I can't sleep without her. The bed is too large, too empty, the house deserted, my arms just... cold. So I toss and turn and curse, then give up and go to her. Except, Siah wakes up as soon as she feels me next to her. Just weeks ago, she would've melted in my arms, seeking me as she slumbered, holding my hand in the dark. And now, she'd rather jump into a fucking snake pit than touch me.

My skin crawls and stings with the rejection.

She has only hate and distrust to throw at me now. No more delicious fear, not a drop of exquisite compliance, absolutely none of her intoxicating belief in me that I am here to make everything better for her.

Hate, distrust, and lust. The magic formula for self-destruction fuel.

It kills me, but I'll take it. Hate is not indifference. The day she turns indifferent to me is the day I'll burn this fucking world to the ground.

Siah might be the one in chains, but I'm the one trapped in a cage of her own weaving. My whole being is attuned to her. She breathes, I breathe. She hurts, I agonize. There's nothing else, *no one* else, out there for me.

"So she knows about me then?" he pushes. "Is she still afraid of me?"

I narrow my eyes at him as I take what I need for our breakfast from the fridge. "She does. Not sure about fearing you, though." I smirk. "I believe her words were '*You can both go fuck yourselves, you conniving lying bastards*'. So make of that what you will." Lining up the eggs next to the stove, I continue, "In her humble opinion, I can take our sob story and shove it up our asses until we taste shit at the back of our throats. Since we're full of it, anyway." I turn to him, crossing my arms across my chest. "She then took a second and told me to thank you. For looking over her, for not dying, and for '*keeping the mindless asshole who only thinks with his narcissistic dick in check*'. I suppose I'm the one with the narcissistic dick."

Elijah snorts in his coffee, shaking his head. "Figures. No wonder she's a writer. She truly has a way with words—I'm touched beyond belief." A foreign smile tugs at my lips. Despite the hollowness in my chest caused by so much uncertainty and years of longing coming to a head, I'm happy, whatever the fuck that means. "Wait until your sister finds out you made Flame&Stake her go-to bar just so you can keep an eye on her."

"She'll live. I won't apologize for protecting her, or anyone else for that matter. What surprises me is that you and the horn dog you call husband kept it in your pants."

The look he gives me tells me I should know better. The problem is... I do. Whatever the reason—loyalty for me or an uncharacteristic exercise in restraint—I'm glad I don't have to find an unmarked plot in the woods for their graves. There's enough of those past the backyard as it is.

I'm well aware I'm a shitty brother. My relationship with Jayme is reduced to two little bullet points—my desire to be a shield between her and James, and her futile attempts at bonding with me. Family and healthy relationships have been unattainable to me before. Before Siah, before my eyes opened to possibilities and hope. So maybe there's still a chance for me and my stepsister.

If Siah forgives me.

If Siah accepts me.

If she'll stay.

"Did you tell her about her parents?"

I nearly cut off my finger as his question slams into me, and I shake my head in response. It's a very fine line I'm walking. The rule is very simple—between Siah and me there's no room for lies. So I've bared my soul to her. Every single dark and dirty secret I've laid at her feet. But there's an art to the madness. Too much, I'll break her. Too little, she'll continue to feel betrayed.

I want to see her free and soaring, not frightened and withdrawing further into that cage she's lived her whole life. My little bird of prey needs to fly. She was not made to be grounded.

"What?" I bark, Elijah's stare burning through the skin on the side of my neck.

He drums his fingers against the dark counter top, the faint thumps grating on my every nerve. "Speaking of Siah's parents... I think I found something." At my questioning raised eyebrow, he elaborates, "Regarding our little murderous friend."

"The Syren?" I breathe in my coffee. "No shit."

"The one and only." Elijah nods. "A pattern."

Back in November, we've been sent fishing. Randomly, throughout the states, a series of men disappeared, all of them over the age of eighteen. If I bring up the statistics, we've been looking for a needle in a batch of a billion identical needles.

Elijah has been running point in the search for this woman. She's wickedly smart and extremely cautious. At first, I wasn't very interested in her. Until I offered to find Siah's parents for her. In a sick twist of fate, Siah's path and the Syren's overlapped. In fact, the very first kill our murderous friend benched seems to have been Siah's biological father.

I'd say it's a coincidence, because in the six years and eight months I've been following my little mockingbird, me and the crazed avenger haven't crossed paths. Not once. That doesn't mean I won't rest easier once she's locked up and away from us. It doesn't mean that I believe in coincidences either.

"What do you see, Eli?"

My best friend has a hard on for puzzles, patterns, numbers. If a sequence is there, he'll find it. And once he does, well... he up and married someone who's able to follow the thread from one end to another. Between the three of us, there's nowhere on Earth someone could hide that we wouldn't eventually find.

"I widened the search, using the parameters we already had." He lifts a hand between us. "Twelve hours between abduction and time of death." One finger goes down. "Always six cuts—neck, tongue, both wrists, chest, and groin." Another finger follows. "Included all states, not just the West Coast." That's three fingers down as he wiggles his wrist in the air. "The hits tripled. The Feds only considered male victims in their profile."

"Women too?" Both my eyebrows spring up on my forehead, and my eyes grow large.

He leans back against the wall, coffee mug held tightly, his knuckles white as he takes a hearty sip.

"It wasn't physical appearance, sex, religion, job, whatever the fuck else." The smile he gives me is absolutely predatory, reminding me of Elijah of before—before the explosion, the burns, scars, and survivor's guilt. "They have all, at one point or another, been suspected of child abuse. And I don't mean there were charges pressed against them. Even if the authorities weren't involved, someone pointed a finger, gossiped about it, or complained in some form or manner. And here we are." He drops the mug on the island and rubs his palms together, his excitement palpable.

"Seems unlikely a killer as methodical and as careful as her would go after someone based on gossip or unverified accusations."

He chuckles ruefully. "Oh, she verifies them, all right. I'm certain I have more resources at my disposal, so unearthing the abuse evidence was quick enough. She might have hit a couple of speed bumps in the road, but there's no doubt she's done the legwork. There's not one fucking innocent on her hit list."

"This should be interesting," I mutter as I chop mushrooms for our breakfast.

The pattern Elijah found only strengthens my resolve not to share with Siah this part of her past. What does it serve her to know her father was a child abuser? Her mother, Rebecca, was a child herself when she had my little mockingbird and Corbin forced her to abandon their baby. He was a cruel piece of shit even then, a groomer. Once he had his fill of Rebecca, he moved on to younger things, trading them in as soon as each of them hit eighteen.

"We've got ourselves a little vigilante. But... that's not all." He's downright giddy, almost as happy as he was the day he married Devon. "I'm fairly certain I know where she's heading next."

I rinse the peppers and grind my teeth. "Just say it, you damned asshole."

"Phoenix."

The knife clatters on the marble floor as my hand jerks.

"I guess I better dust off a suit for the funeral, then. She's escalating, going almost... public. With all the media shitstorm, she's making a goddamn statement." I crouch down and pick up the knife before rinsing it in the sink. Pointing it at Elijah as I dry it, I ask, "I have to wonder, though, is she going after him because of the videos I made public or because of me? Are we still convinced it is a woman?"

"Yup. I'm still gathering the information, but... as with the other cases, the approach was similar. Public place, crowded as fuck, one minute our victims were with their friends or families, the next a woman approached, asked for help, and twelve hours later our good *Samaritans* were dead." He drums his fingers against the island top. "As for your other question, we'll find out soon enough."

I trade the blade for my coffee mug, gulping down a hot mouthful, as I nod my approval. The... coincidences are intriguing, luring. But he'll get me the answers I seek. My duty and my place are to be where Siah is.

Elijah rubs his clean-shaven jaw, grinning like a madman. "Wanna take a break from the hate-fest? Fishing is known to have healing properties for a man's soul, or so I heard. And I really fucking want me a syren."

"My dick's not alluring enough for you anymore?" Devon teases as he walks into the kitchen, dark hair messy, plaid pajama pants low on his hips. He kisses the top of Elijah's head. "Morning, love. Satan." He nods in my direction, and I flip him off before walking to the coffeepot to get one ready for him.

"Morning handsome." I hear Elijah greet him, laughter in his voice. Devon is still on my shit list and will remain firmly there until he apologizes to Siah.

I drop his mug on the island and make my way to the stove to brown the shallots with the peppers and mushrooms. "I heard Phoenix is beautiful in March. You should take your husband, make a trip out of it."

"You're just trying to get rid of me," Devon mumbles, slurping at his coffee.

I shake my head as I stir the vegetables. "Don't fucking tempt me. I still have a plot with your name on it in the backyard. I'm sure Siah will plant some pretty flowers if she feels so inclined."

Elijah clears his throat, probably trying to dispel the tension between the two of us. "Before or after she makes you an orphan?"

I play around absentmindedly with the wooden spoon, pulling the sizzling pan aside to add the chopped tomatoes. "After. Might as well end it all. There's something so beautiful in symmetry. It started with Siah. It ends with me."

With the corner of my eye, I see him standing and walking to me, Devon looming behind him like a dark, pissed-off ghost.

"Do you still need me here?" Elijah claps my shoulder and smirks. "Actually, you do. You're caging a bird instead of setting it free. It's a crime against humanity to ground an eagle. You were never the hunter in this chase, August. So why not show her your true face? Show her that, while for the rest of the world you're an apex predator, in her story—you're the prey."

Chapter Fifty-Two

SIAH

I wince as I stretch, an uncomfortable crick in my neck making me jolt. My back pops as I circle my sore shoulders. The carpet, as soft and as fluffy as it looks, is hard under my back. *Wait. Carpet?*

My eyes spring open as I pat the floor with the flat of my palms. What the fuck? What am I doing on the floor? My heart hammers in my chest as I instinctively curl on my side, my knees drawn tight to my chest. No pull. NO PULL!

I jackknife into a sitting position, the pitch darkness of the room making my head spin. I'm not chained up anymore. There's no rattle of metal links, no buttery tightness around my ankles and wrists. A sinking feeling travels through my stomach as it flips and constricts.

He set me free.

Disappointment weighs heavily inside my chest. Air is hard to come by as I'm trying to make sense of my new reality. He finally got tired of begging for my forgiveness. Is he ready to move on now? This is it? I walk out the door and start from zero as if the last six months, the last six years never happened?

Maybe this is a cruel joke. Maybe August is sick of my vitriol and hatred and decided he no longer wants my forgiveness. Now he'll get his revenge for me enjoying his suffering. He'll leave me permanently in the dark, between four padded black walls until insanity consumes me.

My hands are trembling as I hyperventilate. The collar of my sleeping T-shirt tightens around my neck, strangling me, suffocating me. Wait... T-shirt? HE. CLOTHED. ME.

I heave, the back of my eyes stinging, my sinuses pressuring the bridge of my nose. A sob crawls through my constricted throat, bursting past my lips. "He doesn't want me anymore," I whimper.

Realization hits me suddenly and all at once. Through all the madness and second-guessing my sanity and my morals, the one thing I took for granted was

August's obsession with me. I didn't understand it, but I craved it. I couldn't justify it, but I felt it. To have that last lifeline shatter under my very feet...

I fought for freedom. I fought to be free of him.

Why does victory taste so foul on my lips?

The sheets rustle somewhere to my right, and I startle, crawling backward until my shoulder blades hit a cold wooden surface. The side table is still here, I notice in disbelief. Chains rattle as more shuffling sounds come from the darkness. "Are you crying, little mockingbird?" August growls.

Relief and shock barrel through me. I pad my eyes with the back of my hand, surprised to find them wet. "What sort of mind game is this, August?"

A sigh—deep, dejected, absolutely fucking tired—comes from him. "No games, baby. My watch's on the nightstand. Turn on the lights."

I scramble to do his bidding, a jolt of pain stabbing me through the eyeballs as the bright small screen comes to life, a torch icon right at my fingertips. I tap it gently, and low lights, warm like a sunset, flood my cage.

"What the fuck is this?" I shout, jumping to my feet as I drop the watch on the floor. My heels are rooted to the black fluffy carpet as I take in August in all his naked glory, laying on his back. His long, strong legs half hang out past the edge of the mattress, silver metal rings wrapped around his wrists and ankles.

His eyes bore into mine, serious, solemn, and resigned. There's no cruel smirk on his kissable lips. No teasing wink. His expression is stoic, his heartbreak bleeding in the midnight depths. "This is me setting you free, little mockingbird."

His biceps bulge as he pulls at the chains. The scar of his bullet wound is puckered, red and angry around the edges. He's not as comfortable as I was. His bindings are tight, the back of his wrists flush against the headboard. Apart from a brief movement of his hips, August is trapped. Well and truly trapped. Up and down his chest moves, his ripped abdomen tensing under my perusal. His cock, crowned like the prince he wears on the tip, comes to life against his thigh, lengthening and thickening in front of my eyes.

"The door's unlocked. Your backpack, *untouched*, just past it. I'm at your mercy, baby. I can't get out of these bindings without help. And there's no one else to help me. So it's up to you." The tone of his voice tells me he doesn't have much faith left in whatever connection he thought was between us. And the pain seizing my chest as I witness his wavering faith tells me exactly how fucked in the head I am.

August is giving up on me. He's giving up on us.

I look at the door, then back at him. There's understanding swimming in his eyes. Deep sadness, too. His tongue darts out, swiping against his bottom lip. There's nothing seductive about the gesture, only anxiety and nervous anticipation.

"You have... three choices." He closes his eyes and takes a deep breath. "You stay. You choose me of your own will and want." It doesn't escape my notice the glimmer of hope shining in the golden flecks in his irises. He blinks, and it's gone. "If you woke up this morning and chose cruelty, walk out the door and leave me here. Even if I had someone to call for help, I wouldn't. If I'm out of these chains, I'm coming after you. So I'll stay put. It would be long, probably painful, too. Elijah will know to come look for me in a month."

I gasp and take a step back. The searing agony rushing through each of my nerve endings is unbearable. A world without August... what would that look like? Freedom or just another cage, only bigger?

"Or you can take pity on me." He nods his scruffy chin toward the side table. My whole body is frozen in place. I can't look. I don't want to know what the third choice is. "LOOK, SIAH!" he thunders, the sound crackling between us, charging the empty space separating us with electricity. My eyes dart to where he's indicating. Bitter tears immediately coat my lashes as they snag onto the gun resting against red velvet in a wooden box. The sleek black handle gleams even in the muted light. The danger it poses shimmers against the surface. "I selected it carefully for you. Minimum recoil, silencer, small and deadly, just like you."

My hands clench into fists at my sides. Rage, unlike anything else I've felt before, explodes in the center of my chest. The mental shackles I've placed on myself for years shatter in the face of my ire. August is freeing me of myself while permanently chaining me to him. The motherfucker is manipulating me. These are the choices he's giving me? Him or guilt? Him or murder?

"You absolute fucking bastard!" I screech. "How dare you?"

The shock on his face is priceless. The white of his eyes reddens. "These are your options, little mockingbird. Choose."

"*Choose?*" I mock, making my voice deep and gravelly to match his. "Choose what, August? For you to haunt me for the rest of my life? I either look over my shoulder till I take my last breath or live with your ghost till I'm old and decrepit?"

"IF I'M DEAD, YOU'RE FREE OF ME!" he shouts, and I swear the floor vibrates under the agony in his voice.

I point my finger in his face and shout louder, "You melodramatic, sick son of a bitch!" In one quick breath, my fingers wrap around the handle of the gun and I'm straddling his hips. "You want to die, August? Is that it?" The sleek barrel pushes under his chin. I apply pressure until he is forced to lean his head back against the pillow and look at me through lowered lids.

I ground my hips against his cock, and he groans loudly, unrestrained. "If you think for a second my life is worth anything without you, little mockingbird, you haven't been paying attention," he growls, thrusting his hips up, the jeweled damp head rocking against my throbbing clit.

My nails claw at his shoulder as I lean over him, undulating my ass, circling, teasing, the dainty lace of whatever underwear he put on me roughing up my sensitive flesh. I trail the barrel of the gun over his chin, outlining his jaw, then press it against his bottom lip as I force it into his mouth. The click of the safety as it releases echoes ominously between the two of us. He wraps his lips around the cold metal, his eyes boring into mine, challenging me, daring me.

I smirk despite the tears still trailing down my cheeks, "What if I choose number four, August?" His eyes widen, his brow furrows. I lift myself high on my knees as I scratch my nails over his wide chest, through the middle of his stone-hard abs, leaving four bloody trails in my wake as my fist wraps around his steeled cock. I notch his head at my entrance, pushing my drenched panties aside with a finger. A deep sigh of relief slips past my lips as his crown parts my folds, stretching me, filling me.

We both moan in unison. Me freely and wildly, him muffled and gagged around the gun pressing against his tongue as I impale myself on his length, sheathing him to the hilt. The burn of our joining, the hint of pain in the sea of pleasure, has me rolling my eyes to the back of my head.

I rock my hips slowly, my walls fluttering around him as I adjust to his intrusion. He's so big, so hard, so goddamn perfect. I feel every ridge and pulse as he completes me. I ride him hard and fast, taking him to the very end of me, holding him inside of me as I quiver and gush. I don't let go. He strains against the chains, his abs flexing below me, his hips thrusting up as much as his constraints allow him. The veins in his arms throb underneath his skin. His neck cords, a steel wrist-rest as I press mine against his heated skin.

I arch my back and throw my head, the tips of my curls sprawling against my ass and his thighs. And then I rip the gun from his mouth and press it against my chest as my tits bounce with each powerful sway of my hips. "What if," I mewl as the barbell of his piercing pushes against that special spot inside of me that has me seeing stars and my pussy drowning his cock in my arousal, "I choose number four, and I go first?"

My eyes open as he freezes beneath me. An unholy screech comes from the headboard as it splinters under his hands. His irises are blown, pure unadulterated fear lightning up inside of them. I don't stop my movements. My descent into hell is done with wings splayed open, and my pussy fucked into high heaven. Molten lava courses through me. Stars are born and dying in my veins as my entire Universe explodes in the face of the terror and rage controlling August right now.

The gun flies from my grip as his bound hands wrap around my throat. "The world as you know it will end with you," August promises in a dark voice as he takes my breath away when his fingers tighten around my neck. He pulls me to him, fusing our mouths together while he fucks me like the world ends anyway, right here in bed with us.

I clamp down on him. My skin can't contain the bliss. My body is too frail to withstand hurricane August. He bites down on my tongue, sucking it in his mouth. I buck against him, wild, needy, aching, wanting. When darkness descends over my eyes, I let go.

And I fly.

"Auguust!" My heart seizes, my brain short-circuits as I come all over his cock, his name a prayer and a curse on my lips. And I let myself be caught. "I love you."

He drives himself into me, our bodies fused together as his midnight eyes with golden stars painted all over his irises bore into me. "Little mockingbird, I live and I die for you. Love is too small in the face of what you mean to me," he grits through clenched teeth, finally letting himself fly with me, hot ropes of cum painting the quivering walls of my pussy as he comes.

Barely holding myself upright, I trail my palm over his shoulder, wrapping my fingers around his neck. His pulse is maddeningly racing against my fingertips. "Silly man, dying is easy. Any fool can close his eyes, here one minute, gone the next." He groans, his chest rumbling under me. "Do the hard, terrifying thing instead, August. Live for me. Wake up every day and choose to live."

He shakes his head, chuckling ruefully. "You forget I lost any and all choice the first time you called me a selfish bastard. If I get to wake up next to you every day, there's no other choice but to live."

I lean down and kiss his chin, my teeth nipping at it teasingly. "Tell me, do you kill for me, too?"

He twitches inside of me, our combined lust sticky and hot between the two of us. "What do you think, Siah? Would I kill for you? Would I chop into pieces and roast like prime beef all and any who dare harm you?" He swallows, his Adam's apple bobbing under my touch. I press my thumb in the middle of his throat, savoring his discomfort. Raspy now, the vulnerability thick and heady as he begs me with those mesmerizing midnight eyes of his, August asks, "Would you... kill for me?"

I slump against him, completed and depleted in equal measure. The touch of cold metal against my back coaxes goosebumps to ghost over my skin. My lips press against the center of his sweaty chest, where his heart beats steadily and forcefully against my mouth.

"I caught you, you monstrous prey. And now you're mine, to have and to hold, until death do us apart."

Because... the ugly, harsh truth of the matter is... I would. Oh, I so would.

Chapter Fifty-Three

SIAH

The wheels of my shopping cart creak as I wander through the aisles, mindlessly perusing the shelves. My heels click and clack with each step. But it's not the six-inch red sole stiletto that makes me feel oh so tall. It's forgiveness that does it. Acceptance, too.

I'm ready to start my new life. No more looking over my shoulder, no more cowering in fear, no more making myself small for the benefit of others. Standing tall has never felt so good.

Rounding the corner, my eyes snag onto the colorful rows of boxed cereal. "Oh, what the hell?" I say to myself. Chocolate, Shreddies with chocolate, banana-flavored oats—they all find their way into my cart. I push on my tippy toes, straining to reach the tasteless, flavorless healthy crap August likes to eat in the morning, when I feel it.

It starts slow, a flip of my stomach, if that. My heart stutters and stalls before it launches into a frenzied pound, slamming against my rib cage. An icy chill forms at the back of my neck, curling around my spine, spiraling down as it numbs my limbs. The fine hairs on my arms stand at attention. The burn of his eyes on me intensifies—always watching—as I draw in a shallow breath. *A warning.*

Covertly, I tilt my head. Just a fraction, a subtle movement allowing me to look over my shoulder. What did I just say? Yeah, scratch that. There's a lot of looking over my shoulder in my future. How could it not be, since I'm obsessed with a man who loves to hunt and I, myself, love being hunted?

I could make this difficult for him. Or I could...

"Found you, little mockingbird." I shiver when his minty breath fans over the side of my neck as he presses his lips just below my ear. His arms wrap around my waist, and I lean back into him.

"It's not like Walmart's a maze," I tease.

"You never tried parking at rush hour, then," he grumbles, and I pat his shoulder in a *there, there* gesture.

"What's the point of having a big, burly man if I have to fight for parking?"

August grabs my wrist and spins me in his arms before dipping me over the handle of the shopping cart. He winks as he rights me, and I can't help my laughter. How utterly... ordinary of us. An outsider looking in would see a couple in love. No one could tell that a few weeks ago he had me chained in a cage made just for me.

"Could've ordered online." His tone is gruff, but his mesmerizing eyes are sparkling with humor.

I'm still trapped between the stone-wall that is August and the handle of the cart as he walks me backward, heading to the checkout.

"No can do, hot stuff. Just taking advantage of my newfound freedom."

He rolls his eyes as he steps away from me and taps away at the self-checkout scanner. "I'll never hear the end of that, will I?"

My teasing remark dies on my lips when, out of nowhere, his entire demeanor changes. Midnight-blue eyes narrow, his lips twitching in a sneer. One step, and he looms over me, tall, dark, and menacing, as if thunderclouds surround him. "August?" I squeak.

His arm coils possessively around my waist, pulling me to his chest. I open my mouth to protest, to demand an explanation, when my name is called from somewhere behind me.

"Siah, is that you?" The voice sounds familiar as it trembles over each word. An eerie sense of déjà vu washes over me. His hold tightens around me as I struggle to turn around. Blonde hair, dark-green eyes, and pale sunken cheeks greet me when I finally face her.

"Hannah." My tone is flat, not betraying the sinking feeling churning in my stomach. Henry is gone. I'm starting my new chapter of happiness now. I don't need nor want any reminders of him, especially not from his girlfriend.

She's not deterred by my less-than-warm reception, stepping closer until only the shopping cart separates us. "I'm sorry for..."

"If you're here to tell me you're sorry for my loss, you're wasting your breath," I snap. She shakes her head, blond tresses spilling past her shoulders and over her back. Her wide eyes dart to the man still looming behind me like an immovable mountain, and she gasps.

"I know you. I've seen you at the funeral."

His anger is swift and suffocating. Goosebumps sprout on my skin as if a power surge occurred in our vicinity. Without a thought, I take a step in front of him, plastering my back to his chest. August is a mountain of a man, yet my first instinct is to protect him.

"He was." I hear myself speaking, having no control over my mouth. "He went in my stead, seeing as Henry tried his best to break me into pieces just days before he died, and I was forced to remain in bed and heal."

Hannah maintains our eye contact, although her fingers fidgeting with the hem of her purple jacket betray her anxiety. "I'm glad to see you well, Siah. My being sorry has nothing to do with his death," she hisses. "That night... I knew he was looking for you. I tried to stop him. When I couldn't, I tried to warn you instead." Her eyes well with tears as she sniffles. "I swear, I really tried."

Understanding dawns on me like a block of ice breaking over my head. I got three years of a well-behaved Henry. She met him at the height of his madness. It's not like I can hold her taste in men against her. She didn't know any better. Neither did I.

"You did." August's words surprise me. "I saw your message and was able to reach Siah in time."

As if the weight of the world was lifted off her shoulders, much like me earlier, she stands taller, prouder. Relief is evident in each of the tears falling down her pale cheeks. She brushes them off with the back of her hand, smiling through them. "Thank you." Hannah exhales a watery breath. "I'm really glad you got out."

I burrow deeper into the cloud-soft cushion of the couch, pulling a throw blanket over my knees. A soft glow illuminates the living room, flames dancing lazily inside the electric fireplace. Our dinner plates lay empty and forgotten on the coffee table, the screen of August's laptop flickering dimly right next to them.

Muffled footsteps sound from behind me. I know he's doing it for my benefit. For a man as large as he is, he's stealthy as fuck. We have reached our happy chapter, but us playing out his understanding of how to catch a mockingbird didn't leave me without lingering issues. Everything startles me still—an unexpected noise, him popping out in front of me out of nowhere. It's how our love story plays out—a whole lot of angst, with a healthy side of fear.

A glass of red appears in front of me, and I wrap my fingers around the stem. August bends over the backrest of the couch and kisses the top of my head. "Thank you," I say, smiling at him. The deep burgundy wine sloshes against the rim, and I take a quick sip, so it doesn't spill. "You've been generous."

He rounds the couch, my eyes glued to his flexing abdominals as he lifts my legs with one hand, then plops down next to me, settling my thighs over his lap. Maybe I should make a new house rule where he's not allowed to wear a T-shirt ever—once he makes it past the front door. They look better on me anyway. "You've had a day."

I touch my glass to his. "To turning shit days around."

His dark and gravelly chuckle echoes in the space around us. "I can make that happen," he murmurs as his hand grips my thigh.

"Nuh-uh, Mister. Keep it in your PJs." I laugh as I take another sip, savoring the dulcet cherry notes in the otherwise crisp wine. My brow furrows as my mind wanders back to Hannah. The encounter with her today left me rattled but, weirdly, it also brought me closure. "Do you think she'll be okay?" I think out loud.

"Hmm." August hums as his hand caresses my thigh absentmindedly. "I looked into her today." Jealousy slams hard and fast into me, every muscle in my body locking tight. Maybe it took me a while to get on with the program and understand that August and I are inevitable. But I know it now, just as I know how to breathe—naturally and instinctively. August is *mine*. My eyes narrow at him when a crooked smile curls up the corners of his mouth. "Sheath your claws, little bird of prey." He leans over me, brushing his lips against mine. "I see no one but you."

"You still looked her up," I bite when he settles back on the couch.

"Because I misjudged her at the funeral. She was bawling her eyes out. Either way…"—his hand slashes through the air, as if he's wiping the slate clean—"they haven't been together long enough for him to do any lasting damage. From what I've seen in their exchanges, he was love-bombing her when he needed something and ghosting her the rest of the time. The worst seems to have been… that night."

His last words are growled, carrying enough poison in them to warrant a warning label.

I run my fingers across the tight muscles of his neck, cupping his jaw, and give him a soft smile. "You saved me."

August turns to me, easing the glass from my hand before sliding it onto the coffee table. He interlaces our fingers, pulling me closer to him. "No, Siah. *You* saved *me*. You continue to save me every day." The soft kiss he places on the tip of my nose warms my whole body, butterflies exploding in my belly.

My fingers sink into his silky hair, massaging his head. His dark lashes flutter closed as he leans into my touch, a pleasured groan rumbling from his chest. "So, what now?"

"Now we live, little mockingbird. You'll write your books; I'll orbit around you. I'm yours to do with whatever you please." His eyes spring open, shining with adoration and hope. "You'll marry me and make me the happiest son of a bitch to plague the Earth."

"Is there a question somewhere?" I laugh, tightening my hold on his hair as I tilt his head back.

His tongue comes out to sweep over his bottom lip, and my eyes follow the movement, fascinated. "You want me to get on my knees and beg you, baby?"

I rise from the cushion and straddle his thighs, trailing my nose under his jaw before nipping playfully at his chin. "Oh, you'll kneel and beg for me soon enough."

"Is that so?" He grins as he grips my hips and rolls them against his rapidly growing erection. "When?"

"How about... for the rest of your life?" I don't get to smart my way through his non-proposal when he captures my lips with his, kissing me breathless. His warm, large palms cover my breasts, kneading, teasing, driving me out of my fucking mind. I moan my impatience and...

His phone's ringtone startles me right out of his lap.

"Goddammit," August curses through his teeth. "Come here, baby. Ignore it."

But I know better. A phone call at 2 a.m. is not to be ignored. Even though I haven't spoken to Jayme in weeks, I know she's out on assignment. Our friendship is trembling with holes, but I'll never forgive myself if something happened to her, and we just ignored her call. The slow burning fire below my navel turns into an icicle as the call ends and, immediately, the phone starts ringing again. "Answer it."

He huffs his protest but does as I asked. "Helena, what can I do for you?" Disappointment and relief course through me knowing it isn't my best friend calling.

Her voice is loud enough for me to detect a hint of hysteria, but the volume is still too low to make out any words. Whatever she has to say can't be too bad, because August's eyes sparkle and a wide smile spreads on his face.

"I understand. Don't worry. I'll take care of everything." He nods as her garbled words come once again from the phone. "Got it. When do you think he'll be... released?" His thumb runs circles under my breast, and I squeeze my knees in response. "Of course. Let me know. Siah and I will be there. Get some rest, Helena. This will all be over soon."

His phone drops onto the cushion next to him as he grips my nape and pulls me for a quick kiss. "We just got our first wedding present." I pinch his side, giggling when he yelps. It's what he gets for making me curious, then not satisfying my curiosity.

"Are you going to tell me what the present is or are we waiting for it to materialize on our coffee table?"

The look of horror on August's face is priceless. "Trust me, little mockingbird. We'd have a shitstorm of problems if that were to happen."

"August!"

His midnight-blue eyes roll playfully, the golden flecks in his irises sparkling like lightning strikes. "James St. Andrew was found dead in a motel. Looks like we're planning a funeral first, a wedding second. Fitting, don't you think? With us, both death and marriage are eternal."

Chapter Fifty-Four

SIAH

We're a sad, sad group. And not because the final reddish dust is settling over James St. Andrew and his poor-excuse for a coffin. In fact, between the six of us, not one single tear has been shed.

Itchy sweat drips down my forehead and my back. I'm about two minutes away from ripping my *funeral* dress off me and just strut to the car half naked. Sometimes August's ideas are absolutely ludicrous. If he weren't looking like an avenging angel of death as he looms over James's final resting place, I'd have smacked him behind his pretty head.

The only one looking the mourning part is Helena. With her hands wrapped tightly around her waist and her pale face, she looks positively destroyed. The last two months have been hard on her. Finding out the truth she refused to see for years, and in such a public manner, shook her to her core.

What does it feel like, I wonder, to look at yourself in the mirror and know the extent of the depravity festering in the soul of the man you married?

My eyes dart back to August. I guess I'll be able to answer that question as soon as we return to Seattle. Except, every night I go to sleep, well fucked and well protected, I'll sleep knowing exactly who I'm sharing a bed with.

August St. Andrew is *not* his father's son. But he is dark, twisted, and depraved. And all fucking mine.

"So, who's hungry?" Elijah asks, five heads turning sharply in his direction, where he's leaning against his car. "Oh, don't give me that fucking look. You didn't spend five hours digging your way through a hot as fuck desert to bury a sick son of a bitch. I'm hungry."

Helena snorts. Well, there goes the theory of a mourning widow. She squares her shoulders and turns her back to the make-shift grave. "I could eat."

Devon saunters her way with a shit-eating grin on his lips and throws an arm around her waist. "That's my girl. Let's go feed that husband of mine before he turns feral. He's worse than a menstruating teenager after finding out her quarterback boyfriend has been sniffing around a cheerleading skirt when the munchies hit." He leads her to their car and opens the back door, helping her get settled.

Elijah fists his hand in Devon's hair as soon as he turns around. "Careful now, darling. You'll be trapped with this menstruating teenager for as long as it takes us to complete our fishing trip."

"What fishing trip?" Jayme asks as she stares daggers at the ground covering James.

"Ah, we're chasing mythical creatures and the minds who spawned them." Devon chuckles. My friend's eyes flare in annoyance as she rolls them.

"As far as I know, the Monster of Loch Ness was still safely across the pond. Do you think it magically swam from a landlocked lake to the West Coast?"

August scoffs but doesn't otherwise interfere. I know what their fishing trip is all about. I've seen the map in his office. He'd also told me when we were traveling to Phoenix exactly how James died. Elijah and Devon are on clean-up duty now. And happy as hell about it, too, the freaks.

"Technically, it's not landlocked. If Nessie really wants to pay us a visit, she has a cute little river that takes her straight to the North Sea and the Atlantic." His next words are drowned by an impatient horn. My ears are still ringing as the beeping stops and a car door being slammed closed echoes through the desert. There's that hunger-induced moodiness Devon mentioned.

And then there were three.

"Dickhead." Jayme folds her arms across her chest and tilts her chin, stubbornness dripping out of her. "This is one of those moments when I wished *I* had a dick so I can just whip it out and piss all over his grave," she mumbles, aiming her ire at her dead stepfather. "Good fucking riddance."

August shakes his head, his eyes still narrowed on the freshly covered grave. His face is impossible to read. His irises, a lighter blue than his normal midnight under the desert sun, flash with mirth, there one second, gone in the next. I walk behind him and wrap my arms around his waist, touching my forehead to his sweat-soaked black button down. He circles his long, callused fingers around my wrist, toying with the chain corked around my forearm—my trophy, as he called it.

His strong body is tense, a current of unrest rippling under his skin. I don't know how to make it better for him. The next few months are going to be taxing as we navigate the aftermath of James's death and the circumstances in which he perished.

"Go ahead," he murmurs, "get to the restaurant with the others. I'll follow soon."

I tighten my hold on him. "No. We're leaving together."

He's not fighting guilt right now. It's not grief either. He's fighting his goddamn glee. Two weeks ago, we woke up in the middle of the night as Helena called to tell us that James had been found stabbed to death in a motel room. In the light of his arrest, he made bail as he was waiting for his trial date. August was beyond pissed to find out his father had a secret stash of cash—a big fucking stash. He wanted James to rot in prison for the rest of his days, not live cushy in his home until the trial.

Not even the threat of prison could stop James's depravity. As soon as he found himself free, he went straight to hunting his next innocent prey. Except, this prey was nothing innocent, but a bloodthirsty serial killer, with a penchant for kidnapping and butchering child abusers. A fitting end for my future father-in-law. *Late future father-in-law? Whatever.*

Of course, this only made the media frenzy around James amply and explode. August has spent the last two weeks taking down any and all articles mentioning our names. Our home in Seattle has been swarmed with news vans and reporters. He's fighting fire after fire after fire.

Even with his plate overflowing, he took the time to buy a plot of land in the middle of the fucking Arizonan desert. There's nothing for miles here but rocks, red dirt, wilted plants, and the occasional cactus. Now, an unmarked grave, too.

"He doesn't deserve to rest next to my mother," August hisses. "I hope you rot in hell, you bastard." He pulls on my wrist until I step in front of him. His eyes immediately latch onto mine. "We'll start our forever now."

I smirk. "Maybe after I'm out of this dress and get something in my mouth."

His responding smile is nothing short of predatory. "I have just the thing."

"Actually, before I get an unwanted lesson on how the bird swallows the bee," Jayme interrupts, and I don't miss the apprehension in her tone despite her attempt at humor. I swallow harshly as I stare at August's chin. "Can you drive to the restaurant with my mom and the merry duet of perverted assholes? Siah and I are overdue for a conversation."

His fathomless gaze searches my face. I'm sure he sees the fright there. The longing, too. I miss my best friend like I miss a limb. She has barely spoken to me since she found out about us. Add all the weeks I've been locked up in August's cage and didn't return her brief messages, our relationship has taken a hit. There's a strain to our interactions we've never experienced before. I need it gone. I need my family to be whole.

August cups the back of my head and brushes his lips over mine once, then twice, making me sigh. How did I ever think I hated this man? "It'll be fine, little mockingbird. But don't take too long. I'd hate to have to chase you down... again."

I laugh against his mouth. "We're making jokes about it now?" Taking a step back from him, I turn to Jayme and flip my hair over my shoulder. "That's too bad. I found out just recently that I love to be chased."

His responding growl gets my nipples hard and my panties wet. Jayme rolls her eyes at me, crossing her arms over her chest.

"Now, that's just fucking disturbing." She shakes her head as she climbs in the passenger's seat and waves me in. "Get in the car before he makes good on whatever the heck is passing through his mind right now. Sheesh, talk about things I never wanted to know about my step*brother*."

I slide behind the wheel, sighing in relief as soon as the AC starts, blasting me right in the face. "Where are we going?"

She chews on her nail as she taps one-handed on the screen of her phone. It chimes in her lap soon after. "Elijah sent a location. Let me connect to the GPS."

I pull the car into drive and follow the black SUV in front of us as she programs the coordinates. Until we're out of the desert, they're easy to tail. The problem is when we hit the mid-afternoon traffic once we reach Phoenix.

"So..." she starts, slumping in the passenger seat. "You and August."

My eyes dart to her, taking in the contemplation on her face as she chews on her bottom lip, before returning to the road ahead. "Me and August."

"I get that I left rather abruptly after I found out about the two of you, but... you stopped responding to my messages, Siah."

I tilt my head in her direction. "I was... tied up."

"For three weeks?" The hurt in her tone is unmistakable, and it makes my stomach flip.

My fingers tighten around the wheel, the leather creaking under my hold. "My lack of response had everything to do with me and nothing to do with you. When you left…" I bite my tongue. She doesn't deserve me to lash out. I could've used her support through all this. "Did you know?" I ask instead.

"Know what?" There's defiance now. Well, this could go either way.

"That I wasn't paranoid. That I indeed had someone following me." With the corner of my eye, I watch her reactions, but she gives nothing away. Jayme has an impressive poker face, much like her stepbrother, when she wants to. "That August has been stalking me ever since we graduated."

Her mouth falls open. "Fuck off!" she screeches, slapping at the dash. "He did *not.*"

I lift my shoulder in a dainty shrug. "Take your outrage with August. But… I'm happy to know you were not a part of it." I might have forgiven August, but I will not tolerate any more lies, any more games from the people surrounding me. Too much of my life was wasted living like a pawn. Trapped in a prison of my own making, other people had too much fun locking the doors and manipulating me through the bars. No more.

"You thought I played you all this time?"

"I didn't know what to think, Jay. My reality was fraying at the seams right in front of my eyes. I was afraid for myself, I was afraid for you. The walls were closing in on me. Throw Elijah in the mix, showing up at random times. Not having a clue who he was and how he fit into the narrative… I questioned everyone."

She sighs deeply, and I tighten the hold I have on the wheel, the road blurring in front of me. *Keep it together, Siah.*

"I… I'm not going to pretend hearing you didn't trust me doesn't hurt. Because it does." I bite my tongue as she pauses. As much as I want to defend myself, my lack of faith in her hurts me, too. Her distance hurt, too, even if it was mostly caused by me. "I can't put myself in your shoes, Siah. You've lived through hell for years, and I didn't even know it. The best I can do is hope you have finally found what you're looking for. I hope you're learning that some people have staying power. I'm one of those people. So is August."

"I was planning to leave, you know... after your birthday. Seems like I'm the one who doesn't have staying power. At least, I didn't then." Tears are stinging my eyes, blurring the city lines in front of me even more. I pull over at the side of the road and press the pad of my palms against my eyes. The last thing we need is to crash the car because my body is shaking like a leaf.

"I felt so alone," I say through the emotions clogging my throat. "Not knowing who to trust. Not even being able to trust myself. And then your reaction... I mean... I did worry you'd not be okay with anything happening between August and me."

She wraps her hand around my wrist and squeezes. "Weirdly, I'd always thought August would be perfect for you." Her words land with the power of an asteroid hitting the surface of the Pacific. I swivel in my seat to face her. Jayme's eyes are red, a soft smile tugging at her lips. "I even tried to set you guys up a few times."

I sputter a wet laugh. "No, you didn't."

"I absolutely did. That assignment at Blind Date? I had him meeting us there. But the asshole never showed his face. And you ended up shagging a rando."

My cheeks pink up. *Not a rando.*

"Hell, even at our graduation, I didn't just want him there to support me. But for you to finally meet. The number of times I tried to get us all together is insane." She shrugs now, deep brown eyes glinting with mischief and a touch of sheepishness. "The day we met, I saw a familiar loneliness in you. I've only ever seen it once before... in August. And the more I got to know you, the more I got to love you... I don't know." Jayme takes a deep breath, her fingers twisting in her lap. "I hoped. I continued hoping right until you married Henry." His name, she spits out with a sneer.

"You never said anything. You never voiced any concerns about him at all."

She thumps her head to the backrest, fidgeting in her seat. "God, I wish I had. But you seemed so happy, Siah. And my support, my friendship doesn't come with conditions. I never want to take anything from you."

I lean over the center console and clasp her hands in mine. "You never do, babe. I'm so lucky to have met you. I'm so fucking grateful to you. The distance between us in the past few months killed me. I wasn't in a great headspace. Hell, it's been years since I've been anything remotely myself. But I'll do better by you, I promise."

Jayme wraps her arms around me, and I cling to her. She's been the only family I knew, ever since I walked into that dorm room and found out I was sharing it with her. She's been my rock, my support, my shoulder to cry on.

Both our watches vibrate in unison. "Let's go before he loses his goddamn mind and really chains you to him." She laughs, pulling back from me. "For what it's worth, I'm really happy for you two."

I shift the car into *drive* and merge back into traffic. Relief has me nearly bouncing in my seat. My family has been really put through the wringer in the past months, but we're all slowly healing and growing stronger.

I don't need to know who my parents are. Where I came from doesn't matter. I know who I am now and where I am going. The people I have in my life have chosen me, and I'm choosing them right back. I don't care what my once-upon-a-birth name is. I'm Siah Hadley, soon to be Siah St. Andrew, and I'll proudly wear his name.

As I stop in the parking lot of the bar we're celebrating life at, my door is ripped open. I scramble to unlock my seatbelt while strong arms are pulling me out of my seat. My arms wind around his neck as he ducks his head and hungrily takes my mouth with his. Our lips touch and, for a second, time halts. Everything is suspended into void... my heartbeats, air, the entire fucking Universe. And then he pushes me against the car, his tongue slipping into my mouth as he kisses me furiously, wildly, his whole body wrapped around mine.

August's kisses give a whole new meaning for to have and to hold. He's having me forever. He'll hold me for eternity. Each swipe of his ravenous tongue against mine drives the certainty home. Deeper and deeper until it settles inside my bone marrow.

There's a special kind of safety that's embedded just beneath my skin, knowing that regardless of where I go, regardless of what I do, August will follow. He'll never let me go, he'll never set me free, he'll never stay away.

And I never want him to.

Epilogue

Siah

My blood is foaming inside my veins, bubbling like champagne during New Year's Eve. My heart is racing, pounding relentlessly in my eardrums. An ice-cold shiver peppers goosebumps on my skin, the electric current of the chill seeping into my bones, curling around my spine. My lungs constrict, refusing to inflate. My eyelids spring open, my eyes unseeing. The lack of oxygen finally shakes me awake enough. I jackknife into a sitting position, spluttering and gasping for air. My hands pull at the metal bindings tying them together.

"He's watching me," I croak, my voice raspy, my throat dried out. All the moisture in my body is rushing between my legs, where I ache, I burn, and I need.

I blink as if in slow motion, my eyelids heavy, my eyes gritty, trying to force my pupils to enlarge and my vision to get used to the darkness of our bedroom. I know he's there somewhere, always watching, always following me. My stomach flips, my belly quivers, adrenaline floods my veins, burning through my blood.

The sheets rustle before a heavy, hungry groan cuts through the silence of the night. "Little mockingbird, you're finally awake. Are you ready for me? Is your pussy wet and throbbing, eager to be filled?"

I lean back against the pillow, the strain in my shoulders easing as the bindings grow slack around my wrists, and I let my knees fall open, ready to cradle him. "Why don't you check and find out for yourself?" I moan, tilting my hips up as my back arches. Pure electricity rushes through me as his calloused palms grip my thighs, exposing me to him even more. His nose brushes against my clit, and I jolt, chasing his mouth, needing his touch. He licks a path of sin and depravity across the length of my drenched slit, the scrape of the lace against my overstimulated flesh making me rut against his face. My nipples pucker into tight pebbles, desperate for attention. But he ignores everything, zeroing in on my clit, nipping, sucking, flicking, driving me insane with need.

I'm out in the open, vulnerable, cut apart for *him* to feast on and dissect.

"August, please," I cry out, tethering on the edge, willing him to push me over.

His response is an impatient growl that vibrates through me and makes my belly clench. The thin lace around my hips pulls taut, a sharp burning sensation cutting through my skin before blessed relief courses through me as it snaps and gives way. I moan long and hard as his tongue flicks my clit with no barriers between the two of us.

Passion rises beneath my skin, incinerating any and all coherent thought as he thrusts two thick fingers inside me, scissoring them, twisting his wrist this way and that. He sucks my needy bundle of nerves between his lips and bites down, hard enough to have me screaming, the jolt of pain just the push I needed to let myself fall into the abyss.

"God, August, yes, yes, please, I need more."

He coaxes every drop of my orgasm out of me, his fingers relentless, his mouth without mercy. My hips slump against the crumpled sheets as I come back to Earth with panted breaths and a racing heart. He places a gentle kiss on my inner thigh, slowly removing his fingers from my still quivering pussy. I wince as low lights flood the room, but I can't help the lazy, satisfied smile that spreads on my face as I see him looming over me.

"Hi," I whisper, feeling my chest flush and redness creeping into my cheeks.

August rises to his knees, his cock, thick and hard, juts out. The silver piercing crowning his head gleams as it catches the light in the room. "Hi," he murmurs, fisting himself. I lick my lips, circling my hips against nothing, as I watch him stroke his length from root to tip, thumbing the damp pink head. "Fuck me, you're beautiful. You want me, little mockingbird? Is your pretty pussy still throbbing for me?"

"Yes," I purr, tracing his tensed abs with my toe, then hook my foot around his waist. The chains around my wrists pull taut once more in my futile attempt to close the distance between us.

He strokes harder, his brow furrowing as agony and pleasure dance across his face. "Did you miss me, little mockingbird?"

"Every damn minute of every damn hour."

"Ntz," he admonishes, wagging his forefinger. "Now, that doesn't sound healthy, baby. If anything, you sound obsessed." His crooked smirk is what filthy fantasies are made of—arrogance, pride, and a satisfaction that runs so deep, he bears the scars in his veins.

"That's 'cause I am. Are you going to psychoanalyze me or are you going to fuck me?"

His dark chuckle bounces between the walls of our bedroom, and in a flash he's on me, fist wrapped in my hair. My back bows clean off the bed as his palm connects with my pussy, the sting of his slap making me gush against his fingers.

"Look at you, my little slut of a mockingbird," he growls, praise and awe thick in his voice. I cry out as he slaps me again, this time my achy clit taking the brunt of his punishment. "You like that, don't you? You burn for me. I can do whatever the fuck I want to you, and there's not a goddamn thing you can do to stop me." I moan as his eyes latch onto mine, boring into me, reading every single dirty and depraved thought running rampant through my mind.

He grabs the back of my leg. His fingers, coated in my arousal, grip onto my flesh as he pushes my knee against my chest. We both sigh in unison as he drives himself into me in one long thrust. I throw my head back and tilt my hips, taking him deeper, savoring the feel of his steel length stretching me, filling me, reaching the very end of me.

August is right, of course he is. I burn for him. I'll fly for him, too. But first... he'll make me sing.

"Fuck me," he grits, "God, you take me so well. So pretty, so needy, so swollen around me. I must have been a fucking saint in a previous life to get to be inside a miracle like you." He shudders with his whole body as he bottoms out, grinding his hips against mine. I pull at my restraints, the rattling of chains lost in the symphony of the headboard thumping against the wall, his growled grunts of pleasure, and my blissed-out mewls.

I writhe, I thrash, my soul leaves my body as he pounds into me, his eyes never for a moment leaving mine. He's so strong, so big, I see nothing but him, I feel nothing but him. I live and breathe August St. Andrew.

He throws my leg around his waist, and I clamp down hard, holding him against me as he drives into me in frenzied thrusts that have my eyes rolling to the back of my head. My tits bounce against his chest, my nipples rubbing against the fine hairs peppering his skin, scraping against the sensitive buds, ramping up my pleasure, stoking the fire raging in my core.

August drops his head to the crook of my neck, trailing his lips against the sensitive skin behind my ear, licking and sucking as needy mewls beg him for more. His hips circle and plunge, making stars explode behind my eyelids. The love I have for this man is too big for my body, all-consuming. It bubbles and boils under the surface, bursting inside of me with each drive of his cock. He tilts my hips up as he tunnels his arm under my lower back, changing the angle at which he fucks me.

My walls quicken around him, quivering under the tidal waves ready to wreak havoc through my body. August buries himself into me so deeply I feel him everywhere. "That's it, little mockingbird. Strangle my cock. Look into my eyes and sing my fucking name."

He bites down on my shoulder, and I let go with a scream, soaring high into the sky.

"Auguuuust!"

Oxygen and rationality are taken away from me when he fuses our lips together, kissing me as if my mouth breathes life back into him. I taste heaven on his tongue, a hint of me, a shade of him, and moan my appreciation loudly and wantonly. This chorus is for him and only him. His cock throbs against my fluttering core, and he spills his release into me as he reaches his end and marks my beginning. His hips don't stop pumping until he's expanded every last drop. The mouth ravaging mine grows soft, tender, and loving, peppering my whole face with kisses.

Slowly, he releases the clasp binding my wrists together, and he brings my left hand to his kiss-swollen lips. His midnight-blue eyes sparkle with love and possessiveness as they latch onto my wedding ring, the delicate white-gold chain adorned with sapphires—an exact match of the chain around my wrist and his own ring.

"You're the love of my life, Siah St. Andrew. I'll never stop having you," he murmurs, kissing the ring and the tip of my nose.

"And you're the love of my life, August St. Andrew. I'll never stop holding you," I whisper back.

Who knew ripping a stranger a new asshole over the phone would get me a stalker, a hunter, a family, and a bedazzled cock all wrapped in one handsome and only occasionally murderous package?

Fuck happily ever after. Sometimes all you need is to have and to hold through fears, and heartbreak, and all the worst this life has to offer. And maybe a sturdy bundle of chains.

Acknowledgements

My shower idea book. Yes, yes, that's it. A shower idea. June and July have been... rough months for me. My mental health dipped and ebbed like there's no tomorrow. My creative well dried up. I was... hollow. My anxiety was through the roof, my depression suffocating. Been there, done that, I've the meds as a souvenir. It's an ongoing battle. Sometimes I win, sometimes I lose, and sometimes...

Shower ideas come to life.

I have this very weird... fear of showering when I'm home alone. As soon as I draw those curtains and the water pounds on me, every ghost and monster of horror movies roar to life, and they all have one and only *one* intention. To get to me. So, as my eyes were scrunched closed—because at thirty-one years of lie I still haven't learned how to shower without getting soapy suds in my eyes—my skin prickled. I felt watched. My stomach bottomed out. And chapter one came to life in my mind.

After six weeks of having zero words in my pocket, my fingers ITCHED to write. So I went in—no plot, no names, no two weeks daydreaming of my characters. Just a simple *need* to write write write and an unsettled feeling in my stomach.

I hope you enjoyed August's and Siah's story as much as I enjoyed writing it. They gave something back to me in the middle of the storm raging in my head... they gave me back my love to write even if their story was something new to me that forced me to open up more, allow my fears on the paper more.

And as always, I couldn't have finished this book without the absolutely wonderful people around me.

Bella, your friendship means the absolute world to me. Thank you for putting up with all my freakouts. Thank you for reading every chapter fresh off the press and kicking my bottom into gear every time my fear gets the best of me. Your support and patience have been priceless to me in these dark months of mine.

Most of all, thank you for sharing YOUR stories with me. Officially, on paper, eBook, and for the whole world to see - I'm your number ONE fan.

Jayme, I don't know where I'll be if it wasn't for you. Your immense heart, your endless optimism, your unwavering belief in me... I'm floored and humbled and so intensely grateful. Thank you for putting up with my moods, and my fears, and every single one of my insecurities. You're a kindred spirit, and I thank my lucky stars every day to have met you. I'm in awe of your strength and resilience, and let it be known officially—BRAX IS MINE. There, I licked him, I've claimed ownership. Thank you for giving me "All The Little Things" when I struggled the most and let it be the story that proves strength is a powerful tool when you're alone, but a support system is indestructible.

Annie, Abby, Ashley, Ellie, Frederyque, Silvia, Yvette your support and love have me floored. You're the best **Alpha Reader Team**, and even better, dear dear friends. I'm in awe of each and every one of you and forever grateful to have you in my life.

Ana Maria and Claudia, thank you for being the bestest friends this girl could have. There's no geographical distance that matters when you find your people. Always and forever.

As always, a special thank you goes to Mr. Right. For eight years I've known you, for eight years I've loved you. Thank you for rolling your eyes, but staying in the shower with me and reading the news to me anyway when my anxiety gets the better of me. I don't know what I did in a previous life, but it must have been really damn good, to be rewarded in this life with you. I love you.

The biggest thank you goes to my readers. Thank you for continuing to take a chance on my dream with every page you read. I am overwhelmed in all the best ways for all the love and support I've received so far. It goes beyond my wildest dreams. And it's all thanks to you. You fuel me, give me hope, and keep alive this dream of mine that just one year ago seemed so far-fetched. I hope you found little pieces of yourselves in *To Have and To Hold*, and I hope I've done all of them justice. All my love <3

For the smallest contribution in the grand scheme of things... actually there's no thanking coffee this time. YOU bitter nectar of gods with the smallest hint of hazelnut have FAILED ME big time this round. Because of you, I didn't just take loads of naps. The freaking naps took me. How dare you?!

About the Author

When she's not having a latte in her hands, Alina has a book or her Kindle.

Her time is equally split between her very serious day job, her very fun time writing, and providing Mr. Right infallible arguments as to why it's not her turn doing the dishes.

With a deep love for written word, she woke up one day with characters screaming in her head to be put on paper.

Alina lives in the UK, with her infinitely indulgent Mr. Right (and human dishwasher).

If you'd like to poke the bear and find out more about other novels she's currently writing, please join her private book cave here:

AC's Book Cave

Since procrastination is an effective punishment tool when her characters misbehave, if she's not waiting for a latte to be delivered, she can (sometimes) be found here:

Facebook - Alina Comsa Author

Instagram - @alinacomsaauthor

She promises to be on her best behaviour, whatever that means.

Also By

Lost Hope Series
(small town, contemporary romance)

Lege et Lacrima

Vanilla et Motricium Oleum

Atramentum et Telum Pulvis (Coming soon)

Lux Solis, Fumus et Specula (Coming soon)

Ardor et Glacies (Coming soon)

Standalones
(dark romance)

To Have and To Hold

Printed in Great Britain
by Amazon

62950229R00163